How

Rory Thorne
Destroyed the
Multiverse

How Rory Thorne Destroyed the Multiverse

BOOK ONE OF THE THORNE CHRONICLES

{ K. Eason }

DAW BOOKS, INC

DONALD A. WOLLHEIM, FOUNDER
1745 Broadway, New York, NY 10019
ELIZABETH R. WOLLHEIM
SHEILA E. GILBERT
PUBLISHERS
www.dawbooks.com

First Printing, October 2019
1 2 3 4 5 6 7 8 9

 DAW TRADEMARK REGISTERED
U.S. PAT. AND TM. OFF. AND FOREIGN COUNTRIES
—MARCA REGISTRADA
HECHO EN U.S.A.

PRINTED IN THE U.S.A.

to Colleen, who always believed

Acknowledgments

Writing is a solitary, coffee-fueled endeavor. Getting the book in front of an audience, however, is a team effort, and my team at DAW is the best. (Better than coffee, even.) Katie, Josh, Brittanie, Alexis, Jessica, and the folks whose names I don't know, but who helped: thank you! Extra and evergreen thanks to my agent, Lisa, who always knows what the story needs; to Tan, who always reads it first; and to Loren, always, for being willing to make coffee and cook dinner and rail with me about the evils of the patriarchy. Thank you all. Without you, Rory would not be destroying the multiverse.

Part One

Once Upon A Time

They named the child Rory, because the firstborn of every generation was always a Rory, and had been since the first of that name had cut his way through the cursed briars on the homeworld and saved the kingdom of Thorne—and, incidentally, the princess—from the consequences of poor manners.

That the latest Rory was a girl and not a boy came as a bit of a surprise. The medical mecha scans had been clear. That little flicker on the screen had been proof of Rory's masculinity. And yet, out she came, the blood-slick product of ten hours of hard work, and the little flicker was nowhere in sight on the flesh-and-blood baby.

"A daughter!" said the midwife. She had been an attendant at too many births across the years to be surprised by the mistakes of a med-hex.

The new father—whose name was not Rory, as he was the second son, and the luckier of the two boys born to his parents—stopped himself, only just, from asking if that flicker might've broken off somewhere during the process, or if it mightn't, perhaps, appear at some point very soon. Then he locked eyes with the new mother and thought better. The Consort hailed from Kreshti, a small independent and allied planet on which skill with combat training was considered both a plain necessity (the neighbors were both ill-mannered and much larger) and a mark of personal pride, and the Consort was a very proud woman.

There had not been a daughter born in the Thorne line for ten generations, not since that first princess, the one who had needed her Rory. And thus, no one knew what to call her.

"Talia has the weight of tradition," said the Vizier. "It is her foremother's name, after all."

"A cursed foremother," said the Consort. "I think not. What's wrong with Rory? That's tradition, too."

The Vizier chose not to argue. He pointed out, to a scowling Majesty, that popular fashion indicated that the name *Rory* could function for all genders.

And so it was settled. Mostly.

There was another custom, which hailed from the same quaint homeworld story about magic briars and curses and poor hospitality, which had fallen into disuse, victim of the same lack of girl children in the Thorne line. The Vizier (re)discovered it by accident, while looking for appropriate girls' names among the rare, expensive, fragile paper tomes in the Thorne family library, which had been shipped at great expense from the homeworld when the kingdom had become a Consortium and moved its capital to the planet named for its founding line. That collection of tomes was a mark of pride, a symbol of the age of the lineage, and, according to the King, absolutely vital to the integrity and reputation of the Thorne Consortium. Except for the Vizier, the library received no regular visitors.

The Vizier had gotten his position in part because he had, in addition to a doctorate in arithmancy, earned two graduate degrees in homeworld history and folklore. Finding quaint, forgotten, and neglected customs was his second favorite pastime in the multiverse. Explaining to others the relevance of those ancient customs was the first. Besides, he told himself, he would be remiss in his duties if he did *not* tell the King about the Naming.

He regretted his diligence almost immediately.

"I've never heard of this custom!" The King spun the priceless book and shoved it back across the desk with exactly as much care as he gave his breakfast tray after he'd finished with it.

The Vizier controlled a wince. He turned the book gently and nudged it back across the (imported, expensive, and now slightly scuffed) wood expanse with a fingertip.

"Nevertheless, Majesty. I'm afraid it's very clear. You must invite the fairies to the naming day of a girl child so that they may bless her. You know. Beauty, kindness . . . quick wits," he added under his breath.

The King thrust out his lip. "The boys do all right without that nonsense."

The Vizier did not blink. "Of course, Majesty."

"We invented void-flight and *everything.* No magic involved. No blessings." The King pointed at the 2D 'cast behind his desk. It was a reconstruction of the exact path the first exploratory rover had taken when it made planetfall. A panorama of dull red rocks and darker sand, creeping toward a sepia horizon. The King had set the 'cast to repeat itself, endlessly.

"Do you see that, Rupert? We did that. We Thornes. It's amazing. Phenomenal. *Beautiful.*"

"Yes, Majesty." The Vizier did not point out that the rover had been unmanned. Nor did he point out that the rover's landing site now hosted the void-port, a high-end shopping establishment for off-world visitors, and a full set of embassies, and that the King himself had never set foot on that planet.

The 'cast restarted its loop. The Vizier cleared his throat.

"What? Oh," said the King. He blinked and pressed his fingers over his eyes, creating a nest of fine wrinkles in the skin. "What will the investors think? The Thornes will look stupid. I will look stupid. And the Consort will probably laugh at me."

Oh, thought the Vizier. *That's almost inevitable.* He cleared his throat again. "Call it exactly what it is, Majesty. A quaint custom from the homeworld. Use the Naming as an opportunity to remind your subjects about our origins. Use it as a celebration of our progress."

The King frowned.

"*Thorne* progress, Majesty." The Vizier smiled. He practiced that smile in the mirror every day. Lips curved around just the palest hint of teeth. Eyes firmly blank. "It could be an excellent public relations move. Insist on a reenactment, of sorts. A pageant. If his Majesty will permit, I've taken the liberty of drawing up some names of suitable ladies who might play the twelve—"

"Fine." The King was already glazing over. He flittered his fingers at the Vizier. "All right. Whatever."

"—but I would like his Majesty's advice on who should play the thirteenth."

The King blinked. "What?"

The Vizier rebooted his smile. "The thirteenth fairy, Majesty. She was the one who cursed Talia."

"Then why would we want her? She was bad luck, right? We don't want bad luck." The King grinned, suddenly. "The Consort's mother would be a good choice, though. Ha. No. Skip the thirteenth fairy. Leave that part out. Make the ceremony an *exact* reenactment. I want it perfect. Only." He stopped. "The fairies won't come. You're certain. They're not, I don't know, xenos or something."

The Vizier controlled a tiny sigh. "No, Majesty. They are not xenos. They will not come."

The King glanced uneasily at the 'cast, as if the beings in question might be hiding behind the rust-colored rocks. "Well, but, what if they do?"

The fairy invitations were written on vellum, hand-scribed with genuine ink and a genuine pen in period-specific calligraphy that only the Vizier himself could write, much less read. He could have written the cook's favorite cobbler recipe, or enumerated the King's favorite athletic teams, or made a list of all the bullies he'd survived during his childhood. But being both arithmancer and historian, the Vizier was more than a bit obsessive, and very devoted to detail, so it is no surprise that he wrote the invitations as best he could to the specifications set forth in the record. He had to consult with the court astronomer to calculate the calendar for a single moon and the homeworld's longer solar revolution, and although he consulted with local biologists for local equivalents, he chose in the end to use homeworld fauna.

The Royal House of Thorne
requests the Honor of Your Presence
at the
Naming Day
of the
Princess Rory Thorne
on the
First Day of the Seventh Moon
in the
Year of the Wolf

Lacking the authentic delivery system—sparrows being in short supply, and not well-suited to tesser-hex—the Vizier elected to leave the invitations, neatly rolled and tied with silk ribbons, in a secluded corner of the royal gardens. He tucked them into the branches of the single homeworld tree species that would grow in the light of a foreign sun. It was not a large tree, and the Vizier felt sorry for it, burdened as it was under the weight of the tradition.

He gave the gardener strict orders to leave the invitations alone.

When, three days later, the gardener reported the invitations missing, the Vizier assumed that local fauna (probably tree-rats) had developed a taste for vellum. It was an ignominious end to his labors, but then, he was accustomed to that.

The rest of the guests got the standard electronic invitation, delivered from one impersonal machine to another, and filtered up through the appropriate chain of attendants. It was less aesthetically satisfying, but ultimately more reliable. The Vizier consoled himself with the planning of the actual ceremony: commissioning costumes and choosing which women were best suited to play the twelve fairies in the pageant, where *best suited* meant politically inoffensive, prudent, desirable, and/or necessary, in that order. That was, in the end, a great deal more work than the fairy invitations had been. And it proved to be an entirely wasted effort.

The vellum, ink, and ribbon, however, did not.

On the first day of the seventh moon, which was technically the third pass of the second of the two moonlets, in the year of an animal the only knowledge of which came from old homeworld video footage that only the Vizier and the Consort had bothered to watch, the unofficial Princess Rory Thorne became the official Princess Rory Thorne.

The party was spectacular. All the guests had, per the King's request, come in historically authentic costume. Or, rather, they had tried. There were imported silks and velvets mixed with Martian brocades and leather (from various animals, both native and not) boots. But the overall shape of the garments was correct, and although the Vizier suspected some of the guests might have chosen less than academically reliable sources for their inspiration, he decided he could not complain.

Even the xenos had gotten into the spirit. The foreign attendees, some of whom had too many (or too few) limbs to manage corsets and hose and boots, came as culturally appropriate inanimate objects. The k'bal had come as a five-armed candelabrum, standing two meters tall, with blue carapace showing where the cosmetics had rubbed off. Each head wore a little flame-shaped hat, made of a fine metal mesh that fluttered with each exhale from its cranial vents. There was a teapot, too: an adapted environmental suit for the mirri President, whose daughter-buds had come as little cups.

When the designated hour for the ceremony arrived, the Vizier rang the silver gong. It was a perfect and exact replica, the original having been lost to looters in the initial instability following the first Rory incident, when the homeworld kingdom found itself absent a royal family and possessed of a very large, overgrown patch of briars. The guests obediently withdrew to the great hall's perimeter. The Consort entered with the Princess in her arms. She, too, wore a costume: an elaborate confection of silk and velvet involving a great many laces along the torso. She didn't look happy about it. Her grim-lipped body-maid, in a much simpler garment, stalked along in the Consort's wake, raking suspicious eyes across the guests. Even the gentle little mirri teacups got a scowl.

The King was already in place on a dais, beside the royal cradle—which *was* the original—resplendent in furs and reproduction armor. He beamed at the Consort. At the Princess. At the multiverse in general. After his initial skepticism, he had thrown himself into the Naming Day preparations with startling enthusiasm. The Vizier suspected the armor was to blame. It was heavy, metal, ridiculous, and very manly.

The Vizier edged closer to the King, in case his Majesty needed prompting through the script. He needn't have worried. The King boomed out a formal welcome to his guests, presented the Consort, and oversaw the placing of the Princess into her cradle. Tradition dictated that the guests would, one at a time (as species-appropriate), come to the dais and offer both blessing and gifts to Rory. But first, the fairies.

"I welcome first the guardians of my kingdom, on whose good-will all our luck rests." The King sucked a deep breath. The Vizier spotted motion reflected in the King's breastplate, a pinkish blur, from the far doorway. He turned that way, expecting to see the General-Commander's wife stuffed into her First Fairy robes.

And so the Vizier, man of arithmancy and education, possessor of two degrees in the obscure and overlooked, was the first human being to see a fairy in five hundred years.

She was taller than he'd imagined (because a man does not spend a large slice of his life studying quaint folk beliefs and not wonder what a fairy would look like). She stood at least half a meter taller than the tallest human in the room, which put her at a level with the tallest of the k'bal's cranial stalks. Her dress was an iridescent, impossible close cousin of *red*, and as unlike *red* as stars were to swamp gas. Her skin was faintly pink, the palest echo of her dress. Tiny scales shimmered along her cheekbones, her forehead, the proud arch of her nose. Silver-shot vermillion hair, blasted white at the temples, coiled in a severe knot at the nape of her neck. Her eyes matched her hair, bisected by a single silver pupil. She did not walk as much as she floated across the tile. Not a whisper, not a sound.

She climbed the dais. Took her place on the far side of the cradle. Nodded encouragement at the King.

Who stared saucer-eyed at the Vizier. *But you said they weren't real* warped his lips, fluttered in his throat. Came out as a breathy, strangled, "Wah."

The Consort slid her slippered foot sideways, hard, into the King's armored boot. The Vizier heard the meaty thump and winced on the Consort's behalf. She didn't flinch. Didn't blink, when her husband looked at her.

The King cleared his throat. "Welcome," he said again, to the First Fairy. His eyes clutched at the Vizier. Then, carefully, mechanically, the King welcomed the rest of the fairies. One by one.

By the fourth (aquamarine, angular, and very tall), the Vizier was sure they were xenos. By the ninth (cobalt, whose robes draped in a fashion that suggested rather too many limbs for a human), he was unsure again. By the twelfth (the smallest, pale, and round as the second moon), he simply didn't care. They were beautiful. They were *magical.*

One by one, they approached the cradle. One by one, they offered their gifts to the Princess, who woke up at some point and stared at her visitors with wide dark eyes.

". . . bestow the gift of harp-playing, that you may hold a room rapt and beguile men's hearts and minds." The green fairy leaned over the baby. Tapped her forehead with a small, green finger.

Rory gurgled.

Only one left. The Vizier realized he was holding his breath. Let it go, slowly. His stomach hurt. All this worry for nothing, like most of his efforts.

And, then, from the doorway, came a voice: "Oh, I *see*. You started without me."

The thirteenth fairy had arrived.

She sauntered across the basilica on silent boots, spike-heeled and made of a shiny, very-much-not-traditional material, with silver laces, like wire. She had a shock of pink hair cresting upright along the middle of her scalp. The sides of her skull were shaved bare, and marked with intricate, disturbing tattoos that seemed to move if one tried to look too closely. She wore a black jacket, too big, flapping open, so that the buckles jingled and clinked, and a too-short skirt over too-long legs wrapped in hose that looked like fishing net. The garment under the jacket was the same shade as her hair, and it looked as if it had been slashed by razors. Her skin was metallic, shifting pewter to bronze, flirting with the light. Instead of scales, rings and rivets studded her skin, all polished to a high gleam.

The guests said nothing. Didn't move, as if they worried she might notice them. The other fairies drew closer to the cradle and made a wall of glittering fabric, like martial butterflies. The first raised her vermillion hands and waved her fingers, *go back, go away.*

The thirteenth fairy ignored her. She climbed the dais steps. Paused at the top, and stared at the rest. They wilted aside. Then the thirteenth fairy lasered her attention at the King and the Consort. Dragged her eyes the height and breadth of them.

"Is it custom to begin important ceremonies without all the important guests?"

The King and Consort looked at each other. The King flinched. He scuffed his gaze along the stones and said, as if through a mouthful of velvet, "Well, no. But you weren't invited. So, ah, I'll thank you to leave, now."

The thirteenth fairy's brows rose. The twin rings above her left eye gleamed like tiny suns. "Excuse me? I was very much invited."

"Majesty." The Vizier's voice wisped across the dais. "It's my doing. It seemed—imprudent to leave her out this time."

The King stared at him. Opened his mouth and left it hanging. His tongue wiggled, pink and furious.

"You are welcome, then, Lady," said the Consort. She plucked at her skirts, which was as close to a curtsy as she could manage while gathering herself to leap at the fairy, should she try something untoward toward the Princess.

The thirteenth fairy smiled. The tiny silver ring at the corner of her mouth winked. The Vizier noted that she showed a lot of teeth. He also noted that they were unusually pointed. Sharp, even.

"Thank *you*, Consort." She glanced sidelong at the King. "You would have left me out again."

"I even didn't think you were—"

"Real?"

"That. Yes. And the last time you came to a Naming, you tried to murder the baby."

"I did not."

"Well, you certainly didn't—"

"What? Bring a gift? Is *that* what you think this lot have passed on? Kindness, beauty, a pure heart. Some wits thrown in to differentiate the poor thing from a doll. And the ability to *play the harp*. So useful for a royal scion in this age of galactic empire. Do you play the harp, Majesty?"

"I—no."

"Then why should your daughter need that skill?"

The King seemed to recall who he was, and that people didn't interrupt him more than, well, ever. He drew himself up straight and threw back his shoulders. For a moment, the thirteenth fairy saw the ghost of the man he might have been, and her smile faded. The King mistook that as encouragement.

"I mean," he said, and his tone could have sliced stone, "that my foremother would have died, if you'd had your way, on her sixteenth birthday. You cursed her, *my lady*. I think harp-playing is infinitely preferable."

The thirteenth fairy said nothing for a very long time. The silence squeezed into every crevice and crept into open eyes and nostrils and mouths and breathing tubes, filling mouths and lungs and air sacks and cranial vents.

"Yes," she said at last. "I suppose you would. Your worth does not hang on your ability to please others."

She turned a shoulder to the King and looked at the rest of the fairies. The pink crest on her scalp quivered. The tips caught the light and gleamed like glass. "And *you*. I expected better. Half a millennium passes, they crawl out of their gravity wells and travel all the way here, and all you can do is repeat the old words."

The first fairy spread her hands. "*Here* or *there*, *then* or *now*, they are much the same."

"What they value in a daughter has not changed," said the fourth fairy, pale yellow, whose gift had been clear skin. "Nor," she added under her breath, "have their inheritance laws."

"We understand," added the third fairy, "what you were trying to do, back then."

"We just didn't much like your methods," said the eighth.

"And we are not without mercy." The cobalt fairy drifted a step out of line, like a shadow tracking the motion of an invisible sun. "You will note, sister, that this is the first girl born in almost two hundred years to this line."

The import of that statement took a moment to settle. Then a collective gasp ricocheted through the guests. The k'bal put their heads together, clicking and gusting to themself, while their hat-flames snapped and creaked. The mirri's daughter-buds spun in eccentric, erratic orbits, while the President herself tipped onto her suit's belly and rocked there. The humans covered their mouths, some of them; or put heads together to mutter about *how could that be*. More than one *impossible* bounced off the tile and tapestry before evaporating into uncertainty.

The King's mouth opened. The Consort kicked him, visibly this time, and his jaw clicked shut.

The Vizier heard himself speak. "You're saying—you're saying *you* are the reason the Thorne line runs to boys?"

The cobalt fairy's cloak rearranged itself in what might have been a shrug, or soundless laughter, or the first gestures of a world-ending curse. "You thought it was numerical coincidence? Two hundred years, and not one daughter. That can only be magic."

The King stepped out of range of the Consort's beskirted feet. His knuckles were white on the pommel of the ceremonial sword. "Then why change it now? Why change it for me?"

The first fairy looked at the Consort. "A mother's wish is its own magic."

The Consort blanched. The King turned and stared, but the Consort wasn't looking at him. She was looking at the thirteenth fairy.

"Please. Don't kill her. Don't curse her. *Help her.*"

"I can't be kind. It's not my nature." The thirteenth fairy's eyes were sad above her jagged smile. She leaned over the crib.

The Consort snatched for the King's ceremonial sword. He grabbed her wrist with both hands.

"Wait. Stop!" he shouted, which was equally applicable to both the fairy and the Consort, and equally ineffective.

And so no one heard the thirteenth fairy's wish except the other twelve, and Rory herself.

The thirteenth fairy said this: "I curse you, Rory Thorne: to find no comfort in illusion or platitude, and to know truth when you hear it, no matter how well concealed by flattery, custom, or mendacity."

Then she straightened. She looked at the twelfth fairy, and her eyes were hard and hopeful. "Your turn, sister."

The littlest fairy nodded. She picked up her skirts, dodged a stray foot, and darted up to the cradle. She hooked her fingers over the side and tilted up on her toes. She leaned down and planted the tiniest of kisses on the baby's forehead.

"Well. My sister's ruined any chance you have at easy happiness, unless you sustain a massive head injury in your childhood. How about it?" The fairy paused.

Rory blinked. Then her face collapsed in on itself like a dying star. Her mouth stretched into an event horizon of preverbal rage.

"Good," said the fairy. "I didn't think so." She wiggled her fingers, and a cascade of sparks rained down into the crib. The sparks turned into tiny butterflies (homeworld, not local) and fluttered around the baby's head.

Rory stopped mid-squawk.

The littlest fairy smiled. "All right, then. Here is *my* gift, little princess: that you will always see a path through difficulties, and you will always find the courage to take it."

Which is how Rory Thorne became the woman who destroyed the multiverse.

CHAPTER TWO ≡≡≡

Of Skinned Knees And Birthdays

Human beings are fascinated with time. They measure it out according to celestial motion and ecclesiastical cycles, parse it into increments that accrete or divide to bracket the experience of living.

And they tell stories about its passage, the speed of which is said to vary according to the quality of the experience. The reality, of course, is that time, for all its relativity and proportional relationship to velocity and gravity and physics, marches along at exactly the same pace. Moments of heartbreak and joy, birthday parties and skinned knees, are all temporally equivalent, slotted into weighted categories of memory labeled *unpleasant* and *pleasant*. Sometimes, those categories overlap—a skinned knee might happen during a birthday party—injecting a brief tragedy into a much longer joyous experience.

To Rory Thorne, however, the brevity of the skinned knee would have been pure proof that interesting moments passed too quickly. To her, a skinned knee meant an adventure; but a birthday party meant an ordeal, involving a guest list as long as Messer Rupert's leg (she printed it once, to check), most of whom were adults, all of whom were invited for her father or mother's sake. The few children in attendance, like Rory herself, were stuffed into clothing more suited to formal events than enjoyment. There was cake, yes, but it came at the terrible cost of *sitting still*.

One did not acquire skinned knees by *sitting still*. One did not, in Rory's experience, accomplish anything by *sitting still* except a sore bottom, especially at birthday parties. The great carved chairs to which she was consigned during formal meals had been made for adults, and her chair—carved with long-snouted bushy-tailed beasts with triangle ears and lolling tongues—had grooves in the seat that rubbed her in exactly the wrong places. Squirming didn't help. Squirming, in fact, attracted attention. Deme Grytt, sometimes, would flash her a sympathetic unsmile and shake her head very slightly. Or Messer Rupert would gather his eyebrows over his nose and draw his lips into a little wrinkled raisin of unhappiness and whisper at her to sit still.

At least he said please.

She had asked, at her fourth birthday party, why they had to sit in these chairs.

Her father had leaned across the table—so he could see past the Duke of Somewhere and the See-Eee-Oh of Something and some ambassador who looked human and therefore *boring*—to look down at the end where his daughter's head only just cleared the table's rim. And he had said, in his too-slow, too-loud voice that he always used on her in front of company,

"Because they're family heirlooms, my dear." And he'd smiled. All teeth. No eyes. "Do you know what that means?"

Rory was a smart child. The fairies had seen to that. So although she did not know what an heirloom was, she did recognize when someone else wished she'd be quiet and disappear into the scenery. She knew her father's smile meant *shut up, Rory*. She also knew the other adults to whom she was not related and with whom she did not live were amused by her question. The See-Eee-Oh was smirking, and the ambassador leaned sideways and whispered something to her nearest companion, who snickered.

One of the gifts Rory had not gotten from the fairies was a particular eagerness to please.

"No, Daddy. That's not right." She knew she was talking too loudly for the table, but she had to be louder than the ambassador. "You want people to be as miserable at these things as you are."

The See-Eee-Oh laughed out loud. The ambassador covered her mouth and coughed. The King's eyes rounded like eggs and his cheeks purpled like that vegetable Rory didn't like except when it was fried.

She hadn't gotten any cake, that birthday. And she'd learned there were more ways to get a sore bottom than sitting in uncomfortable chairs. The next year, she didn't ask about chairs or customs. Smile, Deme Grytt said. Say nothing. Messer Rupert had sneaked her tablet to dinner, in the endless folds of his court robes, and slipped it to her so she could read under the table, if she propped her napkin up just so.

That had worked for her sixth birthday, too, only that year it had been her mother who'd smuggled the tablet to the table, when her father had accused Rupert and Grytt of conspiracy.

This year, her seventh birthday, the tablet had been forbidden outright, and Mama was very pregnant and very grumpy and no help at all. The third prong of the triumvirate of awful came when Deme Grytt stuffed Rory into a dress with laces and boning and a much higher potential for discomfort than the chairs presented.

Rory was not happy. "I *command* you to stop this, Grytt!"

Deme Grytt had been her mother's body-maid, before she'd come to *protect*

serve Rory. She knew all about stupid clothing. She also knew all about tempers.

"Hold still, Princess. And you will call me Deme until you're big enough to beat me at spear-throwing."

Rory thought it would be years before she could physically best Deme Grytt at anything except hiding in small spaces. She tried a new approach. Made her eyes big and sad and said, high-voiced, "But Deme, I *hate* this thing. It's stupid and tight and uncomfortable. Daddy must *hate* me."

"Yes, it is, and no, he doesn't." Deme Grytt made it a practice never to lie to Rory. She never lied to Rory's mother, either, but she had come to the Consort's service when they were both almost adults, so it was a matter of respect between them. The Princess, however, had an uncanny knack for picking out unspoken truths, and a very long memory for people who lied to her. So Grytt took a wrap on the laces, and a deeper breath.

"It's meant to be all those things, but mostly it's supposed to make you look pretty. Now, hold your breath. Okay. Wait. There. You can breathe, now."

"No, I can't." Rory frowned past Deme Grytt at the girl in the mirror. She looked like a sausage, in that stupid dress. "Pretty for who?"

"For whom. Some princeling and his self-important father." Mirror-Grytt made a face at mirror-Rory. "Probably some boy they'll want you to marry, someday, for galactic peace and favorable trade routes."

"My father will want that, you mean. Mama wouldn't."

Grytt sighed. There was honesty, and then there was actually encouraging mutiny. A good body-maid—one who had served the Consort for a dozen years, in this place—knew that the former was a rare gift, and the latter was no favor. "Be nice, Princess. He's about your age, and I bet he's not a bit happier to be here."

Rory took exactly two seconds to decide, upon meeting said prince, that Grytt was right. Prince Ivar was

terrified

"—pleased to meet you, and—"

I want Mr. Buttons

"—happy to be here—"

and as uncomfortable in his stiff fancy clothes as she was. He was not a bit pretty, either. He was starched and round and his hair was slicked dark and oily as a tree-rat.

Rory was wiser than she had been, three years ago. She took a fistful of skirt on each side and folded her knees like the paper animals Messer Rupert had taught her to make during Holy Day gatherings.

"I am very pleased to meet you, Prince Ivar." That was a lie, but it was the kind Messer Rupert called being tactful and the kind Grytt called good strategy. Rory thought they were both right. She also thought that if she'd told Ivar that he was really scared of her and that he wanted—what *was* a Mr. Buttons? must ask Messer Rupert—he might cry.

Rory herself didn't cry. Crying was too much like giving up. And she didn't much like other people doing it, either.

Ivar did not cry. Instead, he made fists of his own hands and stared hard at the floor. His body-man, a small round hairless fellow with deep reddish scars along one side of his face and an artificial eye that glowed like plasma, leaned down and whispered something in the prince's ear.

Rory stared at the top of the body-man's head. At the wrinkled flesh where the implant slipped under skin and into bone. The circuits traced under his skin, little metal veins that disappeared under the stiff starch of his collar. She was no stranger to mecha implants. Deme Grytt had some: bolts on her forearm, a plug at the base of her right ear. Lots of people did. So it was not squeamishness or disgust that made Rory recoil from the body-man, or that made her want to get as far away from him as she could manage.

It was fear. Not the sort that crept up on her in the dark, at night, while the palace muttered to itself and shadows against the wall took on the exact shape of the monster from the 'cast she wasn't supposed to have watched so close to bedtime. This was the kind of fear that made koi scatter into the center of the pool and dive under the broad razor-leaves when a dayowl's shadow crossed the water. Threat. A sudden strike, a more sudden end.

An older Rory might have hesitated, or examined the impulse. Fortunately for Rory, Ivar, and the universe, Rory was young and quicker-witted than she was wise. She grabbed Ivar's hand, which felt a little bit like a dead fish. She wanted to drop it, but she didn't.

"We have a koi pond," she blurted. "Would you like to see it, Prince Ivar? We can even feed them. They're very tame."

Ivar hadn't decided yet what he should do about his imprisoned hand. He turned an alarming shade of pink. He held the contaminated arm out stiffly, as if he were trying to get as far away from it as possible. At her question, his face had a tiny seizure.

She thought it was supposed to be a smile.

"Um. If it, ah, pleases my, ah, lady."

No. He was terrified. *Of koi.* She knew the impatience showed on her face. Heard it in her own voice. Messer Rupert would have been

embarrassed to death, my Princess

mortified, but he wasn't here.

"Koi are fish, Ivar. You know. Fish? They live in water. Swim around?" She wiggled the fingers of her free hand. Ivar stared at her, very much like the baby koi did. Round. Unblinking. Unaware of the dangers of dayowls.

She seized on a sudden idea. "They're animals. Like tree-rats, only wet all the time."

Ivar brightened. He looked at his body-man, who seemed to consider. Head cocked, eyes focused somewhere in the middle distance. A man thinking, except he looked more like one of the guards getting orders from the little earbuds. He was *listening* to something, or someone, only he had no earbuds.

Rory's mind shot along half a dozen new vectors. What could she say to convince him, could she just drag this Ivar after her, should she leave him, what could she actually do—

But the body-man refocused on them both. Smiled, a more natural expression on his face than on Ivar's, and said, "Go along, your Highness." Then he turned to Rory and bent double at the waist: "It was very fine to have met you, Princess."

That was truth. And more than truth, that was relief. He wanted them to go, both of them, very much and right now.

The body-man was afraid, too, except unlike Rory, he knew exactly why.

Rory tugged the prince's dead fish hand.

"Come on. Let's go *now*, Prince Ivar."

Because he was a biddable boy, and accustomed to doing as he was told, Ivar came along. Quick steps at first, and then, when Rory made it clear she wasn't slowing down, and that he could either keep up or be dragged, an all-out, clumsy run.

It was during that run that Ivar, who was not a natural athlete, tripped over his uncomfortable shoes, which were too stiff, and fell, and pulled Rory down with him. Ivar scuffed both palms and tore a hole in his trousers. Rory's dress survived, but her knees did not. The tumble laid them both flat, and required some moments of recovery—much fast blinking and brave sniffing and no tears at all from Ivar, about whom Rory had harbored some doubt, and only a wince from Rory herself. But because of those moments, Princess Rory Thorne and Prince Ivar Valenko were essentially unharmed when Ivar's body-man walked into the Thorne palace and detonated himself just past the front foyer.

The shockwave flattened several structures more sturdy than children, and tossed debris about with lethal consequences. The koi, safe in their pond, survived. Twenty human adults, including Ivar's father, King Sergei Valenko of the Free Worlds of Tadesh, did not. Rory's own father, King Philip Thorne, survived the blast for a time, although that was no kindness on the part of the multiverse.

The incident started two wars, one civil and one inter-planetary, and plunged several solar systems into piracy and lawlessness. It was also how Grytt came to have a few more mecha implants, and how the Consort added *Regent* to her title.

And it marked the end of Rory Thorne's childhood, by whatever measure one employs.

CHAPTER THREE ≡≡≡

Neither Apology Nor Accusation

The name the *Free Worlds of Tadesh* was misleading, as it did not describe worlds, but rather a far-flung string of colonies, mining outposts, and massive void-stations orbiting rich, inhospitable planets. Nor were the Free Worlds especially free, being instead a hereditary monarchy whose acquisition (and retention) of those far-flung colonies and mining outposts had come quite often as a result of military intervention and a certain suppression or suspension of freedoms.

The Vizier had much time to contemplate these facts on the journey from Thorne. As the Consortium's official representative, he accompanied King Sergei Valenko's remains (a more apt term than *body* in this instance) and the Prince on the Tadeshi ship that had brought them. It was not the Vizier's first time acting as diplomat, nor even his first time to the Free Worlds of Tadesh. It was, however, his first visit to the Tadeshi capital, an ancient void-station called Urse that threaded an orbit between two massive gas giants, which, in turn, orbited an unassuming yellow star. The massive void-ships were too large to dock at any void-station, even one as large as Urse, and so visitors were obliged to travel by shuttle. Thus, after the ships arrived at the system's gate, through which all tesser-hexing ships came and went, the royal remnants,

Prince, and important visitors faced several hours of sublight void-flight before reaching their destination.

Ordinarily, the Vizier would have used the time to catch up on work, but he considered himself well-versed in the Free Worlds' political disposition already. So he passed the journey by staring at the viewscreens, which piped in a steady stream of images from the shuttle's exterior, and considering the marvels of planets, and the cleverness of humanity for traversing the void. He also contemplated the vulnerability of that clever flesh, defended from aetherless, unbreathable void and lethal cold by metal and arithmancy. And he considered, with considerably more concern, how very *many* Tadeshi warships there were crowded into the system. He knew there was a marine training base on one of the local moons, but these ships were, to his unmilitary eye, rather more than standard, in both number and disposition, than one would need for a training facility, or even for a King's state funeral. They looked a bit like an armada.

The Vizier opened his tablet, without taking his eyes off the viewscreen, and made a note. Then, upon consideration, he added an extra layer of cryptographic hexwork.

He made still more notes upon docking at Urse. He noted that the coffin bearing the King was unloaded first, followed by the dry-eyed Prince, who was clutching a small stuffed animal, and that they were received by the security officers wearing dress uniforms and representatives of the Tadeshi Council. The Vizier, familiar with their names and faces from files and his aforementioned predilection to study, recognized the Ministers of Defense, Commerce, Education, and Foreign Affairs. He did not, at first glance, recognize the handsome blond man wearing councilor's robes at the head of the delegation. He frowned and consulted his tablet. Ah. He frowned a little more deeply. That was Vernor Moss, the new Minister of

Energy, which was a relatively minor position on the Council, and not the sort of person one expected to receive the body of an assassinated king. And if it seemed a trifle odd that Minister Moss would be among those to receive the King's coffin, it seemed even more so that he took immediate, physical charge of Prince Ivar.

The Vizier felt a chill that had nothing to do with the dry, dockside station air, and entertained a momentary wish to turn round and return to the relative safety of the shuttle. Instead, he squared his shoulders and came down the ramp, one more functionary among many, and so unremarked.

That anonymity would not, however, continue. The Vizier expected a request for an audience in the near future. And indeed, that summons came the following morning: a note, real paper (which was its own communication: paper was expensive, and also private, immune as it was to hexes and hacking), folded and sealed, delivered to the Thorne embassy by a black-uniformed Tadeshi security officer. The contents were politically predictable: the Vizier's presence was requested by the Council at such-and-such time, et cetera. The Vizier read it twice, and then started to fold it up. But something about the seal at the bottom struck him as, not exactly wrong, but—no, it *was* exactly wrong. He unfolded the paper and took the summons over to the desk, closer to the small, bright lamp standing watch over his tablet and the small pile of real paper that seemed to proliferate wherever the Vizier tried to do any work, and tilted the paper into light.

The state seal of the Free Worlds of Tadesh was an elaborate thing, curlicues and braids and a slogan written in archaic script in a dead language circling its lower edge. The *royal* Tadeshi seal was identical, except for a tiny set of crossed swords and a crown in what would otherwise be an empty patch just above that slogan. This summons *should* have come with a Council seal at the bottom—that is, the seal without the crown and swords. The Free Worlds had a clear line of succession. If a seated King died, his Queen—whether or not she came from the royal line—assumed the crown. Even without a formal coronation, the Queen was the head of state, and by all rights and rules was the only person authorized to use that seal.

The Vizier touched the very tip of his finger to the crown-and-swords on the seal on his summons. Then he blinked, and folded the paper, and tapped the edge against his fingertips and stared very hard at nothing at all for a long fistful of minutes. He knew the Queen was en route back to Urse from an interrupted tour of the outer colonies, and that she had not yet arrived. So either her entire tour had been a ruse in which the Tadeshi media had been complicit, or someone else was using the royal seal to conduct government business. And if the latter was true—sending, and using, that seal sent its own message.

The Vizier set the paper down gently beside his turing terminal. He considered whether or not he should acknowledge that message when he met with the sender. He would be a poor vizier indeed if he failed to notice a royal seal in place of a standard government sigil; but there was no reason to suppose whoever had used that seal knew *what* sort of vizier he was, or had any special expectations of him, and the seal might be a test, of sorts. A measure of the Consortium's strength and worth, marked by its willingness to chastise a not-quite-ally on the eve of a state funeral. The Vizier considered that his own king was currently badly wounded and lying in a hospital. He considered that his Consort was heavily pregnant, and the only living heir was a princess not yet ten years old. And he decided, in that moment, that it was better to be supposed feckless, and perhaps a bit of a fool, to whomever was using the Tadeshi royal seal, than a threat.

So when the Vizier selected his robes for the meeting, he chose the set with the barest bit of fraying on the left sleeve cuff. He poured a bit of ink out into the sink and rubbed his fingertips in it, until the flesh under the nails turned indigo. He pulled several strands of hair out of their braid and let them corkscrew out of the side of his head as if he'd been caught in a spring windstorm. Then he hexed his aura to conceal strong emotional reactions. Such hexing is standard practice among diplomats, and requires the sort of rudimentary arithmancy one acquires in primary school, and generally takes a only a few seconds. The Vizier, whose arithmancy was considerably more advanced, applied a more elaborate hex that took several minutes. He did not merely wish to conceal his emotions; he wished to present precisely what the observer most expected to see.

Then he went to keep the appointment. Along the way—and it was a short walk from the embassy to the municipal complex, a fifty meter stroll across a wide station corridor and up the ring— he counted the number of black uniforms dotting the otherwise colorful crowds. There were not as many as one might expect, given that the King had died by a Tadeshi assassin. And he noted the unexpectedly few security personnel were inversely proportional to the number of clerks and minor functionaries and liveried servants clogging the corridors of the municipal complex.

The Vizier was a cautious man, disinclined to paranoid imaginings, preferring to amass and analyze all available data before reaching a conclusion. The increased number of servants could be a result of the sheer number of foreign and domestic representatives arriving on Urse by the hour. The paucity of security could be because the screening hexes at the docks were very, very good, or because no one would be foolish enough to attempt an explosion on an aether-station, with merciless void on the other side. Or, he admitted to himself with some reluctance, because the person in charge of dispensing security was unworried about a repeat act of violence, which brought with it a host of questions whose answers promised to be as unsettling as the unofficial armada hovering in the system.

The Vizier passed through the doors, which bore the same royal seal as his invitation, and was immediately hailed—shouted at, really—by a blinking, roundish individual who, having screeched *your excellency the Vizier of Thorne* across a crowded foyer, could not be persuaded to speak above a marble-mouthed murmur while he guided the Vizier through a labyrinth of corridors and finally deposited him in a lush conference room.

The Vizier noted the breadth of the table, and the conservatively beautiful artwork on three bulkheads and the row of portholes on the other. He noted the pair of chairs, and surmised which was meant to be his by its proximity to the door through which he had entered the room, and its distance from a smaller door on the opposite side of both room and table. It was the sort of door a king or a queen might enter through, to avoid hallway traffic. Whoever would come through that door was not worried about assassins or security at all, which suggested either a fool or someone with reasons *not* to worry. Then he sat down, folded his hands on the table, and waited. At precisely two minutes past the appointed time, the Minister of Energy entered the conference room through that small door.

The Vizier supposed he had enough data now to reach a conclusion. He rose.

"My lord Vizier," the Minister said crisply. "How kind of you to agree to meet me."

"Minister," the Vizier said. The social rank between a minister and a vizier was such that a handshake should have sufficed as a gesture of greeting. The Minister had not yet extended his hand, and the Vizier considered for less than a breath extending his. Then he brushed across the Minister's icy blue eyes and bowed instead, his deliberately ink-stained fingers pressed together in front of his chest, as if to a superior. "On behalf of the Thorne Consortium, Minister, let me extend our deepest sympathies and regret for the loss of King Sergei."

"Thank you," said Minister Moss. His gaze flickered over the Vizier, marking every loose hair, every smudge, every wrinkle. One corner of his mouth quirked with a mild, condescending amusement. "Allow me to express our dismay that his Majesty, King Philip, was also harmed in the incident. I trust he is recovering?"

The Vizier hoped his own expression was better behaved. "King Philip is receiving the best medical care our chirurgeons can provide, Minister."

The Minister rearranged his features into a careful mask of regret. "The Free Worlds of Tadesh hope for his swift recovery."

The Vizier bowed again. "Thank you, Minister."

"And please extend our regard to the Consort in what must be a difficult time."

The Vizier blinked and held his bow a half-heartbeat longer while he schooled his own face into obedience. The seal was not the only royal prerogative the Minister was using: he'd assumed the pronouns, too.

"Of course, Minister. I am certain she will appreciate the thoughtfulness. She is hoping to place a quantum-hex call to the Queen on the day of the funeral to convey her personal regrets. I was hoping to arrange that with you today, so that I can advise her Grace of the Queen's availability."

Now it was the Minister's turn for an extra second of hesitation.

Then he flattened his lips into what the Vizier imagined was meant to be a small, pained smile, and which instead looked like the Councilor had eaten something disagreeable. "The Queen is conducting a tour of the outer colonies, and even by tesser-hex, her return will take more time than is seemly for our King to wait for his funeral. We can arrange for a call upon her return to Urse, when I am certain she will be glad to hear from the Consort."

The Vizier forbore a comment that the King was, in fact, beyond inconvenience or scandal at this point. He also forbore to point out that the minimum time between a Tadeshi monarch's death and his funeral was five days, *five*, and that waiting for the Queen's return would in no way scandalize anyone.

Instead, what he said was, "I see." He allowed his hands to flutter like nervous birds.

The Minister of Energy noticed those fluttering hands, and his lip curled just the slightest bit.

The Vizier, in turn, noticed that smile, and his gut coiled into a cold knot, one part fear, two parts anger. Protocol and his good sense said he should wait to be dismissed: the Minister clearly considered himself the ranking official, in possession of both royal seal and royal pronouns, and making an enemy of him would be both easy and dangerous.

But then the Vizier thought about the Princess Rory, who, but for her own disregard for protocol, might have been within the blast-radius when the body-man detonated himself, and he straightened. "Thank you again for your time, Minister."

The Minister of Energy raised one fine, blond brow. "Thank you, Vizier."

And so the first, and last, audience between the Vizier of Thorne and the Minister of Energy came to an end.

The Vizier was a cautious man, fond of evidence. And so he spent the next few days before the funeral making use of the diplomatic access available on the Thorne embassy's turing, and of his considerable skill with arithmancy when that access proved insufficient.

It was because of what he discovered that the Vizier was alone among foreign diplomats and dignitaries who attended King Sergei's funeral to be unsurprised that Minister Moss took charge of the event, and the only one to notice how very close the Minister of Energy stood to Prince Ivar during the funeral and how he hovered, not so much protectively as possessively. Nor was he surprised when reports came that the Queen's shuttle suffered an inexplicable power surge that sent it diving into the sun. Instead, the Vizier quietly arranged for passage back to the Thorne Consortium and departed Urse the same day that Vernor Moss was named the Regent of the Free Worlds by unanimous vote of the ruling Council.

This time, the Vizier spent his journey organizing his notes and observations, and rehearsing his eventual report to the Consort in front of a mirror in his quarters until he was certain of every syllable. It was not his first time acting as Thorne's official representative, but it was his first time doing so for the Consort, and he wanted to impress her with his attention to detail. The old King would have deferred that report for several days. The Vizier suspected the Consort would not, and indeed, she summoned the Vizier to her office within an hour of his return to Thorne.

And so the Vizier found himself delivering his report to the Consort almost exactly as he'd rehearsed it. He stood in front of the desk, which he'd planned; and he had his hands clasped behind his back, which kept him from picking at his cuticles. But he could not stare at his favorite stain on the desk, because the Regent-Consort had covered it with a small pot, in which grew a Kreshti fern. Its silver-blue fronds sampled the air, sifting for pheromones, sending out some of its own, in an attempt to attract unwary insects.

The Vizier recalled that the apparent delicacy of its fronds and stems was an illusion. The only way to kill a Kreshti fern, as the Kreshti farmers well knew, was to tear it out by its roots and burn it. The Consort had been born and raised on Kreshti, and he suspected she and the fern shared that tenacity.

The Vizier finished his report. "That's all, your Highness."

Ordinarily the King would say, "Thank you, Rupert," or, "That will be all, Rupert," or sometimes, a muffled "mrrzzz," at which point the Vizier would wait exactly one minute before leaving quietly so as not to wake his sovereign.

The Consort also said nothing, but she was not snoring, and so the Vizier did not move. Instead, he stared so hard at the little fern that it stretched four of its five fronds toward him and turned a remarkable shade of vermillion.

"That was a fine report, Rupert. Now tell me what you actually think."

The Vizier jerked as if someone had jammed a pin into his leg (which Rory had, once, in her early childhood, shortly after Grytt became her body-maid). His gaze bounced off the fern and landed on the Consort. She had made a little steeple of her first two fingers and rested the point of her chin on the apex. It was a surprisingly disarming gesture, and deceptive, because it meant that she was thinking. A thinking monarch was, in the Vizier's experience, always dangerous. He wished he'd sneaked out while he had opportunity. He wondered if he ever *had* an opportunity. He weighed the wisdom of answering honestly against his experience with the King, who preferred brevity. And, out of reflex, he stalled.

First, clear the throat. Then, raise the brows. Then, adjust both sleeves. And then, "Your Grace?" in the most innocuous tones possible.

She stared at him, night-dark eyes unblinking as a singularity and as impossible to escape.

"Rupert. Sit down. And tell me. What. You. Think."

The Vizier sat. Shot a nervous glance at the fern, which had turned vivid scarlet, and decided on honesty.

"The Minister offered neither accusation nor apology when I met with him. He did not act like a man surprised or bereft by Valenko's death. I think he's responsible, your Grace, for all of it."

"Go on."

"The popular choice for Regent of the Free Worlds was the Minister of Commerce. She declined. So did the second reasonable choice, the Minister of Defense. Together, they nominated Moss, and with their support, the rest of the Council approved his appointment without even a cursory debate."

"Are you suggesting bribery, Rupert? Or conspiracy?"

"It is unclear which, your Grace. Perhaps both."

The Consort raised one half-moon brow. "Samur, Rupert. When we're in private, call me Samur."

The Vizier bowed slightly and hoped the heat crawling up his neck and cheeks didn't show up as red on his face.

"As I said. I have no proof of bribery or conspiracy, nor did I feel it my place to inquire too deeply. Moss had, by the time I departed, already issued warrants for the arrest of individuals he believed responsible for the alteration of the body-man's implants. He is very dramatic, and very persuasive."

"And are those individuals guilty?"

"Perhaps, although I do not believe that is likely." The Vizier tapped his tablet and turned the screen to show the Consort. "Note that they are all former employees of the Science and Research Department. Note, too, that they all either lost their funding in the past two years, or were replaced on their project teams for reasons which seem rather contrived. And note whose authorization is on all of the orders."

The Consort leaned onto her elbows. Swiped the screen, once and again, and frowned. "It seems odd, Rupert, that a minor minister would be signing termination orders for Science and Research personnel and projects."

"It does, your Gr—Samur."

"And it seems unlikely that, even disappointed by their terminations, these individuals would all decide to conspire to assassination, particularly since the King did not terminate their projects. Regicide is a capital crime. If they had conspired, one imagines they would have left Tadeshi space already rather than accepting this exile. And—hm."

The Consort had just noticed, as the Vizier himself already had, that all the accused had been relocated to a half-frozen moon orbiting a gas giant denied any official moniker more personalized than an alphanumeric string. The colonists called the moon Perdition, the planet, Judgment, and the system's star, Sheol. It was, on record, a mining outpost, although not a particularly prolific one.

There were two possible destinations for ships leaving Perdition. One was solidly in Tadeshi territory. The other was Kreshti. This mattered for two reasons. The first was that should those scientists choose to flee that accusation of regicide, Kreshti was their only option. If the Kreshti did grant asylum, then it looked like they approved of—or at least did not mind—the crime of regicide; and given Kreshti's relationship with the Thorne Consortium, and that the Consort was herself Kreshti, it looked as if that regicide might be politically motivated.

And second, Tadesh (before it had collected any Free Worlds) had been sniffing after Kreshti's planetary resources for most of the two hundred years since Kreshti had fought its way free of the Merak Horde. Kreshti had a breathable atmosphere, liquid water, and a relatively hospitable biosphere. While the Thornes were still terraforming dead red planets in the home system, Kreshti were earning their skill with battle-hexes—skills that reminded the Tadeshi in the occasional skirmish that those planetary resources would cost them more than the planet's worth. But as the Free Worlds accumulated, the Tadeshi grew bolder and more certain the cost would be worth it.

It had been the Kreshti's formal alliance with the Thorne Consortium, in the person of Samur, that had guaranteed Tadeshi good behavior. And if Kreshti could be accused of harboring King Sergei's assassins, well. The Free Worlds of Tadesh might be willing to risk an invasion and apologize later. No one liked a suicide bomb, after all, particularly at a birthday party.

There was one final document. The Vizier leaned forward and flicked the screen. "And then there are these, your Grace."

"Requests for asylum to Kreshti. With my aunt's approval already stamped." The Regent-Consort side-eyed the Vizier. "Are these official documents, Rupert?"

"They are."

"Does Urse keep records like this on the public access systems? Because I know that Kreshti does not."

"No, your Grace."

"Rupert. Are you a secret hacker?"

"It is a . . . hobby." The Vizier caught a smile sneaking onto his face. To his surprise, the Consort smiled back. She had a dimple on her left cheek.

"Well *done*."

This time he knew the heat on his cheeks was visible. And the damned fern turned deep yellow.

The Consort sat back, then, and abandoned her smile. She sighed a little and rubbed the nine-month moon of her belly. "Are you aware, Rupert, why I married Thorne?"

Not *the King*. Not *my husband*. Not *Philip*. The Vizier hesitated. As a point of fact, he did know the details of the marriage contract, having helped his Majesty with the finer points of law and Kreshti custom. After a moment's hesitation (and the traitor-fern turning just the slightest bit orange), he said so.

"It was a political alliance, your Gr—Samur. To win your mother and sisters an ally—"

She sliced him silent with a gesture. "My mother used her daughter to *buy* an ally, so that I could, in turn, buy alliances and peace with my children, so that we could all avoid war. It's what sovereigns do. But now—now, we have one king dead, and one dying, and these documents suggest that the man who is now Regent of the Free Worlds both provoked dissent and relocated the dissenters a convenient tesser-hex from the one tiny planet that would, and in fact did, grant them sanctuary, which just happens to be allied to the Thorne Consortium by marriage. Furthermore, you have informed me that the Urse system is full of warships. Would you be willing to wager that the Regent of the Free Worlds killed my husband and his own king, and now he is preparing to declare war on the Consortium?"

"I would never bet against you, Samur."

A ghost of the former smile haunted her lips. "Good to know, Rupert. I will count that a promise. Because I'm not waiting for him. We are going to war."

CHAPTER FOUR

War, Death, And Birth

T hose who do not record history often labor under the misconception that it is easy: events happen, one after the other, fitting together like a well-crafted plot in which the characters do precisely what they must, when they must, to make the story turn out as it should. This is rarely the case. More often, significant moments overlap, crowding each other like geese around grain, each pushing the others aside for primacy. The death of the King of Thorne, the birth of the Prince, and the Consortium's declaration of war against the Free Worlds of Tadesh comprise a trilogy of such magnitude that it is difficult to discern which of them had the greatest impact on the little princess. A conventional recounting of Rory's life might prioritize the dramatic loss of her father, and the more subtle loss of her mother, as formative influences in what was to come.

But in truth, it was Grytt's absence that affected Rory most keenly. Before the explosion, Samur had insisted on daily breakfasts with Rory, and when possible, lunch and dinner as well. Even during her pregnancy, when she was not interested in, or capable of, eating, Samur would sit (complexion waxy, jaw locked and set) at the table with Rory, listening more than she spoke (for fear of what might happen if her jaw were unlocked). But the shift in duties from Consort to Regent-Consort meant that breakfasts became hurried affairs during which Samur stuffed toast into her mouth at a pace that would have drawn criticism, had it been Rory doing the gobbling. Then she was out the door, gone before Rory had got halfway through her own toast—chewing before swallowing, little bites, as she'd been taught. At least *before*, she would have had Deme Grytt for company, should her mother be struck unexpectedly busy.

But now, after the explosion, Deme Grytt was not there, having been wounded and whisked into the medical facility beyond Rory's reach. She had tried to visit. The medic at the front desk had been very firm in her insistence that Grytt could have no visitors, not even the Princess, but that she had been

badly hurt

a little banged up, your Highness, and that she

wouldn't die

would be just fine

If fine meant *in pain* and *all metal and wires, poor thing.*

Messer Rupert, her next most constant companion and tutor, was thoroughly occupied with helping her mother run the Consortium, so Rory's lessons were suspended, pending the acquisition of a substitute tutor.

And so it was that Rory found herself alone for the first time in her life. She thought she should feel lonely, and did, for exactly two hours, at which point she realized that there was no one to observe her loneliness and take pity on her.

That there was no one to observe her . . . doing anything. Well then.

Rory went down to the koi pond first. It was a destination she was permitted to visit alone, so long as she informed someone where she would be. She informed no one. And after skulking along the edge of the pond for several hours—having exhausted her supply of toast crusts, and thus having lost the koi's interest, as well—she determined that no one actually knew where she was, and judging from the lack of household staff swarming about and calling her name—no one cared.

This realization, like the loneliness, was both bitter and sweet.

Next, she amused herself by creeping around the palace. Creeping, because although she could have walked almost anywhere unchallenged, she chose to dress in her least Rory-ish clothing and cling to the edges and shadows. It was a game, at first, to see who would notice her. No one did. So she went down to the formal banquet hall and spied on the contractors who had come to repair the damage. She took stock of the damage herself. The hateful chairs were so much kindling, now. The great table was all burned on one end. And there were dark stains in the polished wood floor that had, she told herself sternly, come from people *bleeding*. Like Father. Like Grytt. Like Ivar's father.

She looked at those for a very long time.

She also looked and looked for any trace of the body-man—a wire, a sliver of steel—but found nothing.

By the fifth day, she had looked up a map to the medical wing on her tablet, and found the staff entrance where the laundry delivery came and went. She was making plans to sneak in to visit Grytt that way—at night, when there was no one to observe her—when there came a knock on her door.

It was well after supper (hers had been soup, a half a sandwich, and solitude), well after the time Grytt would have come in and turned off the lights and confiscated Rory's tablet. When no one had come to collect her tray, she'd decided they had well and truly forgotten her, and told herself that was fortunate, since tonight was moonless and therefore a good time to sneak down to the medical wing.

But then the knock came. Her mind leapt to the immediate conclusion that someone knew what she was planning and had come to thwart her. Then her wits reasserted themselves. It was unlikely, she told herself, that a palace staff that had permitted her to run about unsupervised for days at a time could anticipate this particular transgression.

Her heart continued to crowd up her throat, unconvinced.

She swallowed it, best she could. Blanked the screen on her tablet and stuffed it under her pillow. Jerked the covers up, and then down again, so that her hair crackled and strands of it poked out of her braid. Then she sat up and said, "Who is it?" in her best sleepy little girl voice.

The door cracked open. Messer Rupert's angular silhouette carved into the light spilling from the hall. Like a shadow-puppet. Flat. The effect would have made her laugh, except that Messer Rupert said,

"Rory."

Not *your Highness*. Not *Princess*. Just *Rory*, very gently, as if she were a little girl again. Her heart climbed back into her throat and stayed there. Her voice squeezed past the edges.

"Is it Grytt?"

The shadow-puppet shook his head. "No. No, Grytt's fine. Rory, it's your father. He's—"

Messer Rupert hesitated. He knew better than to lie to her; but he didn't want to be rude, either, and say an indelicate, impolite truth.

Rory spared him that trouble.

"Dead," she said flatly. "My father is dead."

The official press release called his death a tragedy. The whispers around the palace called it mercy. Even Messer Rupert was relieved, although there was grief, too, when he tried (not) to tell Rory the details of her father's passing.

She learned those much later, after she had mastered and misused her lessons in security-hexes for turings and hacked her way into the medical records. The King of the Thorne Consortium died of his wounds without ever quite recovering consciousness. The records say *quite*, because there were times his eyes opened. It is unclear whether or not he realized that he no longer had an arm or both legs, or that his torso ended halfway down in a sleek metal bulb that was mostly wired into the metal shell that did the work of his liver, lungs, and kidneys. What *is* recorded on his medical charts is that King Philip Thorne, first of his name, always ended these windows of consciousness screaming.

In that future time, an older Rory hunched in front of the terminal and read, unblinking, her tears turned to silver rivers in the screen's blue glow.

But when it happened—when the servants haunted the palace with red eyes and swollen cheeks and Messer Rupert went about stiffly, his jaw squared against grief—then, Rory couldn't find a single tear. She knew she *should* cry. She was sorry, certainly, that her father was dead. Sorrier still that so many people—the contractors and the medics and the folk unattached to the household—seemed personally wounded by it in ways she did not understand, a tangle of duty and pride in something much bigger than the man her father had been, something in which they, too, participated.

To them, Rory felt a vague mixture of guilt and obligation. At least their grief was honest. There were others who went around in public with faces mottled and streaky with grief—men who had been to dinner with the King, whom he had called *friend*—who were not a bit sorry. Not quite pleased, exactly; but not grief-stricken, either.

And then there was her own mother, whose weeping—always private, on the other side of doors—held equal parts sorrow and a dark, fierce joy at a freedom she had never thought to feel again.

Even Rory, who had little patience for prevarication, and even less skill at executing it herself, knew that her mother's mixed feelings must remain private. It did not take an adult to understand that. Still, she wished very much for Grytt's advice. She wondered if she dared tell anyone—her mother, Messer Rupert, the koi in the pond—that she missed her father less than she missed Grytt, or if that, like her mother's dark joy, must remain secret.

Lacking any other advisors, she asked the Rory in the mirror. And that girl—oh, a pretty thing now, true to the fairies' gifts, beautiful dark eyes, even red-rimmed, warm bronze skin, hair like a swath of moonless, cloudy night—answered.

"You keep it quiet, Rory. That's what you do."

Rory thought that was something Grytt might have said. She nodded approval at her mirror self, who nodded back.

Then Rory pulled her hair back into a tail, and pressed her lips together, and put her silence on like armor.

She wore that armor for the next four days, as the palace turned itself inside out, preparing for a royal funeral. The contractors would not be finished with the formal entryway in time, and so preparations were made to convert one of the side entrances. More work-people swarmed the hallways. Rory wore her armor through interminable fittings, where maids and seamstresses considerably less contained than Rory herself—Deme Ethel sniffled and leaked the entire two hours—measured and cut and stitched and remeasured, while Rory stood very still and had staring contests with her reflection.

The day of the funeral dawned exactly as grim and dark as the weather-hexes could make it, which is to say, so dark the birds didn't even know it was daylight. Nothing chirped. The tree-rats, who, unlike the birds, knew very well what time it was, hung themselves in the branches and watched as mourners from the city gathered at the fence the entire night. They watched as media crews passed through the guards' checkpoint and crept up the roads to the palace to set up their cameras. They watched, beady-eyed, as the King's coffin and its attendants marched out of the palace through the newly official side entrance. They watched as it marched down the road, toward the gates, past the lawns and forests, until it stopped in front of the gates. Then they listened to the wail rising out of the assembled citizens like the sun, higher and brighter until the whole world seemed painted with sound. And they watched the procession return, by the same route, and the crowd outside disperse. Then, and only then, did the tree-rats come down to scavenge, knowing that any crowd of that size will have members among it clever enough to bring their own food, and still others enterprising and unsentimental enough to set up carts to sell to those less well-prepared.

It was a good day for tree-rats, but not for princesses.

Rory was spared the procession—Messer Rupert oversaw that—but she was waiting when it returned to the palace. There, in the same great hall in which she had been Named, its walls hung with tapestries and screens to cover the unfinished repairs, the whole place smelling of fresh paint and sour incense, Rory stood and waited for her father's coffin. And when it arrived, she stood beside it, through the long hours of speeches by politically important people and monotone rituals by the three official faiths of the Thorne Consortium.

Let us take a moment, then, to describe this coffin, on which so much attention was fixed. It was made of a brushed pewter alloy. Homeworld tradition called for stone, but Messer Rupert had lost his heart for arguing on tradition's behalf. Still, the coffin bore traditional shape: a raised sculpture of the King lying atop it, hands crossed over his chest, his face relaxed as if he were asleep.

It was very lifelike, which made it very horrible and very beautiful. It also made the King seem much sterner and cleverer than he had been, with a geometric jaw and firm lips. It was meant to be comforting, and it was, therefore, exactly the sort of social illusion the thirteenth fairy had equipped Rory to notice. It was like a small rock in one's shoe. Annoying at first, and then painful, and then intolerable.

Rory made a point not to look at her coffin-father's face. She stared just past it, to the worn front edge of the dais. Exactly the spot, although she did not know it, from which the thirteenth fairy had scolded the King. She herself stood in exactly the same spot her father had stood, during that scolding.

It should have been the Regent-Consort's place, but the Regent-Consort was not in attendance, a fact about which her political enemies made much, and which ended up undermining her reign before it had even begun because people will always believe the worst about someone if it's more interesting than the truth, particularly if that person is the least bit different or foreign. It becomes the task of historians to correct those misperceptions with a cold application of fact.

And so: The Regent-Consort missed her husband's funeral because she was busy with an event as inevitable as war and death, though significantly more rewarding. She birthed her second child, a son, eleven days following the explosion, at the precise moment that her firstborn, much-wished-for daughter stood on the dais and listened to the Bishop of Tres intoning dogma about wheels and rebirth.

Rory was not entirely alone on the dais. Messer Rupert stood on her right side, like a tall shadow cast by a rising—or setting—sun. Rory knew he wanted to put his hand on her shoulder, as he did sometimes when he wanted to reassure her. She knew he wanted to stand between her and the crowd and let her hide in his formal robes, as she had when she was very young. She knew he wouldn't dare either gesture, which made her both glad and sorry; but she also knew he was right in his suspicion that she did not need his reassurance.

Because she had Grytt back. That was the best part of the whole horrid day, the joy of which filled Rory's chest and made her heart ache as it tried to decide whether to be sad or happy and ended up just hurting. Deme Grytt had

bullied her way

gotten out of the medical wing to be here. She stood, raw and pink where she had kept her skin, dull brushed chrome where she hadn't. One of her eyes was a tesla, now, blue and bright in a metal socket. It made a faint *whirring* noise as it moved. And it moved constantly. Rory watched the shivers and winces ripple across the faces of the attendees and back again as Grytt's stare passed over them.

So Rory stood between Rupert and Grytt, wearing black crepe and silk in a formal style meant for someone much older. She looked a little bit like a baby crow caught in the rain. But her eyes were clear, and her lips were tightly pressed, and her chin didn't wobble once.

Everyone agreed, afterward, that she had been very, very brave.

When, after eighteen hours in labor, still sweat-soaked and bloody, the Regent-Consort formally entered hostilities against the Free Worlds of Tadesh, and committed her kingdom-by-marriage to war, no one said anything at all about bravery.

Such are the peculiarities of history.

———

The Thorne Consortium had been officially at war for two days before Rory Thorne met her brother. There was no conspiracy on the part of the Regent-Consort to keep her children apart. It was simply an issue of time, availability, and the diligence (the less charitable might say mulishness) of the Prince's nurse.

A monarch in the early stages of a war has much to do, and the Regent-Consort had to fit Jacen's existence into an endless series of meetings and planning sessions. Wars, as it turned out, required a vast shifting of resources, both mechanical and organic; they also required a great deal of funding. The Thorne Consortium was wealthy and well-endowed, so that was not (yet) a concern; but knowing which divisions and battalions and cruisers to put where was a matter of strategy and political argument and long consultation with people who had often conflicting advice.

The Regent-Consort was grateful, in those days, for two things: that she had grown up playing chess and that she had Deme Isabelle to look after the as-yet-unofficially Named Prince Jacen. A baby can be deferred with a bottle. However much their behavior may resemble an infant's, politicians cannot.

Deme Isabelle had also been King Thorne's nurse—an old woman, soft-bodied and sharp-tongued. She had never been Rory's, to her chagrin. Then, the Regent-Consort had insisted on doing her own mothering duties and damn Thorne custom. But this time—with a war ongoing, and a kingdom to oversee—she yielded to tradition and necessity and consigned the Prince to his nurse for large swathes of the day.

Deme Isabelle had never forgiven the Regent-Consort for denying her oversight of the Princess and so, having acquired authority of *this* Thorne child, she was determined to keep it. Part of that authority meant controlling his environment. An infant, of course, does not have many visitors. Jacen had his mother, whom Deme Isabelle had to admit, whatever her grudges; but there were not, at this stage in the Prince's life, a great many others interested in spending time with him. His sister, however, was interested, and here was where the conflict arose.

There were many, many things, in Deme Isabelle's reckoning, that had been done *wrong* in the raising of Rory Thorne. Wild little thing, running about. It wasn't proper. It wasn't *tradition*. Of course, the real source of Deme Isabelle's resentment was not Rory's athletic habits. It was Grytt, to whom the young Princess had been entrusted once she was weaned and toddling, who infected the Princess with her Kreshti ways, allowing a girl-child to run and encouraging her to stick pins in the household staff who displeased her—by which she meant a single, unfortunate incident in which Rory had stuck a pin in the Vizier's leg while he was engaged in attempting to teach her arithmantic hexes. The Vizier himself was usually much on the side of tradition for its own sake, and his relationship with Grytt was an evolving effort; that Grytt's first reaction to the news of Rory's trespass had been laughter, rather than horror, had not helped their relationship. But however inappropriate Grytt's comportment, the Vizier knew that she had not encouraged the Princess to violence. It was just an unfortunately literal child-mind interpretation of the phrase *stuffed shirt*, which Rory should not have overheard and had and decided to test, as one does, with a straight pin.

Deme Isabelle, having drawn her own judgment once, refused to revise it, whatever the actual victim of the incident reported, and upon that belief based her decision to keep Rory Thorne well out of her brother's nursery.

So when Rory knocked on the nursery door, fully expecting

admittance, she was surprised when Deme Isabelle opened the door only half the width of her own body and peered down at Rory and said, "No, dear, I'm sorry," before Rory even got out a word. Deme Isabelle's whole face shone with a delighted malice. "This isn't a good time. The baby's asleep."

Rory did not need the fairy's gift to know that Jacen most certainly was *not* asleep. Babies do not shriek because of wet nappies while napping. Deme Isabelle wasn't even trying to lie. She was just saying no, and daring Rory to do something about it. No. Not daring.

Rory squinted a little. There was *something* the nurse wanted to say. Something fluttering behind her squared-off smirk. She pulled out her best smile and pasted it across her lips.

"I am the Princess," Rory said, in a tone so sweet butterflies would feed upon it, while teeth dissolved into cavities. "And I'm asking to see my brother."

Deme Isabelle did not need the thirteenth fairy's gift to hear *order* instead of *ask*. But perhaps she had been struck by some glamour, for instead of seeing seven-year-old Rory in front of her, she saw instead the Regent-Consort seven years earlier, holding an infant, and she heard the Regent-Consort say, "That will be all, thank you, but I don't need your help."

So it was as much to the mother's memory, as to the daughter, that Deme Isabelle said, "And I'm telling you I'm sorry, but no. Princess."

you'll not be ordering me about, or anyone, now that we have a proper heir, just you wait

Her smile was wide, sharp, entirely sincere, and not a bit kind.

The fairies had given Rory kindness, beauty, and wits. They had neglected to include sweet, biddable disposition. Thus, we might forgive Rory if the temper she had inherited from her mother, which did not much love the word *no* when it was not attached to an explanation, flared up.

Rory looked at Deme Isabelle for a moment longer than was proper for child to look at an adult. It was a staring-down-the-help look, with a good bit of square-jawed stubborn thrown into the mix. In ten years, that stare would provoke results. But Rory's stare was unripe, and Deme Isabelle unimpressed.

The nursery door was shut, harder than was entirely polite for servant to royalty (however young), separating sister and brother.

So.

Rory had become quite skilled at getting into places she should not be, in the past ten days since the attack, and though the nursery door was locked, we must add that it was not secured beyond Rory's ability to hex. (That lesson in lock-picking was Messer Rupert's fault, though unwitting: he had been trying to show a reluctant student the practical applications of theoretical arithmancy, in an effort to head off another pin incident.)

Rory stared at the door. The polished brass knob and keyhole were, like so many other things about the palace, remnants of homeworld tradition left purely for appearance. The actual locking mechanism was a panel on the door which was hexed to recognize, and admit, particular auras. Rory's mother. Deme Isabelle. Baby Jacen.

It was indeed fortunate, Rory thought, that Messer Rupert had recently taught her how family members shared elements of their auras. It was even more fortunate that he had, upon seeing her interest (and rejoicing in it), showed her how her mother's aura and hers, for instance, shared seven of ten frequencies and an unusual double-spiral pattern. It was all numbers, he assured her. The same dread numerals that made up arithmancy also described auras (and, he added, everything else in the multiverse).

She retreated down the corridor, and settled in a tiny alcove with a narrow slit window and a habit of utter neglect. But for this particular afternoon, as the bar of light from its window slanted toward evening and the sky outside deepened to an eggplanty-blue, it had the Princess in residence. She settled into a corner where the cobwebs were not too thick (there was a draft which made it uncomfortable for spiders, if not for young girls) and worked out her hexes with the arithmancy Messer Rupert had taught her, which involved holding her breath until she could see into that first, shallow layer of aether behind the one that everyone could breathe, where auras gleamed as bright as any rainbow. (We should note that holding one's breath is not ideal arithmantic practice as it tends to lead to the arithmancer turning blue and passing out, which the Vizier made clear, and which we repeat here, lest our readers attempt to try this at home.)

Although an aura did have a propensity to particular hues and particular patterns, individual auras could, and did, shift their colors according to the mood and biochemical disposition of said individual. Rory was easily able to match her mother's spiral pattern—only a little tweak to the angle between tangent and radial—but she was less sanguine about the matching of color.

She would eventually learn to identify colors by the numerical designations that governed hue, intensity, and value, which afforded a fine level of control; but the Vizier had started simply, and confined his explanation to a list of simple correspondences. Reds meant strong emotion, love or hate or anger. Oranges, agitation and distress. Yellow was fear or embarrassment; and the cooler shades, cooler emotions (except green, which was generally regarded as unsavory in all its variations, indicating mendacity or hidden agendas). The Regent-Consort's aura had, of late, been populated by more green than was typical, a tinge that diluted the usual blues and blackened the edges of violets. Rory thought her own copy was rather too ultramarine, but she thought it would work long enough to fool the hexes on the nursery door.

And she waited. The supper hour was coming. *Eventually,* Deme Isabelle would have to come out. Or fall asleep. Or—something. Rory hadn't worked out her plans that far, and thinking about them now—after the time already spent on a hex that would get her past the door, and which she badly wanted to try out—only soured her mood even further. Rory was on the verge of attempting to create a new set of hexes, the kind that would give an old woman green spots or make her speak only the k'bal dialect that sounds like dyspeptic chickens, when fate—or luck—intervened.

Although a half dozen servants had walked by the alcove in the intervening hours, not one had looked sideways and noticed Rory. But a Regent-Consort, however preoccupied with meetings, however focused on her tablet and on the subvocalized conversation she was having via earpiece and mastoid mobile, will always notice her daughter sitting in a neglected corner of the palace. And she will read the brow-knit expression (correctly) as a forewarning of mischief, rather than a headache brought on by an excess of dust.

The Regent-Consort stopped. She matched her daughter's frown with one of her own and terminated her conversation with a short pair of syllables. And then she said, out loud, "Rory. For the love of—what are you doing here? Does Messer Rupert know where you are? Does Grytt?"

"No." Rory scrambled to her feet, discovering along the way that hours spent in drafty stone alcoves stiffen even young muscles. She caught her balance on the wall and scraped her knuckle on the brick. The surprise of that, coupled with her general discomfort and threadbare patience, brought tears prickling to the back of her eyes. Her throat sealed around the rest of her answer. Only a tiny squeak escaped. She was horrified. She blinked hard, bit her lip, and tried to make herself stern-faced and grim. She failed miserably.

Her mother's frown deepened. "Rory," she said, and her voice was too gentle for the storm gathering in her eyes. "What happened?"

In a very short time, Rory would learn that the safest answer to that question and its sibling, *what are you doing*, is an ingenuous *nothing*, particularly if there is no evidence to the contrary. At the time, however, she knew only that her knuckle was bleeding, her bottom hurt, and her mother could fix everything.

The words spilled out like rice from a cut sack. "I came to see Jacen, but Deme Isabelle said he was sleeping, only he wasn't, and she wouldn't let me in."

Rory paused for a breath, and considered adding what Deme Isabelle hadn't said, about giving orders and proper heirs, but the Regent-Consort's lips were drawing together like a miser's purse strings. If there had been a Kreshti fern present, it would have turned a deep cerise laced with adamant aubergine.

"Come along," the Regent-Consort said, and took Rory's hand.

Within very short order, Deme Isabelle found the Prince transferred to his mother's arms and herself sent to supper rather abruptly, on the very edge of courtesy.

"If you hurry, you'll be able to eat with the rest of the staff." The Regent-Consort smiled broadly, showing nearly all of her teeth. It would have been a lovely smile, had there been any warmth at all in it. Instead, the effect was rather predatory.

Deme Isabelle dropped an old woman's curtsy to the Regent-Consort. "As you wish, your Grace. Thank you, your Grace."

She crossed stares with Rory. One heartbeat. Two. Then she departed with as much dignity as she could manage. Her stare lingered, even after the door closed, dragging on Rory's skin like old nails.

Rory had never seen hatred before, nor had she ever had an enemy. Her belly felt cold, deep inside, and the space between her shoulder blades itched. It was not an urgent sensation, like her fear of the body-man had been. A more patient cousin, perhaps, like ice on the courtyard in winter, appearing underfoot when you had both hands in your pockets and no way of catching yourself when you fell. Rory rubbed her cheek, remembering that lesson. In another heartbeat, she would have made a note to herself to tell Grytt about it. But then her mother interrupted,

"Here, Rory," and handed her a squirming blanketed bundle. "Meet your little brother."

And in that moment, Rory forgot about Deme Isabelle entirely.

Jacen had the smallest fingers in all the world, and a cap of dark soft hair that wasn't sure if it should curl or simply stick straight out. His beautiful blue eyes, just like her father's, stared up into hers. In that moment, she imagined a future in which she showed him the koi, and taught him to climb trees, and shared the best places to hide from Messer Rupert. Oh, she knew that would not happen for a long time—he was so tiny! so red!—but he would grow. Babies did. He would become a *person*, and he would be her *brother*, and in that moment, Rory thought that was the best possible thing in the world.

Then Jacen screwed up his face and howled and would not stop, no matter how Rory tried to soothe him. He only quieted when she gave up and handed him back to her mother. Then he stuck both fingers in his mouth and stared at her, red-faced and unhappy. Each time she tried to hold him, he howled.

This would become the pattern that defined their relationship.

CHAPTER FIVE ≡≡≡

The Heir And The Spare

Some infants are sweet little creatures, easily pleased and contented. They do not cry often, and when they do, it is for a purpose: hunger, or wetness, or an aggressive burp meandering through their interiors.

Jacen was not one of those babies.

Deme Isabelle insisted, with some pride, that he had "his own mind, he does." Deme Grytt and the Vizier agreed, privately, that Jacen's mind seemed set on whatever the people around him did *not* want, unless that someone was Deme Isabelle. She steered her Prince's desires, and saw to their fulfillment, and because she was his most frequent companion, Jacen grew into insisting on and expecting his own way. By his second birthday, he had learned to throw spectacular tantrums. By his fifth birthday, which was also the fifth year of the War, which had acquired a capital letter and a central importance in public anxiety, the Prince had mastered the fine art of whining. His strategy was simple: produce the most irritating sound, or set of sounds, for as long as was necessary to wear down the opposition and secure whatever it was he wanted.

And what Prince Jacen did not want, at the age of five, was to start his lessons. The Regent-Consort had asked the Vizier to see to her son's tutelage, as he had seen to Rory's. The Vizier privately wondered if he had done something to offend his sovereign. Prince Jacen was currently experimenting with pitch and volume, and had achieved a level of both that, if they did not win him the concessions he wanted (an extra piece of pie from the kitchens, a game, the Vizier's immediate departure), would at least forestall the lesson for some period of time, usually until he ran out of breath.

Jacen enjoyed these battles. The Vizier did not; he was only thankful that Jacen had not discovered straight pins. He made a habit of visiting his first and favorite pupil immediately following his sessions with her brother. It was, in retrospect, unwise, if he meant to keep his ire with the Prince a secret. Because of course when she saw him, Rory knew something was amiss. And of course when she asked him, his perfunctory *fine* rang loudly to her ears as *your wretched brother.*

Rory herself harbored no illusions about her brother's character. She knew she was supposed to love him, and she tried; but she had, by this point, quite given up on trying to like him. She entertained a vague hope she might grow into it, but she found it hard to forgive the effect he had on the people dearest to her. Grytt and the Vizier were made actively miserable by him, while her mother, who held a solid third in her affections, was the only one who appeared to bear any real fondness for him. Jacen's deleterious effect was clearest on the Vizier, whose years as chief and much needed advisor to the Regent-Consort were already threading his hair grey at the temples and carving lines around his mouth and eyes that did not come from smiling.

To see those lines deepen, and know Jacen was at fault, made Rory angry. Because the fairies had given her kindness, however, and because she had not yet learned to rely on violence as a recourse, she sought to repair the defects in her brother's character.

She understood multiverse theory quite well, for a girl of twelve.

Thus, she knew that anything *is* possible. Her miscalculation lay in her assumption that the *possible* and the *probable* are closely related, and in the underlying cause of Jacen's shortcomings.

Jacen had never had a Naming, and thus had never gotten gifts of good character from the fairies. Therefore, a Naming would set him right.

Once convinced of a course of action, Rory was unshakeable. Ordinarily, the Vizier would have found her tenacity endearing. It was, after all, the same trait she brought to bear on arithmantic theory and alchemical formulas, and it made her a joy to teach. It was also the same trait she employed when learning to scale the garden walls and climb around the rooftops, but that was Grytt's particular problem, and watching her handle Rory provided the Vizier with much needed amusement.

He suspected Grytt felt much the same, at present. She was in the corner, shoulder turned to most of the room, running a diagnostic on her left wrist and forefinger, cables snaking from multiple points on that limb to a tablet. She *looked* entirely distracted, but the Vizier knew her better than that by now.

"He needs a Naming," Rory was saying. "I know it's late, but if we held one *now*, the fairies might still come. There's nothing in the histories that says they wouldn't."

"No," said Messer Rupert, for the ninth time in three days. He had counted. And for the ninth time in three days, he added, "It's a great deal of work, planning a Naming, and the sad fact is we don't have *time* right now, and by we, I mean your mother and myself and whoever else would be inconvenienced by your desire to play dress-up."

Once, Rory would have retreated from that tone. Folded in on herself a little and apologized and looked actually guilty for upsetting him. The Vizier felt a pang of nostalgia for that child. This

Princess, with her chin stuck out, bore little resemblance. He considered changing the subject, which would have been prudent; but because he was short on sleep, and shorter still on patience (and because he suspected Grytt was laughing at him, over there in the corner), the Vizier told the rest of the reasons behind his refusal.

"As I told you before, your Highness, there is no tradition of Naming Princes. It has nothing to do with being unfair. It does not mean that fairies don't like boys. It only means that Princes do not need fairy gifts."

He realized, a heartbeat too late, what he'd said, and then it was too late.

Rory pounced. "And a Princess does? Why?"

The Vizier exhaled hard through his nose. Not a snort, which would have meant amusement, but a hard blast like a steam-valve or a teapot on the edge of boiling. His lips were very thin and slightly white on the edges. His eyes were red-rimmed and red-shot and, as a result, extremely green. He flung that viridian stare past Rory.

"Deme Grytt." And when she did not favor him with her attention, "*Grytt*. Would you *please* explain to her Highness why it is we did not, and will not, have a Naming for her brother?"

Grytt tapped *pause* on the screen, arresting the unfolding graph and crimson spill of numbers. Her remaining organic eye rolled one complete, exasperated revolution before settling into the edge of its socket nearest the Vizier. She also blew air through her nose, though far less forcefully.

"I think that Rupert's right, although it's got nothing to do with tradition. It's too late to Name your brother because the point of fairy gifts is to imprint them on the impressionable. I fear the Prince has already chosen his path through life."

Rory threw her hands up. "He's *five*, Grytt."

"Yes. And he's already a little tyrant."

Rory threaded her arms across her chest. "That isn't the *real* reason. I can tell."

Grytt hoisted her eyebrow. "That certainly is *a* reason, and it's just as real as the other." She held up her left forefinger in what would have been an arresting and dramatic gesture, except for the cables dangling from the other three fingers and thumb. "Let me finish, young miss, I'll get to it."

Rory knew Grytt only ever used *young miss* when she was annoyed. *Young miss* meant *you hush and listen, dammit*—because Grytt thought in swear words, sometimes, so clearly that Rory could hear them.

Grytt set the tablet aside. She turned both eyes on Rory, artificial and flesh, cold blue and warm brown.

"Boys don't need fairy gifts, because boys are supposed to be kings. No one cares if a king is pretty. People probably should care if he's kind, but they don't. He's supposed to run things. But you— your job is to make *him* happy and to make his people love you. That's easier if you're pretty and nice. All that business the fairies gave you, that's to make your life easier. Any princess who *isn't* those things will have a rough go."

Dead and sudden silence, as if the world had turned to void.

The Vizier wished very much for a pin. A large pin. Perhaps a foot in length, that he might use to skewer Grytt's tongue to the table. At least Rory, for once, had nothing to say. Her mouth and eyes competed to see which could be wider and rounder and more surprised.

"My *mother*," she squeaked finally.

"Is not a princess, because the Kreshti don't have princesses. But even not-princesses must make political alliances. Do you think her life would be easier if she were kind, sweet, and did what she was told?"

Rory made a little strangled noise in the back of her throat.

Grytt nodded, a little sadly. Then she turned her stare onto the Vizier and tucked one side of her mouth into a wry smirk that said, *That's the last we'll hear of a Naming, then.*

But it wasn't.

It is one of history's little ironies that the Prince did end up getting a Naming, although not the sort that Rory or Grytt might have wished for. It is an even greater irony that the Vizier did not anticipate it: it was, after all, his job to know the homeworld traditions and history, which includes obscure bits of custom that become even more obscure bits of law.

Historians might excuse him: the Vizier had been distracted with more immediate concerns. The War, of course and most obviously. The logistics of waging the War largely fell to the Minister of Defense and the Minister of Commerce, and through them the generals and the merchant fleets and supply lines; but the influx of refugees, the stress of maintaining a wartime economy, and the Free Worlds' alarming proclivity for experimental battle-hexes, ensured that all the Ministers had plenty to occupy them. The Vizier was too wise to meddle in the business of the other ministries; he kept his interaction limited to oversight, requiring frequent reports and briefings, which he then read, collated, absorbed, and discussed with the Regent-Consort long after the official meetings were over. If the other Ministers resented the Vizier's place in the Regent-Consort's regard, they never complained. It meant that they were spared the burden of the endless cycle of finding, hiring, and replacing tutors for Prince Jacen.

———

So when the Vizier received a summons, late one evening, to the Regent-Consort's presence, he was not surprised. The War did not respect anyone's schedule. The venue, however—the Regent-Consort's office, in the business wing—*did* surprise him; for although the Regent-Consort often conducted business late, after dinner with her children, she usually did so from the comfort of her apartments. He supposed that there had been another wave of salacious gossip about their relationship, which, until it died down again, would necessitate several weeks of trekking across the palace at all hours, as well as a suspension of less official association to which Samur's personal quarters were well-suited.

The Vizier passed the evening shift of servants, polishing the floors and defending the old-style 2D portraits from imaginary dust. The sconces flickered with tesla-hex flames, cold and beautiful and guaranteed not to drip wax. He allowed himself a moment to imagine what it must have been like, on the homeworld, when the world was lit by candles, and the night was something to be feared. He made a note to himself to share that with the Regent-Consort—she liked that kind of discussion—perhaps when they finished whatever business she had discovered at this hour. He speculated that it was a general's report on the dispensation of Free World battle fleets, and hoped it was not more bad news out of Kreshti. It seemed as if there might be large-scale crop failure on the northern continent, a blight that no one had seen before. Thorne botanists and arithmancers had been dispatched. But they would not even have arrived yet, so it would be too soon for their report.

The office door whisked aside, sensing the Vizier's aura while he was still two strides away and admitting him automatically. He crossed the threshold as he had a dozen times already today, brain busy with the War, eyes only half-focused on the well-worn path across the carpet, until his gaze snagged on several dots of bright color, and his heart took a sudden plunge into his belly.

The original Kreshti fern was still in its accustomed place on the Regent-Consort's desk. Several of its daughter-ferns also lived in the office: a pair sharing space on the window sill, another tucked between the printer and the quantum-hex viewing globe, a fourth balanced in a wall sconce whose tesla-hex fixture had been removed. At the moment, they were all a vivid orange, making the room look as if an exuberant five-year-old with a large brush had come in and rendered the walls polka-dot.

It would have been a charming effect, had the Vizier not known that orange meant a state of high agitation. Ordinarily, he would have been glad of the ferns' forewarning. The Regent-Consort was legendary, among a staff long accustomed to the Old King, for maintaining her composure. But today, she was standing at the window, staring outward. In daylight, the view of the grounds would have been lovely. At night, the ambient interior light rendered the window a mirror, which meant that as the Vizier entered, the Regent-Consort did not have to turn around to glare at him.

It also meant he could not sneak back out and flee down the hallway. He stopped, instead, as the door snicked closed behind him.

"Your Grace?" It did not seem like a *Samur* sort of visit.

The Regent-Consort did not correct him, which confirmed his suspicion. Instead, she spun on her heel. She marched to the desk, leaned across it, and shoved a tablet down its length, narrowly missing the fern and the terminal. The tablet shot between a pair of 2Ds, one of the Princess and one of the Prince (who could not share a frame happily, and could indeed scarcely tolerate each other on the wide expanse of the desk). In its Regent-propelled rush, the tablet skidded past Prince Jacen's 2D and caught the far corner of Princess Rory's frame, spinning the 2D so that she, and her mother, stared at the Vizier. Of the pair, at least Rory was smiling.

The tablet stopped, finally, a finger's width from the edge of the desk. The Vizier met it there, approaching with caution. The screen showed a great many lines of small, officious print, stacking into columns and punctuated with florid headings meant to imitate handwritten script. It looked official and unpleasant.

"Read it," the Regent-Consort said, unnecessarily. She folded her arms hard across her middle, as if she meant to test the sturdiness of her ribs. The ferns on the desk trended crimson nearest their stems.

The Vizier did so. The small, officious print proved itself to be a legal codex: both unpleasant, and, from the clues left by syntax and phrasing, quite old, from a time when codices were handscripted on vellum and the stars were merely lights in the sky.

"Oh," the Vizier said, when he had finished. "Oh, dear."

The Regent-Consort made a little growling noise in the back of her throat. "Rupert. Tell me this isn't real. Tell me it's nonsense."

"It is nonsense, your Grace. But it does appear genuine. Where did you find it?"

"I did not *find* it. The Minister of the Interior brought it to my attention today. Which is to say, he ambushed me in a corridor with a list of potential husbands for my daughter. He had them arranged by political usefulness, liquid wealth, and raw planetary resources. When I told him I had given no thought to marrying my *thirteen-year-old daughter* to anyone, as she would be Queen someday, he showed me this. He was smirking, Rupert. *Smirking.*"

The Vizier very carefully did not look at her. "I am very, very sorry, your Grace. I regret to admit I did not know about this particular provision."

"Bah." She waved her hand, dismissing the tablet and its archaic codex. The ferns shivered ever so slightly toward aubergine. The Regent-Consort rearranged her face into its habitual composure. The Vizier, who knew her very well, marked the cracks around her eyes, her mouth, in the faint breathlessness of her voice. "It can't be legal, Rupert. The Thorne Consortium has non-discrimination policies for both employment and contracts. Why would succession be any different?"

"Because there have been no girls born to the line since the Thornes founded it. Laws are rarely changed, your Grace, without an immediate and obvious need."

"Well, there's an immediate and obvious need *right now.*"

"No. There is not. You have a son. You remain Regent-Consort, but now you rule for Prince Jacen. If you attempt to change this law now, you will be seen as—" He hesitated. Winced. The fern nearest him drooped and turned chartreuse.

Her eyes were hard and cool. "Kreshti. Foreign. Outsider. Disgracing my husband's memory and shaming his ancestors. Is that about right?"

The Vizier nodded, miserable. "You would also be perceived as playing favorites between your children and, ah, Prince Jacen is quite popular among the people."

"More popular than Rory."

Because they do not know him, the Vizier did not say. *And they do not know her.*

The Regent-Consort said it for him, with a mother's anguish. "Because they have transferred their affection for Philip onto him, knowing nothing of him other than he looks like his father, and that Rory looks like me." She turned away, abandoning all pretense of detachment. "It's a stupid law!"

The Vizier had to agree. But the legal provisions in the antique codex were clear: the throne would pass to the eldest son and the heirs of his body, before it could come to Rory Thorne.

And so, on the eve of his sixth birthday, the age at which boys were deemed sturdy enough to begin bearing the burden of kingship, Jacen Thorne was officially named the Crown Prince, and traded the honorific your Highness for your Majesty.

This did not in any way improve his tendency toward tyranny.

CHAPTER SIX ▬▬▬

Check

Rory Thorne, thus demoted from *heir* to merely *princess*, did not notice any particular difference in her daily routines. She still had lessons with her tutors and lessons with her battle-master (the name she and Grytt agreed upon as more impressive than body-maid). She had meals with her mother, avoided her brother, and made long, introspective retreats to the koi pond. The holidays and public events marched on in their cycle, and she evolved from mere decoration—a child in satin and velvet, perched on a chair beside her brother—to active participant. Still stuffed into satin and velvet, she was expected to mingle with the guests. To smile, and laugh, and

perform like a trained tree-rat

converse with an audience whose judgment was both fickle in its result and certain in its rendering.

Rory developed a sincere appreciation for the effectiveness of a full-sized homeworld harp as a shield against undesirable interpersonal contact. Performance gave her audience an objective and impersonal framework by which they might judge her: *What a lovely rendition of Mzambe's Third Invention, what a strange interpretation of Kinzi's Fugue No. 100, oh, I simply do not like or understand k'bal music.* Thus did the most apparently useless of her fairy blessings manifest utility.

The Princess, by virtue of her position—as a minor, as royalty—did not see the grinding consequences of the War in her daily life, except in the steady invasion of silver through her mother's black hair and the Vizier's gradual transformation from slender to gaunt. The battles never came within a tesser-hex of her home system. There were no near-orbit bombardments, or fuel rationing, or famine; and the palace censors were careful to screen the video feeds to the royal children's chamber terminals.

Rory was clever enough—thanks to the Vizier's tutelage with arithmancy—to bypass the censorship. Her experience of the War, as it cycled through two more long years, came from the public 'casts, alternatively lurid and sensational, sober and thoughtful. She watched in secret, huddled under her blanket with Grytt's tablet in the small hours of the night, until Grytt caught her one evening and instituted a new practice: they would watch the 'casts together, so that Rory could ask questions when she had them.

Grytt was not privy to more official documents, however, as those were classified and protected behind a hedge of crypto-hexes. So Rory, determined to acquire those answers, continued to build on the Vizier's lessons, until one day, after several hours on the hard plascrete bench beside the koi pond, she cracked the Vizier's encryption and hexed her own backdoor into his files. Were she still Crown Princess, she might have asked for, and received, that access legitimately; but since she was not, she would have needed the Council of Ministers' approval, and they had already forbidden her to attend their meetings. They cited vague concerns about security: since Rory would someday marry, they told her, that future spouse might, through her, learn the disposition of the Consortium's military and finances.

What they meant, of course, was *you won't understand any-way, dear* and *you're a princess* and *what does a girl know about war?* More galling: they invited Jacen, as Crown Prince, to attend Council sessions, though no one believed he would actually go. Jacen was eight, too impatient for chess and more interested in playing at war in *Duty Calls* than in doing much of anything else.

So Rory read, from the Vizier's violated files, the field reports from the generals, the briefings from the new Minister of Espionage, and the ever-growing lists of the dead. She read, and taught herself to understand *politics* and *tactics* and *strategy*, supplemented by discussions with the Vizier (for broad generalities) and with Grytt (for specific details).

Her chess game, to the Vizier's delight, improved. So did her *Duty Calls* high score, to her brother's dismay.

Rory also taught herself to understand wartime economics. Included in the field reports were financial reports and projections, treaties and trade agreements, intricate deals and bargains for munitions, and raw materials, and exclusive trading options. She learned which of the vigorously declared neutral kingdoms, conglomerates, networks, and worlds were genuine in that declaration, and which were making secret deals. She learned that the Thorne Consortium had a long-reaching spy network, and a brave, clever military that won most of its battles. But she also learned that the Thorne Consortium did not have limitless resources and was, in fact, nearly bankrupt. The Free Worlds, with their vaster collection of colonies, were winning as slowly and inexorably as the days and weeks of her minority were falling away.

Her sixteenth birthday arrived and departed, with the usual fanfare and several new guests. Men she did not recognize, a Prince and a Count, both from declared neutral kingdoms, and two *junior partners* from prominent Merchant League families, all of whom had substantial resources. She knew who they were, of course. The Vizier kept good files, and these, he *had* shared with her.

"So, ah." His eyes had slid away. "So that you are prepared for your guests."

But he was thinking *damn damn damn* as he said it.

Rory hadn't the heart to interrogate him further. Instead, she read the files and saved her questions for Grytt, who made a face at the list and muttered *open season* under her breath.

"One of them will be my future husband," Rory said. "Do we need the Larish shipyards more than we need the Johnson-Thrymbe fortune?"

"If the harvest on Kreshti's northern continent fails again, we'll need the fortune." Grytt's twisted scar-grimace turned another notch grimmer. "But Kreshti doesn't have two years until your majority. The ship-builder will be a bigger help to the Thorne fleet."

"The Council might grant me dispensation to marry early." Rory was proud of how cool she sounded. She had practiced in front of the mirror, so that her face matched her voice. She knew her brows were level, her mouth relaxed, her eyes half-lidded and thoughtful.

Grytt's original eye rolled in its socket. "Your mother will never allow it."

"Mother may not have a choice."

Grytt brought her mecha hand and her meat hand together on the table, and steepled her fingers in front of her scowl. It was eerily similar to the Regent-Consort's favorite *I'm thinking* gesture.

"Always a choice, Rory," said Grytt. "Sometimes it doesn't look like much, but there's *always* a choice."

Unbeknownst to Rory, such choices were indeed being made, though not in the manner she would have preferred or predicted.

———

"I have an idea, Rupert, but I want you to tell me what you think."

The Regent-Consort was sitting behind her desk, elbows bent, forearms flat, fingers woven together. The ferns were all, down to their tiniest fronds, a vivid orange.

The Vizier, seated on the far side of the desk, glanced uneasily at the ferns. Ordinarily, when Samur claimed inspiration, the ferns were blue or violet or, on occasion, a vivid maroon. Their current carroty hue indicated that the Regent-Consort's idea was one about which she was not happy. And the way she was braced on her desk, as if she must hold it in place lest it cavort about the room, made his stomach knot unhappily around the scraps of his lunch.

He suspected he knew the reason for the orange idea, and both hoped, and did not hope, that it involved what Grytt called an ass-whupping. The Vizier was not by his own nature a violent man. But in this case, he thought he would appreciate watching Grytt (who was quite violent, if permitted) beat the Larish heir and the junior partner from Johnson-Thrymbe five shades of purple. It was not their *fault*, precisely: they were opportunists who sought occasion to advance their own fortunes, like all of their ilk, and they were willing to join their assets with the Thorne Consortium. That would have been true, War or no.

The problem was that the Thorne Consortium could not afford to offend anyone else in the multiverse, particularly not these two. He truly hoped the Regent-Consort was not going to *grant* their intolerable, impertinent petitions. Though of the pair, the Larish boy could at least carry on a conversation. He'd read a book or two. The Johnson-Thrymbe junior partner was exactly as sharp as a bag of wet tree-rats.

Perhaps that meant the Regent-Consort had decided to grant *his* petition. That would be an orange fern-worthy idea. He was glad of the tablet in his lap, so he had something to grip. He wasn't violent, truly, but he wanted his hands around those young men's necks—

He realized, abruptly, that his own breath was the loudest sound in the room. The Regent-Consort was watching, waiting patiently for his acknowledgement. He flushed. A faint, sympathetic yellow tinted the nearest fern before the orange overwhelmed it.

"Ah." The Vizier wanted to hide behind her title, and, by extension, take refuge behind his own. Instead, he made himself sit a little straighter, and said, "All right, Samur. Tell me this idea."

She let her breath go in a rush. "You've seen the proposals from Larish and Johnson-Thrymbe."

The Vizier blinked and dropped his gaze to his lap, and the tablet, and the list. "I—yes, and I think they're entirely inappropriate. To suggest that we grant them special legal exemption to bypass Rory's age of majority—"

"Wait." Samur held up her hand. "*They* didn't seek exemption. Or rather—they did, but both of them did so because my daughter suggested it. *And* she told them how to file it."

"She . . . what?"

"Apparently she's been sending messages. Meeting in secret. Creeping around the koi pond, no doubt, having hexed the security 'bots to ignore her."

The Vizier felt his eyes bugging out. "She didn't meet them in person, did she?"

Samur raised her empty palms skyward in the universal parental gesture of *how should I know?* "Both Larish and Johnson-Thrymbe seem convinced that Rory is personally interested in them. They were *quite* smug."

The Vizier released the tablet from its proxy strangulation and transferred his fingers to his temples. Perhaps, if he pressed firmly enough, he might prevent his brain from bursting out his ears. Perhaps.

"And you are certain this is Rory's doing?"

"Well, it's certainly not Grytt's."

"No. Though if she's aware of this, she should know better." The Vizier began collecting his wits, plucking them from the corners in his brain to which they had fled. "You say they are convinced of Rory's personal interest—so neither knows about the other, is that it?"

"That is exactly it. She's playing them, Rupert. They filed their petitions within hours of each other." Samur's lips tightened to a monofilament edge. "If there are two petitions, of identical merit, then it falls to the seated monarch to decide which to grant, and which to refuse. Or—bless the barbarity of Philip's homeworld traditions—I could make them duel for her hand. Do you think that's what she wants? Boys to fight over her?"

"No. I'm sure that's not it." The Vizier studied Samur's face. He misliked the glassy intensity of her gaze and the brittle edge to her voice. The years since the King's death had blunted his skills at predicting royal outbursts, but those skills had not withered entirely. There was a royal storm coming unless he headed it off.

And so, as if Samur were the King, and allergic to reason, the Vizier spun his answer out like a thick rope: "I think she expects you to choose Johnson-Thrymbe because he's got money that we desperately need to buy supplies and to send aid to Kreshti. That might offend the senior Larish, and cost us the shipyards, except that there are half a dozen Larish daughters, and you still have a son. Offer Larish the promise of that future alliance, and you would secure their shipyards now anyway. Rory, meanwhile, brings in the Johnson-Thrymbe fortune. The only wounded ego in all of this would be the Larish heir, and he's too arrogant to dwell on it for long."

Samur's eyes narrowed. "Is my daughter that clever? Have you *made* her that clever, Rupert?"

The fronds of the ferns closest to the Vizier blanched almost as white as he did. "You don't think *I* suggested this to her! Samur!"

The ferns shivered green, for just a heartbeat. Then Samur took a deep, shaky breath. "No. Of course you didn't. I just mean— she's been a good student. Too good. I think you're right. And I think she actually expects me to go along with this."

The Vizier imagined a rumbling of thunder, and the roiling darkness of clouds above Samur's head, and threads of white lightning. He felt as if he were holding a metal rod up to the sky, daring disaster, and still he asked,

"But you won't, will you?"

"Well. I was thinking, I might make my *own* proposal." Samur paused. In anyone else that pause would have been deliberate drama, meant to force the audience to ask the obvious question, *what proposal?*

The Vizier found his mouth too dry, and his jaw too clenched, to manage. He made a little noise in the back of his throat, instead, and nodded *go on, I'm listening.*

"Regent Moss is fond of power. I plan to offer that to him, in return for a cease-fire. Look." She swiveled her screen to face him. "I've drafted a treaty. A letter. I'm not sure. An *offer*, certainly. It needs the legal, formal language." A breathless laugh rattled in the back of her throat. "I think I've been too forward in my phrasing."

The Vizier found himself leaning toward the screen, his eyes drawn to the words as surely as planets orbit a star. He could no more refrain from reading an offered document than he could refrain from breathing. But a page into it, he did forget to breathe. And by the end, he wished he might unread it, among a hundred other unvoiced wishes.

The Regent-Consort was an educated woman, but she lacked the artifice of a courtier. Her proposal stood as bald and comfortless as the blasted hulks of starships littering Kreshti's sky. The Vizier read it twice. Then he leaned back in his chair and closed his eyes a little bit longer than a proper blink. He opened them to find the Regent-Consort's anxious gaze pulling at him like fingers.

"What do you think?"

"Your aunt will hate it. And you, I think, for suggesting it. It's been an unspoken assumption that Moss was behind the assassinations of both kings. You said as much to your aunt when this war started. To sue him for peace is, well. She will see that as dishonorable. To *marry* him to sweeten the offer, she will see as obscene."

"My aunt is Kreshti's Prime. Her people come first. If Kreshti were not suffering drought, we might continue this war indefinitely, but that is now impossible. My aunt will have to accept the terms or break her alliance with Thorne. She can hate me if she wants. But you, Rupert. What do *you* think?"

The Vizier was grateful that the mother did not share her daughter's propensity for seeing through prevarication. He had the leisure to pick his way among words, to choose the most efficacious, to hide behind a vocabulary as stiff as any shield.

"I think it is a bold move, your Grace, and Regent Moss favors bold moves. I am certain he will accept."

"You don't approve," she said. "I know. But the only approval I need is from the Council, first, and from Regent Moss, after that." She paused, half a beat. Then, softly, intensely: "I will not sacrifice my daughter, Rupert. Not yet."

And so you sacrifice yourself, he did not say aloud. He understood, for some measure of the word. But he could not force himself to say it. Instead, he added another layer of polite armor to his tone.

"I believe that I can revise this document into the appropriate language. I will also advocate personally for this proposal in private meetings with the other Council members. By the time it comes to table, we will have no difficulty passing it." He found he could not look at her any longer. He watched his thumb, rubbing across the polished wood of the chair, as if it belonged to another man. "Then, upon its ratification, I will negotiate with Regent Moss personally, your Grace, to see its realization."

He did not look up as he said it, being entirely absorbed smearing his thumbprint in and out of existence in the wood's polished finish. And so he did not see the Regent-Consort's flinch. Nor did he see the tiniest branches on the fern nearest to him turn black, as if suddenly deprived of all air and warmth.

"Thank you," she said simply, and another frond turned black.

The Vizier drafted the proposal in formal court language and brought it before the Council. His passionate arguments in its favor are credited with its near-unanimous ratification by the Council. Only the Minister of Commerce objected, and that was because she had married a second cousin of the Johnson-Thrymbe CEO.

The terms of the treaty were as legally complex and tedious as is typical of the genre. The Vizier was proud of Rory, that she tried to wade through the document itself. But he could not risk a sixteen-year-old's misunderstanding, not concerning matters this important. And so he visited her quarters one evening after supper, sat beside her at the table on which sat the remains of her meal, and Grytt's, and took on the role of her tutor one last time.

First, he explained, her mother was going to marry the former Minister of Energy and current Regent of the Free Worlds of Tadesh, although the actual governing of the realms would remain separate. Although Regencies were acting as royalty, this position was temporary. Therefore, their marriage would have the same force as a royal alliance, but for only so long as they *were* Regents. Which meant that when Jacen reached his majority, Samur would become Dowager-Consort to Jacen's King. When Ivar assumed the Tadeshi throne, Regent Moss would become—well, probably not the Minister of Energy again, but perhaps something like a Vizier.

Second, and far more difficult to say aloud, was that Rory's betrothal to Prince Ivar of the Free Worlds of Tadesh would be formally recognized, and eventually realized in wedlock when Rory reached majority, to continue the peace begun by the Regencies. But, the Vizier added, that would happen only *after* Ivar ascended the throne.

There was a chance, the Vizier told her, that Ivar might choose to break the betrothal. A king could do that. The Vizier meant to be comforting, and to be comforted, and to impress upon Rory that her mother was hoping—perhaps even counting—on Ivar's objection to his arranged bride.

"Wait," said Rory, and lifted her hand in a gesture so reminiscent of Samur that the pieces of the Vizier's heart ground together like glass. "Do you mean to tell me that *I* cannot break this engagement, but Ivar *can*?"

"Er." The Vizier felt as if he'd been dropped into a lightless room in which were traps—great steel toothy things, able to crush a man like a tomato—lying all about, waiting for an unwary step.

"Yes." He hoped he sounded forceful and certain.

Rory leaned back in her seat—an overstuffed monstrosity of paisley patches, the overwhelming majority of which were incestuous versions of orange—and folded her arms. The effect might have been adorable, or disarming, or a dozen other benevolent adjectives, if her face had not been cold as all aetherless void.

"And my mother is hoping he *will* decide otherwise, but if he doesn't, I'm stuck? *How* is this better than me marrying either the Johnson-Thrymbe or Larish boy?"

There was no good way to answer either of those questions, and so the Vizier did not. Instead, he chose a new approach, one he hoped was perhaps free of steel traps.

"Your mother made the best decision she could, Princess."

Snap.

"Hell she did. *You* don't even believe that."

The swearing was Grytt's fault. *Damn her*, the Vizier thought, oblivious to the irony. He wished for a Rory who could be scolded and lectured about keeping one's composure in the face of supreme provocation. He wished he could give that lecture without hypocrisy. He wished Grytt—who appeared to be the only person Rory would listen to, anymore—would intervene.

He cast a look at her, half appeal, half assessment. She was watching Rory, frowning with more intensity than was customary.

"Rory," she said.

The Princess sat up in her absurd chair, gripping its arms to finger-whiteness. If she had heard Grytt, she gave no sign. "Mother made this alliance to end the war. I understand that. But she mostly did it so I wouldn't have to marry Larish or Johnson-Thrymbe. I get *that*, too, although I wish she hadn't. But then why chain me to Ivar?"

"It was your *father's* intention to wed you to Ivar. Your mother is only renewing that contract."

The Vizier was gratified at a moment's silence from his adversary. Perhaps now she would see reason. His gratification was short-lived. He had forgotten that *teenager* trumps logic in most things.

Rory's chin came up, square and stubborn. "Father might've changed his mind."

"Unlikely, Princess. Particularly after Jacen's birth. Your father would have seen this union as the best thing for the Thorne Consortium."

Another silence. The Vizier took advantage of the quiet, hoping to strike before Rory seized upon some other notion at which to take offense.

"Your father and King Sergei thought that a union between their houses would be the best thing for peace in the sector."

"Best thing? Ivar was afraid of the koi! We're fortunate he never saw a tree-rat. He might've died on the spot of sheer terror. He couldn't keep peace in a graveyard."

The Vizier groped after the last wisps of his patience. "That was a great many years ago. Ivar may have changed. You have."

"He's never going to rule his kingdom. At best he'll be a mouthpiece for Moss. And there's no way Moss will let me go if he gets me." Rory's lips tightened into a razor line. If there had been any ferns present, they would have turned an alarming crimson. As it was, two spots on her cheekbones bloomed exactly that color, as if someone had smudged paint on her skin with a thumb. "Would Ivar have been able to refuse the marriage if our fathers had lived?"

"Not as a Prince, no. The King's word, however, is final."

"And if he refuses me when he is King? What happens to the peace, then?"

"Then the peace must fend for itself."

She snorted, an indelicate, Grytt-inspired noise. "And if *I* don't agree to this marriage?"

"Legally, your wishes have no force."

"So what you're saying is, Ivar's character doesn't matter because he's prince, and since he's going to be king, he can say what happens to me, and so can my mother, while I can't say anything. That's *crap*!"

"Watch your *language*, Rory!"

"I'm not five anymore!"

In that moment, the Vizier saw both the mother and the daughter staring back at him, and his grip on his patience and composure slipped utterly.

Grytt saw it. "Rupert," she said, in exactly the same tone she had used previously on Rory, and to exactly the same effect.

The Vizier matched Rory's volume—indecorous, to be sure, but to *hell* with that. "Then stop acting like it! You are a Princess, and your life is not, nor has ever been, your own! It belongs to your people, to be arranged as the kingdom requires. *Your preferences are of no consequence!*"

Rory plowed ahead with the same restraint shown by meteorological catastrophes and tectonic disasters.

"But if I'd been born a *boy*, I would get a say. And that's *crap*, Messer Rupert."

"Well, you were *not* born a boy. And do you know why?"

"Rupert," Grytt said a little more forcefully.

Rory arched her brows. "Genetics?"

"Rory!" Grytt's voice climbed.

The Vizier pitched his own tones even louder. "Because your mother wished otherwise, and the fairies listened. So thank *her* for your situation!"

He had not meant to say it. He wished it unsaid in the same breath; but the wishes of a trained arithmancer-historian and political advisor do not carry the same weight with fairies as a mother's wishes do.

Rory surged to her feet. The Vizier noted, with a distant corner of his brain, that she had grown quite tall in the last year. Her eyes were nearly level with his.

The color bled out of her cheeks: first the twin spots on her cheekbones, then all the rest, until even her lips were pallid. Then she spun, with startling speed, and snatched a mug off the table. She hurled it at the nearest wall with sufficient force that it shattered into powder and shards and flung the remnants of its contents—tea, it seemed, old enough to be cool—onto everything within a five foot radius.

Not content with a single act of destruction, she reached for the next nearest item of crockery—a plate, this time, with the remnants of supper congealed on it.

"Hell," Grytt muttered, and crossed from her chair to the Princess in a blur that made Rory seem slow and told the Vizier that, whatever the elapsed time since her active service, Grytt retained her soldier's reflexes. She clamped her hand around Rory's arm, holding it, and the plate, steady a centimeter above the table's surface.

"Rory," Grytt said, "That's enough."

Rory tugged against Grytt's hand for another moment. Then she released the plate and burst into tears.

Grytt pulled the Princess into the circle of her arm. To the Vizier, she said nothing. But the look she cast over the Princess's shaking shoulders was sufficiently eloquent.

Pity. Sympathy. *Empathy.*

The Vizier's face felt wet. The tea, no doubt. He did not reach up and brush it away. Instead, he turned and walked out, and let the door shut softly behind him.

The Vizier departed for Urse, to deliver the Regent-Consort's proposal on the following morning, on an early shuttle whose departure neither the Regent-Consort nor Rory attended (although Grytt made an appearance). The Vizier found anger and regret to be poor traveling companions, and it was a very long journey.

Kreshti's Prime publicly ratified the treaty, which, among other things, granted the Free Worlds an exclusive contract for Kreshti mineral rights on the northern continent. This was seen as an act of wisdom and diplomacy, however odious; Kreshti could not break its membership in the Consortium now, after two years of famine and war, and still fend off a large, well-fed, bellicose neighbor. In private, among family, Samur's aunt burned the name-scroll of her favorite niece three times, and declared that no daughter born to that house would ever again bear the name Samur.

The Regent Vernor Moss, to no one's surprise—these things having been settled long since by quantum-hex, which had the virtue of being as close to instantaneous as is permitted by physics, temporarily aligning as it did two fixed locations (unlike a tesser-hex, which, as the reader well knows, folds space to shorten a distance between two fixed points)—accepted the Regent-Consort's proposal. And so the War ended, as many wars do, with a wedding.

Which was, as it happened, the only outcome of the treaty to transpire as intended.

CHAPTER SEVEN

And (Stale)Mate

The Princess Rory Thorne received her first official invitation to a Council session, at long last, shortly after her mother's marriage to Regent Moss of the Free Worlds of Tadesh. The wedding itself had taken place off-world, in a neutral location—a little waypost on the Larish shipping lanes, in orbit around a desultory white dwarf—observed by diplomatic representation from the Merchants League and every free planet, consortium, and kingdom worth the name. Battleships from both parties wove complex and polite patterns around each other, scrupulously avoiding any military incidents while at the same time attempting to intimidate the other side.

The couple spent exactly one night together, to consummate both wedding and treaty, before returning to their respective territories to oversee the end of the War. Further negotiations and settlements took place via quantum-hex, over the course of seven weeks, as the War ended piece by decommissioned piece.

One of the settlements was the dispensation of Thorne assets. It was decided—first by heated argument and then by cold logic—that the Princess Rory should, at the earliest convenience, relocate to Urse. There, the cold logic went, she would be best able to learn the ways of her future subjects, renew her acquaintance with

Prince Ivar, and prepare for a smooth transition after Ivar's assumption of the throne and their subsequent marriage.

"You mean," Rory said, when she heard the news, "I'm going to be a hostage."

"Not just you," the Vizier snapped. Recent events had eroded his polished, political veneer. But where water wears stones soft and round, the War and the Wedding had scraped him into hard edges, brittle and jagged and prone to cut without warning.

"Your mother is sending *me*, too, to be your advisor."

Rory frowned. Grytt frowned. The Vizier, who was already frowning, wished he understood what the look meant, that passed between them. He shrugged a little deeper into his robes, and told himself it was winter draft that made his bones ache.

"The Council wants to see you, Rory, in this next session," he added.

Another look passed between Rory and Grytt.

"Do they, now?" Rory murmured. "And why would that be? Not to ask my opinion, certainly."

"The official agenda is the composition of your household on Urse."

"My *household*? Myself, Grytt—and you?"

"And me, as your advisor. There will also be four security personnel. The Regent-Consort has obtained permission"—it galled him to use that word—"to send along some of our house guard, for appearance. Although your residence, like our embassy, is considered Thorne sovereign territory, you will not live in the embassy compound. You are the princess, not a diplomat."

Grytt stirred and pointed her unmatched eyes at the Vizier, squinting past her nose as if she were sighting down a rifle's barrel. "That's a bit of a middle finger, isn't it? We're saying Rory's not safe in Urse?"

"No." Rory looked thoughtful. "It's about appearances. It's about me looking like a sovereign representative instead of the hostage everyone knows I really am. It's *performance*. Just like when Moss comes here with his matched set of muscle who answer to no one save him."

"Political theatre, yes." The Vizier folded his hands. He made note that Rory used the Regent's surname, rather his title. Indicative of a not-so-secret disrespect, he thought, which might indicate an understandably unhappy sixteen-year-old, or might be symptomatic of a deeper rebellion. Something to monitor, particularly after they took up residence on Urse.

"Presumably that's why I'm suddenly welcome at the Council table, too."

The Vizier hesitated. "The Crown Prince Jacen specifically requested your presence."

"Oh." Rory snorted in a most un-princesslike fashion. "We can't disappoint Jacen, can we? At what, his first meeting? His second?—And where will my mother be?"

The cold throbbed up through the Vizier's bones. "I'm sure I don't know, your Highness. She doesn't keep me abreast of her schedule."

Anymore, he thought. And this time he needed no translation to understand the look that passed between Rory and Grytt.

"Well," said the Princess, after a moment. "That's her loss, then. We're glad to have you with us. Aren't we, Grytt?"

Grytt arched her remaining eyebrow. "We are indeed," she said, with no trace whatsoever of her customary irony.

The Vizier bowed, because that was proper; but he felt a little warmer, somewhere near the remnants of his heart, for the first time in months.

The Vizier had expected the Council meeting to be somewhat perfunctory, Grytt already having assembled a short list of personnel she wanted for Urse, and having already discussed those choices with him at some length. The elder pair of guards, Stary and Franko, had been the old King's personal guard, and brought useful experience; the younger pair, both women and very junior, would provide Rory at least two people close to her own age.

It should have been a simple matter of securing the Minister of Defense's signature on the transfer papers. And indeed, that part of the meeting went entirely as planned. But, as it happened, the Prince had his own ideas about the composition of his sister's household.

"I think a eunuch would be the *perfect* bodyguard for you. No one wants to be killed by a eunuch. You'd be totally safe on Urse."

The Crown Prince Jacen leaned back in the high-backed chair and stacked his boots on the table. In a taller individual, such a posture would communicate disdain and disrespect for those at the table with him, and for the Regent-Consort, his mother, who had expressly forbidden such behavior. But since Jacen was a weedy, unimpressive nine, the elevation of his feet effectively eclipsed his face, and left his audience—the Vizier, Princess Rory, and the Minister of Defense, at the moment, the others having been dismissed—staring at the soles of his boots.

"We could get you one." Jacen's feet waggled back and forth like scolding fingers. "Couldn't we, General Foyle?"

The Minister of Defense had the grace to look uncomfortable. "The practice is illegal in the Consortium, Majesty."

"Right, but it's perfectly legal in the Free Worlds of Tadesh."

Foyle winced. His gaze slunk sidelong until the Vizier noticed it. Then it crept away and settled on the table. "I don't think it's wise to entrust your sister's safety to a Tadeshi bodyguard, your Majesty. That's rather the point of this meeting. To ensure the Princess is guarded by *our* personnel, and to determine who that will be, which we have done, Majesty, to my satisfaction."

"Yes, but—"

Rory shifted a little bit left, so that she could see Jacen's face. She cut him off smoothly. "Thank you for your concern, Jacen, but I don't need another bodyguard. I have Grytt."

Two spots of red bloomed on Jacen's cheeks. "Grytt's only half of anything. Besides. Body-maids are for *Kreshti*. We aren't Kreshti. We're Consortium. And I don't think our new father will want you keeping someone with mecha parts, *especially* after what happened with Ivar's body-man, and *especially* not a Kreshti on top of all that. There are murmurs of sedition on Urse, you know, caused by *Kreshti*."

It was an impressive string of logic, for the Prince. The Vizier suspected Deme Isabelle's hand in the speech-writing. Sedition was a syllable or two beyond Jacen's typical conversational muscle.

General Foyle was frowning, now. The Vizier knew him as a man of formidable intellect and precarious patience. Rory, in contrast, was displaying a remarkable forbearance. No hint of true feelings on her face. *His* training, that. The Vizier felt a gentle sunrise of pride stirring in his chest.

That satisfaction lasted exactly three heartbeats, at which point the Princess ran her hands down both arms, as if straightening her sleeves. In another person, that would be fidgeting, and Rory was certainly capable of that; but the Vizier had spent too many years around Grytt, and around Rory, to be fooled. Rory was checking *weapons*. That she was carrying them at all, in the Council chambers, in the Crown Prince's presence—well, it was certainly illegal, even for another member of the royal house. It was also almost certainly at Grytt's prompting. And because neither Grytt nor Rory believed in empty gestures, those illicit weapons were certainly *not* pins.

The Vizier did not honestly believe Rory would draw steel on her brother. That she seriously considered it, however, he did not doubt at all. And certain as he was of her beneficence, he felt a surge of relief when she gripped the ends of the arms of her chair and spoke.

"Moss is not, nor will ever be, our father."

Jacen's smirk grew wider. "But it's his kingdom. It's his station. And if he says you have to get rid of Grytt, then you do."

Rory regarded Jacen for a long, quiet moment, until the Prince's smirk faded and slipped sideways down his face. Then she pushed her chair back and stood up. Jacen jerked upright in his chair, scraping his boots across the table in his haste to get them back on the ground. Foyle startled in his chair, hands reaching for absent weapons. *Someone*, at least, followed protocol.

If Rory noticed the ripple of upset, she gave no sign. She nudged the table with her hip, just exactly far enough to catch the Prince still sitting. Jacen could only rise now by scooting his chair back, and the conspiracy of thick carpet, wheelless chair legs, and his own royal physique would render that effort conspicuous and undignified.

Rory stared down at her brother, past a nose and cheekbones that owed more to her Kreshti ancestry than the Thorne. Then she leaned over the table, bracing her hands flat. The long tail of her braid slipped off her shoulder and dangled. The Vizier fancied that he could see Jacen's face reflected in the blue-black gloss.

"I will not replace Grytt to suit our mother's husband. If he doesn't like that, then he can refuse to let my shuttle dock, and I will be more than happy to turn around and come back home."

"You can't do that! Mother says—"

"Oh, now it's *Mother says*. Mother's said nothing about leaving Grytt behind. That's your idea, which is why I'm ignoring it. You're not King yet, little brother."

"I will be, someday," Jacen said. "Then you'll *have* to do what I say."

"We'll see," said Rory.

It was unclear to the Vizier whether she meant the conditional phrase to apply to her projected filial obedience or to Jacen's eventual sovereignty. In any case, it proved academic.

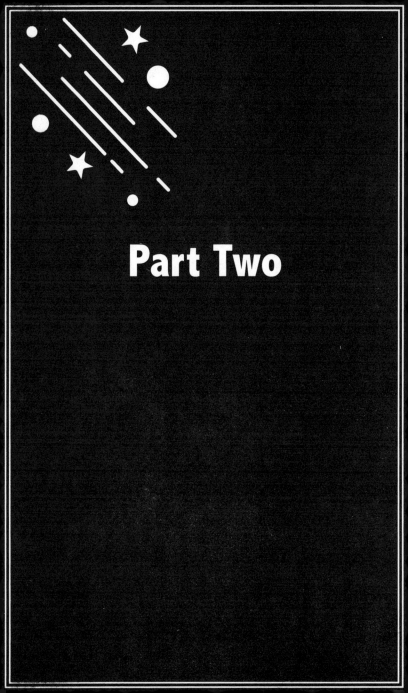

Part Two

CHAPTER EIGHT

Urse

Thorne's sovereign territory on Urse was a double suite, large by station standards, measuring approximately one thousand square meters, comprising two discrete units. The smaller of the two suites housed the four-person guard detail in military luxury, which is to say, very little comfort at all. The larger one was more finely appointed, with three sleeping rooms ("I've had bigger bunks than this," said Grytt) and a central living area ("Wonderful, if we don't mind bumping our knees," said Grytt), with a small, private kitchen, so that they needn't troop to the common mess to dine ("Oh, bother," Messer Rupert had said. "We aren't letting Grytt cook, are we?").

It was a perimeter unit, as well, nested against the outer hull of Urse, at the juncture of two corridors, which meant it had two portholes in the living area. It was, Rory was assured by the Tadeshi staff, a *wealth* of portholes.

"Which is evidently what one calls a *pair*, here on Urse," she muttered to Grytt. "What is one, I wonder? A paucity of portholes? I think we should change the name. Call these two a *prosperity*. What do you think?"

Grytt, who had proved none too sanguine about walking on a deck rather than a floor, or living with a horizon that curved the wrong direction, or a half dozen other things, which she would detail at length with very little invitation, eyed the two

invitations to disaster

objects in question and grunted.

"Hope the seals hold. Leak would pull us right out. Be a contest to see if we freeze before we choke."

Rory did not point out that, should the seals fail, the sudden evacuation of aether would probably draw them against the opening, thus rendering the *pulling* of Grytt's apprehensions into a more violent, gruesome *sucking*, which would then supplant asphyxiation and freezing as the likely cause of death. She also thought any catastrophic decompression was highly unlikely. The porthole seals were so thoroughly hexed against failure that their perimeters glowed to the naked, arithmantically educated eye. Rory had spent some time examining them, with an arithmancer's admiration, before Grytt shooed her away, insisting that she would "mess something up" and "kill us all."

Grytt had completed her mandatory service as a Kreshti marine, to be sure; but, as Grytt was fond of recounting, marines did not have portholes in their quarters, and battleships did not invite hull breach by cutting holes in good steel to improve the scenery. And ship life was, most importantly, temporary. A body could expect, after a tesser-hex or several, to drop dirtside and experience *proper* gravity.

By which, Rory supposed, one might surmise that Urse's gravity was entirely *im*proper, although that was far less true for the station than for any of the battleships that used a gravity-hex instead of basic physics. Urse was an old-style station, one of the first: essentially a giant wheel, spinning around its axis as it rolled an orbit between the planets Bielo and Cherno, called the Brothers, and their unassuming yellow star, Svaro.

After the first seventy times Grytt had imagined out loud some gruesome death, Rory began to think it might have been kinder to leave her on Thorne after all. But when she had suggested it to Messer Rupert, he nearly choked on his tea.

"Whatever makes you think *that*?" he had asked, dabbing distractedly at the damp patches on his robe, while at the same time peering at her from beneath knotted brows. "Have you *taken leave of your senses* quarreled?"

"Not at all. She's just so unhappy here, Messer Rupert."

"Bah. Don't let the frequency or the volume deceive you, Princess. She *isn't any more unhappy than the rest of us* was a marine before she came into your mother's service. Complaints are a marine's version of a counter-hex against universal ill-will and bad luck."

Then perhaps, Rory thought, Grytt should complain even more strenuously.

Outside the prosperity of portholes, the gas giant Cherno, the darker of the Brothers, crept into visibility. It filled the porthole, a massive sphere of hydrocarbons rendered darkish orange and brown by the chemicals in its poisonous atmosphere. Its dozen visible moons glittered like gems that had been tossed into the air and had forgotten to fall again. It should have been imposing, perhaps even intimidating, a childhood monster creeping out of the dark. Certainly Messer Rupert preferred the curtains be drawn when Cherno appeared. But to Rory, the single deep, dried-blood stripe, which sat just a little above the equator, made the planet look like a fat man with his belt too high. A favorite old uncle, instead of a troll.

Or perhaps a fat troll, Rory thought. *Ready to eat princesses.*

"Do you mind if I turn off the lights?" she asked, knowing full well Grytt's mecha eye could see in all wavelengths. And Grytt, knowing full well this was Rory's favorite time of day, grunted what passed for *yes*, when it was just the pair of them with no Messer Rupert to insist on complete syllables.

Rory whispered the tesla counter-hex. The room's artificial, blue-tinted lights winked out, dropping the room into the orange-y glow of sunlight bouncing off Cherno's cloud layers. It was a little like being at the bottom of a pond, looking up. Local opinion considered Cherno ugly. It was, Rory supposed, meant to be a subtle insult, placing her quarters on this side of Urse, for all that she rated a prosperity of portholes.

She thought it a kindness. The brighter Brother, Bielo, was a pale, methane blue, exactly the same poisonous shade as Vernor Moss's eyes. Put *that* outside, and she would have twitched the curtains closed and kept them that way, preferring teslas and cold shadows to even the suggestion of that man watching her.

That Moss did eavesdrop, however, was inarguable, despite the marked lack of actual eaves. Messer Rupert had found no fewer than six tiny spybots in their quarters within fifteen minutes of their arrival. Grytt had promptly destroyed them, in total silence, making sharp *shut up* gestures whenever Rory tried to ask what was happening. Only afterward did Messer Rupert say that he'd expected the 'bots, and that Regent Moss would have expected *them* to find and destroy them; so there might be others, better concealed.

Be careful, Messer Rupert meant. But in Messer Rupert's absence—he was currently in the embassy, performing endless acts of administration and diplomacy—Rory raised her voice and enumerated Moss's moral failings with a volume and inventiveness that would have sent her tutor into apoplexy, had he been present.

Grytt, forever cleaning her weapons (permitted only under elaborate treaty amendments), only smirked.

Rory hoped (but held no hope) that Moss might be scandalized enough to send her home. But she suspected she swore entirely for her own comfort. It was like lighting a match against all of the cold void and holding it close for the warmth.

He had yet to meet her formally. That was either a social breach, or a deliberate snub, and it did not take fairy gifts to discern which. He had not met her shuttle at the dock to convey his welcome. He instead sent a handful of guards—one more than her own complement—and his Prime Minister, who had a prior acquaintance with Messer Rupert, and whose first utterance after *Welcome, your Highness* was a well-rehearsed apology. *The Regent was engaged in important business and unable to break away. Please accept his most sincere apologies and the assurance of a meeting at the earliest possible hour.*

Rory had smiled, inclined her head exactly as far as a Princess should to a social inferior, and told the Minister to think nothing of it, she would be pleased to meet the Regent at his leisure, they were weary from their journey, they were just glad to be here, on Urse.

It was fortunate that the Minister did not possess a version of the thirteenth fairy's gift.

Nor had Prince Ivar sent word of any kind, beyond a generically formal note on the turing terminal in their quarters. A set of five lines, centered on the screen, that said:

Welcome, Princess Rory Thorne, to the Free Worlds of Tadesh.
I hope you find these quarters to your liking,
and I hope to renew our acquaintance soon.
Please feel free to summon staff if you need anything.
I remain your servant, Prince Ivar Valenko

Rory had spent a great deal of the journey to Urse imagining how Ivar might have evolved: whether he'd be taller and dark, like his father. If he'd have developed callouses on his hands, or on his spirit.

There is imagining, and there is hope, and Rory thought it best to remain neutral on that subject. She had not, however, imagined her first communication with him to be a one-way note on the turing.

She had showed it to Grytt, who grunted, and to Messer Rupert, who raised an eyebrow and said, "Hm," and, "The terminal's probably been hexed with spyware. Don't link up your tablets until I've cleared it."

Then they had got to unpacking and arranging, and discovering that Cherno marched across their portholes once a day. They also agreed that they did not want to invite station staff into their quarters for meal preparations if it meant sweeping the place for 'bots every time, and while they had not been forbidden the common dining areas, Grytt did not feel it prudent to explore the station overmuch.

And so, while waiting for Moss's official summons, they learned that Grytt could *not* cook, and Messer Rupert *could*, and Rory had a knack for making curries.

"A fairy gift, no doubt," she had said. "A princess *should* be able to cook. That's pleasing to kings and princes, isn't it?"

"A princess should be more able to eat neatly, without spilling soup on her shirt," said Messer Rupert. "And I assure you, the fairies made no mention of making curry in their blessings—here. Add the cardamom and the turmeric."

The apartment still smelled orange and brown, good match to Cherno's sullen glow. Rory glanced around the room again. Grytt at the dining table. Messer Rupert absent. The turing terminal, left untouched since their arrival, Messer Rupert never quite finding the time to unhex it.

Whereas, Rory was learning, a princess who was also a hostage, being studiously ignored, and thus unofficially confined to her quarters, had a great deal of time.

She sidled toward the terminal. Slid a guilty glance at Grytt, whose chromed half-skull flashed dully as she bent over her weapon. Urse law forbade ballistic firearms—not for any fear of perforating the outer hull, which was far tougher than bullets, but because small high-velocity bits of metal or plastic had a tendency to ricochet in the narrow corridors. As a result, Grytt's permitted-by-treaty arsenal included more archaic blade weapons, the use of which Rory knew well, and the P-370 'slinger, which she did not, and which Grytt currently had in twelve pieces on the table. She seemed occupied. Busy, even.

Rory took another step. A third.

"Get on it, Princess," Grytt said. She tilted the 'slinger's chassis carefully from side to side, peering into the barrels from all angles. "Better to say sorry than may I."

"Do you *always* know what I'm thinking?"

Grytt snorted. "No."

"Just most times."

"You're wasting *your* time. He'll come back soon enough. Best you're done when he gets here."

"Right," Rory muttered, and slid into the chair behind the turing terminal's console.

Cracking a turing's security hex was a great deal more complicated than hexing an aura-scanner. It was all arithmancy, true; but a turing's logic and motivations shaped the sorts of hexes it could accommodate, and most public access turings, and tablets, were basic, simple drones performing a set of limited, prescribed tasks. A simple turing was easy to hex because its motivations were simple: do its job and repeat, without variation. The complications came at the higher levels, with an almost-intelligent collective composed of all the terminals on a network pooling their experiences, which conferred enough originality for the collective to detect tampering with one of its drones. The station's networked intelligence might be overtaxed by the demands on its systems. It might be bored or diligent, suspicious or curious. Rory didn't hold out much hope for that last quality, but she was hoping for the first or the second.

She found her way into the terminal's settings readily enough, with a few taps on the keypad. Then she unlocked its root access, and began a careful exploration of its systems. Very basic, very simple, which was both encouraging and daunting together. She held her breath and slid her awareness into the first and nearest layer of aether, where she hexed a rudimentary sense of curiosity into the turing's code. Not much, not enough that it would start pinging queries at every other terminal on the network, but sufficient that it would seek information of its own volition, at least on particular topics.

Like the current whereabouts and disposition of the Crown Prince, for instance.

Rory squirmed a little higher on her chair, drew her legs up, and reached around her knees to reach the keyboard again. This was the tricky bit, the part where she discovered just how sophisticated the turing collective was—

She let her breath go all at once.

"You all right?" asked Grytt.

"Mm," said Rory, which Grytt understood (correctly) to mean *yes, everything is fine.*

The collective was, in fact, very limited in its resources, which rendered it somewhat stupid. Her little hexed turing terminal was its smartest component, so far. It was also, she discovered, even more limited in its permissions. She poked along its base-code hexes, rendered in neat lines on the screen, discovering the borders of allowability. Poked a little harder in the aether, to see what sorts of locks and barriers the Ursan IT arithmancers had made against intruders.

She was not impressed. She hexed a layer of ingenuity into her turing. A double layer of caution. A smidge of paranoia. And, after a moment's deliberation, a rather sophisticated set of hexes for breaking, entering, and retrieving the information she wanted. This sounds like a complicated procedure, but recall: Rory had been dabbling in security-hexes since childhood, and she had plenty of practice. The Vizier would have been both appalled and proud, had he seen her handiwork.

Then she sat back and set her turing loose and waited, while Cherno loomed outside the prosperity.

The turing terminal beeped.

"Good?" asked Grytt.

"Depends." Rory unfolded her legs and leaned forward onto her elbows. Her reflection filled the monitor, ghosted insubstantial, partially eclipsed by text. "Ivar's on *military* maneuvers. On . . ." She scrolled. Frowned. "On Beo."

Rory had done a great deal of reading about Urse's system, having thought it prudent to know as much about her new prison as possible. Beo was the third of Bielo's seventeen moons, and one of the few which had the courtesy to be solid and warm enough to support a Tadeshi marine training base, while still being poisonous and cold enough to make survival a skill, rather than a guarantee.

"Nasty," said Grytt, who had read the same materials.

"Perhaps Messer Rupert's right about Ivar," Rory said. "Perhaps he's changed."

"Or maybe he hasn't."

"Grytt, be fair. He's with the marines."

"Compulsory service is a rule in the Free Worlds."

"Nothing's compulsory for royalty."

"The future King can't get an exemption, even if he's incompetent."

"But that's an elite base." Rory tapped the screen, as if the impact of her finger on the glass made the facts more impressive. "Doesn't that mean Ivar's elite, too?"

"Might be Moss wants him dead in a training accident."

"Grytt!"

"Moss has two boys of his own. Think on that."

Rory did. She had just sent her little turing to investigate the service records of Vernor Moss's sons when the door alert rang. It was not precisely a ringing sound. More of a raucous howling, as if a dozen tree-rats were trapped in the wires. Rory had not suffered the misfortune of hearing it before, and so she might be forgiven for leaping nearly a meter straight up and out of her chair. Grytt was no less startled. She tipped the table on its edge and had taken cover behind it, the 'slinger's muzzle just peeking over the top.

The door shrieked again. This time, a voice followed, deep, male, and as expressive as new deckplate.

"Princess Rory? The Regent sends his regards. Please open the door."

Grytt stepped carefully around the table, putting herself in front of Rory. She kept both eyes and her 'slinger pointed at the door. "Coincidence? Or did you trip an alert?"

"Coincidence," Rory said, a little breathlessly. She leaned over and swiped the turing's screen blank. "Better put that down before I open the door. Don't want an incident."

"Huh," said Grytt, but she tucked the 'slinger down against her hip.

It was not Regent Moss himself at the door, of course. Instead, Rory found herself chest-level with a uniformed pair of armed men, on the larger side of human genetic variation, alike enough to be clones. The one on the right bowed at the waist, and offered on his gloved palm a little silver scroll stuffed with a roll of what appeared to be *real* paper, tied with a *real* ribbon. An extravagance, a statement about the wealth of Tadesh. A casual gesture of power, meant to intimidate—or, more charitably, a sign of respect, an acknowledgement of her worth.

Rory was not feeling charitable. She inclined her head at the guard and plucked the scroll from his palm.

"Please wait here," she said. It was not *exactly* protocol, leaving the man outside, but she did not think Grytt would appreciate a pair of armed Tadeshi inside their quarters. For that matter, *she* would not appreciate it. Moss would not hurt her, she was (almost) certain; but the large and prominently displayed sidearms on his security did not inspire in her any sense of abiding confidence. These men were *Moss's*, she was certain. Not inherited from Sergei Valenko, and thus not even a little bit Ivar's.

The security bowed again, this time the pair of them, and settled into the professional waiting-on-the-important-people-to-finish-their-business stance.

Rory stepped back and closed the door. Then she locked it, for good measure, and leaned her back against the cool, smooth steel.

"I've got a message," she said, and waved the scroll at Grytt.

"Eh." Grytt tipped her blue eye at the scroll. Waited. Then: "Just paper. It's safe to open."

Rory stared at the scroll as if it had sprouted ten hairy legs and a pair of mandibles. "I didn't even think of that possibility."

"That's why I'm here," said Grytt. She had righted the table, and was in the process of replacing the things that had been innocently sitting upon it and were now scattered across the deck. "I messaged our people. Stary and Franko are standing by. Thorsdottir and Zhang are in reserve."

"Good." Rory shook the scroll out of its case. Her name, complete with title, was scripted and gilded and conspicuous in its solitude on the front flap. Grytt had not been included in the invitation, which was not a surprise. Neither had Messer Rupert, which was.

"He's inviting me to his office. Moss."

"About time."

"Only me. Not Messer Rupert. Shouldn't he also invite the Vizier to a formal, diplomatic meeting?"

"He should." Grytt grimaced. "Tells you something, doesn't it?"

Rory blinked. Frowned at the pretty, formal letters. They looked handwritten. They probably were.

"We should call Messer Rupert."

Grytt's grimace deepened and stretched, drawing her eyebrow and forehead into a vortex of disapproval. "And tell him what, Moss is trying to get you alone?"

"I doubt it's like *that*," Rory said reflexively. She wasn't sure exactly what she was meant by *that*, or what *that* might entail, but she was certain Moss didn't want it. "Maybe he's trying to be courteous. By seeing me alone, he acknowledges me as an independent representative of Thorne, rather than as a minor under Messer Rupert's escort."

"Bah," said Grytt. "He wants you alone and scared."

"Scared? Why would I—"

"You'd be a fool to feel anything else." Grytt gave the grimace one last twist before resetting her features. "You're not a fool."

Rory shrugged, one-shouldered. She had already decided that Moss's real message concerned impressing upon his royal hostage who, exactly, was in charge of the station, and where she ranked in his estimation. Waiting three days. Sending a pair of his own security to fetch her.

"Grytt," she said. "I'm a minor, by Thorne law, and should not go unaccompanied among strangers."

It was Grytt's turn to blink. Then her mouth twisted in a different direction, peeling her lips off her teeth. "Just let me tidy up, Princess."

The Tadeshi escort blinked, in unison, when Grytt followed Rory out, wearing her body-maid livery. They blinked a second time as they marked her half-chromed skull winking from beneath the velvet tam. They didn't blink at all when Stary and Franko emerged from their quarters and took up their positions in the corridor, but their eyes narrowed a little.

"Stay here," Rory told her security. "Grytt will accompany me."

Rory drew herself up and lifted her chin, prepared to turn all objections, but none were forthcoming. The Tadeshi bowed, again in unison, and turned and led the way through the labyrinthine coils of Urse. Rory kept careful track of turns and steps. She had studied schematics of the station, and so she knew that they were not taking her by public route, which was the way she had come— past the stares of residents and shopkeepers and dockworkers— but rather by smaller, less-populated corridors that seemed to run through upper-class residential areas. The residents here moved aside politely and said nothing out loud, but their stares bored into her back like so many steel points.

There were a great many places a person might vanish, back

here. Little alleys. Blank doors. Bulkheads with a paucity of port-holes.

Rory looked straight ahead, and didn't hurry, and wished she had brought her own security. She also wished she had dared to come armed. And she was also very, very glad of Grytt, who certainly had.

Urse had no palace, being a station, but the municipal complex, which spiked the entire height of the station off the primary deck, did a credible imitation. The complex was fronted in a frosted, extremely expensive, one-way hexed diamond compound that glittered in the station lights like an icicle, and its corridors—curved and tangled and not at all like the clean, predictable lines of the rest of Urse—seemed to Rory more like those of a museum than a government facility. Officials flitted the corridors, clustering in alcoves to whisper their business, prancing across the wider rooms to see and be seen. The monarch's office looked over the docks on one side, and across three glass-sided levels of offices, meeting rooms, and lounges on the other. There were curtains drawn across the windows at the moment, of a purple more related to black than to violet, and of a fabric (probably velvet) that sucked the light like a singularity.

Moss had not built it—that extravagance was King Sergei's grandsire's doing—but he had made himself well at home in it. He sat in his padded

throne

executive administrator's chair in his office for a full three beats after Rory entered the room before rising, which was just south of good protocol. At least two of those beats he spent studying Grytt, as if wishing an aetherlock would open up under her feet and remove her from his presence.

Rory listened to the whisper of the ventilation, a background noise on Urse that seemed, when it was the only sound present, like the quiet breathing of something large and invisible in the same room. She looked around the office: a first quick glance to mark the placement of furniture and other heavy objects ("Always look for cover"), and for any openings not as immediately apparent as the door. Monarchs, even those who lived in void, made a practice of having escape routes in case of emergency. Rory guessed there might be a trapdoor of some sort under the desk. The only other solid bulkhead, to the left of the desk, looked like the offspring of a library and a museum, studded with shelves of books and artwork representing all the planets, stations, and assorted colonies of the Free Worlds.

Then, the Regent having still said nothing, Rory took a second, longer look around the room, which ended, perhaps inevitably, on the Regent himself.

If one could wish the nemesis of all that was good and right in the universe to be possessed of unfortunate features in an unpleasing arrangement, or protruding teeth, or pervasive body odor, well, Rory had already been disappointed. She had seen enough holos and 2Ds of Moss to know that his straight nose and high cheekbones and sharp chin were counted handsome by most standards. In person, he smelled like pleasant, clean, manly nothing.

He was, Rory thought, damn (sorry, Messer Rupert) near perfect. He also had more cosmetic-hexes than she had ever seen on one person, and she wondered if he had performed them all himself (unlikely, but daunting if he had) or (more likely) had a small contingent of body-men to do it for him.

She considered, very briefly, testing her arithmancy against his cosmetics, and seeing if sweaty palms, big pores, or halitosis presented themselves. She discarded the notion in the next breath— not because of any fairy gifts of wisdom or prudence, but because Moss chose that moment to rise.

"Princess Rory." His voice was pleasant, its Tadeshi accent musical. His mouth arranged itself into a charming smile, confined to the borders of his lips and the dimple on his left cheek. He tilted his chin down in the sort of greeting monarchs give each other, which does not require breaking eye contact or displaying the top of one's head. "Please accept my welcome, on behalf of Prince Ivar and the Free Worlds of Tadesh, to Urse."

Rory brought out the smile she had honed to perfection on courtiers since her twelfth birthday. She inclined her head, just a hair more shallowly than Moss. A proper Thorne greeting would have included a curtsy, but Rory was disinclined to bend her knee to Regent Moss, and besides, she was wearing the trousers favored by Kreshti women and Ursan residents of all sexes, which rendered curtseys impractical. Instead, she extended her hand, which she intended both as an offer and a challenge, a handshake being, among humans at least, a greeting between equals.

Moss reached for her hand, and for a heartbeat, Rory thought she might have to revise all her opinions of him. Before that little shiver of disappointment could settle into resignation, the Regent caught her fingertips as if they were live butterflies, tipped her hand palm-side down, and brought her knuckles to his lips. His skin was cool, smooth, like plastic. His lips were tepid. His breath, skating across the back of her hand, was hot and cool by turns, as he held onto it for several moments longer than the duration of the kiss.

"You are," he said, smiling past her knuckles, "so very *much* like your mother."

Rory, with a sense of relief, settled back into her prejudicial dislike like armor.

Grytt stirred, in Rory's periphery. Moss's gaze flicked that direction and settled just long enough that his smile shrank and hardened into what Rory thought must be the usual shape of his mouth. Thoughtful. A little cruel.

Then Moss blinked and returned his smile and attention to her. But not her hand, not yet, even as he straightened and drew her arm further over the expanse of the desk, forcing her onto her toes to keep balance. Rory was conscious of the broad expanse of imported wood, with its careful arrangement of tablets and scrolls and documents, a pair of turings, and trio of styluses, arranged by size beside the larger of the terminals. The Regent's territory, and herself suspended over it, trusting her balance and dignity to the pressure of his fingers on hers.

He squeezed her hand gently. "I am so very pleased to
have you
make your acquaintance, your Highness, and to have you
keep you
here on my station."

Rory marked Moss's use of the personal possessive pronoun. Then she plucked her fingers out of his hand and thumped back on her heels. She had to retreat half a step to catch up to her balance, which both irritated (it looked like retreat) and relieved (*oh good, another meter between us*) her. Thus removed to a safer distance, Rory pressed her soles firmly into the textured deckplate and dropped her chin in a gesture Messer Rupert knew well. Had he been present, he would have stared warning at her with such force as to leave tiny holes in the side of her skull.

In another age, the thirteen fairies might have wished wisdom on the young princess, as it is often a necessity to the happiness of princesses and queens, who must manage their male counterparts. And so the twelfth fairy had intended to grant Rory that gift. But with the thirteenth fairy's modification on the traditional death-wish, the twelfth fairy had elected to ameliorate the curse with a counter-wish, and to let wisdom happen in its own time, a companion to age and experience. Perhaps she was herself unwise in her choice of counter-wishes, or perhaps she expected Rory's elders to be forever at hand to guide the Princess through her youth, or perhaps she thought that, in the end, wisdom is wasted on youth. Who can say, with fairies?

Thus it was that Rory—superb harpist, fine singer, as kind as wishes could make her—was, by Moss's contrivance, without her best and wisest advisor when her own wisdom failed her.

"Thank you," she said, with the barest sincerity, and three measures too much briskness for proper etiquette. "But where is Prince Ivar? I had expected him here to greet me."

There should have been at least one *your Grace* in that query. Her tone should certainly have been, if not demure, then at least respectful. Instead she sounded in that moment like the least fortunate amalgam of her father's arrogance and her mother's temper— in other words, entirely like a monarch.

Grytt cleared her throat. The tiniest cough, as if she'd mislaid a bit of air and had to snatch it up again. It was a Messer Rupert sort of noise, and it generally meant *think carefully* or *you just said something stupid*. Coming from Grytt, it probably meant *shut up* and *check for cover*.

Regent Moss never looked at Grytt. Not a flicker. Instead his Bielo-colored eyes rested on Rory until she fancied that she could see her breath smoke in the chill.

"Prince Ivar regrets he cannot be here," the Regent said finally, softly, all the music of his accent sunk flat. "He is presently engaged in other activities."

Truth and truth. Rory nodded. "Go on."

Grytt sighed.

Regent Moss traded his greeting smile for a leaner, sharper

model. "On Beo, as it happens. In your recent reading, surely you came across that name."

Rory's mouth, a few steps ahead of her wits, dried up. She swallowed. The fairies had not stinted her intellect or her cleverness. She knew a trap when she saw one. And she realized she had nearly stepped into it with both feet.

"Beo," she repeated, trying the syllables like a new flavor of sweet. And then she did something she had never done before in her life: pretended to be stupider than she was. "Isn't that one of the moons?"

To her ears, her lie sounded bright and false as sunlight before a storm. The Regent did not appear to notice.

"Yes, Princess, it is a moon," he said, as if explaining that Svaro was round and yellow, and also, void is very cold. "Beo belongs to Bielo. It is a cold place. Toxic atmosphere. There are only certain times a pilot can reach the moon's surface at all, with the gravitational vagaries of its neighbor moons and Bielo itself. And sometimes storms on the planet unsettle the radiation in the area, which makes flying even more hazardous. Your arrival coincided, unfortunately, with one of those storms. Prince Ivar

has no idea you're here

does not want to risk a pilot, but he did not believe it was appropriate to keep you waiting any longer, lest you think us poor hosts. So he asked me to offer formal welcome."

Rory swallowed past the thumping in her throat. "Oh. I—oh. It's just, I was so looking forward to seeing him."

Moss blinked and frowned, ever so slightly. Then he bowed exactly as far as was proper, one ruling Regent to a Princess who wasn't the heir to her kingdom, and smiled. "I am certain you will see him soon, Highness. I will do everything in my power to make it so."

CHAPTER NINE ═══════

In Which Appetites Are Both Whetted And Spoiled

A second, silver-scrolled invitation arrived that very next evening, just as Grytt was clearing away the remnants of supper. It should be noted that we say *evening* out of habit, a custom grown from the regular cycles of revolving planets and horizons and a distinctly dirtside perspective; but stations, of course, do not have proper days and nights. They have shifts, because a station never sleeps, and so station schedule divides the old homeworld more-or-less twenty-four hour day into three equal segments.

Rory, who was trying to accustom herself to Urse's terminology and nomenclature, self-corrected *evening* in her head to *early second shift*.

Messer Rupert, already seated in the living area, studiously ignoring the panoramic darkness in favor of the contents of his teacup, raised both head and eyebrows and consulted the chronometer on the wall, staring at it as if it might reveal to him the motives behind such a late visit.

Grytt did not bother noting the time. She set the dish she was carrying down, carefully, on the narrow strip of synthetic wood that passed for a kitchen counter, and, drying her hands on her trousers, headed for the door. Although her 'slinger was back on the dining room table, a thin ceramic blade nevertheless managed to find its way into her hand in the short distance between kitchen and door.

"Rory," said Grytt.

The Princess nodded. "Go ahead. Open it."

Grytt did. Outside, in the corridor, stood another matched set of Tadeshi security. This pair was smaller, slimmer, and darker than the first, but still several orders of magnitude larger than the average human male. They looked at Grytt, and at the slim blade in her hand. Then the one on the left, distinguishable by a faint scar on his chin, said,

"Good evening."

He pronounced the second word carefully, as if it were carved of jet and might cut his lips if he spoke too quickly.

"And a fine second shift to you," Grytt snapped. She held out her unarmed, mecha hand. "I'll take that metal tube you're carrying."

Someone other than Grytt might have been pleased to note a frown—very slight, but distinct—on the security man's face, as an indication of shared circumstance: he, too, was just a person doing his job for superiors who ordered visits at unreasonable hours. Grytt, however, divided the world into My People and Those Others, and the first group was quite selective.

"It is for the Princess Rory," said the second security guard, whose chin was quite perfect.

Grytt, who had been imperfectly featured even before the bomb, peeled her lips back in a warning smile. "And that's who I'll give it to."

"We have orders," said Imperfect Chin. An unripe irritation thickened his Tadeshi accent, corroding his polished consonants.

Grytt's teeth gave up any pretense at friendly expression. "So do I. Anything you have for her Highness comes through me."

Messer Rupert sighed, very faintly. Rory thought he muttered something about *pissing contest* and decided she must have misheard, since Messer Rupert did not swear. Then he threw her a look that said, clear as any speech, *You'd better get involved.*

Exactly, thought Rory. She came out of the kitchen and stood, just enough out of true with the door that the guards could see her shadow on the bulkhead, but not her actual person.

"Who is it, Grytt?" she said, loudly.

Grytt raised her own voice, but did not turn her head, so that she was half-shouting in the guards' faces. "Messengers

lackeys

from the

bastard

Regent. They've got a message for you."

"Well, take it, then," Rory said. She was beginning to agree with Messer Rupert's assessment of the situation. The mood at the door was getting ugly. And while she could admit an improper thrill at the thought of seeing Grytt beat the hell out of Tadeshi security, she knew that a diplomatic incident might lead to Moss expelling Grytt.

Fortunately, Tadeshi security did not appear inclined to force the issue, either, with the resident foreign princess having spoken. Perhaps Moss had given them orders, too. In any case, they withdrew without another word, leaving in Grytt's mecha hand an open-ended metal tube with a roll of what looked like paper inside. She closed her fingers around the steel. Held it up to her blue eye and peered at it from all angles.

"Excessive precaution," murmured Messer Rupert, who had

not moved from his chair. "They're hardly going to wire it with explosives."

Grytt snorted. "And what you doing over there, then?"

"Necessary precaution," said Messer Rupert. He had, in fact, been performing his own examination, eyes half-lidded, pretending disinterest while he whispered his hexes and examined the aura-prints on the steel. Moss had touched neither the paper nor the metal, though his presence slicked both items with a greasy rainbow shimmer. Having ascertained there were no spybots, he returned his attention to his tea. "Well, Rory. What does it say?"

The Princess considered that *pissing contest* might well apply to the dynamics of her household, as well. She tipped the tube and shook the message into her hand.

"It's an invitation to a formal dinner for you *and* me, Messer Rupert. For tomorrow evening."

He nodded serenely. "About time. Not unexpected."

"Grytt's not on the invitation."

"One imagines Regent Moss wants his silverware used for its original purpose, rather than subverted into proxy solutions to the *in situ* weapons ban."

"You ever *seen* a shrimp fork?" said Grytt. "Wicked tines. Pluck an eye out, neat as you please."

"Except for the blood and viscera, I imagine, yes. *Very* neat."

Rory settled against the narrow lip of the porthole and leaned her back against the polysteel. Cherno's light made the creamy paper look rusty. Or bloodstained.

"I suppose I can't refuse," she murmured. She didn't think Messer Rupert or Grytt would hear her, being engaged in their own conversation, and of course she already knew the answer. The invitation was polite summons, nothing more. She would have as much choice in attending this dinner as she ever had for one of her birthday celebrations.

"Course you can't," said Grytt, proving yet again that her mecha ear was more sensitive than the standard biological organ. And as Rory gathered up the wisps of breath to say yes, yes, she *knew* that, Grytt added, "You got to scare hell out of them, Princess. Kick 'em in their expectations."

"Indeed," Messer Rupert said soberly. "As much as it pains me to say this, Grytt is correct. Regent Moss imagines you to be a child, both in fact of age and of experience, an impression reinforced by your recent encounter."

Rory sighed, winced, and braced herself for another one of Messer Rupert's devastating disappointed looks. Instead, he produced the smallest, thinnest smile Rory had ever seen, razor-sharp with malice. "He believes himself to have the advantage. You must disabuse him of that notion."

"Oh, he has an advantage over me. Really. He has the best cosmetic arithmancers I've ever seen."

Grytt snorted. Messer Rupert's smile warmed a few degrees. "And what other advantages does he have?"

"He's very powerful, and he won't give that up easily. Or at all, I think." Rory thought she understood, suddenly, what must have happened to Ivar's mother. She also understood why Messer Rupert was always pinching the bridge of his nose and sighing, and why he had the lines around his mouth, too, the ones that didn't wrinkle up when he smiled. "Poor Ivar."

"Indeed." Messer Rupert nodded. "Poor Ivar. And yet here is your advantage: you and Ivar are both what he is *not*, and can never be. You are royalty. And if you marry Ivar, then someday, you will be *his* sovereign."

Rory blinked. "I hadn't thought of that."

"He has." Grytt snorted, and waved off Messer Rupert's warning glare. "We're assuming he's going to let it get that far. Marrying Ivar."

"He's hardly going to assassinate me," said Rory. She wished she sounded more confident in that declaration.

"Of course he isn't," said Grytt. "Not this close to the cease-fire. Nobody wants more war. But you could have accidents. And *Ivar*, hell, I'm surprised he's made it this far."

"Oh Grytt," Messer Rupert murmured. "Shut up. Rory, listen. Regent Moss is a dangerous man, yes, and I do not believe there are many things which would give him pause, should he need to do them to get what he wants. Including, yes, your assassination, Ivar's, mine, and Grytt's. However, I *do* believe that your health is in his best interests."

"At least until Ivar rejects me. And even if he doesn't, I am only necessary if Moss thinks he can control me, too."

"Oh no. You're more precious than that. Regent Moss has two sons. Any hope he has of maintaining power here will need royal legitimacy, or he will face an internal rebellion. Urse may be cosmopolitan enough to imagine a life without sovereigns, but there are others in the Free Worlds who hold royalty to be divine."

"Like . . . a god?"

"Like a god."

Rory considered that. And said, for the first time, with real anticipation, "Then I suppose I should worry about what to wear."

In the end, Grytt's advice ("Wear battle armor. Carry a sword.") lost to Messer Rupert's more conservative counsel.

"Consider the effect you wish to achieve, Princess." He weighted the title, both in volume and stress. "You are both a representative of your kingdom and the future Queen of this one."

"Not officially. Not yet, anyway."

"Not at all, if you appear dressed for war—shut *up*, Grytt—and whatever your feelings on the betrothal, Rory, the treaty rests on its realization."

"I know." Rory's teeth creaked, clenched as they were against an argument that would serve no purpose except upsetting Messer Rupert. "But I'm not sure about wearing *that*."

On Thorne, formal affairs were conducted in approximations of traditional (and archaic) homeworld garments, all dependent on an excess of fabric and extra hands to help stuff, prod, and arrange their wearers. The women's garments were even more elaborate, having even more laces and alarmingly little fabric in some places, countered by even more alarming arrangements of skirts. Several examples had travelled with Rory, none of them of her choosing, all of them snuck into the baggage by maids undoubtedly following her mother's orders.

Or, she thought, eyeing him suspiciously, Messer Rupert's.

Which gave her an idea.

"I could go in a robe."

"Ah," said Messer Rupert. "No. A robe isn't appropriate for a princess."

"What he means is," said Grytt, "only men with more brains than wits wear dresses. Armor," she added, under her breath, "is far more sensible."

"Learned men wear robes, yes," said Messer Rupert, crisply. "Political officials. Arithmancers. Men who are *not* warriors. But not women, on Thorne."

"Because you Thornes don't want women smart *or* armed."

"Grytt—"

"The whole point of a robe," said Rory, "is that it *isn't* a dress. I don't mind the skirt part." She flicked her fingers at the current offering, spilled along the length of the couch like wine from an upended goblet. "But I'm afraid to breathe in that thing. I'm afraid I'll pop out. I know that's the point—that the dress makes people—"

"A particular *kind* of person," murmured Grytt.

"—imagine that, not that I *actually* will."

Messer Rupert's lips wrinkled a bit, as if he had bitten into something sour. A muscle ticked in his jaw. "Quite."

"I don't think Moss would care if I walked in there naked. But his sons will be there, and—" Rory shuddered. "Do I want them to think about me like that?"

Grytt snorted. "They will anyway, unless their preferences lie elsewhere."

"I have heard no rumors to that effect." Messer Rupert tapped his fingers on the table in no particular pattern, which meant he was considering the merit of Rory's objections. "It would be useful for the Regent's sons to find you attractive."

"She will be, unless you put a bag on her head."

"Or put her in battle armor," snapped Messer Rupert. "Which I believe was your suggestion. And a robe is going too far in the other direction. We don't want her to appear sexless." He caught Rory staring at him, and a red deeper and more dramatic than the dress crept up his neck and settled in two bright suns on his cheeks. "My apologies, Rory, I—"

"No, I understand." Rory rubbed her forehead, kneading the skin in slow circles. "No one is interested in my education or my arithmancy. You advised me to remind Moss that I am not a child, and while I'm sure this particular choice of garment will affirm that I am past puberty, I think it will also raise a new set of reasons for him to dismiss me."

"Battle armor," Grytt said, under her breath. "Listen, Rupert. There is nothing says she has to wear traditional Thorne anything.

What do they wear around the station, to formal events? Or have you even bothered to notice?"

"I haven't *been* to any formal events," Messer Rupert said, in a voice that could wither leaves on the branch or congeal fidgeting courtiers to stillness. Then he looked at Rory and sighed. "You're right. Absolutely. I am sorry, Rory. I will do what I can to procure you formal wear that is both Ursan and more comfortable, if you wish, but I do not think we can do so before the dinner. One of these dresses will have to suffice. And consider this, too: I did not say you must disabuse the Regent of his preconceptions *yet*. It may be useful to have Moss underestimate you for a time."

Rory waited for Grytt's retort. Instead, the battlemaster-turned-body-maid grimaced as if whatever sour thing Messer Rupert had sampled had found its way into her mouth, as well.

"Strategy in that," she said, eyeing Rory. "Needs patience, though. Think you can manage that? Keep your mouth closed, maybe, this time?"

This time it was Rory's cheeks that warmed. "Yes."

"Then I say wear the black one. It's got fewer skirts, and there's a gather in the bodice for a little blade."

"Absolutely *not*—" Messer Rupert stopped himself. Blinked at her. "How do you know that?"

"Oh, don't look at me like that. I can't hex, but I can sew. You know Samur always carries steel on her person, Rupert."

Messer Rupert's nostrils pinched white. He glared at Grytt.

"Yes." It was the shortest, sharpest *yes* Rory had ever heard.

Grytt, unsurprisingly, ignored his discomfiture. "You didn't think Samur got a palace seamstress to tailor her dresses, did you? You think the old King would've let that go?"

Messer Rupert's mouth flexed a little. "I don't think he had any idea, actually."

"Right." Grytt rolled her flesh eye. "Don't you fret, Princess. I brought a knife that will fit, too."

Rory set aside her worries about necklines, gravity, and the occasionally inconvenient necessity of drawing deep breaths while wearing a bodice. "My mother carries a knife?"

"Of course she does. A Kreshti soldier always carries a blade."

Rory sat down, heedless of the audible wrinkles her bottom carved in the dress's voluminous skirts. "My mother was a soldier?"

"Sure. Compulsory service."

"I knew that. I thought she might've gotten out of it, or, you know. She never said anything about it."

"Of course she didn't. You'd've asked to be a soldier, too, and started a civil war. She gave me to you, instead. Personal trainer to the Princess." Grytt chuckled.

"Rory can*not* carry a weapon into the Regent's presence. Or Ivar's. You'll cause an incident. There will be spybots all over the palace against weapons."

"I never said it'd be steel, did I?" Grytt grinned. "Don't worry, Rupert. Metal's not the only thing you can sharpen. Besides. I got it this far, you not knowing, or the bloody 'bots. Moss won't know, either. But you'll have to be careful, Rory. It'll hold an edge until the sun dies, but it's brittle."

And so it was that Rory arrived at her first formal reception on Urse *welded*

laced into a black velvet dress, with a finger-slim dart of bone and hex-grown diamond for company, snug in its Grytt-sewn sheath. Rory kept her fingers balled at her side, to resist both checking the blade's presence—which she could feel very clearly running a line from sternum to navel—and making fists in her skirt, which only small children or nervous adults did. The knife was entirely invisible from the exterior. Rory was quite certain of that. The slightest bulge, and Messer Rupert would have insisted she leave it behind.

Besides. She was, she told herself sternly, not nervous.

The Princess was also not alone among skirt-wearers. At least four diplomats from Lanscot were in attendance, wrapped in swathes of an itchy-looking fabric that concealed their bodies from knee to forehead, leaving only eyes and mouth exposed. The garment, traditional to the Lanscottar, evolved as a response to the climate of the planet's habitable zone, which was cold, wet, and generally miserable. The colonists who live there take great pride in surviving the inconvenience, and in pointing out that at least Lanscot had breathable atmosphere and, despite its propensity to precipitation, was actually quite fecund. Further, the planet possessed a rich collection of native flora quite edible for imported livestock, the husbandry of which formed the backbone of the Lanscottar economy, which survived on meat and wool exports.

Rory thought the Lanscottar must be very warm under all that wool, and very stubborn to continue wearing it, when most of the other guests eyed them sidelong, wearing little superior smirks with which Rory was quite familiar, having grown up among courtiers. She resolved to visit Lanscot at the earliest opportunity, with as much public fanfare as she could manage.

Most of the Tadeshi women wore slim-fitting trousers and shirts that rivaled Rory's own bodice for minimalism, without the boning and laces to make sure that everything inside stayed that way. The presence of so many steep necklines was both reassuring and disconcerting. Some kinds of familiarity only serve to reinforce the depressing truth that people everywhere are capable of developing the same foolish customs. At least the Lanscottar costume rendered everyone equally unappealing.

The upshot, however, of the sea of plunging necklines, was that no one was making a special effort to stare at Rory. She squirmed away from Messer Rupert relatively early, and explored the reception at her own pace and leisure. She was partly aided by the venue itself. There were trees, and bushes, and great vines holding the multiple levels together like twine. It was, Messer Rupert said, a favorite place for diplomatic meetings which, while not precisely clandestine, were at least largely proof against both 'bots and traditional eavesdropping. It was also, he had added, after a moment, quite popular among young couples for, ah, well. It was just popular. Tonight, for the reception, there were tiny teslas strung through trees, which winked like little white stars caught among the leaves, and rendered the overall ambiance somewhat crepuscular.

Rory spent longer than was strictly proper with the Lanscottar, who seemed pleased to have the foreign princess's attention, and genuinely delighted to go on at length about the habits of their sheep and the cleverness of their dogs. Rory, who had never had a dog, and had only a passing academic knowledge of sheep (ate grass, made wool), made an excellent audience. She was perhaps halfway through a recitation of the exploits of a dog named Robbie and a clever sheep-thief when she heard Regent Moss call her name from a distance that required him to raise his voice to attract her attention: something, she had been told, a ruling scion *never* did.

Well of course, Rory thought. He's no scion. He's a jumped-up Minister with delusions of royalty and a talent for seizing power.

Rory examined that moment of smug condescension. She considered, briefly, ignoring him. Pretending she had not heard him, engrossed as she was in the tales of a clever canine and his woolly charges. Indeed, she did not turn at once.

But the Lanscottar *had* heard, despite all the layers of wool. The tallest, a woman named Maggie, straightened first, her eyes flashing past Rory's shoulder. The other three followed suit, stiffening to their full height, chins migrating upward and outward, under their woolens, until the face-wrapping stretched tight. Rory guessed there were tight, square jaws hidden under there. Their eyes, all four sets, were hard and flat as deckplate.

"The Regent," muttered Maggie.

"Aye," hissed the shortest Lanscottar, whose wrap was a particularly startling combination of reds, blues, and bright green lines.

Rory made a note to check the history of diplomatic relations between Moss and the Lanscottar when she got back to the suite. She also revised her assumptions about the logic and inconvenience of Lanscottar dress customs. The facial wrap alleviated any need to keep one's feelings off one's face. In a court environment, that could be a very useful concealment.

Then, thus forewarned, she turned around.

The Regent was alarmingly close already, and, even more alarmingly, not alone. A pair of young men trailed in his wake, both alike enough to each other and to the Regent himself that their identities were easy to ascertain.

"Princess," said Moss, with a precisely correct bow. "You are looking lovely this evening."

Rory smiled, her very sweetest, and dropped into a Thornestyle curtsy, arms spread, chin lowered, chest just so slightly outthrust. Her gaze remained fixed on Moss, unblinking.

"Regent. What a delightful gathering."

"You are too kind, Princess." He tilted his head. His gaze wandered over the Lanscottar, and his lip curled. "I see that you have found some of the Free Worlds' more, hm, eccentric inhabitants. The Lanscottar do love their stories, and those stories are very diverting. I hope you've enjoyed them."

His tone suggested that, whether or not she had, her time with Robbie the very clever dog and the sheep-thief of the Clarster Moors had come to an end. Behind Moss's shoulder, the young men traded sly, knowing looks. The taller of them kept trying for Rory's eye, slinging his smirk at her like a grappling hook.

Rory wished for more room in the bodice, so that she might take the deep and slow breaths necessary to douse her temper. Then she turned a shoulder to Moss, and looked back at the Lanscottar.

"Thank you for the conversation," she said. "I look forward to hearing the rest of Robbie's tale at a later date."

"Your Highness," said Maggie. The Lanscottar bowed, of a piece, and shuffled away into the arboretum. The smell of over-warmed human and wet sheep trailed after them.

"Much better," muttered the taller boy. "You don't have to flatter them, Princess."

Rory had practiced this particular gesture a dozen times in the mirror. Chin up. Shoulders back. Eyebrow . . . just the one on the left . . . up, up. *There.*

"I'm sorry," she said crisply. "I don't believe I know you."

The taller boy's cheeks turned red. The shorter one caught his sniggering in his hand, which he turned into an unconvincing cough when his father turned to glare at him.

A cold little smile took up residence in the corner of Moss's mouth, as if it were trying to get as far away from its wearer as possible. "Indeed. My apologies, Princess. Allow me to introduce my sons, Merrick and Jaed."

Merrick and Jaed shared their father's striking good looks: blond, both of them, tall and wide-shouldered, with narrow hips and long legs. Merrick was the taller, the one with the sense to blush. Jaed was perhaps four centimeters shorter, which he made up for in the increased breadth of his shoulders. His hair was perhaps two shades darker, as well, bronze rather than gilt.

Rory suffered the obligatory hand-kissing, all the while battling twin impulses of regret and relief at Grytt's absence. Not that Grytt could have done anything about the social niceties. She did catch sight of Messer Rupert, trapped on the edge of the room. His expression suggested he wished Merrick and Jaed reduced to insectivore amphibians on the spot.

Unfortunately the only remedy to Rory's situation was diplomacy. She decided she'd have to rescue herself.

Rory plucked her hand out of Jaed's fingers (still damp from his coughing) and took a neat little half-step back, twitching her skirts to their widest circumference, making a border of velvet and lace that, together with custom, would keep young men just out of easy hand-grasping range.

"I am delighted to make your acquaintances," she said. "Regent, your sons do you credit."

"They are at your disposal, Princess. They would be delighted to show you around Urse at your earliest convenience."

Rory folded her fingers together at her waist, smiling from one Moss to the other. She waited until Jaed opened his mouth, and then said, "How kind. Do you both also serve with the Tadeshi marines, like Prince Ivar?"

Merrick blinked. Jaed, caught open-mouthed, remained in that condition. "Uh," he said.

"No, your Highness," said Merrick. His fine brows had drawn together.

"Oh?" Rory affected surprise. "But I understood that service, here in the Free Worlds, is compulsory. Or is that only for Princes?"

Moss's face transformed, becoming all ice and hard angles, anger and a malice that raised chill-pimples along her exposed flesh. Then he pinned his lips into a smile, and Rory wondered if she'd seen the lapse at all.

"Your Highness, I have some good news. The Prince is here, on Urse. He will be joining us later this very evening."

A suspicious person—or one, perhaps, raised in a court environment and tutored by a vizier to believe that people were capable of all manner of deceit, and one was only prudent to suspect it—might have wondered at the promptness of Ivar's arrival. And indeed, Rory did wonder. She also retained enough wit to refrain from asking.

She checked the disposition of her smile, shined it up a bit, and dipped again into a curtsy. Merrick's and Jaed's gaze slipped from her face. Their chins mirrored the dip and rise of their gaze. Regent Moss's eyes, however, stayed steady, and Rory found herself fighting an urge to blink and look elsewhere as she said,

"Thank you, Regent. I appreciate the extraordinary efforts to which you must have gone, retrieving Prince Ivar from that dreadful moon."

"Not at all, Princess. It was no trouble."

Her heart would have sunk, had the dress permitted. Instead it fluttered unhappily, battering itself against bone and bodice.

It continued to do so for the next nearly hour, while Merrick and Jaed attached themselves one to a side and steered her through the twinkling trees. For Rory, however, the magic of the evening was quite extinguished. The lights instead seemed dim, the shadows ominous, and every hiss of the doors made her start and turn, craning past branch and bough to see if this time the arrival was Ivar's.

She had begun to imagine his arrival as the event which would give her excuse to shed her escort. She had begun to imagine him as, well, her *rescuer*. She wasn't entirely certain how a rescue would look, having never before imagined needing one, and in truth, she needed no rescue now. Merrick and Jaed, while vexing, hardly offered her any danger. But perhaps she can be forgiven for the lapse, having never before been pursued quite so aggressively or so trapped in anyone's (or in this case, anytwo's) company.

And then, very suddenly, the moment arrived, and reality and Ivar made their entrance. The arboretum doors labored open, letting station-cool air invade the warm, somewhat humid arboretum like a snake across the top of a bare foot. The reception's murmur faded to the sort of expectant quiet that seems to hum, at the limits of one's hearing.

Rory stopped, forcing Merrick and Jaed to stop, as well. She rearranged herself, stretching onto her toes and tilting alarmingly sideways—using a tree for balance, much to Merrick's visible disappointment—to catch a clear view of the door.

A middle-aged man in Valenko colors, velvet cut in the local Ursan style, stepped into the doorway and paused, looking dramatically around the room.

"Prince Ivar Valenko," the herald shouted. His voice filled the arboretum, nudging the trees aside, filling all the aether. No sooner had the heraldic echoes died than Prince Ivar Valenko stepped into the arboretum. He blinked at the teslas. He blinked at the trees. His glance skipped from face to face, wide-eyed, until it found the one it sought and settled. Then he blinked again, decisively.

Regent Moss approached, bowed, and said something Rory couldn't hear. Then, using the Prince's elbow as a rudder, the Regent guided the Prince into the arboretum and unerringly in her direction.

As we have noted, Rory had allowed herself only a small, prudent measure of imagining, where Prince Ivar was concerned. She had not wished to begin their relationship with any preconceptions. There were facts, which one might read on a dossier. There was the added knowledge of the Prince's deployment on Beo, and the basic expectation of the sort of young man who might serve on dangerous off-world bases. Even the most diligent and practical of minds might be forgiven a *little* fantasizing, in those circumstances.

But then that mind was confronted by the reality of the Prince, which proved only that dossiers were, at the end, merely data, and as such were vulnerable to arithmancy or good old-fashioned fabrications.

Prince Ivar did not enjoy the same cosmetic arithmancy as his Regent. Nor did he display any of the physical symptoms of a man accustomed to martial exertion. He did not march. He shuffled. His body expanded into the folds and corners of his garments much as Rory imagined rising dough would, if it were dressed in a velvet coat.

"Your Highness," the Regent murmured. "May I present the Princess Rory Thorne."

Ivar blinked at Rory. His right eye appeared to harbor some sort of minor infection. It was red, watery, and a little bit swollen. Rory tried not to look too closely at it. Instead, she gathered up every scrap of the etiquette Messer Rupert had drilled into her.

"Your Highness," she said.

"Er," said Ivar. He stared at her outstretched hand as if it were a live snake studded with mines.

"You must forgive his Highness," said Regent Moss. "He is unaccustomed to courtly manners." Moss waited half a beat, then leaned down and said against Ivar's ear, "Kiss the Princess's hand, your Highness."

Jaed suffered another small coughing fit. Moss ignored him. Ivar did, too. He set his jaw and took Rory's hand, still behaving as if it were a reptile wired with explosives, and brought his lips to a parchment's distance from her knuckles. She felt the warm brush of his exhale on her skin, thin and shaky. Then he let go as if the snake had caught fire and begun reciting poetry at the same moment. His eyes were a little wide and glassy.

"Your Highness."

Rory dipped into a curtsy, intending a gesture of depth and dexterity befitting a monarch, and to buy herself time to gain control of her features.

The tiny knife in her bodice had other ideas. It poked into her belly as she folded, its sharp tip threatening the integrity of Grytt's sheath, and Rory straightened more quickly than she'd intended. Ivar hadn't had time to turn away yet, and so he, like Merrick and Jaed, was still staring at her. Ivar, at least, was looking at her face, his own mouth wrung out, his watery eyes blank as a koi's.

Protocol, in this case, dictates that a monarch-to-be should speak first. Rory gave that exactly two seconds' consideration, apologized in her head to Messer Rupert, and said in a strong, clear voice:

"It's good to see you again, Highness."

Ivar's mouth wrung even tighter, tighter, and then snapped slack. "Right. Er. Yes. Very nice to see you again. Er. Your Highness." He cast a hopeful gaze at the Regent, like a man on the rack imploring his torturer to please, yes, just crank it back a couple of notches.

Ordinarily the thirteenth fairy's gift came to Rory as a whisper, one that she felt, more than heard. A certainty in her belly, and in her heart. But this time was not ordinary, the whisper was a shout, and Rory's head fairly rang with the echoes.

who is she why is she looking at me no one said what I should say WHO IS SHE

She was a little dazed as Regent Moss steered the Prince away, and toward a waiting knot of courtiers. She managed the appropriate murmurings of leave-taking, and the barest and most pathetic of curtseys. She guessed, from the looks Merrick cast at her, that her discomfiture was visible.

"Princess," he said. "Are you all right? Do you feel faint?"

To be fair, lest one believe Merrick more of a churl than is warranted, his hesitation to inquire after the Princess's well-being was born of native custom. It is not polite to acknowledge others' distress, in the Free Worlds. He should have pretended ignorance, while waiting for Rory to gather her wits. By acknowledging her distress, Merrick feared he was rendering insult.

"Fine," Rory said; and under the camouflage of that same custom, Merrick dismissed the terseness of her response as an indication that yes, he *had* insulted her. He sagged back a step, quite crestfallen, his magnificent shoulders bowing inward like a tree coated in ice.

Jaed, who had observed this exchange, calculated his own position improved by his brother's failure. He took a step closer to Rory, and risked the barest of finger-touches to the inside of her elbow.

"We're lucky the Prince came at all," he said. "Must've had someone helping him with his buttons."

There were fifteen separate, egregious breaches of etiquette in that statement. Rory drew as much breath as the bodice would permit, half to settle her wits, half to fuel the stinging rebuke she meant to deliver. But the little bone blade, its sharp edges unimpressed by Grytt's stitching or the sturdiness of its sheath, and quite put out by all the curtseys, took the opportunity to part both the leather and the very first layer of flesh just above Rory's navel.

It was not a very great discomfort, but it was startling, and it was exactly enough to divert Rory from her planned outburst and channel her into a much more succinct utterance.

"Oh, shut up," she snapped, and Jaed was startled enough to do just that, which left Rory a few moments to ponder the reasons for her distress.

The fairies may have neglected Rory's wisdom, but they had not stinted her intellect. And what she had concluded was this: that this unfortunate boy-man wasn't Prince Ivar at all.

She wasted no time in reporting that, at the end of the dinner, having spent two full hours in proximity to the man in question, and thus being quite certain of her conviction.

"I'm telling you, it's not Ivar."

It was the fourth time Rory had said as much, in the space of thrice that many minutes. The Vizier cast the same sort of look at Grytt as a man might at a sturdy tree with sturdy branches hanging over a raging river, in which there was exactly one slippery rock to which said man clung, desperately, while the current tore at him.

Grytt only cocked her eyebrow at him, those sturdy branches waving just out of reach.

The Vizier sighed. "Yes, Rory, so you have said."

"Well, what are we going to do about it?"

Rory folded her arms in a most alarming imitation of a five-year-old. The Vizier felt the first stirrings of a headache. He probed carefully the borderland between eyebrow and flesh along his eyesockets. The Princess was not given to flights of fancy. That she was disappointed in her betrothed was understandable—the boy was a bit of a mess—but her reaction was entirely out of proportion.

"Rory. Listen. I understand that Ivar is perhaps not what you had hoped for—"

"Oh *hell*, Messer Rupert." The Princess, having been freed from the twin confines of bodice and public observation, tossed her arms toward what would have been skyward, in a place *with* a sky, and sent her gaze after them. It was very much her mother's gesture; but while Samur often followed such gestures with entreaties to her family's ancestors and the old gods of Kreshti, Rory only made frustrated noises at the impervious steel plates.

It was just as well, the Vizier thought, that the daughter did not share the mother's faith. If the Kreshti ancestors or their gods *were* lurking and listening in the maintenance tunnels between decks, then Rory would be disappointed in their impotence. The Vizier knew that all too well. He had burned incense and lit candles to every god still worshipped in Thorne, and a few besides, including the old Kreshti gods, and still, his Princess was here, awaiting marriage to a man so odious to her that she had regressed to childish fancy to excuse it.

"Messer Rupert. Are you even listening to me?"

He was not, as it happened. He debated the wisdom of saying as much, and had reached the conclusion that yes, he might be permitted a display of irritation, when Rory spoke again.

"That's. Not. Ivar. He had no idea who I was. None." Her eyes bored into him, bright as the power indicators on Grytt's 'slinger. Full charge.

Messer Rupert rubbed his forehead again. His hands, perpetually chilled here on Urse, granted some small measure of relief from the thump on the other side of his skull. "Perhaps he simply did not recognize you," he said carefully. "It has been a great many years."

"You don't even believe that. You think maybe he's stupid. And maybe he is. But even if he *never* checked a holo or a 2D, he should remember me. And he didn't. Not my face, not my name. Nothing. Messer Rupert. How could that be?" Rory crossed the floor— princesses did not *stomp*, or that is exactly what she would have been doing—and stopped in front of him. He pretended not to notice her impatient feet, and continued to massage his forehead.

"The last time Ivar saw you, his father died in an explosion. Perhaps he has repressed the memory."

"*I* didn't." The feet shuffled, then stilled. A shadow darkened the Vizier's already limited field of vision as Rory leaned down, putting their faces on a level.

"This Ivar's a fake. An imposter. Moss is . . . I don't know. Passing him off. Keeping the real one prisoner somewhere."

The Vizier looked at her from within the cool frame of his hands. He fancied he could feel the headache pushing against his fingers. "Do you have *any* idea how fantastic that sounds?"

Rory's already stubborn chin thrust out a little further. "I do know. But I'm serious. It's not wishful thinking, it's not me being upset that this Ivar's a, a—"

"Dullard? Because I find that somewhat upsetting, myself." Rupert sat up, bringing his face out of the plane it shared with Rory's, forcing her to stand up and step back. "I had hoped this boy would have grown into a worthier man. I am disappointed. As are *you*, Rory. But that does not therefore mean this Ivar is an imposter."

"The fairy gift made it pretty damn clear he is!"

"The fairy gift. Rory, honestly." The Vizier fired a glare past his Princess's left hip. "Don't you have *anything* helpful to say?"

Grytt, who had been rubbing at a spot on the kitchen counter with more vigor and intensity than any stain deserved, left off her labors with an expression somewhere between grimace and grin. "We all saw the fairies. And the girl's got a gift for seeing through nonsense. Admit that."

"I'm standing right here," said Rory.

The Vizier ignored her. "So you think Ivar's an imposter, too?"

Grytt shrugged and leaned back against the counter. Her fingers, flesh and metal, curled around the edge. The Vizier hoped she was not leaning half as hard as she appeared to be; she was not a large woman, but the implants made her heavier than she appeared, and the mecha hand was more than a match for the plastics that comprised station furnishings.

"The prince I remember wasn't much, but that doesn't mean anything. I'm saying, it's damn convenient for Moss, that the heir's a bit of a mess. Makes it easier for his boys, if he does grab for power. No one's going to miss Ivar."

"That's what *I* thought."

"Rory, please. Don't crow. It's unbecoming. And loud."

"Sorry, Messer Rupert."

She was, too. That was genuine regret on her face, and guilt, because Rory Thorne, in addition to being gifted in ascertaining social truths, was also relentlessly kind. And whether that kindness came from the fairies—whose reality the Vizier doubted, sometimes, despite the evidence of memory (his, Grytt's, Samur's)—or whether it was native to Rory herself, well, the result was a young woman of whom the Vizier was very fond, who did not deserve the troglodytic Prince to whom she was bound, and who, despite her distress, was sincerely sorry to have upset him.

The Vizier found himself angry at the rules and customs that shaped the world in which he moved. He found himself wishing that, just this once, the most unlikely and fantastic explanation was the true one, and that he could spare Rory a betrothal that, unwelcome before, had become intolerable.

And suddenly, he realized that he could—if not spare her, at least *try*. But he was the Vizier, whose task and talent was offering advice, and guiding kings and regent-consorts and princesses into making the best decisions available—oh. Well then.

He caught Rory's gaze. "If you are *certain*, Rory, that the young man is not Ivar, then what would *you* suggest that we do about it?"

Rory blinked, and some of her certainty drained away. "Do?"

"Surely," Rupert went on, "you are not making much of this fact for the sheer joy of hearing yourself complain. Nor, I presume, are you doing it under the expectation that Grytt and I will figure out how to fix it for you."

A man of lesser quality, dealing with a girl of lesser quality, might have been hoping to discourage Rory by issuing such a challenge. The Vizier, however, knew his princess very well, and he knew how she responded to complications.

"If," said Rory, after a moment, "if there were a plot to conceal the true Prince, if Moss hasn't just killed him outright—but Messer Rupert, what if he has?"

Rupert cocked his head. "He may have. But the fact remains, Rory, you believe we do not know the truth of Ivar's situation, *whatever* it is."

"I—yes. True. All right." Rory's eyes narrowed. They skipped away from the Vizier's face, wandering instead across that ghastly striped planet that was even now swelling in the porthole, rusty in its radiance. "I think such information would be hidden, obviously; but it couldn't be totally secret. There would need to be a conspiracy of some kind. One man couldn't do it alone. And they couldn't be keeping him *here*. But if they're keeping him elsewhere, there must be . . . I don't know. Records. Evidence." She paused. The planet striped her face with glowing bands of rust and sienna and, if a man were superstitious, blood.

"Communications would have to go through the quantum relays unless they were on actual paper and carried by courier."

Grytt grunted. "So we need to find this courier."

"No. Well. I don't think there is one." Rory turned back to her body-maid and grinned. "Paper is immune to hexing, but it's fragile and expensive *and* it takes up a lot of space. A courier would be less secure than just erasing the data on a local system, too, because they could be intercepted or killed. So I think any secret information will be in the turing collective somewhere. And even if it's been erased, that doesn't matter. Data's never really gone. There's always a ghost. A really good arithmancer can find the ghosts and reconstruct the information."

"Huh," said Grytt. "You that good, Rory?"

"Not me. Messer Rupert." She turned to face him, finally. "That's my proposal. That you hex the turing and find out what's happened to Ivar. And then, once we know that, we can decide what to do next. Will you do that?"

The Vizier thought about the ways in which this endeavor could go extremely wrong: miskeyed hexes, arithmancers more clever than he, Valenko's dead queen, and accidents, and how very far Urse was from Thorne. He thought about how very many things could happen to a man, even a diplomat, even a vizier, so far from home.

Then he looked at Rory, and imagined a future in which she married the man he'd met in the arboretum, and he said, "Yes."

CHAPTER TEN ═══════

In Which Things That Can Go Wrong, Do

There is no consensus, among arithmancers or people who write about arithmancy, exactly how best to describe it. An art, say the more romantic. A science, say the practical. The most succinct explanation, and the one most popularly repeated, came from a k'bal arithmancer named Ptt'nikki, who recorded the *Arias* (now considered the foundation for the art school of arithmancy) before the Vizier's ancestors had quite figured out fire. In the *Arias*, which function more like a series of fables than a treatise, there is a tale in which the universe acquires a gender and misplaces her chastity and, in her quest to recover it, acquires some of the more basic arithmantic principles. Although the translation is not entirely accurate, since k'bal do not have fixed characteristics linked to their four genders and three sexes, the popularity of the tale suggests that there is, among arithmancers, a sense that one is conversing with a universe that has an opinion, and that if one wants to succeed at arithmancy, one should employ a degree of flattery, trickery, or raw talent.

The mirri word for arithmancy translates simply as *magic*, which, while counted superstition by everyone else, seems to suit the mirri just fine.

The Vizier belonged to the more scientific of the arithmantic camps. He regarded the universe as a puzzle to which he had, if not the ultimate solution, at least an accurate and detailed set of instructions for solving. And besides, he had more than a passing familiarity with the Ursan turing's collective, having hexed through its defenses once before, during King Sergei's funeral. He had, at that time, laid down some backdoors, arithmantic hatches worked into the turing's code against the eventual necessity of his return. He congratulated himself, as much as a man of the Vizier's modesty ever does, on his foresight and on his memory, for recalling the precise placement and arrangement of his hexes.

Unbeknownst to the Vizier, the turing's collective also remembered him.

Rory was not surprised when the Vizier settled himself behind the primary console and got to work at once, almost before the echoes of his affirmation had faded. She was surprised, however, to find him still hunched over the console the following morning, chin on one hand, while the other pecked irritably at the keyboard. His eyebrows had drawn together, wrinkling the skin between them into valleys and peaks of concentration. His cheeks seemed more hollow than usual, the lines around his eyes much deeper. His gaze did not even flicker as she came into the room. She watched, for a minute, to be sure that he blinked.

He did, but not often. Rory frowned. "You should," she began, but Grytt touched her shoulder.

"Let him work," she said. "You know how he gets."

"Hungry," said Rory. "And dehydrated."

"And grumpy," agreed Grytt. She eyed the Vizier with something like approval. "He's *fine*."

"Huh," said Rory, and performed her own hex, simple and tiny and unobtrusive, shifting her perception just a little bit, so that she could see the aura emanations in the aether. True to Grytt's prediction, Messer Rupert was indeed *fine*, although his orange band was brighter than usual, and the red more intense.

"He's worried," said Rory. "And . . . angry. I think. Or strongly annoyed."

"Right. Like I said. He's fine."

Rory rolled her eyes. "Well then. I think I'll just go take a walk around the station today. Visit the embassy. Wander the arboretum."

Grytt stopped smiling. "Are you serious?"

"Yes. Actually, I am." Rory paced the length of the room. Once. Twice. She paused on the far end, pressing her back against the wall. "Last night marked my formal introduction, didn't it? Everyone officially knows I'm here. So there's no need for me to stay locked up in here like a mirri during estrus."

Grytt snorted. "You're just testing him now, aren't you? See if he'll hear you and sputter a bit?"

"Maybe." Rory frowned. "But that does raise a question. Do you think we need to stay with him? I mean, *can* we leave him alone?"

Grytt studied the Princess a moment, and considered how easy it was to forget how old she was, and that young women of her temperament did not do well in confinement. The history of her father's homeworld was testament to that. Grytt did not blame the fairies, particularly, for having skimped on Rory's patience. Grytt had seen the fairies, to be sure, but she did not accord them the same regard as Rupert or Samur. They were people. They had some pretty impressive tricks. Good for them. Rory's impatience was more easily explained as *Samur's daughter* and *sixteen* than any oversight on the part of xeno guests. She was worried, she was bored, and that made a bad combination, by Grytt's reckoning. She was certain the Vizier would agree.

"We don't have to stay here with him, but someone does. And don't think about assigning that job to me either, Princess. Waste of time, leaving me here. I can have our people on the door. Thorsdottir and Zhang, maybe. It's junior work. They can make sure no one comes in and finds him like this. If he does manage to remember to eat, he can manage on his own."

"Excellent." Rory powered up her tablet and logged into the network, trying not to look as relieved as she felt. "I'll tell the embassy we're coming."

They returned just before the dinner hour. The suite was unlit by anything other than Cherno's rusty glow, and as a result, mostly composed of the ominous shapes that familiar furnishings wear in the dark. Messer Rupert was still hunched in front of the turing. His right hand lay sprawled across the keys. Every few seconds, his fingers would move. His eyes had screwed into slits, dry and miserable behind the outraged puffiness of his eyelids.

A muscle in his jaw ticked in time to his heartbeat.

There was a cup in the sink with a dark, congealed puddle at the bottom, and rings of the same color dotting the counters, proof that Messer Rupert *had* moved during the day.

Grytt made a noise in her throat and fetched a rag.

Rory folded her arms and stared at Messer Rupert. She wanted to tell him about her day: the meticulous tour of the embassies, while messages sizzled through the aether, office to office, until the Tadeshi Minister of Entertainment arrived and requested an audience with her. She wanted to tell him about holding that impromptu meeting there in his office, playing princess, negotiating and flattering and, when those failed, bullying her way into a more complete tour of the station, and access for herself and Grytt to the private gym where the highest-ranking citizens took their exercise. She wanted to say, "I had to throw a bit of a fit, Messer Rupert. They didn't want to grant permission for Grytt. I had to say she protects my virtue. I thought she'd laugh outright, but she didn't, and I *made* them agree."

And she wanted to ask him, in a very soft voice, so that Grytt could pretend not to hear: "Did I do okay?"

Instead, she touched Messer Rupert's arm, very gently, and sighed, and went into the kitchen to make a curry.

It is not for nothing that arithmancers were once called wizards, before Jabir Ibn Hayyan transcribed the treatises of Trismegistus, and imposed reason on superstition. It is also not for nothing that arithmancers tend to gauntness, poor nutrition, and (historically) the keeping of apprentices in lieu of proper caretakers. And it is not for nothing that said apprentices believed their masters (and occasional mistresses) to be wiser than they were: for although the eyes, and the body, and the bulk of an arithmancer's attention is engaged in whatever aetheric layer he inhabits, he can—and does—still experience the physical world. Aural and olfactory senses are unimpeded, although the importance assigned to their reports is at the arithmancer's discretion.

Thus, the Vizier was aware of Rory's presence, and of Grytt's. He was not half so oblivious as he pretended, or as Rory imagined, which, if one did the math (which the Vizier did, being an arithmancer), meant he could hear roughly all of what happened, even if his visual faculties were otherwise engaged. This is the drawback of arithmancy (if one can coax an arithmancer into calling it that; there are those who insist that it is no *drawback*, but rather a feature, albeit an occasionally inconvenient one): to see the mathematical structure which underlies the universe, one must shift one's perception into the layers of the aether where that structure is visible. The Vizier liked to imagine the process as analogous to taking steps. One step to see auras, two for a simple hex (the sort that might help an industrious young princess to shift her own aura, for instance), three for more complex hexes (the sort an industrious, *devious* princess might employ to open a locked keypad, or which a diligent, dutiful Vizier might use to destroy a spybot).

The Vizier had never taught Rory arithmancy requiring more than three steps, although he fully expected she could work out for herself how to do it. She was exactly the right kind of stubborn for arithmancy.

The Vizier himself was many, many more steps than three into the aether, so far that his physical body seemed to belong to someone else entirely. This meant that his fingers on the keypad were abominably slow to obey. It also meant that he had sunk through enough aetheric layers that he could *talk* to the turing, for some version of the word. Their dialogue was algorithmic, numeric, arcane.

Rory and Grytt's audible return was insufficient to tempt the Vizier to respond to them; but the smell of frying spices reminded him that the Princess made very good curries, and he had not eaten in a long time, by a body's reckoning. And so, thus reminded of his mortality, the Vizier began the process of stepping back out.

It was during this process—tedious, complicated, and largely uninteresting except to other arithmancers—that the Vizier discovered a tiny line of code lying on his path. It looked like a shadow, or a smear, or the imaginings of tired eyes. Except that he had no actual *eyes* in the aether, and whatever the fatigue of his body, the Vizier's mind was sharp and aware. He paused to examine the code-line. Faced with his full attention, it vanished.

He reconsidered his self-assessed exhaustion. Began to turn away, to step through another layer of aether—and spotted the code-line again, in the corner of his perception.

The resulting surge of adrenaline made his distant body twitch and gasp, and his face turned an alarming shade of red. The Vizier, unaware of the physical changes, heard only Rory's alarmed, "Grytt! What's wrong with him?"

And Grytt's cool, grinding, "He's coming out of it, that's all. Make him some tea—that stuff in the green and brown box. Two scoops of it."

A dozen aetheric steps away, the Vizier rose and backed away from the code fragment. He continued on his path. This time, he paid attention to the edges, where the turing's architecture gave shape to the aether. Another code-fragment lurked in the crack. And another. Translucent from the corners of his perception, transparent when he looked right at them. Very, very tiny, like single threads. And, as he pretended not to look too closely—mobile, too, eeling along the borders, dipping into the turing. *Following him.*

The Vizier paused, while the kitchen erupted in metallic banging—cabinets, teapots—and the sound of running water, and indulged a surge of despair. Then he turned his aetheric head side-long, and shot his hand out, snatching one of the code-fragments from its perch on a corner of mainframe, where the entertainment datastream ducked under the wide tube of personal communications. He pinched it between his not-fingers. Peered at its sequence of hexes.

Then he queried the turing. It insisted there was no fragment. There was nothing at all, where the Vizier wanted it to look. It suggested that the Vizier was imagining the fragment. It asked if he wouldn't rather play a nice game of chess.

The Vizier sighed. Then, patiently, he directed the turing to find and eliminate any samples of code that looked like *this*. He repeated himself seven times before he realized that the turing was not being especially obtuse; it actually could not *see* that particular series of hexes, even if he broke them out of sequence, even if he asked for separate elimination of each portion of the code.

This indicated that a very talented arithmancer had overwritten the turing's quantum collective at the root level. It also indicated several other unfortunate corollaries, the most pressing of which was the probable limit on the Vizier's continued corporeal freedom and the measures which station security might take to curtail it, since he had almost certainly alerted that same talented arithmancer to his trespass already.

So the Vizier hurried back, faster than was wise. The nearest analogy might be jumping from a very tall bridge into a very deep lake, only backward, while inhaling water and hoping to achieve the bridge's apex before he drowned.

It was, in short, exactly how an arithmancer was *not* supposed to traverse the aether.

The Vizier slammed up into his body with sufficient force to break several blood vessels in his nose, compress his lungs to empty, and bring his teeth together unpleasantly hard.

"Oh, look who it is."

The Vizier grunted at Grytt. His head swiveled toward the kitchen noises, and he commanded his body to follow. His shoulders attempted to obey, thrusting his palms onto the desk and propelling him out of the chair. His knees mutinied. His hips simply ignored him, and continued taking up space between his thighs and his pelvis.

The chair squirted out from behind him, squealing across the decking before fetching up on the rug. The table might have bolted in the other direction, except that Grytt caught it on her thigh.

"Careful." Grytt steadied him with her metal hand under his elbow. The Vizier had the impression she could have carried him if necessary. His perceptions, still stretched from his aetheric journey, marveled at the unforgiving metal fingertips, and the pattern his sleeves made in his skin where those fingertips gripped. He felt the tiny capillaries in the crease of his elbow break, and the slow leak of tiny bruises—

Grytt shook him, not a bit gently. He blinked back to himself, and found his eyes and hers uncomfortably close.

"Rupert. You're scaring her. Focus."

He squinted at the kitchen. There was a new smell layering the ambient. Something green, and bitter, and noxious.

"Uh," he said.

"Tea," said Grytt. "I had Rory start it, when you blanked out. Said it would help you. Don't know if it will, but it gave her something to do."

The Vizier blinked. He became conscious of something wet running from his nose to his lips. He probed at it with the tip of his tongue. Salty. Metallic. *Red*-tasting.

Grytt made a face at him. "Oh, ancestors. Stop that."

She lowered him into the seat far more gently than the expression on her face indicated and dabbed at the blood on his face with the edge of her sleeve, ignoring his monosyllabic protests about staining the fabric.

"It's *black*, Rupert, that's why I wear this color." She guided his own left hand up to his nose, pinched his fingers together over the bridge, and squeezed. "Hold that."

After a moment's critical observation, she decided he could be trusted to follow directions, and left him. The Vizier heard her voice, pitched too low for comprehension, buzzing counterpoint with Rory's lighter tones. He decided to take advantage of the moment's respite to summon his scattered wits, give them a stern scolding, and send them back to their posts.

In the meantime, he rediscovered the fingers of his right hand, and sent them to calling up onto the turing's screen the fruits of his arithmancy. By the time Rory and Grytt arrived from the kitchen, the Vizier had half a dozen windows stacked on the screen, each with a file already saved to hard memory. His nose had also stopped bleeding, which was fortunate, as he did not want to try to conduct a conversation with his nostrils pinched shut. He checked for blood and, finding none on his skin, nor in the immediately visible vicinity, rested his hands on the edge of the desk and hoped no one noticed their trembling.

The Kreshti ancestors may have been listening to his prayers, just this once. Rory, for all her perspicacity, did not remark on the Vizier's unstable appendages; never one to ignore available reading material, she instead turned her attention to the contents of the screen. She leaned down, sending her braid slithering dangerously close to the teacup she cradled in both hands.

The Vizier eyed the steam rising out of it. He misliked the smell.

Rory hooked a nearby chair with one foot, dragged it over, and navigated her backside into the seat, all without looking. The Vizier, who had not yet reestablished speaking terms with his lower extremities, found himself a little envious of her casual athleticism. He pretended to lean back to grant the Princess better vantage; in truth, he could manage either that, or slumping; and as the slumping brought him closer to the noxious cup in her hands, he chose the former option.

"Who are these people?" Rory scrolled down the list. She paid no particular attention when Grytt came and stood behind her, except to note the gleam off her brushed metal skull reflected in the tablet's screen.

The Vizier's desiccated voice crumbled around the syllables. "Research scientists. An alchemist, a physicist, a biologist—"

"Oh! Wait. Here. I'm sorry. This is for you." Rory pressed a teacup into his hands, filled to dangerous volumes and spewing foul odors. He looked past his reflection to the bottom of the cup. It was obscured by the silty sludge already collected there, undoubtedly from whatever toxins had sloughed off during brewing.

He sighed, and sipped without comment.

"Wait." Grytt reached for the screen. Her metal hand hovered, unmoving, a precise quarter centimeter away from the alchemist's name. The screen's glow leapt into the cracks and crevices of her fingers, greening the metal where the gleam was brightest. The Vizier could just make out the mecha hex whispering to itself at the joints, and where metal married flesh.

"Wait," Grytt said again, although the screen had not moved. "I know her. She's one of the refugees. On Kreshti. She's one of the people who asked for asylum. She's one of the damn reasons we *had* a war."

The Vizier nodded and swallowed his mouthful of tea. It tasted exactly like it smelled.

"Yes. So are the others. All of them were involved in cryostatic research at the same facility in Tadeshi territory, and all of them had their projects terminated by then-Minister Moss just prior to King Sergei's assassination." The Vizier paused for another swallow. His stomach muttered and shifted, like an old cat wanting nothing more than a nap in the sun and finding himself beset by kittens. "When I first discovered the connection—and I made your mother aware, Rory—I did not know that these researchers shared more than a physical location. I, and she, assumed they were the Regent's political enemies, or otherwise inconvenient to him, and he was maneuvering to take them out of play, first by exile, and then by accusing them of regicide."

The Vizier paused for breath. For once, neither Rory nor Grytt had anything to interject, and he realized with a quiet shock that they were waiting patiently for him to continue.

So he did. "It turns out, the researchers also shared a project: a type of cryogenic stasis unit, presumably for medical applications, with an obvious appeal to the commercial sector as well. I thought it was odd that Moss would scrap such a potentially lucrative project, and indeed, he did not. He appropriated it to Defense, after removing the original researchers and assigning new personnel. The records indicate that Defense has continued its development."

Another pause. Another breath. The noxious tea had chased the aether chill out of his bones, which was pleasant; but its apparent intention to declare war on his digestive stability was far less so. The Vizier measured the distance to the lavatory against the obedience of his limbs, and hoped his stomach was more stoic than current impressions indicated.

Rory leaned in until her nose—entirely her mother's, the Vizier thought, aquiline, on the lovely edge of that category—nearly touched the screen.

"Okay, so Defense—that was at the beginning of the war. What happened with the research?"

"As far as I am able to discern, it was relocated to the facilities on Beo, and there it has remained."

Rory jerked so violently that her elbow endangered the teacup, clutched as it was in the Vizier's hands. "That's where Ivar's supposedly stationed."

"Indeed," said the Vizier. "That does not seem coincidental."

"It's supposed to be *medical* cryostatic research." Grytt frowned. "That makes no sense at a top-secret military base. Research of any kind doesn't make sense there. It's a training facility."

"I concur. And the layer of hexes surrounding the data was far beyond simple security."

Rory had sat back in her chair and curled up, arms wrapped around her drawn-up legs, chin balanced on her knees. She squinted at nothing in particular.

"That's where Ivar is, isn't it? In cryostasis. They're holding him there, on Beo, in suspension."

"Perhaps. Although I am hesitant to assign any certainty to that conclusion. We don't *know*, Rory. He might be on Beo, in cryostasis or otherwise. But that does not explain the young man currently on Urse, nor does it explain Moss's motives in initiating this alleged deception in the first place."

Rory pursed her lips at the word *alleged*. The Vizier anticipated an argument: saw, in fact, the flash of defiance in her eyes. Then she blinked, and took a pair of breaths, and although the skin around her lips was tight, when she spoke, her tone was even, reasonable, cool.

"So why didn't the exiled researchers tell the Kreshti about their project?"

"Perhaps they did not know what Moss intended to do with their research."

"Or they didn't want *us* to have it, either," Grytt said. "They're Tadeshi refugees out of favor with the current administration. They haven't given up *being* Tadeshi."

"Grytt."

"What? You think that old bit about *the enemy of my enemy is my friend* is true? Bah. Just means you have more enemies. Besides. We wouldn't know if they *did* tell. Not like the Prime tells your mother everything. Maybe the Kreshti do know about it. Maybe they've got it, too." Grytt shook her head slowly. "Whatever it is. Rupert. What is it?"

"You are assuming I overcame the security hexes."

"I am assuming you managed something for all your lounging around."

"You mean, besides the information I have already delivered?" Grytt glanced at Rory. "I mean—"

"I know what you mean." The Vizier did not often interrupt; the event was so novel, it startled Grytt into quiet. The Vizier took a heartbeat or two to revel in that small victory. Then, as his stomach performed another maneuver better left to zero-g, he winced, sighed, and told the truth. "I was not entirely successful. Although I did retrieve the information, the probability is high that I was detected while doing so."

Rory stared at him. Although her jaw dropped wide enough to liberate any exclamations of horror or accusations that he was not being entirely honest, no sounds emerged.

The Vizier gave her a small smile, in thanks, and inclined his head a finger's width. "There is a very skilled arithmancer on the Regent's staff. Perhaps several. Better, I fear, than I am."

"Hell," said Grytt. It was the mildest of her expletives. She then added to it with several others less tame.

As vivid (and anatomically unlikely) as some of the expressions were, the Vizier had to concur with their sentiment. He nodded at Grytt until he caught her gaze. "If I was identified, they will arrest me."

Grytt made a noise in her throat that the Vizier decided to classify as a *snarl*, although it held more menace than any animal's utterance that he had ever heard, including the Kreshti ice-banshee, whose aggressive vocalizations could actually cause the human neural net to overload, leading to a temporary paralysis (a very unfortunate discovery for the first film crews attempting to document its breeding habits, as was the subsequent realization of what exactly the ice-banshee eats).

"Well," said Grytt. "They can try."

"Grytt," the Vizier began. He was going to tell her that her priority was Rory, that she could not risk an interplanetary incident, that the situation was fragile. What came out instead was, "Thank you."

Improbably, that silenced her. She stared at him, her brown eye round and distressed.

"They may not realize it was you," said Rory. She had lowered her chin until she was peering up from under her brows, as if she meant to head-butt the universe if it thwarted her. "Moss already suspects *me* of hexing the system."

"It is more likely he blames me for that, as well. I do not believe he considers you a capable enough arithmancer. I also don't think they will come here, since it is Thorne sovereign territory. Most likely, they will apprehend me while I am in transit to the embassy."

"They can't just arrest the Vizier of Thorne. There's diplomatic immunity!"

"You mean rules," the Vizier said, very gently. "The sort of rules that might prevent a man from seizing a throne from a child by assassinating both of his parents."

"The same rules you think he'll follow by not storming our doors."

The Vizier considered that. "I think he will count the cost of apprehending me here as too high, and too obvious. The Regent is not a direct man. He prefers artifice and subterfuge. A pitched battle—in which he might lose a number of people, and in which the Prince's fiancée could be injured or killed—would be an unnecessarily public performance."

"Fine," said Rory, after a moment. "Then I will accompany you, whenever you go to the embassy. *That* is Thorne territory as well. Whenever you are in public, Messer Rupert, I will be with you. Then Moss won't dare to act."

As we have noted, the fairies did not gift—or curse—Rory with prescience.

CHAPTER ELEVEN

In Which It Becomes Clear That One Should Always Ask Grytt

There are several schools of thought regarding the proper balance between the rights of monarchs and the rights of their subjects. There are those anti-monarchists, such as Li and Francher, who advocate for a legal system maintained independently of the monarch himself, so that the law of the land (or ship, or station, as the case may be) applies to all citizens more or less equally; and indeed, this practice is the one most widespread in regions of void belonging to the Merchants League. But there are still traditionalists (particularly Herrick) who insist that the right of the monarch must be absolute, and supersede any other laws or customs. The monarch becomes, in Herrick's system, a de facto deity, wielding the power of life and death, with no other legal check on his behavior than his own will. It is an appealing theory if one is the monarch, and rather less so if one is anybody else. It is also no accident that the historically preferred methods of dealing with this sort of monarch have been violent and rather permanent.

The late King Sergei Valenko had been a strange combination of progressive and absolutist. On the one hand, he had attempted, via legislation, to codify the law of the Free Worlds, favoring the rights of individual stations and planets to self-govern under their own laws and customs. But at the same time, he had been famous for overriding the wishes of his own Council in other matters, the most infamous of which was an edict forbidding the establishment of an elected Free-Worlds-wide Tadeshi Parliament. The proposals (for there were many) included provisions for elections based on colonial population, economic significance, and longevity of membership in the Free Worlds. King Sergei's edict objected to those proposals as invitations to tyranny, and castigated members of his Council by name for their transparent self-interest in promoting the power of their own houses or homeworlds, while limiting the powers of others.

It may be that Valenko's future biographers will posit that the King was, by being a tyrant himself, attempting to eliminate the politicking and maneuvering among his nobles—using tyranny to combat tyranny, if you will. They will almost certainly notice that Vernor Moss is not one of the council members named in that edict, but whether his ascension to Regency is attributed to a general inoffensiveness, or to the cleverness of his maneuvering (or whether the King is portrayed as doomed idealist or ravening despot), will depend on the prevailing political winds at the time of the writing.

It will almost certainly *not* be noted that, among the works in the Regent Moss's office, was a copy of Herrick's *Treatise on the Rights of Kings*.

Although Rory had been in Moss's office, and had in fact glanced over his shelves, including the one on which Herrick's *Treatise* resided, she was unfamiliar with the work itself, or with its author. The fault for this, if fault it was, could be laid at the feet of the Vizier. There are only so many hours in a week, and because the Vizier himself was quite familiar with Herrick (and several dozen more political theorists of whom no one has ever heard except other academics), *and* because he had taken for granted that he would be available to advise Rory, he had elected to leave Herrick off her reading lists.

Had he chosen otherwise, perhaps Rory might have noticed the book in Moss's possession, and drawn the obvious conclusions; and perhaps she might have mentioned its presence to the Vizier. Then they two together may have been better able to see the pattern in Moss's Regency thus far, and to make predictions about its future trajectory.

Or they could have asked Grytt's advice, which no one ever did, at least on matters of politics.

While this seems like a logical decision, it should be noted that, while she was not familiar with Herrick, or with Li and Francher, Grytt was very familiar with Kreshti history, and by extension, with seminal Kreshti writers. She would have recommended Rory read Kahandir, who, as one of the revolutionary founders of Kreshti, had a great deal of advice about tyranny, and the varying stages and methods of dealing with it.

Grytt would also, if asked, have shared her opinion of *diplomatic immunity* and the likelihood of Regent Moss adhering to rules which he had not made himself (in that, she might have been in agreement with the Vizier); and she might have been able to verbally prepare Rory for what she foresaw as inevitable.

But, as we have noted, no one asked her.

Grytt was not offended by that oversight. She proceeded with the preparations anyway. She made certain that she had the unauthorized 'slinger, loaded and charged, slung around her hips on the following morning. She also made certain that she briefed the morning's escort personally, reflecting as she did so that it was a pity that Stary and Franko were not a better representation of the original purpose for which militaries had been designed. Oh, those men were adequate at their martial skills, even competent. But it seemed to her that those soldiers in service to the royal household had achieved their positions largely because of familial influence, or because they were especially good at polishing boots and keeping their uniforms crisp; and it was not Grytt's personal experience that the actual business of fighting (which was often attended by bleeding) had much to do with shiny footwear or creased trousers. When Samur had granted her free choice of the barracks on Thorne, Grytt had selected the best of the lot, and sacrificed to her ancestors that she never need *use* them in a manner to which they were unaccustomed.

Grytt, like the Vizier, did not place a great deal of faith in the intervention of ethereal beings; she also knew that, under unusual circumstances, soldiers, like weapons, might surpass all expectations, or fail dramatically. It was her responsibility to predict the outcome. Stary and Franko were the most experienced of the staff and the ones Grytt would want at her back in a pitched battle. They were the best at following orders: told to hold the corridor, they would do so or die trying. But they also possessed the same mental acuity and flexibility as a bag of wet mice. Some days, the Princess would need well-armed, violent wet mice. But this was not one of those days.

And so, this morning, Grytt selected the two most junior staff. The first, Thorsdottir, was a big-boned farmer's daughter from Thorne's northern continent. She was painfully aware of her common birth, and apparently unaware of her uncommon talent. She was also much smarter than anyone gave her credit for (except Grytt).

The second, Zhang, came from a comfortably connected upper-middle-class merchant family. Her mother in particular had expressed great dismay when she enlisted in the royal guard instead of becoming a lawyer. Much of Zhang's unflappable composure, for which Grytt had selected her as much as her martial skill, had developed as a bulwark against constant maternal disappointment. Zhang, in her turn, harbored an unsecret worship of all things Grytt. The reason for Zhang's fascination had nothing to do with the several rumors circulating around the barracks (ranging from lascivious to aggrieved), and everything to do with Zhang's own paternal grandmother, who had been a Kreshti marine killed in a skirmish with pirates. To Zhang, Grytt was the nearest thing to Grandmother she might ever meet.

Grytt collected Thorsdottir and Zhang in the antechamber. She pretended to inspect their uniforms; and indeed, the pair were polished and crisp. They were also armed, to the limit of the treaty, with 'slingers of the same make and model as Grytt's own. Grytt had seen their marksmanship scores, and had no doubt of the steadiness of their hands; she had also seen their service records, and knew they had never fired a weapon in combat.

She was counting on both of those things. She explained—with capital letters and complete sentences—the scenario she predicted would take place that morning, or if not that morning, sometime Very Soon. She outlined several possible outcomes, identifying which of those she, Grytt, considered optimal, and which ones—indeed, all the others—were Completely Unacceptable. Zhang and Thorsdottir did not interrupt, which Grytt had expected. They also did not blink, which she found disconcerting, not least because she could see the doubts crowding behind their eyes like children at the sweet-shop window.

She waited through several moments of rigid silence, after she had finished, before she asked, "Are there questions?"

Zhang looked at Thorsdottir, who winced a little. "No, Guard-Commander."

"It's just—" Thorsdottir blurted, and stopped when Grytt looked at her. "Nothing, ma'am."

Grytt made a grinding noise in her throat reminiscent of large, ill-used machinery.

"Just say it," said Grytt. "Whatever it is. However stupid."

Thorsdottir did not look happy, and for a moment Grytt thought she would refuse to answer and make another apology. That might have been the prudent response, for an ordinary guard to an ordinary captain on an ordinary day. Indeed, Stary or Franko would've done exactly that. Grytt held her breath, just a little. The Princess did not need ordinary.

Then Thorsdottir's jaw squared off into a stubborn angle. "You're asking us to defy the Princess, Guard-Commander."

"I am."

"That's treason."

"It is, if you're strict on the meaning. Seems to me it's our job to keep her safe, even if she's determined otherwise. All goes well, she won't give any orders. If not—our job is to keep her alive and unharmed."

"Right," said Thorsdottir. "I hope it does go well, then."

Grytt almost smiled at her, and stopped it just in time. The smile sighed and went back into seclusion. The more familiar grimace took its accustomed place, perhaps a little smugly.

"Huh," she said. "So do I." But she didn't really expect that it would.

And, of course, it didn't.

There were six Tadeshi security waiting in the corridor in front of the Thorne embassy. The morning crowds eddied around them in the same way fish avoid rocks in a stream, and the security paid the crowds exactly the same attention as rocks pay to fish. They were placed at intervals so that they might observe every possible approach to the embassy's big front doors, over which protruded a single, smooth black hemisphere: the security camera, with Thorne security personnel somewhere behind the walls watching its feed. Grytt was familiar with the range on that particular model, and was not the least bit surprised that the Tadeshi security ranged themselves just at the edge of its limit, where they might not be noticed by personnel inside.

Nor was she at all surprised to see the security; the Regent's men patrolled the station at regular intervals, and residents (of which she only grudgingly considered herself) grew accustomed to their passage. Near the embassies, the concentration became somewhat higher. And truthfully, Grytt had anticipated an increased presence this morning. But six. Well. That seemed excessive. Or flattering, if she was fool enough to imagine the quantity of armed men waiting near the door was any reflection on *her*, or on the skill of the Princess's guard.

As we have noted, Grytt was no fool (although the battle-wise portion of her wits insisted otherwise, if she continued walking into what was *clearly* an ambush). The six were more likely a reflection of the importance of their task, both as gesture and advertisement. Moss, Grytt reflected grimly, had probably calculated exactly how many security one could dispatch to arrest a Vizier to both intimidate and ensure compliance. He wasn't a fool, either.

That Rory's *entire* guard detail numbered two fewer than that half dozen, no more than two of which were permitted, by treaty, to accompany her (Grytt counted as body-maid, rather than guard), indicated to Grytt that Moss intended his six—of the more massive sort, this time, thick-limbed and tall—to remind Rory of how very powerless she was, in Urse.

As a general tactic, Grytt approved of intimidation. As a specific tactic pointed at *Rory*, well. It would not have been a method Grytt herself would have chosen, unless she actually desired the opposite result; teenagers, in her experience, possessed a near universal tendency to defiance. She was surprised that Moss, who had dragged two sons through their teen years, would discount that tendency. Then she wondered if it was merely Rory he discounted.

And then she gave up wondering at all for the meantime, because the Tadeshi security had finally noticed their approach. They drew together and ranged themselves in front of the embassy's entrance—inside the camera's range, now, so close to the doors that no one might get round them. Now the passersby noticed; they scuttled and darted, clearing a nearly perfect half circle of conspicuously empty deck.

"Oh, dear," murmured Rupert.

"Hell," muttered Rory.

"That took long enough," said Grytt, with her usual tone and volume. There was a small chance the Tadeshi might hear her, but they were not her audience. She couldn't see Zhang, bringing up the rear as she was, but she thought she heard a little snort. Thorsdottir, on point, grew a bit straighter, and her shoulders a bit more square, until she appeared as formidable as any one of Moss's bully-men.

Grytt spared a moment's regret that she did not have six Thorsdottirs before remembering that it wasn't just Rory and teenagers who responded poorly to intimidation. She took a pair of deep breaths, held them, let them go, and looked over the opposition. Six Thorsdottirs or sixty: this wasn't about numbers (which was fortunate; one need not be an arithmancer to see who had the advantage) or firepower (which was also fortunate, as the Tadeshi had 'slingers with greater range and capacity), but strategy.

Grytt played a wicked game of chess, but she preferred the pieces to be wood or metal or plastic, and not flesh and bone, particularly when the opponent had only pawns on the board. Moss might be willing to sacrifice. She was not.

One of the Tadeshi differentiated himself by stepping forward and raising his hand in an archaic, universal gesture (among bipeds; the same gesture had, early in relations with the k'bal, nearly resulted in an unfortunate incident).

"Please stop," he said, in a tone that indicated he expected compliance, as a figure of authority speaking to an ordinary citizen.

Rory, of course, would have ignored the order, but to do so would have entailed treading on Thorsdottir's heels. So she stopped and looked directly at the security officer.

"Good morning," she said, in a tone that clearly conveyed *get the hell out of my way.*

The senior security officer frowned down at her. He made no attempt to look at his fellows; clearly he was in charge, and had no doubt of his orders. How nice, Grytt thought, to be so certain. She could see what he could not: there were nervous glances darting among the men in the back row. They were truly remarkable for their sameness. Broad shoulders. Dark hair. The same solid cheekbones and jaw that suggested a skull perhaps thicker than average. A matched set of toadies, all with the same strict orders and marked lack of imagination.

Grytt revised her opinion of Moss. He was not trying to avoid a conflict. He was trying to provoke one. Pawns ranged against a future Queen.

"Mm." Rupert cleared his throat. He sounded a little bit hoarse. "Is there a problem, Lieutenant?"

Senior Toady hurled his full attention at Rupert like a drowning man lunges for a rope.

"Lord Vizier Rupert of the Thorne Consortium," he said too quickly. "You are under arrest for acts of sedition and treason against the Free Worlds of Tadesh. If you will come with me."

"He will not," Rory snapped, before Rupert could say anything. "He is a member of my staff, and out of your jurisdiction. Now move aside."

The Vizier's hands stretched and knotted at his sides. Grytt fancied she could hear the creak and pop of tendons. He was trying to catch her attention; Grytt felt his stare pulling at her, willing her to look back.

She ignored him.

"The Princess needs to stand aside," said Senior Toady, after what appeared to be a moment's strenuous thought. He sounded faintly aggrieved. "We are here for the Vizier."

Rory raised her chin and tossed her braid back over her shoulder. "And I have said already, you won't have him."

She started forward, as if expecting the Tadeshi security to turn into smoke, or at the very least, step aside. Since neither was likely to happen, and because there is a certain loss of dignity if one's sovereign runs into armed and armored men, and because Grytt had prepared her for just this eventuality, Thorsdottir stuck out an arm. Rory swatted it with all the effect a kitten might have moving a stone lion—which is to say, not aside, as she had planned. She was forced to stop a second time.

Grytt, now a bit behind Rory, watched irritation creep redly up the back of the Princess's neck, and watched her shoulders expand around a deep breath. There was a chance that breath, when released, would be quiet and take all Rory's anger with it, but Grytt was not willing to take that gamble.

"Your Highness," she said.

The title, rather than the tone, struck Rory like a small sack of stones. The Princess turned, yielding up a meter of space, and Grytt moved into that gap as if it were the most natural thing in the world. Thorsdottir's arm dropped, and Grytt found herself chest to chest—or rather, chin to chest, as she did not possess Thorsdottir's prodigious height—with Senior Toady. She squinted her living eye at his uniform as if inspecting for lint.

"I need to see your orders . . . Lieutenant. Before I will even consider permitting you to take the Vizier into custody."

Rory let out a tiny gasp. Grytt braced for an argument, for a counter order, for a scene of such drama that 'cast writers from five systems would request the security footage for inspiration for the next generation of entertainment programming.

Then she *heard* the Princess's teeth grind together, and the moment passed. Grytt wondered if Rupert had whispered something to her, or whether Rory was just saving up for a spectacular outburst.

Senior Toady, oblivious to the nearness of his miss, twitched a little, whether from revulsion (Grytt wore her best ugly scowl) or apprehension (she was within easy reach of his person and his sidearm), Grytt could not guess. She did know he could not retreat any further without stepping on his own men. *They* worried her more: five hands hovering over their 'slingers with an eagerness which suggested they were not just ready for action, they were *expecting* it.

Grytt was no arithmancer. She could not read auras. But her metal eye had a web of hexes that welded it to her flesh and her nerves, and it provided information a plain, human eye couldn't. Right now, it was displaying thin translucent cyan lines plotted over the standard visual input, probable trajectories for 'slinger bolts fired from each of the Tadeshi, to their most likely targets.

Grytt did not like what she saw.

"Orders," Grytt snapped. "Surely you have them."

"I. Yes." Senior Toady retained enough wit to raise his left hand in a *wait and hold* gesture. The other five retained enough discipline to freeze exactly in place while he fished into his breastplate with his right hand and produced a wafer-slim, flexible tablet.

Grytt made a great show of reading it over, although she got little more than the Vizier's name and title prominently displayed at the top, and Regent Moss's name, title, and elaborate signature at the bottom, and a great morass of Tadeshi legalese in between. The ancestors and Rupert might understand it; Grytt could only hope Rory could figure it out, given time.

She rolled the tablet into a tube, tight as the plastic would permit. "Thank you," she said. "Lieutenant—what's your name?"

He blinked. "Malvar."

"Malvar." She made a face as if the name tasted bad. "Fine. We'll expect you to treat the Vizier with every *possible* courtesy, you hear me? Because this"—and she pointed the rolled tablet at his face like an angry finger—"this is someone's very serious mistake, for which the Princess and the Vizier will expect a very serious apology. A *personal* apology, Lieutenant."

Senior Toady Malvar jerked his chin down in what might have been a nod, if every cord on his neck had not been standing out like steel cables. Then he broke stares with Grytt.

"Lord Vizier," he said. "If you will come with me."

There was a shuffle behind Grytt that sounded like a tall, slight man trying to come forward, and a significantly smaller and more athletic young woman perhaps holding his sleeve or otherwise impeding his progress.

"It's all right," Rupert said quietly. And added, "Princess."

Then he brushed by Grytt, glancing down as he did so. She marked the pulse beating in his throat, and the beads of sweat on his lip. And she saw the message that flashed across her metal eye, hexed there by an arithmancer trying to walk, surrender, and hex at the same time. It was not up to Rupert's usual eloquence, but the sentiment was clear.

Grytt nodded, to show him she understood. And then he was past her, and past Thorsdottir's broad-shouldered perimeter, and surrounded by Tadeshi uniforms.

"Tell the Regent," said Rory in a brittle, spiky voice, "that we are *displeased* with this action. Tell him that we will expect an explanation *immediately*, Lieutenant Malvar. Do you hear me?"

"Your Highness," said Malvar, and bowed a little more than the requisite angle. He seemed quite happy now to retreat, leaving the embassy doors unobstructed.

It was a long walk from those embassy doors, through the gathering knot of distressed embassy personnel, through a small labyrinth of embassy corridors. The Vizier's office lay at the end of the main floor corridor, beside a tiny arboretum with a slender little copse of Thorne-native trees, hexed within a centimeter of their genome to survive in the canned air and cold light of Urse.

Rory waited until the office door whisked shut before she said, "Grytt," in a voice that immediately filled the room, crowding into corners and the gaps in the decking, snatching every scrap of warmth and replacing it with a chill more profound than deep aether. Her mouth worked around what she meant to say next, trying on half a dozen demands, exclamations, and accusations.

Grytt watched as *how dare you* and *what the hell were you thinking* and *what have you done* tried, and failed, to be the first words out Rory's mouth. She was mildly surprised when Rory turned instead to Thorsdottir and Zhang.

"Out," she said.

"Stay," said Grytt. "You're going to yell at me, they can hear it."

"I was going to yell at all of you, but it's not their fault. It's yours."

Thorsdottir looked at Zhang, who looked at Grytt, who grimaced. "If you mean they followed my orders, then yes."

"I don't need guards who follow *your* orders, I need guards who follow *mine*."

Thorsdottir's cheeks reddened. Zhang flinched. Grytt wished the damned fairies had given Rory a blessing about think-before-speaking. But even fairy gifts might be powerless before teenage tempers.

Grytt, however, was not. "And you'd've ordered what, Princess? That we fight back? Say we had. Then what? A firefight in front of our embassy, three on six."

"Moss's men would have stood down." But Rory did not look so certain, now. Her brows crowded together. "They wouldn't have risked *me*."

"No. Not you. They're good enough to miss you completely. But *Rupert*, now. You think a bolt in his skull wouldn't solve a few of Moss's problems? So sorry, Princess, we didn't *mean* to kill him. Firefight. Accident. This way, he's alive and unhurt."

Rory's face resembled a Kantarin deathmask, gone smooth and blank. Only her eyes flickered, like a tesla with a short in the wire. "And a prisoner."

"Alive," Grytt repeated. "Which he wouldn't be, if you'd got your way. Or your guards, either. I'm half metal. Hard to kill. But Thorsdottir and Zhang have all their original parts. Best for you, and for them, if they keep them."

Rory said nothing.

Grytt blew her anger away in a gale-force sigh. "Listen. Moss set you up. That lieutenant wasn't any diplomat. He was greener than five-week-old cheese left in the sun. He was *supposed* to provoke you. And me, I imagine."

"It worked."

"It did. It would've worked better if you'd gotten your way and started a fight. Moss is good at this game. You need to get better."

It took Rory a moment to swallow whatever retort had lurched up her throat. It took her a moment longer to blink her eyes clear. She held out her hand. "Let me see the orders."

Grytt handed them over, with small swell of pride.

We did okay with this one, Rupert.

But of course Rupert was not here to see it. Cold fingers stirred through Grytt's guts. Rupert, in Tadeshi custody. She came as close as she ever did to fidgeting, while Rory scanned over the arrest order.

"Conspiracy against the sovereignty of the Free Worlds of Tadesh. That's suitably broad and dramatic-sounding, isn't it? And treason's a capital offense. They wouldn't dare execute him. But they could exile him. Or." The Princess glanced up at Grytt. "Put him on an unlucky, accident-bound ship. Perhaps malfunction during the tesser-hex. Perhaps even pirates."

"Rupert would hate pirates."

"He would." Rory almost smiled. Then the moment passed, and the shape of her jaw reminded Grytt entirely of Samur. "I'm certain he'd never make it home. Moss doesn't want Messer Rupert here, but he *damn* sure doesn't want him back with my mother. I mean, that's why he came with us in the first place."

Grytt found a sudden fascination with the desk, scrupulously organized and deliberately impersonal and, therefore, obviously and entirely Rupert's. "He came to advise you, Princess."

"Of course he did. He also came because my mother couldn't

keep him on Thorne, with all the rumors around. Not after she was married."

Grytt pretended to study the spines of the books—real books, dear ancestors, a small, heavy, expensive-to-transport fortune right there—on the single shelf behind the desk. She gave up, being unable to read half the titles, bloody pretentious script—and shifted her attention to the paneling on the bulkhead. The wood—synthetic, highly polished—threw back reflections which, to a normal eye, would be only ghosts. To Grytt's mecha eye, however, such details were easily resolved. Rory's faint, rueful smile. Zhang's plain horror. Thorsdottir's credible attempt at blank-faced.

"Rumors," Grytt repeated. She wasn't doing as well as Thorsdottir. Her own reflection told her that.

"Grytt." Rory's lips quirked. "I'm sixteen, not seven. *Everyone* knows about my mother and Messer Rupert. Which means Moss does, too."

The cold fingers in Grytt's gut turned into fists. She caught herself considering the logistics of forcibly retrieving Rupert from the detention block, and gave herself a stern scolding for even entertaining the idea. Drop that spark in this environment, she'd have the whole lot of them planning something magnificently stupid.

Rory was nodding slowly, as if she could hear what Grytt was thinking. "Moss will expect some kind of reaction out of us. So what do I do, Grytt? File a *complaint*? Call my mother?"

"What would Rupert tell you?"

"That isn't fair."

"Nope."

"He would say, try diplomacy. No." Rory shook her head. "He would say, 'Be sneaky, Princess. The Regent will expect you to act like a child and throw a tantrum.'" Rory laughed, softly and breathlessly. "Which I damn near did. Which I still want to do."

Grytt, who shared the Princess's desire for inappropriate, emotionally driven action, found herself momentarily without any wise—or unwise—advice.

The moment should have passed, silent and unnoticed, except that Thorsdottir cleared her throat.

"Ah. If I might interject. There's something to be said for tantrums, your Highness."

Rory stared at her. So did Grytt. Only Zhang seemed unsurprised; she might have been smiling, just a little, but with Zhang, it was hard to tell.

Rory frowned, in a manner which indicated concentration, rather than ire. "What do you mean?"

Two spots of carmine appeared on Thorsdottir's cheeks. "Only—it's the audience that matters. For some people, seeing the Princess very upset might seem like an opportunity."

Rory blinked. "For what?"

"For intimacy," said Zhang, and startled everyone. "To gain your confidence, your Highness."

"People," Rory repeated. "You mean Merrick and Jaed."

Thorsdottir forgot to be nervous. "I do, your Highness. Or rather—one of them. Both might cause a different problem."

A moment of quiet passed, and then another. Then a slow, sly grin crept across Rory's face. "They won't come within a meter of me with you around, Grytt. Fortunately, I am so angry with you that I am ordering you to go—oh, elsewhere. The detention block, so that you can keep an eye on the Vizier's well-being. You are to return there every day until he is released."

"Huh. That news will travel."

"Yes. Straight to Moss. And he'll think I'm being a child, throwing a tantrum. Also, you being there will probably annoy him, especially when you do return every day. And then." Rory looked at Thorsdottir and Zhang. "Then I will go for a walk somewhere Merrick will be—the arboretum, maybe?—so that I might just *happen* to encounter him in my vulnerable state."

"That's a dangerous game. Relies too much on coincidence. And the boy's not stupid."

Rory snapped a glare at Grytt. "I don't care about his brains. I care about his ambition."

"Your Highness," said Zhang. "Jaed may be a more opportune target."

Grytt looked at her. Rory looked at her. Then Rory said, "What makes you say that?"

Zhang cast her gaze at Thorsdottir like a cat scrabbling for balance on an unexpectedly narrow windowsill.

Thorsdottir uncurled a little smile. "Your Highness, let me explain. We see Jaed in the exercise facilities when we're there. He's usually alone. Merrick, however, is *never* alone, anywhere."

"The second son," Grytt said thoughtfully. "Might be jealous of his brother. Maybe you could use that."

"Jaed." Rory performed a credible imitation of Grytt's grimace. "Jaed," she said again, as if sampling an unsavory dish for a second time, to confirm the initial opinion. Then she clamped her jaw tight. "You said *usually* alone. Who comes with him?"

"Young men of his age. Nobles' sons, I'm guessing, Highness. But there appear to be no particular bonds among them."

"And no women. No girls."

"No, Highness."

"Oh, stop that," Rory muttered. "My name is Rory. In private, when it's just us, call me that. And if you can't stand the informality, at least leave off with the *your Highness* business. Grytt only calls me that when I'm being a fool."

Thorsdottir and Zhang traded a look that partners only develop after some time working together—or more rapidly, if they are the junior-most members of an elite detail.

Thorsdottir cleared her throat. "Should we do that also? Call you by title when we think you're being unwise?"

"Yes," said Grytt. "You should."

Rory strangled a laugh in the back of her throat and stuffed it into a dark corner where its body would never be found. "Yes. Although be very sure I'm being stupid, first."

Zhang and Thorsdottir traded solemn stares.

"Yes," Zhang said, after a moment.

Grytt worried that a smile might stage an escape and take up residence on her face, where its very incongruity would attract unwanted attention. So she scrubbed it away with the back of her hand, under the guise of scratching her chin, and cleared her throat.

Three pairs of eyes landed on her and waited, expectantly.

"Since you lot appear to have the tantrum-planning well in hand, I suppose I should begin my exile from your favor, Princess." Grytt glanced at the chronometer on the wall. "They've got him in detention by now."

She did not add, *If they took him there. If they didn't just dump him out an aetherlock,* but something of the thought must have leaked onto her face. Whatever brief relief Rory might have been feeling evaporated. The Princess looked as if the last traces of childhood had sloughed away.

"Keep him safe, Grytt. Hear me? That's not an order."

"I know what it is," said Grytt. She stabbed a nod at Thorsdottir and Zhang, who snapped a pair of matched salutes.

Ancestors have mercy, they were young. And Rory was even younger. Grytt felt every one of her years settle into bone and joint, where she still had them, and into the borders between meat and metal, where she didn't. The alloy replacements, wrapped in arithmancy and alchemy, remained oblivious, impervious. Not unlike the young, she thought.

And may these particular young be just as resilient.

Then Grytt took her leave, making certain to hit the door on her way through—as it opened too slowly—and to stomp through the foyer, past the same knots of personnel as had heralded her entrance. She was no thespian, but she had never found it particularly difficult to mislead people if you simply fulfilled their expectations.

If anyone had asked Grytt, she might have admitted that Rory's adoption of Thorsdottir and Zhang—the beginning of her *own* staff, of people who would be hers, first and foremost—had been her goal all along. But as usual, no one did.

CHAPTER TWELVE ═══════

In Which The Princess Negotiates

I t is assumed, by those who claim maturity (which should not be conflated with wisdom), that a rational adult wants stability, predictability, routines. It is further claimed, by those same mature folk, that one of the markers of youth is adaptability, a flexibility of mind and spirit which enables a person to acclimatize to changes in routine, circumstance, and habit. Those who can endure, and eventually overcome, the instability, are admired for their resourcefulness.

Those individuals who *seek* this instability are deemed fools, children, or adventurers; and it is generally assumed that an individual will either grow wiser, grow up, or expire.

Stationers, like most people, live and die by schedules. Urse was no more or less typical of that than, say, Thorsdottir's farming family. But where Thorsdottir's youth had been marked by celestial motion and season, and had been subject to, and victim of, random acts of meteorology, Ursan time was marked in arbitrary shifts, in which there was no visible variation. Oh, perhaps a planet might swing past outside a viewport, or the constellations might shift through their accustomed patterns; but life *inside* the station did not vary. There was no weather, no sunrise, no sunset, no clouds. The rainshowers in the arboretum did not count, since they occurred on a precise schedule (like everything else) designed for the optimal health and well-being of the botanical residents. When an inspired horticultural arithmancer attempted to hex the plants through seasonal cycles, producing changes in foliage color and profusion, so many complaints and queries were filed that the Minister of Education was forced to conduct a public symposium on the impact of planetary motion on plant life, including invited botanists from each the Free Worlds that supported vegetative inhabitants, native or immigrant. The symposium ran for three days and at rather substantial expense, the results of which were an uptick in the number of students studying botany, an increased consumer demand for houseplants, and general apathy from the general public, who were relieved that the garish new leaves would soon fall off and grow back a proper, predictable green.

There are rumors that the arithmancer was removed from her post and exiled to Lanscot, doomed to spend the remainder of her career studying various subspecies of a particularly tenacious shrub that did not mind the dismal conditions. There are other rumors that place her in the Tadeshi embassy on the mirri homeworld, where the flora was small, round, and extremely toxic; and still a third set of rumors have her fleeing to Kreshti, where she assumed a new identity and achieved a comfortable living growing ferns. The precise details of her fate are less important than the actual fact that, shortly after her experiment with seasonal hexing, she no longer resided on Urse.

This fact mattered to several people. Three of those four were her friends and colleagues. The last one was a child—and, as such, still curious, bored, and seeking instability—who spent as much time as possible (excessive amounts, by his father's reckoning) in the arboretum. The arithmancer had discovered him one afternoon in the stand of ornamental cherry trees, collecting the fallen petals and weeping; he was convinced that the trees, in losing their flowers, must be dying. He was a very small boy, and shy, and rather weedy himself. His affinity for plants seemed rather natural to the arithmancer; and having found an audience interested in the habits of ornamental flowering trees, she waxed loquacious on the subject. She thought, when the boy finally departed, that he would not return.

She was wrong. He returned the following day, just after mid-meal on the first shift, and she introduced him to orchids. On the fifth visit, they had moved on to Kreshti ferns. Soon the boy knew every plant species in the arboretum, and had amassed the sort of obsessive expertise in a subject only possible for children and doctoral candidates.

The boy's father, newly risen to the post of Minister of Energy, did not share his son's newfound fascination with flora, nor did he encourage the boy's declared intention to study botany and become a horticulturalist, at the least, or an arithmancer-horticulturalist, which was his highest aspiration. His father insisted, rather, that he play sports and achieve some measure of physical formidability. The boy resisted strenuously, first overtly, and then covertly. The father, preoccupied with his career and his elder son, who was altogether less disappointing, declined to expend the energy required for a sustained conflict.

For a time, it seemed that the boy might achieve his goal after all.

But then the incident with the seasons happened, and the arithmancer disappeared, and a new horticulturalist—one with no skill in arithmancy—took over the care of the ornamental cherries and the orchids. The new horticulturalist owed his appointment to recommendations of, and favors from, the Minister of Energy; so it was also unsurprising that he was uninterested in further encouraging the boy's interest in plants. He was quite firm, quite clear, and quite unkind when he asked the boy to please, let him get on with his work, he had *no time* for a child.

It was then that Jaed Moss—no longer a small boy, but still weedy—ceased regular visits to the arboretum and instead developed an apparent interest in more appropriate pastimes. Vernor Moss had not yet imagined Regency in his future, but hoped that his sons might cement their influence with the young Prince, who was more fishy than weedy, and not especially inclined to physical pursuits, either, though the King was working on that. Minister Moss did not bother to ask his younger offspring the reason for the change, assuming that it was his influence behind it and that his son was, in fact, growing up, wiser and less curious all at once.

Which was how Jaed Moss came to frequent the station's elite recreational facilities with the same zeal with which he'd once frequented the arboretum, and how it was that Zhang and Thorsdottir encountered him there with sufficient regularity that his schedule figured into Rory's plans for freeing the Vizier.

Unfortunately, Rory was unaware of Jaed's earlier interest in either arithmancy or horticulture; had she known, she would have approached him as a natural ally instead of as a challenge to be surmounted and saved them both some distress. But such information is not stored in turing archives, and Jaed did not maintain a close circle of friends from whom one could glean such information. Rory instead spent days plotting with Zhang and Thorsdottir how best to make contact and then manipulate events to her advantage.

The opening moves of the plan involved an encounter with the Regent—the predictably ineffective diplomatic protest of the Vizier's arrest, followed by a predictably ineffective personal appeal. A second (ineffective) personal appeal followed, this time in public, following a "chance" encounter between the Regent and the Princess on the very populated thoroughfare in front of the embassies. Observers—and there were many—made note of the Princess's obvious distress and of the Regent's apparent impassivity and, his critics noted (for the Regent did have critics on Urse), even *impatience* when he refused her request to "at least let me see him!"

Various media outlets reported the encounter, accompanied by opinions and editorials and several heated comment threads. There was even 'caster footage, and a few still-shot 2Ds, in which the Princess's features were scrutinized for signs of stress and grief, and at least one insisted that her "eyes were red" and she had "obviously been crying." The commenter, in that case, seemed sympathetic.

Grytt, who was spending her days in exile down in the detention wing, prevented from seeing the Vizier by two sets of locked doors and a somewhat nervous set of security personnel, watched the reports on the detention block 'caster and smiled, which made the security even more nervous.

Rory, when she saw the 'casts, shared a tight little smile with Thorsdottir and Zhang.

"Now," she said, "the game gets interesting."

On the eighth day of the Vizier's incarceration, Rory made her first visit to the recreational facilities. Although her visit went unreported by the official media, private residents did make note, and thus Rory's appearance was semi-public knowledge as rapidly as those residents could connect with the turing.

The Regent was informed very shortly thereafter that the Princess Thorne was in the main recreational facility, among the citizens, practicing tum'mo by herself on a rug in the corner of the main studio while her guards—the same two young women— batted each other about in one of the practice rings. It was a break in routine which the Regent assumed was meant to irritate him and to garner favorable publicity in hopes of swaying public opinion in her favor. She was succeeding in both cases.

Although the Regent entertained the possibility that the Princess's new public presence could tempt an assassin, he did not divert any extra security of his own to see to her safety. He was far more concerned with the Kreshti body-maid on near permanent installation in his detention block. He was concerned, too, that he uncover the depths of the Vizier's transgression, which meant a slow and thorough sifting of the turing for all arithmantic meddling by his chief arithmancer, and reading the subsequent daily updates. Monitoring those situations was a better use of his resources, he was certain, than a teenage girl who, for all her histrionics, seemed unlikely to attempt violence and whose growing popularity with the Ursan citizens limited the likelihood of violence attempted against her.

By the time the Regent realized his mistake, it was far too late.

Though she was no soldier—having never experienced anyone screaming profanity into her face, among other distinctions—Rory was well-versed in the handling of 'slingers, staves, and small bladed weapons, as well as the basic hand-to-hand skills taught to all Kreshti at puberty. On Thorne, Grytt had overseen her training—an unpleasantly rigorous regimen of calisthenics and a regular repetition of drills—as far as a Princess's schedule would permit. But even that had ceased, upon arrival on Urse, when the Vizier deemed the practice inappropriate and suggested Rory confine herself to her practice of the one hundred eight tum'mo, which one could perform on a small rug in a relatively small area in one's quarters.

You mean a Princess isn't supposed to sweat.

Not in public, Rory.

Or fight.

Not—

—in public, yes, I understand.

Not merely in public. Fighting leaves marks, and you will be scrutinized whenever you are in public. People will wonder about bruises, and they will usually wonder exactly the wrong thing.

Rory's martial competence, therefore, was only a fraction of her guards'. She had discussed with Thorsdottir and Zhang the advantages of resuming that training now, and *damn* decorum.

Thorsdottir was horrified. "We can't just *hit* you."

"Grytt doesn't suffer from that concern."

Zhang raised an eyebrow in an uncanny imitation of their subject, and said, somewhat ironically, "We are not Grytt."

"And we can't just let you win, either. Anyone who knows anything about fighting would see what we were doing, and that would not help you."

"Or us. It cannot be seen that the Princess's guards are—"

Rory raised her hand, then, and interrupted. If Thorsdottir or Zhang had possessed Rory's particular gift, they would have heard *I am so tired of proper I could spit acid or cry or cry acid.*

Instead, they heard only, "I understand."

Rory followed their advice, the first several visits, bringing her tum'mo rug and ensconcing herself in the corner where the mirrored walls afforded her a good view of the room, and afforded everyone a good view of her. She practiced her tum'mo, all one hundred eight postures, while Thorsdottir and Zhang collected bruises, sweat, and no second looks as they tossed each other around on the mats. Zhang, Rory noted, was quite good. Quicker than Thorsdottir. But Thorsdottir was strong and patient, and willing to take a few hits to land one.

Useful information, Rory thought. Meanwhile, anyone observing her—the Regent's security, at least—could dismiss her as a competent tum'mo practitioner, with all the threat that did not imply.

Also useful. She reminded herself that it was better to be thought *less* than *more*, though her pride prickled and her tum'mo suffered. She had never been self-conscious before. Now she was painfully aware of everyone watching-but-not-watching, out of the corners of their eyes, in the edges of the mirrors.

Practice, she told herself. *Breathe.*

And she did, as the days crawled past. The Plan, which had taken on capital letters in her mind, passed into its second stage and stalled there.

There was no sign of Jaed. He had either broken his pattern, or changed it entirely or—

Practice. Breathe.

Rory practiced, and breathed, and sweated (in public), and began work on Plan B. She had formulated a method by which she might use her harp to strike notes approximating the frequency of the alloy comprising the station's interior walls, and hex that approximation into an exact match, and use that to weaken the detention block walls around the Vizier, so that when she crawled through the ducts and appeared in the cellblock, she would be able to get him out of the cell itself, when Jaed resumed his schedule.

Rory, Zhang, and Thorsdottir walked into the main studio and there he was, grimacing at his own reflection while he swung a single, metal ball in an arcane pattern around his torso.

His eyes, a shade greyer than his father's methane-ice blue, flickered toward Rory and lingered. The line between his brows, which might mark intense concentration or severe myopia, deepened. He sat up a little straighter on the bench. Rory, attuned through her recent, constant, vigorous tum'mo to the body's myriad ways to carry tension, noted a sudden tightness in his shoulders, a stiffness in his spine.

She noticed, too, that his gaze settled on her exactly as long as it took to ascertain that yes, she was looking back, before he looked away.

She rearranged her grip on the tum'mo rug, and remained exactly where she was. She considered the plans thus far. She was *supposed* to proceed to her corner of the room and commence with her practice. She was *supposed* to cease and desist shortly after Jaed himself was finished, and from there, contrive to encounter him in one of the corridors near the equipment storage areas, while Thorsdottir and Zhang ensured that the corridor remained empty for the duration of the conversation.

Rory was, as previously noted, rather short on patience.

"Go on," Rory murmured to her guards. "It's all right. I've got this."

Thorsdottir and Zhang looked at each other. Thorsdottir considered taking the Princess's arm, or bodily moving in front of her, or something. Instead, she said, "Please, Princess."

Rory looked at her, and for a heartbeat Thorsdottir thought she had succeeded in preventing whatever it was Rory was about to do. Then Rory winked.

"Trust me," she said, and lifted her chin, took a tighter grip on her rug, and walked straight across the room. There was no doubting her destination.

Several other patrons in the facility also noticed the Princess's trajectory. Heads turned, with varying degrees of subtlety.

Thorsdottir groaned, very softly. Zhang said several words in a combination of such creativity that Grytt, had she been present, would have been impressed.

"What do we do?" whispered Thorsdottir.

Zhang shook her head. "Nothing. Watch."

"This will be all over the station in an hour."

"Optimistic."

"Grytt's going to kill us."

"Certainly."

Jaed, too, noted the incoming Princess. He froze, mid-lift, for several breaths, and blinked. Then he set the kettlebell down on the bench, stood, and turned.

"Princess," he said, while she was still several strides away. A greeting. A query. The first touch of blades in a fencing match. He bowed at the waist, which, while entirely appropriate for formal events, looked absurd in its current context.

And not just the bow. All of it. Everything. Rory was suddenly struck by their reflection: the Princess of Thorne and the Regent's son, wearing exercise kit, which in neither case left any doubt of their wearers' physiques and exposed large swaths of skin, and yet they were both armored in etiquette and plastic smiles as if they were stuffed into lace and velvet.

Rory stopped at a radius that indicated she wished for quiet voices and private conversation. "Jaed."

And with that, she broke five rules of protocol. Or seven, if one was adhering to Sangeline's *The Proper Princess*, which Rory had been given as a child (by a distant, well-meaning relative) and which she had promptly buried in the garden.

Every head in the room, except those of Thorsdottir and Zhang, ducked back to its business, although the noise and clang of the usual pursuits seemed strangely muted as everyone strained to listen.

Jaed looked down at her. His eyes were a little wide, his mouth pursed and puzzled. Off-balance, Rory thought. A little nervous. His face was flushed, from recent exertions or embarrassment or a combination thereof.

"Princess," Jaed said again, firmly. "What a
unwelcome interruption
pleasant surprise."

Rory had been about to apologize for interrupting him. She reconsidered, with fairy truth ringing in her ears. She wondered, suddenly, if Jaed had someone else who might also hear about this meeting. She had assumed—and what had Messer Rupert told her about assuming? And Grytt?—that he would *want* her attention. Instead, her presence might be as unwelcome to him as his was to her. Perhaps that was why he'd been so awkward that first encounter, speaking rudely about his Prince and examining her physical attributes without subtlety: he'd been trying to discourage her or assure himself that she would choose Merrick, when she chose.

When. *If.* There was a danger in thinking that the Regent's plans would come to fruition, that she would remain here, lending legitimacy to an upstart sovereign while his father ruled the Free Worlds of Tadesh. That she would have to marry one of his sons. *This* son.

She was taking too long to respond, she knew that: standing there, mouth partway open. Jaed misread the delay. She watched as suspicion hardened his features. His eyes narrowed, and a smirk snapped into place on his lips like a shield.

"The customary response is *no, the pleasure is mine,* your Highness."

choke on that and lie to me

Fairy gifts collided with etiquette, knocking Rory's words sidelong against the back of her teeth. He was angry *already*—at her, perhaps. At the situation. The gift was not clear. Years of courtesy and courtiers tried to reassert themselves, offering apologies and excuses. She had offended, well and true, and whatever she thought of him, she needed to repair that offense. She needed his help. Soothe the temper, stroke the ego.

lie to me

She shook her head, and took a breath, and shot a quick glance at Thorsdottir and Zhang, in the mirror. Then she drilled a glare at Jaed with such force that his smirk shattered.

"Where have you been?"

"Excuse me?"

"You heard me. I've been looking for you. Here, every damned day."

He stared at her. Reflex tried to rebuild his smirk and failed, settling instead for a half-melted scowl.

"I bloody well know that."

"So you were avoiding me."

"Yes."

"Why?"

His lips thinned. He cast a glance around the room, at heads bent to their particular exercise, at necks stiff with the strain of holding heads tilted *just so*, to catch every word. He leaned down, close enough that Rory could see the sweat of his interrupted exertions, collected in beads along his hairline. Close enough that she could smell him, skin and sweat, and not the chemical propriety of perfumes and soap.

"You want something," he said, in a tone that would have been intimate if it had not been so brittle. "And you want me to get it for you. So you can save your breath. I won't help you."

"Won't, or can't?"

He considered that. "Both."

Truth. Rory folded her arms, and noted that this time, Jaed's eyes didn't leave hers. It was a point in his favor.

"Why not?"

His lips pressed flat. The expression made him look older,

pushing him into the grim twenties, out of the borderland of nineteen.

"Because my father doesn't take advice from me. He definitely doesn't do favors for me. Whatever my father's got on your Vizier, it's worth more to him than I am."

Truth again, or at least he believed that it was. The bitterness was palpable.

Rory's eye caught movement in the mirror: Zhang, cutting a graceful path across the room, managing to look as if she weren't at a near jog. Thorsdottir hovered near the door, wearing a grimace even Grytt could envy.

Jaed noticed Rory's distraction and turned to look. And so they were both watching, as Zhang arrived and inserted herself into their conference.

"Perhaps this conversation would be better continued less publicly, *your Highness*. Or." She paused and bowed slightly. "More quietly. Your Highness."

Rory nodded at her. "Thank you, Zhang. Will you walk with me, Jaed?"

"No. Your Highness."

She blinked. "What?"

"Not accustomed to hearing *no*, are you?"

"And you're not accustomed to being able to say it."

He shrugged. Temper flickered through his eyes, like heat lightning behind clouds. "I can't help you. I said that."

"Your Highness. My lord," said Zhang, a little desperately.

Across the room, Thorsdottir closed her eyes, squared her shoulders and her jaw, and (having reopened her eyes) started across the room with a great deal less grace and a great deal more force than her partner. Jaed's eyebrows rose. "Is she going to drag *me* away, Princess, or *you*?"

"Possibly both of us."

His smirk battled gamely for possession of his lips against the flat line of real anger. "What did Merrick say, that made you desperate enough to try me?"

"I haven't talked to Merrick. Why? Would your father listen to *him*?"

Jaed's face went through contortions that seemed to indicate a mouthful of sour marbles or a live mouse. "He might. Why *didn't* you talk to Merrick first?"

"Because I knew where you'd be, and I knew you'd be alone."

Jaed laughed soundlessly. "Well then. I'm

never anyone's

your first choice. What a surprise."

Rory's stomach turned on itself. For the first time, she thought the thirteenth fairy might have cursed her, after all. She decided that the shreds of propriety were not worth preserving, nor was pride, and laid her hand on Jaed's bare wrist. His skin was warm, damp, and a little sticky.

"Please, Jaed. My lord. At least talk to me."

He stared at her hand. At Thorsdottir, incoming. Then he offered a small smile, wary and crooked, neither weapon nor armor. "Fine, then.

already in trouble, make it count

We'll walk."

"Thank you." Rory removed her hand, carefully and deliberately. Her palm tingled. She wanted to scrub it on her pants or make a fist of it. Instead, with the same care and deliberation, she permitted it to hang back at her side.

She turned just as Thorsdottir arrived. "We're going for a walk," she said. "I'm sorry. It's going to interrupt your exercise."

"Your Highness," said Thorsdottir, and bowed. The look she

cast her partner was grim; the look she dropped on Jaed was of such severity and delivered from such proximity—they were of a height—that he let out his breath in a little surprised gust.

And so they left together: the Princess of Thorne, her guards, and the Regent's second son. Notes were made of the marching order (the larger guard first, the smaller last), how the Princess and Jaed walked abreast, how they looked at each other (not at all, while they walked), how the guards looked (unhappy), where they walked (out of the main room, and then out of the facility altogether), the Princess still carrying her rug and wearing her tum'mo kit, the Regent's son bare-armed in a shirt whose hem was curled and frayed with age and abuse and damp with drying sweat.

At least twenty illicit 2Ds were taken on personal communication devices, all of which appeared on the turing net within a quarter hour. Versions of the conversation—of which only snatches had been overheard, however public and obvious the expressions—found their way into personal correspondence and board postings, and at least one anonymous gossip column attached to the major media outlet on Urse.

About these developments Rory knew nothing and would not for some time. She was, however, conscious that their perambulation was accreting attention in the same way an avalanche gathers snow.

"Shall we go to the arboretum?" she asked. "It's somewhat secluded."

"No," Jaed said, rather too sharply. And added, under his breath. "I hate that place."

The fairy gift said otherwise. Rory tucked that contradiction away for later examination, carefully, mindful of the sharp edges.

"Then where?"

He looked down at her and shook his head. "Let's just walk. It's harder to listen in on a moving target."

Since her arrival on Urse, Rory had learned a great deal about the limits of 'bots, which, being stationary, had a fixed radius in which their surveillance was effective. For her, the knowledge was a matter of necessity, if not for survival, at least for privacy. She hadn't expected Jaed to know it, or care about it . . . or *need* to care about it. Another bundle of knowledge, then, stashed for later.

They passed, at that moment, in front of the observation porthole which overlooked the passenger terminal. The porthole itself was huge, easily a dozen meters long, a strip of transparent alloy, the production of which was a trade secret in the Free Worlds, as it was a major export, as well as a testament to the skill of its alchemists. Bielo hung blue and baleful in the upper corner, casting cerulean shadows across the ships tethered to the station, reaching cold fingers into the station itself. One of its moons—Beo, perhaps?—swung over the equator, a single dark dot marring the blue.

Rory stared back at Bielo, and tried not to think about the vastness on the other side of the porthole and the great swaths of unbreathable, unbroken void between her and Thorne, with exactly as much success as one trying not to think of pink elephants when one is instructed not to do so. She drifted to a halt, her brain determining that, with no one to oversee the placement of her feet, it was better to simply stop.

Jaed made note of the Princess's expression. He would have smirked, a quarter hour ago, with the void-born's contempt for the provinciality of the planet-born, and offered insincere (though sincerely delivered) platitudes: how awesome the view, how frightening, and oh no, you never got used to seeing *that*.

Now he held his silence, and his smirk, and watched the Princess stare, unblinking, at Bielo's icy curves. After a moment, he said, "You had no choice, coming here."

"No."

The silence returned, but this time it was a softer thing, and warmer. Rory looked past the planet, into the ghosts of herself and Jaed Moss in the portal. They appeared only as shapes, dim lines drawn on the black, with no eyes or discernible features. They might have been any two people, admiring (grimly facing) the view.

But of course they were not *just anyone*.

She shook her head, and blinked the planet away, and resumed walking. She expected Jaed would follow her, though she did not look back and check. She considered what she would do if he did not, if she would turn around and return to him.

Then she felt him arrive at her shoulder: the movement of displaced air, the smell of his sweat, the sense of another person closer to her than most people could, or would, approach. A princess did not just go walking, did not take casual strolls with her friends, because a princess did not *have* friends. She had bodymaids, guards, teachers, viziers.

She had never thought of herself as alone, until now. It was a revelation.

It was easy to imagine that Jaed Moss might share that same sense of isolation. The fairy gift hinted at it. That isolation might become a place of empathy, a shared condition of their rank. A patch of ground in which friendship might grow, if one were exceptionally optimistic or under the impression that the neat reality of stories is also true.

But she did not like him, and although she had not tested her theory against the fairy gift, she thought he did not much like her, either.

Well. *Like* was best confined to food, not politics.

"My lord," she said. "I did mean it. I do need your help."

"Jaed," he said. "Call me Jaed. Princess—"

"Rory. Please."

"Rory." He inclined his head. "Assuming I can help you—and understand there're limits to what I'm *able* to do—it won't come free. I think we need to be clear about that."

Rory closed her eyes, trusting the invariance of the decking under her feet and Thorsdottir's broad-shouldered presence on point to keep her walking straight. She forced breath past the cold weight in her chest, like a solid stone where her heart should have been.

"Of course."

She would have been five kinds of fool, on whom all of Grytt's pragmatism and Messer Rupert's careful tutelage had been wasted, if she had come to this encounter without imagining—in her own mind, not sharing with Thorsdottir or Zhang—what Jaed Moss's help might require, and what she would be willing to pay.

At least Jaed was *honest*, saying that. A princess could do worse than *honest*.

That she did not want to bargain with Jaed Moss (or any Tadeshi) was as true as the First Principles of Arithmancy. She wanted (wished!) to free Messer Rupert, and from there, to break her betrothal, to go *home*.

But even a princess, or perhaps *especially* a princess, knows the futility of some wishes.

CHAPTER THIRTEEN ═══════

Keeping Faith

Whole human religions are founded on the principle that the multiverse is, in whole or in parts, sentient, and interested in the well-being of its inhabitants. Sages and philosophers debate the soundness of those beliefs, and write elaborate treatises on their conclusions. Arithmancers and alchemists eschew all debate on the multiverse's awareness or intention, and instead hold forth on its nature: regular, predictable, bound by rules. (Here we necessarily exclude the philosophies and religions of the various xenos—k'bal, vakari, tenju, alwar, mirri—as even a summary of their disparate faiths is beyond the scope of our work here, and whose opinions on multiversal sentience vary as widely as their biologies). Neither sages nor alchemists lay much stock in superstition, the definition of which includes whatever phenomena or conditions run counter to the popular theories of the day. Superstition, they say, is for the uneducated.

It is unclear precisely where fairies fall in those classifications, and perhaps it is they, and not the multiverse, responsible for subsequent events involving Rory and Jaed. Whatever the case, the unfolding of those events seems to indicate a particular sense of the absurd and ironic, which would indicate that, if the multiverse is itself sentient, it has a peculiar sense of humor.

Grytt typically returned from the detention center to the Thorne apartments at the first-shift supper hour, or a little later. She did this for two reasons. One, she found her presence unsettled the second shift security when they arrived to their posts and found her already waiting. And two, it allowed Rory ample time to prepare supper after completing her own self-imposed work day at the embassy. Rory had declared cooking to be *relaxing* and *therapeutic*, where most of the relaxation and therapy came from the swift violence of chopping and the sustained aggression of frying, boiling, and baking. Thorsdottir and Zhang had learned quickly that offers of help, while tolerated, were somewhat unwelcome, and that the Princess was best left alone in the kitchen, and approached only upon Grytt's arrival.

Given the stress of the day, Thorsdottir expected the Princess to prepare something elaborate, involving a great deal of mincing and slicing, and the application of high heat. But upon her return from her walk with Jaed, the Princess planted herself at the turing and remained there, unmoving, looking uncannily like the Vizier had on the afternoon before his arrest.

Thorsdottir and Zhang had not actually *seen* the Vizier on that fateful day, but they both knew arithmancy at work when they saw it, and they surmised that Grytt would not be pleased to arrive home and discover the Princess engaged in dangerous activities from which her guards had not prevented her.

"Though if Grytt wants to stop her," Thorsdottir muttered to her partner, "she's welcome to try. *I'm* not that brave."

Zhang, having exhausted the day's conversational stores already, only nodded. She shared her partner's concern. The Princess's very public performance this afternoon had generated a great deal of traffic on the public networks, and at least two separate mentions on unrelated 2D broadcasts, including four minutes of amateur video of Rory and Jaed walking past the passenger terminal promenade and pausing at the porthole, while the program's host commented with plastic intimacy about the significance of the romantic reconciliation after the tiff in the recreational facilities.

When it was clear that Rory was engrossed in whatever arithmantic mischief she'd found, Thorsdottir—whose mother had tried, very hard, to raise a respectable daughter—pushed back her sleeves and began assembling a soup out of the remnants of earlier meals and the last bits of unused ingredients. It was, she reasoned, likely (inevitable) that Grytt would return in a temper, and even more likely that she would (correctly, in Thorsdottir's reckoning) blame Rory's guards for failing to protect the Princess from her own impatience. What exactly they could have done, she and Zhang, to prevent Rory's actions, Thorsdottir would not have been able to articulate; but it was her professional experience that no one ever *did* ask the bodyguards, and besides, royalty's task was to govern kingdoms and consortiums, not itself.

So she was surprised when Grytt arrived and said, the split second the door had closed in her wake, "You realize that your little performance today has the turing net brimming with speculation about your affair with Jaed Moss?—Oh *hell*, tell me you're not hexing that turing."

Rory, absorbed in exactly that, did not answer.

Then, and only then, did Grytt round on Thorsdottir. "*Tell* me she's not hexing that damn turing."

The partners looked at each other.

"She is," said Thorsdottir. "But she assured us it was safe."

Grytt folded her arms and planted herself in front of Rory's desk, so that she stared down past the turing's screen and directly at the Princess's face.

"Safe is the ground underfoot and a gun in the hand. Safe is not a damn turing in this place. Which you *know*, Rory Thorne."

The Princess did not remove her eyes from whatever held their attention. But her mouth tightened, and she heaved out a sigh of excessive volume that one did not require a fairy gift to understand as *I am busy, please shut up.*

Thorsdottir made herself very busy with the soup, lest her stillness attract Grytt's ire. Idle soldiers, in Thorsdottir's experience, were *always* a target.

After the soup was well on its way to boiling, and Zhang had crowded into the narrow space to offer her own expertise ("I think maybe salt?"), and the pair of them had sprinkled and sniffed and stirred as much as they could—then, finally, Rory pushed her chair back from the desk, producing an unlovely squeal of metal on metal.

She looked up at Grytt, who had not moved, for a long unblinking and unsmiling moment.

"I do know," she said. "And it is safe. And I am *not* having an affair with Jaed."

"Since when does something need to be true to have everyone believing it?" Grytt shook her head. "I'll bet your new friend is getting an earful tonight from his father. Maybe his brother, too."

"Bah," said Rory. "He's not my new friend."

"Not what it says on the network."

Rory pulled the end of her braid around and examined it thoughtfully. She began to unravel the fastening, and, having done so, started to unweave the braid, combing the strands out between her fingers. Her voice climbed into a high, false innocence. "Since when does everyone saying a thing mean that it's true?"

Thorsdottir had grown up on a farm that, among other things, kept sheep, which were a particular favorite of the local bear-cats. To protect the sheep, therefore, any farmer with wits kept several of the large, thick-furred dogs bred especially for that purpose. Those dogs, when confronted with a bear-cat, made a sound very much like Grytt was making now.

"Don't you make a game out of this, Rory Thorne."

Thorsdottir wondered if her duties as bodyguard included protecting Rory from Grytt. Zhang's expression, when she checked, suggested that Zhang shared her worry.

The Princess herself appeared unconcerned. Rory flicked the half-undone braid aside and leaned forward onto her elbows. "No joke. No game. *You're* the one who told me that the best plans don't survive contact with the enemy."

Grytt appeared to consider the classification of Jaed Moss as *enemy.* "You're telling me you had a plan. Well. That's something."

"I'm telling you Jaed was hostile. Charming him—which *was* the plan—wouldn't't've worked."

"And now?"

"Now he's agreed to cooperate."

Grytt chewed that information over, rolling it from cheek to cheek, flesh to metal, before swallowing it. "And that will explain why you're hexing this turing?"

"I'm not," said Rory. "At least, I haven't yet. But I do have Jaed's pass-string."

"You have—" Grytt squinted through her flesh eye. The metal one, lacking an eyelid, whined in its socket. "We're all going to end up neighbors to Rupert. You think his father doesn't spy on him, too?"

Rory smiled with the minimum possible number of muscles

necessary for the expression. "No. And neither does he. But he'd like to be . . . unspied upon. So I volunteered to look over his pass-string for hexes. *Which* I found, and removed."

"And what do you get, in return for this labor?"

"Another pass-string. Preferably the Regent's. Maybe one of his Ministers'."

"Hm. He's stealing for you, now?"

"He is."

"Fascinating."

"Not as fascinating as what I found out with only *his* set of clearances."

Rory paused, for half a beat. Grytt raised her eyebrow. The princess added another pair of muscles to her smile.

"The royal apartment is not drawing sufficient power for any inhabitants, unless Ivar likes it dark. Nor is it drawing any water from the system. Therefore, the Crown Prince is no longer on Urse."

"You found that out with Jaed's pass-string."

Rory inclined her head. "Resource consumption isn't top-secret information. It's just restricted to government ministers and certain mid-level employees, which happens to include the Regent and his sons. That's . . ." She glanced at the screen. "Approximately two thousand people, give or take. Besides. It's a simple hex to make my access just now, with Jaed's string, look like the third-shift clerk in charge of tracking water consumption in the first through fifth levels. The *significant* information is that Ivar's not here. Nor can I find any records of a shuttle—military or otherwise—departing for Beo."

"If it was a royal shuttle, there may be no records."

"I thought of that. But there *is* a regular supply run that goes from here to Beo. It's dependent on celestial motion and local atmospheric conditions. The last supply run was cancelled because of the storms. *Nothing* has left Urse for Beo because nothing can land on Beo right now. Not supplies. Not Ivar. So where is he, Grytt?"

"How should I know? I can almost keep track of you." Grytt side-eyed Thorsdottir. Then she crossed toward the portholes and glared out. Cherno had wandered out of sight, leaving only a carpet of stars and a great deal of unbreathable void to absorb Grytt's scowl.

"I suppose whatever pass-string you get from Jaed will help you find out where Ivar is. Is that the plan?"

"That is the plan."

"And then what?"

Rory shrugged. "Then we continue with the terms of our bargain."

Thorsdottir braced her hands on the counter, prepared for the mother of all eruptions. She was surprised, therefore, when Grytt did not ask, and in fact only shrugged.

It was Grytt's experience that diplomacy, which was a nice way of saying politics, was a lot like war, except the enemy could not be dispatched by a well-aimed bolt. Political methods, Grytt thought, were uglier and more damaging, particularly to the wielder; she would have spared Rory that experience a while longer, if she had been able, but necessity dictated otherwise. Grytt saw no point in fretting over it, or in asking questions the answer to which she might not like. She and Rupert had done their best with the girl. Best let her get on with it, and trust her to handle herself. She turned her attention to the kitchen, to Thorsdottir's soup and the serving of supper. Soldier or politician, mecha or princess, everyone needed to eat, and she was hungry.

———

Had anyone inquired of the Vizier his opinion of the multiverse's sense of humor before his incarceration, he would have waxed enthusiastic on the subject, citing multiple obscure texts and authors, and very likely enjoyed himself. Now, however, confined as he was in a detention block somewhere in the nether regions of Urse's municipal complex, he found his opinion distilled to the more pragmatic *there is no bad luck, only bad choices*, which he'd read on a poster in a professor's office once during his undergraduate studies. He had thought that notion absurd at the time. Now, he was less certain.

His choices had landed him here, after all, where *here* meant locked in a cell with a bunk, a sink and a toilet, and four blank, deliberately depressive bulkheads in dimensions just a shade too close to be comfortable. Through the single, small window in the door, he could observe another depressingly blank bulkhead across the corridor; over which lurked a single, obvious camera, a black globular eye that almost certainly had its twin in one over *his* door, and probably several less visible cousins besides. The cell had no 'caster, no terminals, no tablets. The guards had divested him of all personal belongings, including his robes, and given him a set of coveralls, just the wrong side of scratchy and the same color as his breakfast porridge.

So his choices, he thought, might require a little scrutiny.

In the first few days of his incarceration, the Vizier balanced his time between examining those choices and dreading the future. Rupert did not suppose Moss meant to torture him, exactly; there were statutes against that, to which every human collective, empire, kingdom, and corporation was signatory, and besides, torture didn't work especially well unless the goal was to inflict suffering. While Rupert suspected Moss possessed the cruelty sufficient to order pain for its own sake, he did not think the Regent would be inclined to expend that effort just to hear someone scream.

No one came.

Rupert's meals—the aforementioned porridge at what he thought must be first shift, and some twelve hours later, a sandwich of dubious origins, or a bowl of something edible with spoons (no knives or forks here)—arrived through a slot in the door (at the bottom, so that he must crouch to retrieve the tray, like a supplicant or a servant), and later departed the same way. He attempted once to crouch down and peer out the slot; he saw only a mecha's chassis.

And still, no one came to see him. No one asked him any questions. No one arrived to present themselves as his solicitor. He might have, except for the meals, been entirely forgotten. Rupert could think of at least three statutes to which the Free Worlds of Tadesh were signatories that forbade solitary confinement of exactly this sort, except in the cases of pathogenic contagions or persons so dangerous that they could be classified as pathogens themselves.

Perhaps he should be flattered the Regent considered him such a danger. Instead, he felt unequal measures of self-pity, regret, and grim vindication. It had indeed been his choices that had landed him here. He could have accepted the offer for post-graduate studies in arithmancy instead of choosing the serve his Consortium, been a researcher instead of a diplomat. He might've managed to convince Samur to forego the alliance with Moss and to marry Rory to Larish instead, in which case the Consortium might have won the war with the Free Worlds (but, ugly but, Rory would be wedded to the Larish boy and travelling the void with the Larish fleet and he'd never see her again except by quantum-hex viewing ball). And of course he could have refused Rory's request to hack the station turing, but then it would be her here in this cell, not him.

Grytt would have told him to quit whining, he thought. Grytt would have insisted he get off his sorry, narrow backside and do something. He wished she were here to tell him that, so that he could point at the blank bulkheads and the brazenly staring 'bot and demand of her how, exactly, he was supposed to do anything, should he beat things with his fists, like she would? And she would say—

The Vizier blinked. She would say, *Do what you're good at, Rupert.*

So the Vizier attempted arithmancy.

It was a small hex, simple, meant only to discover if there were, in fact, other auras present in the corridor (guards) or the other four cells (other prisoners) or, as he was beginning to suspect, if it was only mecha and 'bots in the vicinity. But as he closed his eyes and slipped past that first aetheric layer, he encountered—not unexpectedly—a layer of counter-hexes, not only on the bulkheads, the door, and the deck, but also woven thick in the aether of the cell itself. He could see them plainly enough, like a minefield of equations that would alert someone if he attempted to bypass them. He tried a deeper layer, and another after that (and so on, until he knew he'd reached his limit) with the same result. Then he withdrew into his body and the first pressings of a headache. At least none of the hexes was actively attempting to breach *his* defenses, which was curious, and a bit of a relief, since he had not yet thought to put any into place.

So he did that next: laid a bulwark of hexes designed to deflect simple readings of auras, to conceal his own, to alert him if someone attempted to remove them. And then, no one having yet arrived to challenge him, Rupert made an attempt at the enemy hexes. First to brush them aside, and then, when that (predictably) failed, to counter them outright.

To his credit, he managed to disable one before the rest converged on him like a swarm of angry hornets. The subsequent shock-stings of counter-hexes startled him out of his usual composure, eliciting a yelp and a short, profane expletive. Then, breathing a bit faster now, and sure he had amused whoever was watching the 'bot feeds of his cell, he dabbed the blood off his nose, settled onto his bunk, and laid his palms on his crossed thighs. Surely now, someone would come, and the isolated waiting would end.

And still, no one came.

It was at this point that Rupert realized the solitude was the torture, and that he was in real trouble.

We will not linger on the details of the Vizier's suffering endured in the subsequent days: how his mind, deprived of external stimulation, invented scenarios in which terrible things had befallen Rory, or—even worse, because they were even more impossible—scenarios in which he was rescued by Samur herself appearing at his cell door.

In truth, Rupert suspected that Samur did not even know what had happened. Moss controlled the station's communications, and so could determine what information left Urse, and he almost certainly would not send Samur a message, nor allow Rory or the Thorne Embassy to do so (or intercept one if they did). A ship might carry the news, but it would have to be going toward Consortium territory, and Rupert knew that Urse was at least two tesser-hex gates from the Consortium border by the most direct route. And even if she did hear of his plight, what could Samur do? He had broken Tadeshi law. He might be subject to recall under treaty and diplomatic immunity, but he could just as easily be reported dead in custody, or in transit (and what if Moss had done so already?). He was also not sure Samur would invoke treaty on his behalf, not when he had been so careless. Except he had not been careless: the hex that had eluded him on the Ursan turing had been first-rate, the sort of thing he wished he could have encountered in an arithmantic trade journal, dissected and discussed in theory. He had been out-hexed, that was all. It happened. But the multiverse has never been conceived of by anyone, xeno or human, as forgiving.

As for other sorts of rescue, well. Grytt was too smart to use force on a station in which she and the guards were entirely outnumbered. He knew that Rory would continue to try to get him out by whatever means available to her. He did not hold out much hope that she would be able to do so. And so, given no alternative, he sat on his bunk and meditated in between fantasies of rescue and bouts of self-recrimination.

Then, finally, someone came. Rupert was unsure of the exact day or hour—he had no way to mark time's passage except by meals, and he'd lost track of those—but he knew it was more than ten days, and less than, oh, twenty.

He had only a few moments between the pneumatic hiss of the door's mechanisms and its subsequent opening to prepare. His mind leapt first to the certainty that it would be guards and that his time for interrogation had finally arrived. His heart, spurred by grim anticipation, galloped around the confines of his chest. He stood up, under some half-formed instinct that it was better to meet one's fate upright.

The door opened. A single individual stepped through the open gap neatly, quickly, and the door whisked closed so quickly that the gust of its passing disturbed the otherwise pristine drape of his tunic. His clothing was typical stationer, unremarkable in its style, though its superior tailoring marked the wearer as rather well-off. He bore no obvious weapons.

An assassin, thought Rupert, and on the heels of that, *how dramatic*, followed by a conviction that the multiverse might possess, if not a sense of humor, at least a sense of the absurd. But then a hex attempted to breach Rupert's own hedge of defenses. It was tiny and innocuous, intended to probe and map defenses rather than to breach them. After a few frustrated moments of finding no gaps in Rupert's defenses, the hex withdrew.

It was then that Rupert concluded the multiverse had a genuine sense of humor after all. The attacking hex had be so stealthy and well-designed that, had Rupert been beset by distractions (such as, oh, anything else), he would have overlooked it completely. But because he had noticed it, he had also noticed its basic structural similarity to the hex in the turing which he'd overlooked and which had resulted in his current predicament.

Rupert gazed at his visitor with new interest. He was a smallish man, trim and tidy, possessed of a thin mustache and an even thinner pair of lips. Thoroughly unremarkable, if one were to pass him in the corridors. Rupert wondered idly if he had done so, and simply failed—again—to identify the threat. One's attention just slid off the man. Or would have, if there had been anyone or anything else in the cell to look at.

Like hex, like arithmancer.

Rupert's voice rasped from so many days of disuse. He hoped his wits were not similarly disposed. "I must congratulate you. It was an excellent hex, the one in the turing. I almost did not see it at all. Was it your creation?"

The arithmancer (whose name was Ashtet-Sun, which he did not share with Rupert but which we shall reveal here to give us something to call him besides *the arithmancer*) gazed at Rupert with a combination of irritation and incredulity. "Yes."

"Then you are here to gloat, perhaps? Well. You have earned it. I am not sure how you managed to divide the sum of the first two variables without—"

"I am not here to discuss hex-string theory with you."

"A pity, since that is the only thing I am prepared to discuss with you."

Ashtet-Sun regarded Rupert through narrowed eyes. "I told the Regent that this wasn't the right approach to take with you. This cell. Solitary confinement. I said it would make you defiant."

In that, you are wrong, thought Rupert. The solitude had been well on its way to cracking him. Ashtet-Sun's appearance now was an unintended boon for his sanity, but it also bespoke, well, something else, which he might turn to his advantage. Impatience, perhaps. Curiosity. Something that brought the Regent's arithmancer here, deep in second shift, without armed escort, and if it was not vanity—

Ashtet-Sun hissed through his teeth. Impatience, then. Rupert felt another sally against his hexes, another attempt to read his aura, which his defenses repelled. He waited for his visitor to attempt to break his hexes down with force. That attempt did not come. Instead, the other man shifted unhappily from one foot to the other, as if the deck beneath his soles were growing warm.

"My countermeasures remain intact. So how are you getting past them?"

Rupert raised his eyebrows. "I assure you, I have no idea what you are talking about. I understand that response is cliché and expected in these circumstances. Nonetheless, it is true."

The reader may here be suspecting—correctly—the correlation

of Ashtet-Sun's arrival with the discovery that someone using Jaed's pass-string was rooting around in the turing. Ashtet-Sun was certain that someone was not Jaed, since Jaed was not the sort to take an interest in water consumption in the Prince's apartments. Rupert harbored no suspicions of Jaed, but he was certain that whatever had alarmed Ashtet-Sun, it was Rory's doing, and the very idea filled him with dread. This man was a skilled arithmancer, and Rory was not his equal. She was going to get herself caught—

Rupert gave himself a mental shake. Whatever Rory was about, she was succeeding so far. His visitor appeared to be in a state of some agitation, asking vague and unformed questions the way a man might if he was thinking aloud. He was also alone, without guards. That begged asking why, but Rupert already knew the answer. His work as Vizier had taught him the reading of people, with or without the corroboration of an aura or a convenient Kreshti fern.

"You're afraid."

Ashtet-Sun stared at him. "Why would I be?" he asked in a brittle voice that said that Rupert had gotten it exactly right.

"Because if it is not me responsible for whatever is happening, then you don't know who it is."

"Of course it's you. You and that body-maid, somehow."

"You mean Grytt? I haven't seen her. You know that." Rupert gestured at the bulkhead, the deck, the overhead, the presumed surveillance 'bots. "Besides. She is no arithmancer."

"She doesn't need to be. All that hexwork on her prosthetics." Ashtet-Sun's fingers flicked vaguely at his face and head. "She could be transmitting something. Or receiving it. Or hexed to explode."

The Vizier began to suspect how the assassination of two kings on Thorne had been managed via the body-man, and perhaps by whom. It took every scrap of skill and experience to keep his face and voice diplomatically bland. "You made no error with the hexwork in this cell, and you've missed no secret transmissions. You may assure the Regent that I am secure and that, whatever prompted you to come here, I am not responsible for it."

Ashtet-Sun stared at him, two parts withering, one part anxious, and pressed his thin lips to bloodless invisibility.

Rupert felt a small surge of hope. "The Regent doesn't know you're here, does he? He doesn't know about whatever it is that has you so disturbed. And you don't want to tell him. You're afraid of what he'll say. Or of what he'll do?"

Ashtet-Sun did not bother with a response. He simply turned on his heel and departed, which was eloquent confirmation enough.

The Vizier stared for a full minute at the closed door. Then, when he was certain the 'bot would be recording again, he began to laugh: not the raggedy gasps of a man halfway to breaking, which he had been half an hour before, but deeply satisfied chuckles which were out of place in solitary confinement, and which Rupert hoped would spark unease in his captors. (Which they did. The guards observing him were in fact so disturbed that they filed a report, flagged for the Regent's immediate attention, the delivery of which spoiled Moss's dinner.)

Then the Vizier returned to his meditation, only this time, it was interrupted by imagining what it was Rory was doing, and taking pride, and hope, from that.

Ashtet-Sun was a careful man, bordering on paranoid. He performed a second, third, and fourth extensive review of his hexes in Rupert's cell, none of which revealed any weakness or possible way that the Vizier could have wormed his arithmantic way through them. Perhaps that reassured Ashtet-Sun, or perhaps it further inflamed his paranoia and dread of the Regent's displeasure. Regardless, it is not recorded that he ever reported his visit with the Vizier to Regent Moss, nor alerted Moss to his suspicions.

There are two things we might conclude from this encounter. First, that skill with arithmancy is in no way connected to good judgment; whatever the Vizier's errors in overlooking Ashtet-Sun's clever hex in the turing, Ashtet-Sun committed a much greater error in visiting the Vizier. For although Rupert gained no physical advantage from the visit, nor any new information, he did acquire hope, and that sustained him through the long, lonely days that followed.

The second is that the multiverse does have a sense of humor after all.

CHAPTER FOURTEEN ═══════

The Brothers

J aed had, as a child, believed that the multiverse, embodied in the persons of father and brother, bore him a particular grudge. This certainty had only been cemented by the Arboretum Incident, in which his budding arithmantic aspirations (which, ironically, might have eradicated his belief in personal multiversal malice entirely with further study) had been pruned. If there was luck, and it was *his*, it would be bad.

Thus we see the dangers of superstition, which can prevent a man from examining the details of an unfortunate situation by causing him to imagine instead himself a victim, helpless to change his circumstances.

In his defense, Jaed had had little opportunity to exercise independence. But today, during his negotiations with Rory, he decided that his bad luck might be related to the heretofore unsubstantiated suspicion that there were hexes on his pass-string and not to a universal bias. She had suggested the possibility, this foreign princess, before revealing, in the subsequent conversation, that she was also an arithmancer. Not particularly accomplished, she said, certainly not an expert. But she had been taught, and so, to Jaed's thinking, must also be capable of teaching.

He revised his terms for their alliance, which he had not—fortunately—yet uttered. The Princess accepted, after a moment's hesitation, and after repeating, and being sure that he understood, her level of expertise.

For the first time since the arboretum's single, unfortunate autumn, Jaed had experienced a surge of—well, *hope* might be too strong a sentiment. Optimism, then. Let us call it that.

"Jaed! I want to talk to you."

It sounded very much like the Regent's voice; and, like the Regent's, its tone suggested that its content should be obeyed. But of course it *wasn't* the Regent. It was Merrick, and his voice had preceded him around the corner, as if he had known Jaed was in the passage. He did not wait for a response—Merrick never waited for anything—and he rounded the corner at a brisk, angry pace.

That he wanted a confrontation was obvious.

Jaed was accustomed to doing what Merrick wanted. It was a habit to which he gave little thought, having seen no particular alternative that did not come with painful consequences, and Jaed was not fond of pain. They had not come to blows since their early teens, when Jaed had been much smaller, but the habit had stuck.

And still. The day's events had been unexpected, and he was not ready to set aside that strange, fluttering sensation in his chest. Rory was right about the hexes on his pass-string. He hadn't thought of it—hadn't thought to think of it—but how else, when he had done his very best to be unpredictable in his timing, coming in well past the dinner hour, and coming through the servants' entrance, would his brother know to find him here? It did not occur to him that Merrick might have been waiting (his brother was not that patient), nor that he might have spies among the servants (any spies on the staff belonged to his father). It was, without doubt, the pass-string, which he had used both in the restaurant where he'd had his dinner, and on the lock at the servants' door.

If the Princess of Thorne kept her word (and possessed sufficient skill), this particular vexation would not trouble him much longer. Jaed clung to that thought in the same way that a man cornered by bear-cats clings to a convenient stick. Unlike that stick, however, he could make no use of the thought as defense or as weapon.

Jaed leaned his forearm on the bulkhead, between a pair of plexi-sheeted 2D portraits of himself and his brother, formally attired, taken on their respective eighteenth birthdays. Visitors remarked, invariably, on the brothers' similarity. Like mirrors of each other, they said. The same cool eyes. The same strong jaw.

Looks, Jaed thought, were not everything.

He sighed, loudly, and ran his tongue over his teeth, which served to loosen both the organ and his jaw, which had clamped at the sound of Merrick's voice. Then he took a firm mental grip on his metaphorical stick, and attacked.

"What do you want, Merrick?"

His brother stopped a scant meter away. His hair, his clothing, were entirely in order. Only the two spots of pale pink on his cheekbones indicated his level of agitation.

"I think you owe me an explanation."

Jaed waited a beat too long, and took small satisfaction as the pink deepened to crimson and slunk down into Merrick's collar.

"About what?" he asked finally, in his best bored voice.

"Do you have any idea what a spectacle you've made of yourself? And don't you *dare* act like you don't know what I mean."

Jaed pretended great interest in the patch of carpet just under his left foot. He pivoted the heel back and forth, examining the pattern. It was some expensive imported thing, from outside the Free Worlds. Kreshti, perhaps, from before the War and the various embargoes, and somehow overlooked in the general purge of all things non-Tadeshi. More proof, he thought, that the Regent couldn't know *everything*.

"I'm sorry. Who elected *you* our father?"

Merrick leaned forward and hissed, "You be grateful he's not down here himself."

"I'm surprised he isn't. Did he send you to do the interrogation, or is this your own idea?"

Merrick's mouth bent in disapproval. "*He* thinks it's a stunt on her part, and that you're playing along to embarrass him."

"If Father doesn't think it's that important, I'm not sure why *you* do."

"I think." Merrick clipped his teeth together in front of what he'd meant to say next. Jaed watched him considering his next words. Plotting them.

Jaed had played enough chess—with Merrick, with the Regent— to know the look. To know that he was likely going to lose a major piece on the board, very soon. He reminded himself that his queen (oh, the joke there) was her own agent, and smarter than his father or Merrick suspected. *That* was his secret.

"You think Father is wrong?" he prompted gently, as though coaxing a reluctant child to tell the truth about the drawings on the wall. "Is that it? You think Father made a mistake?"

Merrick let that pass. His temper was receding, somewhat, restoring his skin to its typical, glacial shade.

As within, thought Jaed, *so without*.

Merrick's voice, too, had dropped several degrees. "I think you're playing along to embarrass *me*."

"Seems like it's working. You're embarrassed."

Merrick arched an eyebrow. Irritation and impatience vied for supremacy in his narrow, pale eyes. "She wants something. What is it?"

"My company."

"This isn't a game, Jaed."

Of course it is, Jaed thought. *That's exactly what this is.*

And it was one in which he was not assumed to be a player. He was accustomed to being a pawn. He was not accustomed to being entirely discounted. He understood that Merrick fully expected to end up with the victory—the Princess, the Free Worlds, the sum of their father's ambition. That didn't surprise Jaed. What did was Merrick's apparent distress over the contents of a conversation to which he had not been privy, and over which half of Urse was amusing itself with speculation.

Jaed tried on his own smirk. It felt small and crooked. It *felt* like a failure.

Merrick stared at him for a moment. Then he said with the inerrant aim of an older brother, "She doesn't like you, you know that, right? She's using you. So just tell me what she wants."

Jaed felt the warmth bloom in his cheeks. He felt a much more intense heat in his chest, pushing against his heart, his lungs, his ribs. He knew that the reason he played chess so poorly had less to do with his failure in strategy than it did with the skill with which his brother could provoke him, and his own inability to counter that provocation, particularly when that taunting rang true.

He tried. He took a deep breath and held it, and counted to five. He thought about the pass-string, and about the Princess, who had been *very* angry, he was sure—but who had not lost her temper. He envied that discipline. He wondered if it was natural to her, or a product of the arithmantic teaching. He wondered what he might have been like, by now, if the horticulturalist had stayed.

He wouldn't need Rory Thorne to teach him arithmancy, that

was certain, or to un-hex his pass-string, but she *could* give him that freedom. If he was patient.

A second breath came and went. Jaed watched the muscles flex in his brother's jaw. Merrick possessed their father's restraint, most times. Something had shaken it. It wasn't that Merrick was afraid to lose, Jaed realized then. It wasn't even that he was afraid to *look* like he was losing. He was afraid he *had* lost something, and that something was Rory Thorne.

Jaed turned that thought over and over, like a gift whose wrapping is so exquisite that you don't want to destroy it in the opening, so lovely that it seems better than the gift itself.

Then Merrick committed what would prove to be a small, and ultimately significant, long-reaching mistake. He tipped his head back and laughed. "I'm not stupid. Neither is Father. Neither is the Princess. The only stupid one here is the one who believes her. So I'm asking you again, what does she want?"

Or rather, he would have said, *what does she want*, except that Jaed's right fist interrupted him.

It was not an elegant move, nor particularly adept; Jaed lacked his own personal Grytt, and his martial education had been limited to his year of compulsory service (which he *had* served, but on Urse in the local garrison), in which the finer skills of hand-to-hand combat are not emphasized as much as obedience and conformity.

Merrick had undergone the same service experience; but unlike his brother (whose attendance in the gym was a solitary endeavor), he had pursued the martial arts, enlisting several of his father's security in private training sessions. It was a small matter for him to elude Jaed's strike: a simple slide of the foot, a shift of weight. He could have remained out of reach, and continued to retreat, thus avoiding an actual conflict. But he'd had a difficult day. Bad enough that he was (entirely) certain that to a good portion of Urse, *he* looked like the losing suitor. But there was the (small, miniscule, tiny, ridiculous) chance that he really was. And to *Jaed*.

It was intolerable.

So Merrick handled his outrage and insecurity in the time-honored way of young men, and determined that, whatever the object of his desire's preferences, he would settle the matter with violence, here and now, with his rival. He grabbed Jaed's outstretched arm at the wrist, stepped in close, and folded it the elbow, wrenching it up and behind Jaed's back. Then he nudged Jaed in the back of the knee and guided him, at rather unsafe speeds, face-first into the deck.

Jaed had a new opportunity to study the carpet from a closer perspective. It smelled a bit dusty. It was softer than it looked, grinding against his cheek. And the orange was really alternating threads of yellow, crimson, and a disturbingly iridescent pink.

If pain had a color, he thought his shoulder might be exactly that hue, with bright filaments spreading toward his elbow, across his back, and up his neck with each heartbeat.

Merrick leaned on his shoulder, which transformed the bright pink into waves of garnet, magenta, vermillion. Jaed bit down on the instinctive yell. His eyes squeezed closed, hot with tears that were more physiological than psychological, and no less shameful for that.

"I want," said Merrick, "You. To tell me. What. She. Said."

Jaed collected several tiny bites of air and spent them all at once. "She doesn't like you, Merrick. That's what she said. She said, *I don't like your brother, Jaed, he's a bully.*"

"You're lying." Merrick rearranged his grip on Jaed's wrist, pulling it higher between his shoulder blades, leaning a little more heavily across his brother's back.

The pain burst into seven shades of blinding white. Jaed

slammed his cheek into the carpet, trying to gain enough leverage to dislodge his older, heavier sibling. When that failed, he spent the remainder of his breath suggesting that Merrick attempt an anatomically unlikely pursuit.

And shortly after that, when Merrick readjusted his grip a third time, Jaed's howl ricocheted off the carpets and the framed art, finding every exposed metal surface and echoing. It sounded as if someone were tearing his arm off.

It was not very much later—the noise of the conflict having alerted municipal section security, whose arrival and intervention Jaed credited with his shoulder's continued presence in its socket—that Jaed arrived back at his quarters.

His terminal was flashing. He stared at it, caught between his desire for a handful of painkillers and his curiosity. It might be a blistering missive from his father or a terse summons to which he could not plead exhaustion or ignorance. Although why the Regent would concern himself at this hour with the private violence of his sons—now, after a childhood filled with it—Jaed could not figure.

The strange fluttering reappeared in his chest. He had never seen a living bird, but if he had, he would have imagined the sensation feeling very much like wings. He held his right arm very carefully against his ribs—perhaps he should have seen the chirurgeon, but it *moved*, didn't it? That must mean it was all right—and crossed to his desk.

He stared at the green light. It blinked back. Then he tapped the keypad, one quick, left-handed strike.

The message appeared, from—he blinked, and squinted, and leaned forward. From *himself*.

He opened it.

This message is secure. So is your pass-string. My code is below, if you care to reply. -RT

Jaed grinned. Then he sat down at the turing. It took him some effort, one-handed, but he was determined. He copied his pass-string from Rory's message, and used it to open another screen on the turing. He input the code. He had no way of knowing whether or not she'd done what she said. No way of confirming the absence of hexes that would, if still present, alert his brother and his father to his sudden, uncharacteristic interest in their schedules and appointments.

He then acquired that which he had promised Rory. And having done so, he employed his clean pass-string one further time, and sent her a message.

Meet me in the plaza dining area at thirteen hundred. My treat. -JM

Then he turned off the turing and sat alone and in the dark, and, for the first time in his life, imagined his future.

There is some debate, among those to whom etiquette is an art, whether it is proper to inquire after obvious injury and blemish, or to maintain the fiction of not noticing. The Tadeshi custom, particularly acute on Urse, is to pretend not to notice. On Thorne, the matter is more open to debate. Rory was a skilled political performer, and the damage to Jaed so apparent—even across the dining plaza—that she had ample time to consider the merits of each. On the one hand, Jaed was a prickly sort, who might not appreciate someone noticing what was, in Rory's Grytt-honed experience, the fruits of a round of fisticuffs. He didn't *look* like he'd won, but then, as Grytt was fond of saying, Rory had not yet seen his opponent. And on the other hand, he might welcome solicitation and sympathy from . . . well, *her*, Princess and ally and young woman.

She resolved to stay quiet, and to let Jaed himself set the tone of the encounter. Say nothing, unless he did.

Her guards, however, suffered from no need for impassivity.

"Great Mother," Thorsdottir murmured. "He's taken a beating."

"Mm." Zhang pursed her lips. "Look at his hands."

Thorsdottir understood immediately. Rory took a moment longer, having little experience with beatings.

"There's nothing wrong with his—oh."

"An ambush," Thorsdottir offered. "From behind."

"His brother," said Zhang.

"Merrick? No way. I mean, he just seems—" Rory censored the vapid *nice* she had been about to utter, and said instead, "Jaed's his little brother!"

Thorsdottir and Zhang side-eyed her. Then Thorsdottir, who had been raised one girl child amid many boys, said, "Older brothers can be a special kind of monster. Besides. Anyone else who laid hands on Jaed would be in prison, and the incident would be all over the media. So it happened somewhere private, which limits the perpetrators."

"Ambush." Zhang made a little clucking sound in her throat.

Rory considered that. She also considered the reasons an older brother might do *that* to his own sibling (she bore no especial love for Jacen, but she had never seriously entertained notions of doing him harm). She hypothesized several causes, and concluded that she would simply have to violate one school of etiquette, risk Jaed's ire, and simply *ask*.

Thus resolved, she sped up, striding with purpose across the plaza. It was a long walk. Jaed had chosen a table near the bulkhead, a freestanding unit that, from the bright lines on the decking, had been a meter closer to its neighbors in the very recent past. She pretended not to notice observers, or the sudden flicker of handhelds as diners adjusted their screens for potential 2Ds or perhaps even recordings. She smiled, just a little, as Zhang twitched toward a particularly quick movement, frightening the holder of the handheld into dropping his device and pushing his chair back a screeching half-meter.

Jaed stood, rather stiffly, to greet her. Rory noted that he held his right arm very carefully, as if the shoulder itself could not move, the hand curled into a solid fist. She noted the especial bulk of his sweater today, and how the knit and cable might conceal a wrap. She wondered where the alchemists were, and the chirurgeons, to leave him in such discomfort.

Perhaps *they* had not. Perhaps he had chosen it. Pride, perhaps.

He tried to come around the table, with obvious designs on pulling out her chair.

"I have it," she said, waving him off. "That's not a Tadeshi custom, is it?"

Jaed frowned at the chair, and at the Princess settling herself into it. Then he sat back down. "No. Yes. Only among the aristocracy. It's an archaism."

"Ah." Rory looked around at the neighboring tables. She glanced at Thorsdottir and Zhang, who were in the process of dragging an unoccupied table to a strategic point from which they could observe, and intercept, anyone approaching.

"It's the same on Thorne. An archaic custom. It's also rather widespread among the population at large, between those romantically associated, as a sign of regard." She folded her hands on the table and smiled. "On Kreshti, everyone oversees her own seating, unless one is an infant or an invalid."

She watched Jaed turning that over. "Neither of which applies to you."

"Indeed. Nor are we romantically associated. I prefer other demonstrations of regard."

His mouth—bruised and a little swollen, on the same side as the black eye—quirked up at the corner. "Such as?"

"First I must earn the regard, no?"

She sat back and looked around at the plaza. Then she whispered, under her breath, a tiny optical hex, which bent the light in her immediate vicinity in such a way that any images would be blurry. She whispered another, to introduce static to any recording.

Jaed watched her intently.

"You're doing it. Hexing. Arithmancy."

"I am."

"I can see the shimmer. What'd you do?" He smiled: a flash of real, unguarded delight.

Rory was startled by how young it made him seem. She found her own face responding, and admonished it to withdraw into cool dignity, with mixed results. "Gave us a little privacy, assuming no one's got hexes on their handhelds or a 'bot."

Jaed's face also appeared to have remembered its task as indifferent mask. He sat back. The smile settled into a crumpled little shadow of itself. "What a convenient
I want to learn that
skill."

Rory inclined her head, said nothing, and allowed him to interpret her silence in whatever manner he chose. She used the time to study his face. The bruise on his cheek was exquisite, appalling, like a storm boiling over the mountains, promising agricultural ruin in exchange for a pyrotechnic performance. His eye on that side was a little swollen and a lot bloodshot, and somewhat uncomfortable to look at.

So that was the eye on which she focused, until Jaed realized what she was doing, at which point he dropped his gaze.

She struck in that moment of self-conscious vulnerability. "What happened?"

Jaed, she saw, was undergoing the same dilemma: whether to put forth the polite untruth of *nothing*, or to tell her. She spared a moment's wish for the latter and a second moment to wonder why it mattered.

Then Jaed leaned forward onto his elbows (most of the weight on his left side), which brought their faces rather closer than any interpretation of etiquette would deem correct.

"Merrick and I had a fight. Over you, of course." Jaed's clear eye flashed like a mirror in sunlight. "He was embarrassed by our discussion yesterday. He thinks you're up to something."

"That's why he hit you? Because *I'm* up to something?"

"That, and he thinks it indicates a personal preference on your part."

"Why should that bother him?"

Jaed looked at her as if she had suddenly sprouted a live goose on the crown of her head. "He's jealous."

True, said the fairy gift.

There was another *why* trying to force its way past her lips. Rory swallowed it. She was familiar enough with popular literature to recognize that men were not so different from bulls or rams when it came to courtship, more concerned with each other's opinions than those belonging to the female of the species. Jaed would no more understand the *whys* of that than he would the intricacies of the arithmancy behind tesser-hex gate theory, and it would do little good to ask him.

But ancestors, that *bruise*. It was, upon more thorough inspection, scored with tiny striations, little stitches of blood holding the flesh together. Rory caught herself reaching for it. She stopped when she felt the heat coming off it and when Jaed visibly steeled himself.

"I won't touch it," she said, at the same time as he said,
"It's a carpet burn. I did it to myself, trying to get him off me."
He smiled. It looked like it hurt. "No luck."

"So he just hit you because, what, we talked?"

"Because I made him look bad. He thinks. He's just so damned
smug. He just assumed he'll get everything he wants." Then he
added, a little defensively, "You don't understand."

Rory made a very un-Princesslike noise. "You have not met *my*
brother. So who *won*?"

"Merrick." Jaed's gaze wandered away. "He's better than I am."

Etiquette, courtesy, *kindness* dictated she offer reassurance to
Jaed: tell him that Merrick was not better, that he was morally
deficient, a bully, that physical prowess was not the sum of a
man's worth.

The moment passed, and took a handful of its associates with
it. Jaed took a visible breath and refocused his attention on her. He
was really quite bad at masking his feelings. In that, he was entirely not his father's son.

That realization made her like him a little more.

Rory leaned forward and, before Jaed could flinch, broke her
promise and traced the edge of the bruise from his cheekbone to
the corner of his mouth. The skin felt both spongy and very hot.

Etiquette had a script for moments like this, too: queries so
obvious ("Does it hurt?") that their truth is never in question, designed to allow the responder to (re)assert his own manhood ("Oh,
it's not that bad.").

Jaed was braced, obviously, for one of those social stupidities.
Rory could see him preparing his own polite untruth, his stare
drilling past her, his jaw knotted tight enough she worried he
might crack his teeth.

She said nothing, and neither did Jaed.

She banished, in that moment, any lingering fantasies about Merrick Moss. Whatever the quality of his behavior toward her— courteous, even kind—this revealed another side of his nature.

That was disturbing. Even more disturbing, her whole chest felt hot. Her heart fluttered, too small for its boney cage, and her lungs felt squeezed into fists by the pressure of that heat. It was not affection. It was not sympathy. It was *anger.*

It was not at all in her plans.

Jaed cleared his throat, then, and sat back just out of reach, neither fast enough to be rude, nor far enough to declare her familiarity unwelcome. He folded his arms, very carefully, tucking the right fist underneath the left elbow.

"I got your message. *Obviously.* I took my pass-string out for a little test run."

She raised a brow. "And?"

Jaed shrugged, left-sided. "They haven't arrested me."

"Would your father do that?"

He thought about it. "He might, to make a point. But probably not. It might be too embarrassing to the family. You and I are an *item* now. People are watching."

"And everyone's going to say you and your brother fought over me."

"True." Jaed pulled out a very public smile, lips pulled back over his teeth, eyes wrinkled up at the edges. To observers, battling the blur of her hexes, he would seem genuinely happy. "I have something for you."

She matched his grin, and added a head-tilt. "Oh?"

Jaed shifted onto his elbows again. This time the right hand, still a clenched fist, migrated partway across the table. She noted the white knuckles, unmarked, that her bodyguards had noticed at once. Jaed hadn't landed a punch.

"Take my hand," he murmured. "The right one. Do it. Keep looking at me."

She slid her hands around his. His skin was cool, smooth, stretched rigid over tendon and bone. She noted the raised tendons in his wrist. Guessed there was muscle locked all the way up. "You holding a live fish?"

"What?" He blinked. The smile slipped a little, then recovered, teeth bared. "No. Here."

He twisted his fist in her grip, uncurling his fingers, rolling the tiny datastick from his palm into hers. "My father's code. I lifted it from some private correspondence between him and the Minister of War, so it's definitely his, not some secretary's."

Rory stifled her first impulse, which was to ask what the contents of that correspondence had been, and said instead, "Thank you."

Jaed's smile widened, as if she'd said something especially sweet. His eyes held all the warm malleability of diamonds. "My side of our deal," he said.

Rory flashed him the brightest, most practiced smile in her arsenal. Then she leaned back, taking her hand—and the datastick—with her. She thanked Ursan practicality that her trousers had pockets, easily reached when a young woman's hands retreated into her lap in a spasm of shyness, or propriety, or whatever an observer chose to interpret. She kept them there, glancing not at all surreptitiously around the plaza, before letting them creep back onto the table.

Empty, of course. Both of them. She let Jaed see that. His tiny, real smile reappeared for an instant, too small and too transient to be visible through the hex. That pleased her, for reasons she did not care to examine too closely.

"All right," she said. "Now it's my turn. We'll start simple. Have you ever seen an aura?"

CHAPTER FIFTEEN ≡≡≡

In Which A Plan Is Made

The semi-public liaisons between Jaed and Rory continued for a tenday before the Regent summoned Jaed to a meeting in his office. During that span, the Regent's second son and the Princess of Thorne conducted daily rendezvous, often for several hours at a time, to the delight of the public 'nets and the celebrity gossip channels, which speculated on the romance and on the Prince's eventual reaction, or whether he knew already, and how this whole business might resolve. The turing nets crackled with footage: 2Ds of the Princess and Jaed in the public dining plaza, live digital of them strolling through the station (attended by the Princess's guards, who, it was noted, no longer included the one with mecha parts).

There was much excitement about the nature and cause of Jaed's injuries, which faded from spectacular purple to a more cosmetically concealable green-yellow after several days (and several applications of alchemical lotions). So when Rory and Jaed appeared together at the public recreational facilities, where Jaed accepted lessons from the smaller of Rory's guards, the one obviously of Kreshti descent, public opinion declared that his injuries must have been the result of a training accident—perhaps with this very guard—which inspired further rumors of extensive private contact, of which the sudden publicity was only the latest stage.

The Regent had discovered Jaed's injuries along with the rest of Urse, when he saw the footage of his younger son and the Princess sharing a table in the dining plaza. He had watched, fingers steepled, eyes flat. Then he had sent Merrick a terse invitation for a brief before-supper meeting, in which he said only, "You will not assault your brother again. You will, in fact, avoid contact with him, and you are, under no circumstances, to be alone with him. Good night."

Jaed knew his brother had been summoned, and he knew exactly how long the meeting had taken (five minutes, fifteen seconds). Rory had shown him how to hex Merrick's pass-string, so that it reported his brother's movements to him.

"The better to avoid him," Rory had said, with a wry little half-smile.

And the better to spy on him, thought Jaed, and proceeded to do both.

Jaed guessed, from the meeting's brevity, that his brother had not been permitted to make any appeals or excuses. He also guessed, from Merrick's continued activities over the subsequent days, that he had garnered no punishment. That was cause for both relief and worry. Jaed was not eager for another encounter with Merrick, but he also did not trust his father's intervention. He told Rory as much, under his breath, when they met at the recreational facility the following afternoon.

"My father's up to something," he told the back of her hand, as he brushed his lips across it in a gesture performed especially for the recording devices they both knew were concealed in gym bags left carefully open, *just so*, all over the room.

Rory smiled. Jaed was beginning to dislike that particular expression. It reminded him of alchemically produced gemstones: beautiful, glittering, and ultimately artificial.

"Oh, I'm sure," she said, scarcely moving her lips. "What, though?"

"No idea." He released her hand, making note of her unscuffed knuckles. He supposed she was not allowed to train with her guards. He had, so far, only trained with Zhang, although today he was supposed to face Thorsdottir. He eyed her sidelong, and wondered if she would permit him to scuff his knuckles, or if she would beat him flat in front of everyone.

Thorsdottir let him get scuffed, as it turned out, and his knuckles were red and tender when his father's summons came.

At your earliest convenience, the message said, which was Father for *now*.

Jaed thought he knew why. Footage of his lesson with Thorsdottir had topped even the hand-kissing on the boards today. He had scanned through some of the comments and marveled at the sheer volume of experts in martial tactics living on the station. He wondered if Rory ever bothered to read the reviews of their performances, and what she thought about them.

He resolved to ask her, assuming his father didn't have him under house arrest by third shift. Jaed hadn't been confined to the family wing of the municipal section since the Arboretum Incident, which had cemented his father's suspicion that the practice of restricting a child's freedom as a means of punishment confers as much suffering on those who share quarters with the perpetrator. No. If his father knew he was learning arithmancy, Jaed reckoned he might well end up on a marine transport to some distant colony world. Or to Beo, with Prince Ivar, which would actually be worse, Prince Ivar being as stimulating as a sack of wet socks.

But his father *didn't* know. There was no way he could. The Regent was not omniscient, he was irritated, and therefore Jaed could expect a reprimand (not his first) and an extended period of his father's cold-as-void disapproval (also not his first), after a short treatment of sarcasm and withering disdain (the pattern holds here). All he had to do was endure it in silence, listen to his father's condemnation, avoid answering back.

He had never been good at listening.

Jaed cycled his turing down and checked himself for respectability. Then he took himself to his father's office. He could have gone the back way, using private corridors. He chose instead to take the longer, public route: out the main doors, across the promenade in front of the embassies, past a half-dozen 'bots, some of which belonged to Tadeshi security, some of which belonged to their respective embassies. He made a point of cutting close to the Thorne Consortium's embassy, within range of its 'bot. If his father did decide to discipline him by curtailing his freedom, he wanted a record on systems uncontrolled by the station's turing, so that Rory would know what had happened.

Jaed did not actually consider what Rory would do with such knowledge. He also did not examine too closely his own desire for her to think well of him. He especially did not consider whether or not she would actually *care* if he disappeared, beyond her own inconvenience.

He made a point of looking at the lens of Thorne embassy's 'bot, in passing. Then he passed out of its range, and into his father's domain.

The public wing of the municipal complex was predictably empty. It was perhaps two hours past the shift-change, too early for meal breaks, past the usual hours for official business. The transparent-walled offices were empty, reduced to dormant turings and desks in varying states of order. Jaed listened to the muffled echo of his boots on the decking. When he'd been small, he and Merrick had chased each other through the corridors, slapping their feet as loudly as possible, laughing, reveling in the echoes. The game always ended with misfortune, either in the person of one of the long line of grim nurses charged with managing their childhood, or with a slip on, and subsequent collision with, the deckplate. The latter tragedy had most often afflicted Jaed, as he was the smaller and less physically gifted.

Jaed eyed several places where the deckplate seemed a little darker, stained with youthful missteps, and stifled the urge to run through the corridors again. No doubt if he tried, security would converge in triplicate from one of the opaque offices that studded the corridor like missing teeth in a smile.

The three transparent walls of the Regent's office were unsurprisingly also dark, the alloy hexed to an impervious matte grey. The doors, however, sat partway open. It might have been an invitation, if the Regent were a different man. Instead, the gap looked to Jaed like a mouth, ready to snap shut. His father's secretary had already gone home. His desk was visible through the gap, empty and sterilely neat, as if the office had already eaten him.

Jaed knew his father was watching. The 'bot's unblinking black compound eye glittered over the doorway. The Regent was on the other side, probably frowning, waiting in a facsimile of patience for Jaed to come in.

For a handful of heartbeats, Jaed thought about turning around and walking out. See how far he got. See if he was faster now, if security came after him. But this was Urse, and a station does not offer much chance in the way of escape.

He stepped through the doors, and crossed the empty antechamber. The second set of doors, the one behind which his father waited, were closed. Another, identical 'bot stared from its perch above them. Jaed was unsurprised when the door did not open. The keypad glowed red for *locked*. His father would expect him to stop and request access, like any other subject seeking audience with the sitting substitute monarch.

Jaed closed his eyes, aware that his father would interpret the gesture as fear or hesitation, and practiced the simple hex Rory had taught him, summoning the symbols on the backs of his eyelids. They remained when he opened his eyes, ghost images marking the border between the layers of aether. He took a last breath and shifted his awareness across that border.

Then he touched the keypad, producing a subdued chime.

The doors slid apart, silent as judgment.

"Jaed," said the Regent. "Come in."

Jaed did so, and for the first time, looked at his father through an arithmancer's eyes.

Rory had told him it was a simple hex, both in execution and in results. Auras were merely indicators of a person's emotional state, faint bands of color that varied in intensity based on the subject, the subject's mood, the arithmancer, and the amount of ambient light.

"It's not very impressive," she'd told him, when he'd tried it out that afternoon. "I hope you aren't too disappointed."

He hadn't been, his delight so obvious that Rory's own aura had picked up and reflected his enthusiasm, in shimmering bands of blue, purple, turing-text cyan. Thorsdottir's aura had been less enthusiastic, a vivid and disapproving sienna, which only grew brighter when Jaed had grinned at her. Zhang's had been cooler, muted, exactly what Jaed expected to see from his father, who was the coldest person Jaed knew.

So his first glimpse of his father's aura startled him: a pyrotechnic display of jagged orange, shot with unhealthy pinks. Jaed had a moment to contemplate it before a slick void of bottomless black devoured the aura and slammed him out of the hex, settling reality over him with a jolt that made his teeth ache.

A counter-hex. Of course his father had counter-hexes. Stupid to imagine otherwise. But instructive, too: orange was agitated, pink was the border of real upset, and their brightness indicated that the Regent was very distressed, indeed.

Though he didn't *look* distressed. He sat behind his desk, his cheeks and chin limned green from the turing's screen, his eyes as cold and distant as the planet hanging outside the porthole.

"Sit down," he said.

Jaed shook his head. He locked his hands behind his back to keep them still. His throat, arid with this unaccustomed defiance, snagged his voice on the way out and tore it ragged. "I'd rather stand."

The Regent nodded slowly, as if an invisible someone were murmuring expected information into his ear. "Then by all means, remain standing. Do you know why you are here?"

Jaed knew this ritual, the rules, the inevitable conclusion. He must confess—fault, error, accident, poor judgment. A tiny upwell of anger trickled from his belly, burning the back of his throat.

He lifted the uninjured shoulder, a gesture calculated to irritate with its apparent carelessness. "No, sir."

The Regent blinked. "Do you imagine that I am a fool, Jaed?"

"No, sir."

"Good. Then I choose to believe that you are not, either. I wish to discuss your new relationship with Rory Thorne." The second brow climbed to meet its fellow. "Unless you expect me to believe you two have been carrying on some secret liaison, prior to the Vizier's arrest?"

Jaed frowned. He wished he had the courage to say, *believe what you like*. Instead, he said nothing.

His father's mouth turned up in humorless smile. "Your brother believes you've been sneaking about, outwitting us both."

"Maybe I have."

"I thought we agreed there are no fools in this room." The Regent leveled his brows and leaned forward on his desk, hands folded neatly, calmly, as if he were discussing a dinner menu. "I was beginning to believe the Princess was plotting something truly worrisome, even without the Vizier. Instead, she has behaved, if not predictably, at least conventionally. She's looking for an ally. She chose you."

The Regent laid the very slightest emphasis on the last word, almost imperceptible, unless the listener was a younger son attuned to a father's disapproval. Jaed was prepared to hear it and for the familiar ache in his chest. He clung to his anger like a drowning man clings to a broken plank, believing himself saved even as the sea's chill soaks into blood and bone.

"Let Merrick beat me again. Maybe she'll change her mind."

The Regent smiled, all the way to both sides of his mouth. "She won't. Your defeat made her *more* inclined to you, but that only works once. If it becomes a regular occurrence, her pity will turn into contempt."

Jaed's ribcage, which had constricted alarmingly around his heart and lungs, expanded. Air rushed into his lungs, lingered a moment, and rushed out again, bypassing his wits entirely. "She doesn't pity me."

"Of course she does. You should thank Merrick for that. Now she sees him as a bully, and I don't believe she'll ally with someone she despises, no matter what it gains for her. The Princess is a clever girl, but she is not her mother."

Jaed ground his teeth together. He could feel the anger rearranging his features, stretching the healing bruise, cracking the scabs on his lips. He told himself he would say *nothing*, that that was always how his father won, that *he* would win this time. He reminded himself that his father, for all his appearance, was also upset. Those orange spikes in his aura might be because Jaed had surprised him, because Merrick had disappointed him, because he needed the weaker of his sons when he would prefer the stronger.

The Regent nodded, as if Jaed has spoken aloud. He leaned back and examined his younger son with the same detachment as a sculptor confronted with a flawed block of marble. "She chose you," he said again. "We shall have to work with that."

Jaed pressed his lips together. He tasted blood from the split, and added to it, biting hard on the half-healed wound. Then he raised his chin, and met his father's eyes, and asked, in a solid approximation of composure, "Work with me how, exactly?"

"Well. You tell me. What does Rory want from you? Or rather, what does she think you can do for her?"

"She hasn't asked for anything."

"Jaed." The Regent shook his head. "No fools in this room."

"She wanted me to ask you to release the Vizier. I told her you wouldn't listen to me."

"And she said?"

Please, *please*, the 'bots could not record auras. Rory had told him lies showed glowing and toxic green.

"That I was her only hope. That she would do anything I asked."

The Regent blinked. "And what have you asked for, so far?"

Jaed said nothing, very carefully. He did not blink, very carefully. He dragged the corner of his mouth back and up into an unkind, knowing smirk, and tasted fresh blood.

The Regent made a sound like a leaky airlock. "Perhaps she is more like her mother than I thought." He tapped his first two fingers together. "So, having delivered her side of the bargain—she did, I presume? Yes. So. She will expect you to make your request to me. Which you are doing, right now."

Jaed side-eyed the 'bot on the top of the bookshelf, a matte black geometric wedged between a leatherbound copy of Herrick's *Treatise on the Rights of Kings* and a mirri gazing-globe. He fancied he could see his own reflection, and hoped he looked cooler than he felt.

"Does that mean you'll release the Vizier?"

The Regent looked at Jaed for a long moment. "What use would she have for you," he said finally, "if she got what she wanted?"

"What use will she have for me if I can't deliver?"

"You will. We simply need her to realign her desires in a more appropriate direction. I believe Ivar should return from Beo to begin preparations for his coronation and his marriage. He needs to acquaint himself with his future queen." He looked at Jaed and waited.

Be quiet, be quiet, be—

"How will *that* help? She'll just ask *him* to help her, and what if he says 'release the Vizier?'"

"Jaed." The Regent raised his eyes ceilingward for a moment, then closed them, and waited through a pair of breaths. "Do you think Rory wants to marry Ivar?"

"No. But he's the Prince, she has no choice—and I think she *will*, regardless. Especially if he'd get the Vizier for her."

"There will be no Vizier to get," the Regent said, in exactly the same tone as he might pronounce on the wetness of water. He gathered his lips into a razor-edged moue. "Rory is a devious girl. She intends for you to care for her, do you see? To bear for her some affection. You two have made quite a spectacle of yourselves. How much of that is genuine, Jaed?"

Jaed swallowed. Shrugged, while his eyes slid sideways. *Treatise on the Rights of Kings*. Mirri gazing ball. A red leather-bound book with Kreshti script. He clenched his bruised knuckles.

"Ah. I see. You believed her, didn't you? Thought she was growing fond of you? That is what she wants." The Regent sounded like he was smiling, as if each word were silk, slipping through his teeth. "And so, we will let her believe she is succeeding. You will rescue her, Jaed, from Ivar."

It was an absurd idea. Jaed couldn't rescue himself from Merrick. And Rory had Zhang and Thorsdottir and *Grytt*. Rory had herself, for that matter. Ivar might need rescuing, if he laid hands on Rory Thorne.

If she protested, which she wouldn't, if they married. He could picture the look, that grim set to her mouth, like the one with which she'd propositioned him, a mere tenday ago, which he had not seen on her mouth since. That had been *desperation*, with a liberal strand of *hope*. He imagined that expression settling into her face, soaking into her eyes, becoming *duty*.

Jaed's stomach did a fair approximation of a singularity, drawing into a single point of bile, sucking all the air out of his lungs until his heart flopped and hammered in his throat. His cheeks burned.

The Regent watched him closely, a tiny, malevolent pleasure flickering through his pale eyes like light over ice. "I think," he said after a moment, "we can agree, you and I, that the royal marriage should not take place."

And, by extension, neither should the coronation. *That* was treason. That was also, when Jaed thought about it, not much of a revelation. He'd *known* his father was ambitious, and he'd never actually been able to imagine Ivar on the Tadeshi throne.

That spot had always been Merrick's. Except that *Merrick* would need Rory to hold a royal seat. And Merrick didn't *have* her. *Neither do you. She doesn't love you.*

But that didn't matter, did it? She needed him, or at least his influence. She had sought him out for that very reason. And if *if, remember that, if*

his father was correct, and Rory saw him as nothing more than a tool, well, he did not need to concern himself with *her* feelings. And if she actually liked him—that did not need to change. She would prefer him to Ivar. She had to.

Jaed's future, newly imagined, shuddered and split. Suddenly there were new vectors, new possibilities. He closed his eyes. The memory of the hex equations lingered on the backs of his eyelids, almost too faint to read.

"Are you listening to me, Jaed?"

He opened his eyes, and for the first time, met his father's gaze without fear.

"Yes."

CHAPTER SIXTEEN ═══════

In Which Plans Change Abruptly

Grytt was not often surprised, either by circumstance or by human behavior. But when she encountered Jaed Moss lurking in a side corridor, out of which he came more quickly than prudence might indicate, she was surprised in both senses.

The mecha eye made note of him first, flashing red threat on its HUD, reporting speed and trajectory that suggested a body *approximately one-point-eight meters tall and seventy-odd kilograms, probability: male* coming at her out of a passage that, at this point in second shift, was always empty. Although her endocrine system responded with increased adrenaline and accelerated heartbeat, Grytt did not jump back or cry out. She did as her training and habit dictated, and struck first: to pin the assailant to the wall with momentum and metal, reserving an option to inflict further harm.

Jaed would have acquired several new bruises, at the least, and some time with the chirurgeons, at the worst, had her mecha eye not identified him *Moss, Jaed* before impact. She promptly downgraded him from *threat* to *nuisance* and arrested her own forward motion in the same moment.

Jaed, to his credit, took a step back and raised both hands, palms out, presumably in some attempt to reassure her that he was no threat. Or perhaps he had realized exactly how close he'd come to making intimate acquaintance with the bulkhead. Both things were true.

There were protocols for addressing the Regent's offspring. Honorifics. Rupert would know what they were, but Rupert was where he'd been for the past twenty days, locked in solitary detention and beyond anyone's asking. That knowledge did not predispose Grytt to patience.

"What do you want?" she snapped.

The younger Moss boy blinked, clearly unaccustomed to being addressed in that manner. Then he tipped his head sideways, back down the corridor from which he'd emerged so precipitously.

"Can we step back a little bit? I've disabled the 'bots in this corridor."

Grytt forbore the obvious *how*. She guessed Jaed was putting his new, unhexed pass-string to good use. Or rather, to some use, the goodness of which was subject to debate. This was, after all, the Regent's younger son inviting her into an unmonitored patch of naked decking and bulkhead, into which he expected her to go on his assurance. She was not concerned for her safety. She could see, with the mecha eye, that the corridor was empty and devoid of hatches, doorways, or other strategic openings that might conceal a triad of Tadeshi security. But she did not have Rory's fairy gift, and she smelled *trap*.

She shook her head. "We can talk here."

Jaed closed both eyes. His jaw clenched. Then he took a visible breath and looked at her again. Credit to the boy: he did not flinch from her face.

"We can't. We could be seen."

"Better to be alone with the boy chasing Rory, then. Me. The Kreshti mecha-maid. That won't seem suspicious, especially when you reappear with new bruises."

Jaed blinked again. "No," he said. "I mean." He licked his lip again, and shook his head. "I'm not trying to set you up. I'm trying to warn you."

"Why?"

He retreated a step into the passage, where, presumably, the 'bots would not be watching. "You're supposed to say, about what?"

Grytt slid a foot closer to the passage and pitched her voice to follow him. "And I'm saying, why warn me, and not the Princess?"

Unless, she thought, sudden and horrible. Her mecha hand whined into a fist. "Has something happened to Rory?"

Jaed turned a visible two shades more pale. "She's fine! As far as I know, she's *fine*. I came to you because I knew you'd be here, now, coming back from the detention block, and I can't just walk into the Thorne compound and demand an audience. Thorsdottir would kill me."

"So I'm less terrifying and more convenient than Thorsdottir?"

"Rory can't know. If she does, she'll do something stupid. Now will you *listen*?"

"'S what I'm doing," said Grytt. "Start talking. My lord."

Heat flowed across his cheeks, settling on the points of the Moss trademark cheekbones. Handsome boy, Grytt thought, and wasn't sure whether it was boon or curse that he did not share his father's intellect.

"My father thinks." Jaed looked up as if reading a script off the ceiling. "He thinks Rory's trying to use me to get the Vizier released. So he wants the Vizier gone. Off Urse. There's a shuttle set to depart for Beo during third shift. The Vizier will be on it."

Grytt grimaced. Of course, that made sense. One did not just *kill* a Vizier and ambassador from a recent enemy with whom the treaty ink (metaphorically speaking) was scarcely dry. And one did not deport him, either, when doing so would put him right back in Samur's confidence, her court, her bed. But:

"Why move him now?"

Jaed generated a grimace comparable to anything Grytt's own features could manage. His fingers flexed, clenching on air. "My father thinks Rory's using me to get media attention. That she's going to make some public appeal for the Vizier's freedom and he'll have to *do* something. And she's popular, so if he says no, he'll look bad."

"He cares what the public thinks?"

Jaed regarded her with surprising seriousness. "He does. He has to."

And the Regent's solution to Rory's popularity was to send the Vizier to Beo before Rory could ask for anything. Assuming, of course, he arrived at all, and did not suffer an accident like Ivar's mother, whose shuttle had joined the glittering dust rings around the darker Brother. Grytt had investigated the official reports. Accident, they called it. Mechanical failure, exactly the sort that regular maintenance was meant to prevent. Grytt supposed Tadeshi mechanics made mistakes only when the passengers were more convenient dead than alive.

Which Rupert would be. Grytt glanced both ways. No one coming, either direction, and the 'bot at the corridor's end was angled at the main thoroughfare and the second shift public. She closed the gap between herself and Jaed mecha-quick, fetching up damn near on his toes. She thrust her face into his.

"What do you think I'm going to do? Storm the docks? Conduct a jailbreak? Ambush the guards when they transport him? You think I'm that stupid, my lord?"

Give the boy still more credit: he flinched, but he did not even break eyelock. His throat moved. He moved his right arm—slowly, very slowly—and lifted a tiny datastick between their two faces. "This is my father's pass-string."

She cocked her head, eyeing the datastick like a bird examining a particularly unappetizing insect. "What am I supposed to do with that? Besides get myself arrested. You notice I don't look much like the Regent."

"The 'bots won't record you."

Rupert would know if that were true, or even possible. *Rory* would know. Grytt wished for both of them, and added a wish for fresh strawberries, while she was at it, for all the good wishes would do.

She snorted. "Oh, so it's a *magic* pass-string."

"It's my *father's*," Jaed said. "He doesn't like the 'bots recording his movements."

Grytt had little doubt of that; a man of Vernor Moss's political ambition would require secrecy. She was also in little doubt that the laws of the Free Worlds frowned upon clandestine, off-record movements of its highest ranking officials. She harbored *many* doubts that his younger son would have gotten his hands on it unnoticed, unless Moss was a great deal less careful than she thought. Or Jaed was a great deal more clever.

Jaed interpreted her silence as a prequel to acquiescence. "The detention block's guarded. That might be tough to manage. But the shuttle's docked in R-5. No security until they bring the Vizier in."

"How many crew on the shuttle?"

"One pilot."

"And how many security?"

"Three's standard."

Grytt raised her eyebrow. "The *Vizier* is a standard prisoner?"

"He's high profile, but he's not *dangerous.*"

That was certainly true. Rupert was not a violent man. He was extremely unlikely to intimidate a pilot into taking him somewhere other than Beo, even if Grytt put a 'slinger in his hand and glued his finger to the trigger.

"The Vizier's no pilot. Neither am I."

"The shuttle's got a smart turing. The Vizier could use that to get off the station. Hex it."

Oh, boy. If you think arithmancy is some kind of magic, you will be sorely disappointed. Grytt didn't say it. Nor did she reach for the data-stick.

Instead, she ran the calculations in her head. If Rupert could hex the turing and get the shuttle to the edge of the system, he could message one of the Consortium warships patrolling the border. They could come get him. Transfer him. Leave the Tadeshi personnel and equipment unharmed. *If* she could subdue them without being identified. *If* she could convince Rupert to leave Rory on Urse.

Grytt set the collections of ifs aside. Rupert was the arithmancer. She had a soldier's mathematical sense that measured force and strategy, and in that, the numbers came down in her favor as long as they were on Urse. But:

"What stops your station from shooting the shuttle down the minute it clears the station?"

"That pass-string. The station will log my father on board. The shuttle's military. It doesn't have to clear through the usual channels."

"Well," said Grytt. "You've thought of everything. Except why I should believe you."

Jaed's face tightened, pulling swollen flesh white and tight over bone. The scab on his lip cracked again with the force of his scowl. "I'm not lying to you. I don't want Rory to get hurt. Losing the Vizier will do that."

Grytt had no fairy gifts. She had often pitied Rory for hers. Now, she began to see the usefulness. Rory's well-being might be a genuine concern to him, but Grytt could think of half a dozen ulterior, parallel, and subordinate motives that had everything to do with what was best for Jaed.

Grytt *was* certain that her presence, and Rupert's, were perceived as impediments to the Regent's control over Rory, and by extension, to any influence Jaed might hope to wield. Their disappearance, together, would be seen as good fortune, a gift from the multiverse.

Grytt was a woman committed to her own survival; no one survives battles and bombs and the hex-grafts of mecha parts who is not. She had also spent her adult life in occupations in which her life was not always her priority. But since her own tasks were better accomplished *alive*, she was expected to exercise good judgment in the risks to which she exposed herself.

In her judgment, Jaed Moss was, if not a *bad* man exactly, not a strong one, either, and not the brightest star in the firmament. Were it only her welfare at stake, she would walk away. But there was Rupert, who, if Jaed told the truth, would be beyond reach and rescue in very short order, and, if Grytt had to lay odds, not long for this life after that. This would be the only opportunity to retrieve him.

And there was Rory, the other variable in the equation, the most important, whose health and happiness were Grytt's concern in equal measure. Rory would, if Grytt reported Jaed's offer, insist on effecting a rescue. Rory would, if Jaed subsequently offered her the pass-string, attempt the rescue herself, citing the same reasons: they would not have another chance like this, and Rupert would die if they didn't act.

Grytt was certain the Princess of Thorne must not be apprehended with the Regent's pass-string, attempting to hijack a shuttle and rescue the Vizier. That sort of incident could rekindle a war, or win from Samur concessions detrimental to the Consortium. So if Jaed was lying, well, better it be Grytt caught up in it. If she ended up in a cell beside Rupert, then Rory would have an opportunity to play hero and rescue them both.

Grytt plucked the datastick out of Jaed's fingers with her own, original set. For a moment their skin touched. His, she noted, was cold and clammy, with what was almost certainly nervous sweat. That made perfect sense. He was betraying someone. She just didn't know who.

Grytt was pleasantly surprised when she arrived at the R-dock without having encountered Tadeshi security. She was delighted when, upon her entering the pass-string, the door marked *Restricted* slid open with a pneumatic sigh and no further protest. She had expected klaxons at least.

She couldn't tell if the 'bots were awake and aware and merely ignoring her, or if they were napping; but the continued absence of security lent credence to Jaed's claim.

The third option—that security was already waiting in the dock—seemed much more in line with her customary expectations of Moss trustworthiness.

Whatever Jaed's ultimate intention, he had directed her to an entrance at the high-numbered end of the R-wing. It was a long walk to R-5. She checked, for the third time, her regulation (and thus underpowered) 'slinger, and kept to the edges of the corridor, to maximize her own angles should the ambush arrive sooner than the shuttle bay. The doors, pocked at uneven intervals along the bulkhead, accreted in her wake, each one a potential source for the enemy. She resisted the urge to keep checking back over her shoulder, and relied upon her senses, both mecha and meat, to warn her.

It was a little funny, how fast she fell back into wartime thinking. She had been Rory's age when she had fought her first skirmishes against pirates, and it had been nearly that many years since her last real combat. Her opportunities for action in the Tadeshi War as body-maid to a child-Princess had been limited to particularly rough games of hide-and-go-seek in which Rory, at Grytt's encouragement, learned to set traps.

It felt a little like that now, creeping along these passages, caught in the strange certainty that she would, in fact, be surprised. She could only hope that she had enough warning to act, rather than react. On her side were the hyper-awareness of adrenaline and the HUD in her eye scrolling a litany of sit-reps. The ancestors, too, maybe, if they hadn't washed their hands of her years ago.

On the opposition's side—well. Everything else.

R-5 arrived, finally, a lone door in a wide expanse of naked bulkhead, offering a hint to the size of the space on the other side. A shuttle bay or a storage vault. Or perhaps, Grytt thought, a room of Tadeshi security, all set and aimed at the door.

She tilted the mecha half of her head toward the metal. The audio reported nothing unusual: the faint echoes of ventilation, the hiss of Grytt's own breath through carefully reconstructed nasal passages, the nostrils of which flared wide in an old human reflex, held over from days in which danger carried a recognizable scent. Now she smelled the deliberate nothing of station aether, scrubbed clean by ventilators and alchemical hexes.

Grytt hesitated, turning the datastick over and over. Then she pushed it into the keypad, and flattened against the bulkhead, and was grateful her mecha hand did not sweat on the butt of the 'slinger. The door opened promptly into a small, metal room, with an identical set of doors on the other side. A tesla blinked expectantly on the interior door.

An aetherlock. This was, indeed, a shuttle bay. And past the second set of inner doors, which opened just as easily, sat the shuttle.

It was a medium-small craft, perhaps ten meters long, and a third that high. Wedge-nosed, angular, unlovely, its belly swollen with subcutaneous shafts terminating in neat, angled holes. And there, on the top: a bristling nest of sensors, like cat whiskers. Grytt was not familiar with the model, but the type, oh, she knew that very well. A troop transport, designed for a single pilot, who would guide the craft from an aether-sealed, armored forward compartment, unreachable from the interior cabin during flight. The shuttle's otherwise smooth lines were marred by raised metal ridges, where internal irises could, and would, cinch shut in case of hull breach.

The whole thing looked a little bit like an insect. A mecha insect. Probably a wasp, Grytt thought sourly, or some other stinging, biting representative of the genus. There, at the rear, if one wished to press the visual metaphor, if not the functional, was the stinger: the ramp extended, the rear iris open and withdrawn into the frame of the shuttle.

Grytt stepped into the bay. The inner hatch closed behind her. Nothing happened, for long enough that she became convinced that she was, indeed, alone. She raised the 'slinger anyway, and linked the HUD in her eye to its targeting system. Then she took a five-minute approach to the rear of the shuttle.

It was empty. It was also not *entirely* a troop transport, any longer. The interior furnishings had been changed. There was an apparatus which looked like a coffin, clamped to the deck and tilted upright, with a transparent plate across what would be the upper third of a resident's torso, with a complicated array of gauges, pads, and teslas studding its exterior. It was currently open, its interior teslas dim. A set of cables, each as thick as Grytt's forearm, ran from strategic points on the not-really-coffin into what appeared to be a generator grafted onto the shuttle's bulkhead. Its teslas glowed a serene, steady blue and emitted a faint electromagnetic hum. It was, to Grytt's reckoning, an entirely separate power unit, independent of the shuttle's own systems. Interesting. A substantial power source meant for a device that would, when activated, require constant, uninterrupted current. Upon closer examination of the hardware, she discovered not one, but four distinct temperature gauges, three of which concerned themselves with ranges more suited to preserving ice than flesh.

Had Grytt been an alchemist or an arithmancer or some other learned expert in the associated fields, she would have concluded that this could not in fact be a cryostasis unit: everyone knew it was impossible to make one this compact. Fortunately, however, Grytt was less concerned with *possible* than *right here in front of me*. She recalled that Moss had commandeered and relocated to Beo a cryostasis project, and that this shuttle was a refitted military unit based in that very place. And finally, Jaed had insisted that Rupert would have a standard escort, which was far better explained by a cryostasis unit than a belief in the Vizier's capacity (or lack thereof) for personal violence. A frozen arithmancer was no threat at all.

Grytt harbored a suspicion of any technology which appeared magical in its deployment, and which had not been tested by seven wars and seven hundred years, or at least someone whose opinion she trusted. This contraption might well be Rupert's new prison, if it did not kill him on freezing. Or thawing, assuming Moss bothered with it. It might be simpler to keep the Vizier in stasis indefinitely.

Grytt distrusted assumptions only slightly less than she distrusted embryonic technology. And still, she recalled Rory's own hunch, that Ivar's location and disposition were Beo and in cryostasis, respectively. It looked more likely, now. She was still not inclined to visit the place and confirm the suspicion.

Rupert, of course, would find it all *fascinating*. He would probably want to examine the unit. He'd be trying to figure out how it worked right up until it *did* work and arrested his wonderings altogether.

Grytt resolved that wouldn't happen. Not if she had to sabotage the unit herself, which—

The aetherlock clicked. The door whispered to itself, sliding along its track, held its breath, then whispered itself closed again.

—would wait until she'd dispatched the new arrivals.

Grytt settled her own silhouette in the deep shadow cast by the cryotube. The remaining seats, by virtue of their military shape and utility, included ample storage capacity underneath. Grytt was slightly larger than a duffel, but she was infinitely more flexible, and it did not matter if her bottom third blocked the aisles or not. She flattened onto her chest, belly, and hips, cocked a knee sideways, and sighted down the length of her 'slinger. The mecha eye attempted to acquire a target in what it identified as an empty expanse of hangar. A crate, an oddly-shaped shadow, the bright line between deckplate and bulkhead—

And there: a pair of boots, accompanied by legs and pelvis and, yes, finally a torso. The point man. Like all Tadeshi in Grytt's immediate experience—which is to say, those serving as station security, rather than as infantry—he wore a black uniform composed of a light anti-ballistic weave, but no real body armor, and no helmet. He was armed with the standard issue Tadeshi 'slinger, larger than her own, but still a sidearm model. And of course, he had two partners.

Thus she was outnumbered and outgunned, but not significantly so. She engaged that most useful of skills, patience, and waited. Number One crossed fully into her sights before the second appeared, and then the third, holding between them a tall, narrow figure in a shapeless coverall the color of four-day-old porridge.

Grytt's human heart—surprisingly sturdy, having survived the blast that killed Rory's father, almost unique among her organs to have done so—flopped against her composite ribcage. She had known very well Rupert was alive and unharmed; but the visual confirmation made her very glad of the mecha hand's immunity to foolish, unnecessary physiological responses. *It* stayed steady, while her wits recovered (it did not take long) sufficiently to observe Rupert's condition more thoroughly.

His face was obscured by a holographic static veil, projecting from the collar around his neck. Grytt could hear the sonics from across the hangar. Buzzing, crackling, whining at a pitch that seemed to get between her teeth and her jaw and vibrate.

Anti-arithmantic measures, she surmised, and noted that his lateral escorts each had a hand on him, though not tightly. For partial guidance, rather than support, which meant he must have limited audio and visual capacity.

She hoped it would be enough, coupled with his native wits, to get him on the ground when the firing started, before a bolt achieved the same effect. Both guards wore their sidearms on their free side, which suggested that, should a firefight occur, neither would be hindered in participating, except by Rupert's physical presence. How much that mattered to them was not something Grytt wished to discover.

She adjusted her HUD to a smaller target, entirely unarmored, let all her breath go, and fired the split instant she got lock.

The first bolt planted itself in a strategically vulnerable area of the point man's cranium, producing a brilliant spray of fluid that hissed as it passed through the Vizier's veil. That sufficed more than any shout might have to warn him to reduce his own silhouette. He dropped, nearly as fast as the stricken point man, to a prudently prone position. His security were unconcerned with his sudden movement, having their own attention occupied by this change to their reality. That they had been attacked was fairly obvious; but such a realization, while easy to make, is harder to resolve, particularly when the mind attempting that resolution is stuck on what is believed impossible versus what is actually happening.

The nearer Tadeshi resolved his situation rather more quickly than Grytt would have wished, and, having dived for cover behind his deceased comrade, proceeded to sling a pair of bolts at the open back of the shuttle. One of them bored through the seatback above her. The other ricocheted off the bulkhead twice before exhausting its momentum and clattering to the decking. Grytt, herself occupied with sudden adjustments, fired at the far security and took his leg out from under him, clipping his calf and spinning him back and away from Rupert. Not the target she'd intended, but the result was sufficient.

Grytt fired again, this time for cover, and scrabbled into the wedge of shadow beside the cryostasis unit. She wormed herself flat against the bulkhead's curve. Another brace of bolts gouged the decking where Grytt's face and torso had been.

That made four. Two more, and the shooter would need to re-load, unless the man she'd dropped was *also* firing, in which case—

Two more bolts entered the shuttle in rapid succession, from different vectors.

To hell with counting. Grytt held her breath, and primed her 'slinger, and very carefully walked her right fingers blind up the cryotube until she felt the panel's smooth polyplate. Memory told her there were three buttons. She felt her way across them. One. Two. Three. She had no idea in what order they should be pressed to activate the unit, or in fact what their purpose was.

She pressed them all.

The unit beeped, loudly, and Grytt dove across the shuttle, be-hind the already perforated seats, as two sets of 'slingers unloaded again, this time punching holes into the cryotube, which promptly commenced wailing and flashing two colors of light and spraying crystalline plumes of coolant across the shuttle's interior. The am-bient temperature plunged into a credible imitation of Midwinter at the Thorne palace, complete with spitting precipitation and treachery underfoot.

Grytt's human eye prudently closed. Her mecha eye, unblink-ing, adjusted its perception from the now obscured, convention-ally visible spectrum into the longer bands. The two Tadeshi—and Rupert—were bright and hot through the cloud. She knelt and shot at the nearest, one-two-three, into his chest. The resulting spray from his body cooled to rapid invisibility.

The far security, the one she'd only winged, steadied himself on his knee and aimed at her, clued in by muzzle-flash. She launched herself for the far front corner, where the angle of door and bulkhead might offer her some cover.

Her foot stepped squarely into a smear of coolant and crystal-lized water vapor. She had a moment to register *I'm slipping* and employed it to turn her shoulder and retain her grip on the 'slinger, in contravention of reflexes which would have dropped the 'slinger to prevent the subsequent teeth-rattling impact with the deck-plate. She spun mid-air, landing meat-side down on shoulder and elbow, and skidded gracelessly across the open deck before her hip came down and friction stopped her, fortunately short of a cranial impact with the wall, and unfortunately far short of the any cover, and *most* unfortunately, on her side facing *away* from the shuttle hatch.

The coolant chose that moment to exhaust itself. The last traces of it drifted down, riding aether gone suddenly still. Grytt had a clear view of the emergency kit bolted to the shuttle bulk-head, and the placard with pictographic instructions for what to do in case of rapid depressurization.

At least I won't have to deal with that, she thought. Her back was exposed, the coolant's foggy shield was *gone,* and—

There came a single, decisive shot. Then a second and third, in rapid succession. A man shouted, or tried to: the utterance turned rapidly soggy, ending on a gurgle.

Grytt blinked at the emergency kit. Her body registered no damage. *She* wasn't bleeding. Interesting. She rolled over, driving her mecha knee into the decking for leverage, and came up ready to fire.

The Tadeshi were all down. Rupert was picking himself up, two knees and one hand for balance. In the other, he held a 'slinger. The collar, unfastened, dangled from his neck. He peered at the shuttle.

"Grytt! For the love of—*Grytt,* are you all right?"

"I just started a war," Grytt said, standing up. "I hope you're happy." She picked her way down the ramp, careful of the glassy smears of liquid.

"Horrified. Thank you." He looked at the 'slinger, and at his hands, and then at his coveralls. Then he put the weapon down, very slowly. "You're not hurt?"

"No. Thanks to you." She holstered her 'slinger and, with both hands, twisted the collar the rest of the way off Rupert's neck. She turned it in her hands.

"You got this off?"

Rupert touched the raw patches on his neck where the collar had been. "Evidently."

"Mm." She dropped it to the deck and stomped on it with the mecha foot, hard enough to rattle her own teeth. "There."

Rupert stared at her, blinking rapidly. His eyes were red-rimmed and a little swollen. "I may have killed someone."

"You did."

"Oh," he said, faintly.

Grytt grabbed a fistful of coverall at his shoulder and hauled him upright. Then she shoved him, gently, toward the shuttle.

"We've got to go."

She jogged across the hangar to the aetherlock, jammed the pass-string into it, and keyed it to *sealed*. Turned back and saw Rupert standing there, eyes closed, chin raised, as if he were looking up at the inside of his own skull. He was an arithmancer. He might be doing just that.

"The lock won't hold," she said. "Not forever. There're probably eleven alarms going off right now. *Move*, Rupert."

He opened his eyes. "And go where?"

"Into the shuttle. Come on." She paused only long enough to scoop up the Tadeshi 'slingers. She shoved two of them into her waistband, which exhausted the fabric's ability to accommodate stolen weapons, and held the third loosely in her left hand. Her right, she used to take Rupert's elbow and half-steer, half-drag him up the ramp. He had never been a bulky man, but his bones felt sharp under her hands. "Didn't they feed you?"

"I wasn't especially hungry. Grytt. I repeat: *where* are we going?"

"Off Urse. Shuttle's set for Beo. We're not going there." She waved the datastick at him. "Moss's pass-string. It will get us past Control. Make sure they don't shoot us down. We get to the system's edge, we can signal one of our ships. Might take it awhile to get the message and come through the gate, but I don't see much choice."

"And how will we do any of that?"

"There's a smart turing in the cockpit. You can hack it. Can't you?"

"Let us hope so." He squeezed his eyes closed, as if against a particularly bright light. "We can't come back here. To Urse."

"No."

His eyes opened. His gaze this time was clear and sharp, like razor glass. "And what about Rory?"

Grytt hesitated. Then she peeled out a layer of truth, and said, "She'd've come herself, if I would've told her. Which I didn't."

He drew a breath, held it, hissed it through his nose. Anger and anguish fought for supremacy across his features, twisting lips and pinching nostrils and sending his brows crashing together and retreating again.

Grytt offered a sympathetic grimace. Then she got on with the business of making their escape. She cycled the door seal. The ramp rose slowly, eclipsing the carnage in the hangar, reminding her of closing jaws. Not a comforting thought. Not one she would share with Rupert.

The shuttle shuddered. The interior lights dimmed and shifted, lighting along the creases of bulkhead and deck, bulkhead and ceiling, casting the whole space into muted greens and yellows.

The engines. The *pilot*.

She bolted for the cockpit hatch, splattering puddles of fully liquid coolant underfoot, and, upon arrival (a coolant-assisted skid-slam into the bulkhead) stabbed the datastick into the pad. She had grown accustomed to the immediate, compliant green. The pad remained stubbornly red. The iris remained closed, squeezed tight like an eye against bright light.

Or a fist. Grytt punched the hatch, mecha to metal. The impact sent warning twinges along every hex-point that anchored alchemy to flesh. The door sported knuckle-shaped gouges. Her metal knuckles sported door-colored scuffs.

"That won't help," murmured Rupert.

"There's no one in there. I *checked*."

"Of course there is. The turing." He shouldered her aside; or rather, he inserted himself beside her and waited. He could no more move her than a sheet of paper could defeat a rock. But he could probably finesse the locks if she moved aside, which she did, swearing a steady stream of paint-blistering invective that would have delighted Rory.

Rupert pursed his lips, unimpressed, and leaned down to peer at the lockpad. Then he closed his eyes and did whatever it was arithmancers did while normal people contemplated further violence against inanimate objects.

The shuttle shivered. The teslas on the external door panel turned red, indicating depressurization underway as the aetherlocks cycled.

"Rupert, it's taking off."

"Yes, Grytt, I know."

Grytt's heart, still perfectly human, rattled between synthetic lungs which, despite the tightness in her chest, continued to inflate and contract steadily, refusing to allow the luxury of panic.

She hated void-travel. She hated it when there was a pilot, and a dozen redundancies in case of disaster. This was the worst-case scenario she could conceive other than being flushed out the aetherlock without a hardsuit.

And if Rupert couldn't outwit the turing, they *would* go to Beo, which would end much the same way, except with a fight beforehand, for which she was woefully underarmed. Her 'slinger, carrying half a load, the three partial loads in the Tadeshi weapons, and an arithmancer, to land on a hostile base of *marines*.

The aetherlock option seemed suddenly a little more appealing, until she examined the shuttle's interior and discovered that both of the emergency hardsuits had taken damage in the firefight. She fingered the splintered poly-ceramic. She might be able to get *a* whole suit out of the two. Might.

"Rupert."

The shuttle rocked and wobbled aetherborne, stabilizing after a moment. Then it lurched forward, threatening Grytt's balance and tipping Rupert away from the lock for a slipping, scrabbling moment.

"You did that on purpose," he murmured. "Bad turing."

Grytt fingered one of her stolen 'slingers. If they landed on Beo, one bolt more or less would not matter. But here:

"Rupert. Will you have better luck *in* the cockpit?"

"Likely."

"Then move aside."

He looked at the 'slinger in her hand, and his eyes saucered. He turned sideways, covering his head, as if mere flesh and bone were proof against bolts. As if she would *miss*, at this range. The larger Tadeshi bolt punched easily through the lockpad, throwing sparks and little shavings of plastic and polycarbonate amalgam. Grytt stuck her mecha hand into the hole. The bolt had gone most of the way through the pad on the other side. A small matter to push it clear. A slightly larger matter to wedge her fist, and then her forearm, into the hole. The angle was unhelpful, but the mecha wrist did not suffer the same motile restrictions as its human analog. Its fingers were not as sensitive for feeling blind, either, but her target was a lever, not a button, and *there* it was.

She grunted and pulled. The hatch irised open to reveal an empty pilot's seat and a front console occupied by a turing with a small screen and a rudimentary input pad, attached by a web of cables and bolts. A bank of teslas blinked in a pattern discernible to the turing itself, and probably to Rupert.

"It's annoyed," Rupert said.

Grytt hefted the 'slinger thoughtfully. The box did not look particularly shielded. "So am I."

"Patience. That's our pilot." Rupert eeled into the single chair, propping his legs up on either side of the turing in a most indecorous fashion.

About time, Grytt thought, and wished his lapses in propriety coincided with less desperate situations.

The shuttle changed direction slightly. Acceleration pushed Grytt partway back into the main cabin.

Rupert merely grunted. He did something to the console's remaining controls, and the turing's small screen blinked awake. Grytt frowned at the orange grid and the tiny readout scrolling down the far right edge.

"Central Control just cleared us," said Rupert. "Evidently this *is* a regular run to Beo. See? Those four digits there indicate—"

"Rupert."

He sighed. She marked again the new sharpness to his shoulders, tenting through the coverall and settling over the knobs of his spine.

"I have no live communications. Grytt. Does Rory actually know what's happened?"

"No," said Grytt. "There wasn't time to tell her. We can send a message once we're clear. Assuming we *get* clear. If we have to land on Beo. . . ." She grimaced. "I'll try and do something with the hardsuits, in case we need them."

"Of course." He offered her a smile both crooked and sympathetic. Rupert knew as well as she what would happen if they landed, and what *could* happen, and what must not.

Whatever happened now—Rory was on her own.

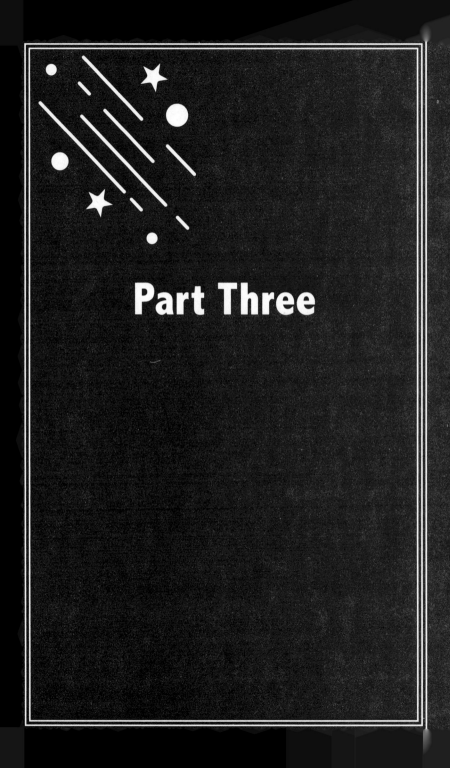

Part Three

CHAPTER SEVENTEEN ≡≡≡

Scientia Potestas Est

I t is common wisdom that the small hours of third shift are best avoided by persons who wish to maintain cognitive function during first and second shift, which is when most business is conducted. It is also common knowledge that teenagers, while quite fond of sleep (as a concept, in general, and in practice on days when their schedules begin early), will forego it when sufficiently motivated. In general, that motivation takes the form of peer social gatherings or illicit and unwise behavior unapproved by the local adults (and sometimes all three together at once). Rory had no interest in, nor access to, peers. She was, however, quite willing to engage in illicit and unwise activities, particularly in the absence of Grytt or Rupert to insist that she turn off the turing and go to bed.

It was Grytt's absence that had inspired her deliberate insomnia. That Grytt had not called was understandable. She did not trust the communications for anything more important than *please pick up some noodles on the way home.* Security had logged Grytt's departure at the accustomed hour, but after that, she simply vanished, somewhere between the detention block and the main promenade. That was worrisome. One did not simply *lose* a person like Grytt.

Rory had sifted through the detention records, and security, to ascertain whether or not Grytt had been arrested, detained, or somehow otherwise delayed. She found nothing.

Rory was not the same caliber arithmancer as the Vizier. He had a post-graduate degree in its theory and application, and many more years' experience. He could, and did, and *had*—which was how they'd caught him—traverse the aether on more levels than she could. But he had also, in his last foray into the turing, left a set of hand-scribed notes on the hexes he'd discovered. She also had Jaed's pass-string, the Minister of Finance's, *and* the Minister of War's. Rory made good use of all of them, and manufactured for herself an amalgam of the three pass-strings, composed of clearances and wrapped with the same hexes that Messer Rupert had identified. The turing did not notice her passage. Flat out did not. Could not, as long as she did not disturb anything.

She also took into account Messer Rupert's warnings, and the clear evidence of his arrest, that Urse had at least one extremely talented arithmancer working its security. As a concession to safety, she kept her communication to the turing limited to material interface of keyboard and screen. It was rather like trying to paint while wearing mittens, but it was safer than spreading her consciousness out through several layers of aether.

You see, Messer Rupert? I'm being careful.

To which her inner Grytt said, *Not enough, you're not.*

Rory had some words for that internal Grytt, mostly having to do with *where are you* and *dammit, come home.*

"There's nothing in security," Rory announced, and wondered why the news did not do anything to ease the tightness in her chest. "No alerts. Nothing. No hospital admissions, either, that look pertinent."

Zhang paused in her tidying of the living room. Tidying was

Zhang's way of coping with stress. Thorsdottir preferred to cook. And thus, in the past several hours, as Grytt grew later and later, Thorsdottir had prepared an elaborate cake, a tray of muffins, and sufficient lentil soup for, Rory was certain, at least a dozen people. At Rory's announcement, she emerged from the kitchen, clutching the rag with which she had been wiping down the counters for the past twenty minutes. They didn't look as if they felt any better, either.

Rory glanced at the chronometer. "You two should go to bed," she said. "I'm going to keep looking. If something happened, I think there'll be some try at covering up the information. So I'll just dig a little bit."

Thorsdottir and Zhang looked at each other a long moment while Rory pretended not to notice. That they wanted to marshal some objection was obvious; and it was equally obvious they, like she, wanted to know what had happened to Grytt. And they, like she, knew that if she *did* get into trouble, well, it wasn't the sort that 'slingers and martial arts could solve.

"All right," Thorsdottir said. "We can send Stary and Franko over."

"No."

"There are rules," Thorsdottir said, doggedly. "You can't be left alone."

"I'm aware of the rules." Rory sighed. Stary and Franko were large, uniformed presences who always called her Princess and Highness and snapped salutes. They were, in Grytt's words, *sticklers for protocol.* They were suitable escorts for, oh, the embassy; but there were reasons they did not come along on liaisons with Jaed, or to the gym. They might not know what she was doing on the turing, but they would know she shouldn't be doing it during the small hours of third shift. Thorsdottir and Zhang knew that, too, but they wouldn't argue.

"Stary and Franco need to stay where they are," said Rory. "You can tell them Grytt hasn't returned—I imagine they know that already—but that we don't know where she is. That's what I'm trying to figure out. Tell them that, too. Then get some rest, because I think tomorrow's going to be busy."

Thorsdottir steeled herself visibly. Rory sensed an imminent *Highness*. She held up a hand.

"If Grytt doesn't return, you two can move in tomorrow. But in the meantime, just trust me. I am looking for Grytt, I won't do anything stupid, and if I need you, I'll call."

Thorsdottir looked at Zhang. Then her shoulders sagged. "All right."

"I'll make you a pot of coffee," said Zhang.

Thus fortified, Rory settled down to do some serious arithmancy. It stood to reason that, had Grytt been apprehended doing something untoward—and there was no doubt in Rory's mind that *had* there been an arrest attempt, there *would* have been physical damage—there would be some sort of record, somewhere, in the hospital files. She was most afraid that said records would be in the morgue records, and so she began there.

She did not find any mention of Grytt, or of Messer Rupert, in the morgue subfolder. She expanded her search, looking for information specifically tagged as official, diplomatic, or restricted. No Grytt. One small file on Messer Rupert, dated from his arrest, making note of his general health. There was a second entry, dated three days ago, making note that he'd lost two kilos since his incarceration, and recommending more aggressive measures to ensure that he did, in fact, eat, and was not attempting some sort of hunger strike.

Rory reread that file twice, and made special note of the attending chirurgeon for her future attention. It was probably not his fault, exactly; the Regent was the sort of man to hold a chirurgeon responsible for his patient's health. But there was a small knot of anger in her belly, keeping company with the worry, that did not care if the chirurgeon had had a 'slinger pressed to his temple while he examined Messer Rupert. She had a name, now, and if this was a man Moss trusted to look after his valuable prisoners, then he might have access to other interesting patients as well.

She soon discovered that whatever his other skills, the chirurgeon was no arithmancer. The hexes on his personal files were rudimentary, the sort non-arithmancers purchased and installed to give themselves the illusion of security against *real* arithmancers. It was somewhat surprising, given his access to sensitive personnel. Here was the Regent's medical file, and Merrick's, and Jaed's. She paused, debating the relative merits of further investigation.

And it was in that pause that she spotted a folder named *Valenko, Ivar* that was so marked with *forbidden* and *access restricted* hexes that Rory revised her opinion of the physician's arithmancy, until she realized the hexes bore the same trace-markers as the ones Messer Rupert had cataloged. The work of the same arithmancer, *the* arithmancer, the one who had caught Messer Rupert.

Rory sipped her coffee, burned her lip, and frowned. The layers of security seemed absurd, even for royal records, unless there was something dramatic in Ivar's file. Perhaps he had some debilitating, progressive disease. She examined the small surge of hope that produced and frowned at herself. There must be something important in the files, anyway, that meant they, alone of everyone's, had to be hexed to inaccessibility.

"Time to take off the mittens," Rory told the coffee cup. Then she set it down and slid it halfway across the table, safely out of spilling range.

Messer Rupert had taught Rory his preferred method of traversing the aether, which involved stillness, quiet, focus, breathing, all activities to which children are not generally suited, even Princesses. If he exaggerated the degree to which one must have quiet, focus, stillness, well, he could be forgiven for it, particularly when his Princess had proved herself more stubborn than impatient, when it came to arithmancy. He had been trying to protect her, as much as the locks in the Thorne palace, as much as anyone's privacy when an adolescent commenced observation on everyone's auras.

Rory suspected Messer Rupert's motives already, having seen the speed with which he had extricated himself from the aether. She had also made note of the nosebleed, his complexion, and the hour he'd spent in the small hours of third shift, heaving up what little supper he'd managed to eat with as much quiet as a man could manage while he was turning himself inside out. So there was, she reckoned, some merit to slow, deliberate arithmancy, and in adhering to the steps one already knew.

She sat still, and took deep breaths, and let her gaze slide soft-focus. The first layer was simplest. The contents of the room acquired an extra shadow, a little border of white noise that meant unliving synthetics. Her hands, however, were spidered through with faint yellow threads, which meant she was nervous.

She breathed carefully, slowly, until the yellow disappeared. Then she fixed her gaze on the terminal's screen. It had no aura, being both synthetic and unsentient. Rory stared past it and through it, until its physical shell gave way to a wire-frame version of itself, through which she could see pathways composed of light and unreflective blocks of hardware, tiny circuits she could disrupt, overload, reroute—or repair, if, as Messer Rupert had admonished her constantly, she would just use her powers for good.

All good, Messer Rupert. Promise.

She had not often attempted this third step, and never without him there to observe (and, should she require, assist). Her heartbeat fluttered. Her aura, already an arithmantic step back, flared hot. It would be red, she thought, and orange. She willed it cool. Will herself back to calm. Then she fixed her gaze on a light path, and focused.

Imagine the atoms, Messer Rupert had told her. *Imagine them floating in void. Then* see *them, and see past them.*

Rory's eyes kept locking onto the glowing lines, until their images burned white on the back of her eyelids. She blinked, and breathed, and held *still*: Grytt's teaching, as much as Rupert's.

The one in control wins the battle.

She was not certain that was true, exactly, but it was good enough advice. Certainly the one who lost control lost the battle very quickly. And this was just a layer of aether, small step, nothing difficult, if one counted simple stepping both inward and down, until she shifted perception to a place on the other side of those floating atoms, where the wire frame resolved into strings of symbols and numbers.

The hexes, from that vantage, were easily seen: errant equations wrapped around honest data like chokevines strangling trees. The preferred method of dealing with chokevines involved sharp hatchets, wielded with some care, lest the host be likewise damaged. Rory employed the arithmantic equivalent, rearranging the hexes—a changed command here, a parenthesis relocated—until she convinced the hexes that she had legitimate access, and the layers of security peeled open like bogflower petals during rain.

To her credit, Rory hesitated. The Vizier had taught her arith-mancy, but he had also taught her ethics. This was an invasion of a man's privacy, in particular, the man she was intended to marry (whatever her own opinions in the matter). She would be privy to information he might not choose to share with her, knowledge of which she would have to conceal from him. It was not a good foundation for a relationship. It was also illegal, by Tadeshi statute. The Regent could—well, if not exactly arrest her, move to restrict her freedom; he could even dissolve the marriage contract and return her to Thorne.

She considered that. Then she opened the folder.

Inside were four files, each named *Valenko, I,* each with a dif-ferent datestamp. She opened the earliest, and largest, first. It was a medical chronicle of Ivar's minority, an unremarkable list of ill-nesses and treatments. What was interesting, however, was the extensive alchemical analyses of his blood and his humors, cross-referenced with childhood events. He tended toward melancholy, with a surplus of yellow bile linked to his parents' deaths. A note from his physician indicated optimism that, given time, the Prince's humors might rebalance. He was young, after all. But each subsequent evaluation revealed no rise in sanguinity or phlegmaticism. Upon his early enlistment at sixteen, the Prince was severely melancholic. There was a note, by the same physi-cian, that the mandatory service should be waived, or at least de-layed. There was a subsequent order, signed by the Regent, accepting the Prince's early enlistment so that his service would be completed by his coronation.

"Well," murmured Rory. "So much for medical advice."

The apartment made no comment.

She scrolled to the next file, expecting a mid-service evalua-tion; and indeed, it *looked* like Ivar's bio-alchemy—severe melancholy, punctuated by choleric outbursts in response to stress—but the numbers were not exact, even to Rory's untrained eye.

Within acceptable parameters, said the notes, with an accompanying list of deviation percentages and analyses. Then followed several subfiles, chronicling basic health checkups, including blood alchemistry, over the span of nearly a month. Rory was no physician, and her knowledge of anatomy was fairly basic; but she judged that the falling percentages of whatever the long, technical sounding words were, in some columns, and the rise in others, meant nothing good. The last page confirmed her suspicions: it was a post-mortem, complete with 2D stills.

Rory sat up in her chair and said several words Messer Rupert would not have approved of. That was *Ivar's* body on the table. Or at least it had Ivar's face, the body itself showing the marks of autopsy and extensive, invasive medical examination. Another Princess, one whose body-maid was not half-mecha, who had not grown up during the War, might have felt faint, or queasy, and closed the file. Rory kept looking, despite the shock rattling in her chest.

But Ivar was not dead. Or rather, *this* person, this corpse, could not be Ivar, unless the Prince she'd met wasn't actually the Prince. She had suspected as much, and, being now almost seventeen, experienced a momentary surge of vindication. Messer Rupert had doubted, and here was proof—

Of what, Rory?

She sighed. Proof of something untoward, certainly; but the exact *what* remained unclear. The project Moss had reassigned and relocated to Beo had been about cryostasis. There hadn't been anything mentioned about cloning, which this certainly seemed to be, and which, to her knowledge, was alchemical fiction, not alchemical fact. And yet, the files suggested otherwise, and she had two more to examine before she could think of settling on a conclusion she could share with Zhang and Thorsdottir (and Grytt, please, Grytt, too).

The remaining files looked much like this second one: a detailed chronicle of a version of Ivar, all culminating with massive biological failure and an autopsy. The last file, the fourth, had a commencement date approximately eight days prior to the formal reception at which she had been presented to an Ivar who clearly did not remember her, which made perfect sense because he'd been a tenday old at that point. *His* autopsy had taken place on Urse, exactly four days after the reception. The file noted that there was some improvement in longevity, with several hypotheses offered for further testing.

Further *testing*. Either Ivar was alive, then, or samples of him were, on Beo. Rory had never been so conflicted about being right before. Imagining Moss's monstrosity was one thing; confronting it in hexed files was quite another. On the one hand, she had proof of his perfidy, and of Ivar's victimhood. On the other, were Moss to discover what she knew—well. He was not the sort of man to stop at violence, clearly.

She had to secure Messer Rupert's release, immediately. He was too vulnerable in the Regent's custody, both as a guarantee against her good behavior, and as a potential victim himself. She could make Grytt understand that, surely.

She exited the aether hoping to find Grytt standing over her, scowling and demanding to know what exactly she thought she was doing. Instead, she had only a headache and a tepid cup of coffee for company.

Thorsdottir and Zhang found Rory in much the same condition the following morning, although the contents of the coffee cup had changed twice in the interim, and the headache had been exacerbated by a three-hour nap on crossed forearms.

Thorsdottir looked Rory over. "You haven't slept," she said, by way of greeting.

"You haven't, either," said Rory.

"No," said Zhang. She frowned at the coffee pot, which was empty, and began to rectify that situation. "We briefed Stary and Franko on our situation. Then we strategized."

Thorsdottir jerked her chin at Rory's turing. "No word from Grytt?"

"I was about to ask you that."

"She hasn't called in. Stary and Franko reported nothing either, on the usual channels. No security alerts to which *we're* privy. If the Tadeshi got her, you'd think we'd've heard. It's like she fell off the station."

"She might have," said Rory. "A shuttle that left the station at oh-one-hundred, destination Beo. I found an entry in last night's log."

"Why would Grytt go to *Beo*?"

Rory dropped her face into her hands. The bones felt hot, too heavy for her skin to hold. "To rescue Ivar, maybe. But I don't know how she'd've found out, and if she *did*, why she wouldn't tell me."

A moment's silence, in which Rory imagined Thorsdottir and Zhang sharing one of their looks again, the ones which meant, alternately, *what does she mean?* and *I wish Grytt would say something right about now.*

Rory expected she'd see the latter a lot more frequently, unless Grytt performed a miracle and appeared at the door. She expected no miracles forthcoming today.

"Prince Ivar," said Rory, before Thorsdottir—it was almost always Thorsdottir—could ask, "is a prisoner on Beo. They're cloning him. Or his genetic material. I *assume* he's still actually alive, but I can't prove it. I can, however, prove that he's on Beo. Would you like to see?"

Zhang abandoned the coffee pot, having set it to its task, and came briskly to her partner's side. The pair of them leaned over the desk as Rory rotated the turing so that they could read it.

"Took me most of the night to get these copied and unhexed. See? Three Ivars, all with very brief lifespans, all clearly clones of the original."

Rory was gratified to see her guards' faces go from dubious to horrified. This time it was Zhang who spoke first.

"Why would Moss do this?" she asked.

"If he marries me to Ivar, only it's an Ivar-clone, I'll be a widow in a matter of weeks. At which point I am Queen Regent, in need of a new husband, and there will be Jaed, very conveniently. At that point, I imagine the original Ivar will die for good."

"So you *can't* get married. It's not just a matter of preference anymore."

Rory leaned back. Her neck creaked. She was certain she could feel her brain moving in her skull, heavy with new knowledge. "I don't see that I can avoid it, unless we can rescue Ivar, the *real* Ivar, and bring him back here. I don't think the Regent can continue to hold power if everyone sees what he's done."

Leave aside, Rory thought, that her suggestion would cause a civil war.

Thorsdottir lifted a single forefinger, drawing Rory's attention back out of her own skull. "And you think *Grytt* went to rescue Ivar?"

"I don't know. If she found out about him, then she should have told me. And I don't know how she would have, because this took *me* most of the night, and I'm an arithmancer, *and* I have Messer Rupert's notes." Rory sat up a little straighter, and named the fear that was pressing icy fingers into every corner of her chest. "I did find an entry in hospital records from late third shift. It wasn't to emergency services. It was to the *morgue*. The details were hexed, but." She shrugged. "I got a look. It wasn't Grytt, unless they lied in the records. It *was* three dead men, all Tadeshi security, all dead from 'slinger shots. They were found in the same bay that the shuttle was in, the one that left for Beo."

"Three bodies," murmured Zhang. She sounded impressed.

Thorsdottir, in a complete reversal of roles, said nothing. She squinted past the turing as if the aether itself might yield up an answer.

Rory knew better. She'd been plying the aether most of third shift. "I know. The bodies in the bay sound like Grytt's doing. But that means she killed enemies under truce. That's an act of *war*. Why would she do that? Why would *you* do that?"

Thorsdottir looked as serious as Rory had ever seen her. "To defend you. I can't think of another reason."

"To defend yourselves?"

Zhang caught her breath. "Yes," she said, while Thorsdottir frowned and clenched her jaw. "Unless our deaths would serve your interests."

"Would you surrender?"

"No," said Thorsdottir. "Unless, same thing, our surrender would serve your interests."

"So Grytt obviously knew something," said Rory. "And she acted on it. *In my interests.* And if she *knew* about Ivar, then she might've gone to Beo. This makes me more worried than ever about Messer Rupert. If Grytt's gone and done something violent. We need to get him *out*. But we can't just fight our way into detention. And even if we *did*, then what? We can't just bring him back here. Can anyone fly a shuttle?"

Zhang frowned. "Franko is a pilot."

Thorsdottir wrinkled her forehead. "So're you."

Zhang peered down her nose at Thorsdottir, which was no trivial accomplishment, given their vertical disparity.

"I have a *provisional* license."

Thorsdottir made a very Grytt-like noise in the back of her throat and rolled her eyes. "And top rank in your class."

Rory held up a hand. "So you *can* fly."

Zhang sighed, and favored Thorsdottir with a look that suggested, were will the only criteria, flames could, in fact, shoot out of her eyes. "Yes. For atmospheric craft only. I am not at *all* trained for voidships."

"We are not stealing a shuttle," Thorsdottir said firmly. And then, less firmly, "Are we?"

"No. Maybe. Not yet." Rory closed her eyes. The insides felt gritty and hot. Grytt would act without orders, certainly—but she acted in defense of Rory, always. So the knowledge Rory needed, more than anything, was what threat had prompted Grytt's actions and whether that was related to the three bodies in the morgue. If Grytt was responsible, then relations between Thorne and the Free Worlds of Tadesh might be in jeopardy. Rory was certain that the Regent did not want another war; but he could use an incident that resulted in shots fired and dead Tadeshi citizens as leverage. Her marriage to Ivar was supposed to wait until she was eighteen, but under certain circumstances—say, the death of Tadeshi personnel caused by her own Kreshti body-maid—that rule could be waived, with permission from the Thorne sovereign. Samur wouldn't like it, but she'd probably agree: Samur didn't want a war, either, and she would be furious at Grytt for putting her and Rory and all of Thorne in a vulnerable political position.

So this action could result in a *faster* marriage to a cloned Ivar, with even less time to maneuver and formulate a new plan that would not involve marrying anyone. It was, by all appearances, a foolish, even treasonous, thing that Grytt had done. Except Grytt wasn't a fool or a traitor.

The only thing Rory did know, already and for certain, was what Grytt would say to plans of absconding with a shuttle and flying to Beo to rescue Ivar with no guarantee that he was alive, and it would be heavily punctuated with *your Highness* to remind her that she was being an idiot.

"No," Rory said. "Definitely. No. No stealing shuttles. We'll have to manage this some other way. First, we have to figure out where Grytt is."

Thorsdottir made a face reminiscent of someone who has a mouthful of slivered glass and vinegar. "The Regent might know."

"The Regent might. I don't want to ask him yet, though. I need to see Jaed—"

At that moment, the turing flashed a warning. In the very next, both Thorsdottir's and Zhang's comms buzzed.

Zhang answered. Frowned. And said, before Rory could ask: "That was Stary. We've got three station-security inbound."

"Well," Rory murmured. "I guess we'll be asking him soon."

CHAPTER EIGHTEEN ═══════

The Perfect Leaf

Much conversation, both literal and literary, has been expended on the economic and temporal investment made by individuals before they present themselves in public. Whole industries depend on it, from cosmetics and clothiers, who recognize a lucrative opportunity when they see it and attempt to cultivate that market, to comedians and pundits and religious figures (often difficult to distinguish from one another), who find their own profit in mockery of individuals who expend their time and effort in what are often called vain pursuits. The irony in this phrase is the assumption that such pursuits *are* vain—which is to say, that they are wasted effort.

A princess knows better, though it is only the wiser princesses who understand that clothing and presentation are as much a weapon as an expression of conformity to public expectation. Messer Rupert and her mother had, over the years of her adolescence, impressed upon Rory the need to present an appropriate face and figure, not for social conformity, but for camouflage.

You must control their focus, Messer Rupert had said. *Show them what you want them to see.*

Grytt had said, *Be like a mantis-lion. Match the foliage. People want to see a leaf, let them see a leaf. Surprise is your ally.*

That latter advice had, in Rory's childhood, led to an attempt to wear nothing but green for a fortnight and long hours spent in the gardens, leaping out of the foliage at inopportune moments and startling the groundskeepers. It was shortly after that incident that Messer Rupert explained *metaphor*. But the lesson had stuck.

Today, she needed to be a mantis-lion. The Regent needed to believe she was Rory-the-leaf, until she ate his head. Well. Perhaps not that, exactly: until she demonstrated, through nonviolent means, that she was an ally whose goodwill he needed, as much as—no, *more* than—he needed her mother's.

She also needed to be able to lie today, because although Messer Rupert had taught her that personal honesty was a virtue, he had also said political dishonesty was a necessity.

So before she got dressed, Rory took a guilty detour into Messer Rupert's quarters. He had not brought much in the way of personal items. A Kreshti fern. A small embroidered pillow. And a small personal trunk which was fortunately *not* hexed, so that she needn't feel even more wretched for breaking into it.

Messer Rupert was both an arithmancer and a historian by training; but he was a politician's advisor by profession, and as such, Rory knew he kept odd hours and, on occasion, resorted to alchemy to maintain his alertness. She was not the slightest bit surprised to find a small packet of stimulant capsules in the corner of the trunk, wedged beside an innocuous bottle of painkillers and an unopened bottle of aftershave.

Having acquired—she refused to think of it as *stolen*—the capsules, Rory retreated to her own quarters, to the mirror, and assessed her condition. She currently looked like someone who had not slept more than three hours in the past twenty-four. She *needed* to look like a fully-rested someone unconcerned with the absence of her two closest advisors.

There were not enough cosmetics in the world for that, though a Winter Nights mask might suffice, if seasons mattered on a void-station, if the Free Worlds bothered with such things.

Rory chose dark items from her wardrobe, strategically close-fitting in some places and draping in others. She coiled her usual braid into a knot on the back of her neck, as Kreshti women do when they've achieved majority. She wore an elaborately embroidered vest and a wide belt, and blacked the rims of her eyes and turned the dull smudged exhaustion into grey-painted shadows.

The Vizier, had he been present, would have caught his breath, seeing Samur in her daughter. Grytt, had she been there, would have raised her remaining eyebrow and nodded approval, for the same reason. Rory, having only a mirror and her own perception, thought she made an excellent leaf.

The three black-clad security were waiting at the end of the tiny corridor that led to the official Thorne compound on Urse. It was three blonds, this time, strong-featured and long-limbed and conspicuously armed. They had clearly been waiting awhile; they were looking everywhere but down the corridor, shifting from one foot to another, heads tilted together in a private conversation. Stary and Franko had emerged from their quarters and stood just inside of the corridor, armed and armored and, from the shade of red on the back of Franko's neck, very angry.

"Hell," said Zhang.

Thorsdottir said something more scatological.

Rory said nothing. Her first impulse was to go right back inside, which of course she could not do, because she was no longer five and the Tadeshi would not go away if she pretended they were not there.

"Thorsdottir," she said. "Back inside. *Now*. Wait until we're gone, and they're gone. Then go find Jaed, and tell him what's happened."

Thorsdottir did not look at all surprised, which indicated she had either expected something like this, or she was becoming accustomed to Rory's improvisations. "And then?"

"I may need a rescue," said Rory. "Use your judgment."

"Princess," said Thorsdottir, and ducked back into the flat.

Rory took a breath deep enough to feel, and thus reassure herself, that the tiny Kreshti knife was where it belonged, tucked in the band of her undergarments, where the wires inherent in the garment's structure would (according to Thorsdottir and Zhang) conceal the extra metal. Its placement also rendered it ineffective for urgent defense; but Rory did not expect violence from Tadeshi security in a public area, not against the Princess of Thorne, darling of the social networks.

Which meant she needed to get herself out *into* a public area, and quickly.

"Follow me. Stay behind," she said to Zhang.

Rory plastered a very practiced, public smile across her lips. "Good morning, messers," she sang out, and increased her pace.

The Tadeshi turned their heads as if controlled by the same puppeteer. The foremost—who seemed the most relentlessly medium of the three, adorned with the two-pip insignia that marked his superior rank—opened his mouth to possibly return the greeting, and more likely issue a command. When he realized that the Princess was coming at him at ramming speed his mouth remained open and empty. Whatever plans he'd had for this encounter, a royal charge was not among them.

He locked eyes with Rory, holding her gaze for a heartbeat before turning his head and issuing orders to his own men. They yielded ground and backed up into the main thoroughfare, so that the midmorning traffic broke and eddied around them, leaving a small area unoccupied and demarked by a triangle of black uniforms.

"The Regent requests your presence at once," Two-Pips said. His vowels were stiff, his tone condescending and, worse, utterly confident of compliance.

Rory tilted her head. Her smile hardened a fraction. "You're mistaken, messer. I requested *his* presence, to which you are here to escort me. But you have arrived unexpectedly early, and so I will need to stop along the way, to procure breakfast."

The three looked at each other. Evidently the care and feeding of the Princess had not been part of their briefing. Nor, evidently, had they been briefed to expect a princess who was less than accommodating and gracious. They had likely been told to fetch her, escort her, expect no difficulty—because Rory had not, in her tenure on Urse, shown that tendency.

Rory tossed her head back and took a step forward—conservatively, this time, in case the Tadeshi were done with retreat for the morning.

They were. Rory found herself an uncomfortable half arm's length from a uniformed chest. She suffered a sharp, irrational stab of annoyance that the Tadeshi were, as a general rule, taller than average, even at their most medium.

"I'm sorry, Princess, but we must insist," said the chest's owner. "The Regent's command was very specific. We are to deliver you to his office at once."

As if she were an order of take-out. Rory stared at a speck of lint on the unbroken black and wished for laser beams in her eyes. She knew she should acquiesce. Leaves did not argue, and after all, the Regent's office was her intended destination as well, and she had been concerned he would refuse to see her. But her nerves were raw and her temper threadbare and she disliked Two-Pips' tone.

She lifted her chin and stared past the tip of her nose, dismissing her smile. "You forget your place, messer, and mine. I take no one's commands. If you wish to drag me, bodily, to the administrative offices, then you are of course free to try. But you will attract attention. And you will likely find it more costly than you are prepared to pay."

Zhang inhaled, sharp and quiet as a knife. Perversely, it was a comfort.

Rory's smile returned, sudden and false as sunlight during a rainstorm. "So I recommend that you wait until I procure my breakfast, at which point you may escort me to the Regent, or we will create an incident in which you will not appear sympathetic. Clear?"

Two-Pips looked as if all his breath had been stolen out of his lungs. Red crawled up from his collar, staining his neck and cheeks, creeping across his forehead. He clamped his teeth together as if he meant to crack them. "Yes, Princess."

Zhang let her breath go.

Rory raised a hand, flicking her fingers as if at a persistent insect. The Tadeshi uniforms parted like curtains. She walked between them briskly, to better conceal the fledgling tremor in her knees. There was a pastry vendor nearby, who sold passable crêpes. She pointed herself that direction and hoped her stomach would cooperate.

The Tadeshi remained where she had left them, talking amongst themselves in low voices. Probably with the Regent, too, over comms.

"They will either arrest us forthwith," muttered Rory, "or we will be permitted to carry on as if nothing at all is amiss. So. What would you like for breakfast?"

Zhang looked as if she had a mouthful of observations. She swallowed them. "Princess." Another breath. "They're coming."

"So they're not looking at the apartment anymore."

The corner of Zhang's mouth lifted, just a little. "No."

"Then let's keep their eyes on us, shall we? Because I suddenly don't feel like crêpes. But there's an excellent patisserie two sections up-ring from here. What do you think?"

"I think the Regent is going to be annoyed."

"Tragic."

Zhang chuckled, and matched Rory's pace.

Thorsdottir felt a bit like a child, holding the door propped a crack, using a mirror to peer down the corridor, as if she were playing hunt-and-hide with her brothers, dreaming of the day when she would join the Royal Guard and acquire all manner of exciting equipment. Bolt slingers. Hex-casters. Spybots. Some of which she had, and others of which Stary and Franko did, in their much smaller apartment (which would now be much less crowded, once she and Zhang had officially relocated to Rory's flat). They had the best Thorne could provide, within treaty, and a little without, because Grytt had proven herself an able smuggler, with a false-bottomed trunk in her room that housed several pieces of wartime equipment. And still, here Thorsdottir was, crouched in the doorway so as to leave no silhouette, with Rory's silver hand mirror.

Sometimes the simplest tools worked best. She watched Rory and Zhang step through the security escort, heading toward the refreshment vendors. She watched the security escort huddle together for a moment before they moved, in formation, to follow.

And it *was* following, rather than pursuit, because they weren't moving fast. No urgency.

Thorsdottir let her breath go. She eased back into the apartment. The Princess had said, use your judgment. Thorsdottir knew her judgment was exactly why she was here—both on Urse, and on the Princess's personal guard detail. Grytt had told her as much. But *judgment* was easier to define when it was a matter of detecting threats and managing the Princess's personal space out in public. This version of *use your judgment* involved mental muscles Thorsdottir hadn't used since her hunt-and-hide days.

A soldier learns, during her basic training, to robe and disrobe with great haste and efficiency. Thorsdottir was out of her uniform and into a pair of unremarkable trousers and a dark sweater of Lanscottar wool in the same time it took most people to open a drawer. The sweater had been intended for her brother, back on Thorne, and as such, was too large for her, which made it perfect for concealing the very small, very illegal 'slinger, taken from Grytt's stash of contraband, muzzle down at the small of her back. Its cartridges were unmarked, which was worrisome; if she was forced to use it, she and her opponents would both be surprised at the force and content of the charge.

She checked the corridor again before exiting the flat. No Tadeshi security team. She took her time getting up that corridor, staying close to the bulkhead, observing the crowds for any sign of alarm or unusual distraction. Nothing. She was not entirely surprised, when she poked her head into the main thoroughfare, to see no sign of Rory, Zhang, or the Regent's men. She only hoped their absence was due to the Princess's plan—whatever it was—and not the Regent's impatience.

I might need a rescue.

Thorsdottir hoped not, if that rescue somehow involved Jaed

Moss. She didn't like her Princess's apparent trust in him. He was Tadeshi. He was a *Moss*. And he was, unfortunately, the closest thing to an ally Rory had on Urse, outside of her own dwindling household.

Thorsdottir set her worry aside. Her mother had said there was little sense in borrowing trouble before it arrived at your door. Her mother had also said, when Thorsdottir enlisted, that there was even less sense in *looking* for it. But that was the point of hunt-and-hide, wasn't it? Looking for trouble, or trouble looking for you, depending which side of the game you were on.

Thorsdottir stopped at a public terminal four intersections down-ring of the Thorne quarters. She keyed in Rory's pass-string, which Rory had insisted she and Zhang memorize ("Grytt knows it. So should you."). Then she typed a text message into the keypad, one finger at a time. She'd participated in the crafting and sending of several such missives, over the course of Rory's alliance with Jaed. She thought it sounded authentic.

Meet me at the observation porthole by the recreation center, 1130. -RT

It would get him out of the umbrella of his father's security, at least. There was something to be said for un-royalty, that it could go wherever it liked without escort. And he would come. If he didn't she would find him and drag him bodily to Rory's aid. Thorsdottir was fairly certain that was not Rory's intent; but she found herself hoping for an opportunity, nevertheless.

Thorsdottir herself did not expect to make it more than two intersections before discovery and apprehension, and was somewhat surprised, therefore, when she made it to the observation porthole without incident. She had imagined herself something of a celebrity: clips of her sparring match with Jaed were all over the network, and yet here she was, walking the Ursan mid-first-shift corridors with scarcely two glances from passersby. But she had been in her uniform, then, hadn't she? And now she was just another woman walking through the station.

Jaed arrived at the rendezvous two minutes early, hair still damp and curling, clothes sticking to him in the places that were most likely to be wet, if one had been rushed with a towel. He leaned against the railing, breathing a little hard, and let his head hang from his shoulders as if it were too heavy for his neck.

Thorsdottir detached herself from her hiding-in-plain-sight patch of bulkhead. She could have approached obliquely, allowing him time to notice. She came from the back instead.

"Thought you'd be late, did you? You are."

Jaed spun quickly, one hand still on the railing, the other dropped loose at his hip. Thorsdottir noted the improvement in balance, the way his knees stayed under his hips. The speed with which he turned.

And he looked tired. Bruise-blue under his eyes, pastier than usual, even for a station-boy. Thorsdottir, whose skin bore a permanent scattering of freckles from a childhood in the sun, thought he looked like milk. Bloodless. At the commencement of their acquaintance, Thorsdottir equated appearance with actuality; but she had spent almost as much time around him as Rory had, and exchanged bruises with him, and had revised her estimation of his worth as an opponent, if not quite as a human being.

He frowned at her. "Thorsdottir?"

It was Thorsdottir's experience that, having asked an obvious question, people did not expect an answer; and if one wasn't forthcoming, would answer it themselves, and save her the trouble of follow-up conversation. She raised a brow.

"It's the uniform," he said. "Or the lack of it." His frown deepened. "What's going on? Where's Rory? Where *is* your uniform?"

"In reverse order: the flat, possibly under arrest but more probably leading your father's men on a merry chase through Urse, and that is what Rory's trying to discern."

"Under *arrest*?"

"Possibly. Can we please move this conversation elsewhere?" She made an idle flourish with her fingers. "'Bots have ears."

Jaed's frown sunk all the way to scowl. He closed his eyes. Thorsdottir watched his hands clench on the railing, the muscles lock all the way up his arms. Arithmancy, she guessed, though he seemed to expend more effort at it than Rory.

"Now they don't," he said, after a moment. He sounded like he'd forgotten to breathe. "We're safe."

"You're sure."

"Yes." His eyes opened, wide and pale and indignant. He didn't like to be challenged. She knew that. It was exactly why she did it. They were of a height, another thing he did not like. It took effort for him to stare down at her. "Now where's Rory?"

"Your father sent security to collect her. She's stalling. It's working, for now." Thorsdottir cut her glance sideways, toward one of the public monitors. "Don't see any breaking news about the arrest of the Princess of Thorne. I take that as a good sign."

"Why are you here, then?"

"Orders." She grimaced. "Rory wanted me to tell you what she found out last night."

He frowned. "Her Highness."

"Only when she's being unwise. So to me, right now, she's Rory, even though she asked me to find you. Now listen, *my lord*. Will you?"

Color smeared across his cheeks. But he kept his teeth together. Nodded, once and sharply.

Thorsdottir gritted her own teeth. There was no time for storytelling. "Grytt didn't come home last night. Rory stayed up checking all the hospitals and security reports. She found reports of a fight in a shuttle bay, and dead security. She *also* found Prince Ivar's medical records and hexed her way into them. He's a clone. Or he's been cloned. Point is, the man she met here on station wasn't the real Ivar. *He's* on Beo, if he's even alive. She thinks Grytt might've found out, and that's maybe where she was going. She wanted to ask your father about it, but his men were waiting for her this morning and *what* is wrong with you?"

Jaed's face had evolved as she spoke, shifting through phases like a moon. The final phase was a disturbing shade of grey, as if he were already dead and cold. It reminded Thorsdottir of her brother's face, the time he'd run to town for a power convertor and bear-cats had gotten into the sheep. He might not've been able to stop a bear-cat, but he hadn't been there to try, either.

Thorsdottir recalled an incident in her childhood when a cow had kicked her twelve-year-old self in the chest. She felt exactly like that now: as if she might never draw a full breath again.

"You knew."

"No. Not about the Prince." Jaed held up a hand. "Listen to me, all right? I knew about Grytt. That was my . . . fault. They were moving the Vizier last night. I told Grytt. I, ah, gave her my father's pass-string, so she could do something about it."

Thorsdottir had never been this angry before. She had also never been this calm. "Where were they moving him?"

"Beo."

Of course. "When did you tell Grytt about it?"

"Early second shift. She was a little late leaving detention. I intercepted her maybe two cross-corridors up-ring from there."

Thorsdottir chewed over the information. It was a good explanation for Grytt's absence, and for the bodies in the shuttle bay. Not for the shuttle's current location, however, or its passengers.

"And how did *you* know about the Vizier's transfer?"

Jaed pressed his lips together. "I was poking around my father's files."

Thorsdottir had brothers, and she had learned to sniff out the truth in much the same way she learned to cross a barnyard. Lies, in her experience, had a great deal in common with cowpats. They stank, and you didn't want to step in them.

She wished for a good pitchfork.

Jaed's gaze had slunk sidelong, and was roaming the vista on the porthole's other side with practiced disinterest. Thorsdottir considered arguing with him. She considered grabbing him by the neck and shaking him. She said, instead:

"The Regent told you about the transfer, didn't he?"

Jaed folded his arms and hunched. He found something on the floor to stare at, and did so with determination. "He said moving the Vizier would make it easier to control Rory. He didn't suggest I tell Grytt. That was my idea. I *think* he wanted me to tell Rory. Or he thought I would. At the time, I just thought he was telling me his plans. Confiding in me." Jaed closed his eyes. The bitterness was palpable. "I told Grytt because I was *afraid* to tell Rory. I thought she'd do something stupid."

Thorsdottir couldn't argue with the logic. She and Zhang could have *your Highnessed* until they were hoarse: if Rory thought the Vizier was in danger, she'd have done something. Grytt had saved everyone the argument and just . . . acted.

Thorsdottir sidestepped an upwelling of panic. It was one thing to *suppose* they were Gryttless on Urse. It was another thing to *know* it. Rory was down to her and Zhang for advice, and desperate enough to send to *Jaed* for help.

But if Jaed was right, then the Regent hadn't expected Grytt's actions. Which meant he hadn't expected Jaed to tell her. He'd expected Rory to find out, and to do something precipitous, and to be in a great deal of trouble, and thus at a disadvantage, which Jaed had spared her.

"You did the right thing," Thorsdottir said.

Jaed's eyes popped open. He stared at her as if she'd grown wings.

"I'm serious. If you'd told Rory, then you're right. She'd've done something. Then the Regent really *could* arrest her. He may have even planned on that. But you told Grytt, and she—I don't know what she did. I bet your father doesn't, either. All he knows is that three of your security are dead, the shuttle's missing, and Grytt and the Vizier are probably on it."

"You think they're alive?"

Thorsdottir thought about it. "Yes. No help to Rory, now—oh, stop it. That's no criticism. They're not dead. That's most important. She'll think so, too."

Jaed's brows drew together. He would be awful at poker, Thorsdottir thought. Every thought that went through his head traveled across his face. She hadn't realized he *had* that many thoughts. It was an encouraging revelation.

"He must think Rory's responsible. That she ordered Grytt to attack. That's an act of war."

"Until she tells him otherwise. Then it's going to be *your* act of treason."

He lifted his gaze and his chin together. "Better he blames me."

Perhaps there was hope for Jaed yet. Thorsdottir directed her gaze through the porthole where Bielo hung, pale and monstrous. Two of its moons tracked across its face like mobile freckles. One of those might be Beo. Grytt and the Vizier could be on it. Ivar, or a part of him, certainly was.

"Listen. Rory showed me the files about Ivar. Your father's been cloning him."

Jaed gaped at her. "What?"

"You didn't know?"

"No. *No.* That makes no sense."

"It makes all kinds of sense. Clones have a short lifespan. Rory thinks the Regent means to marry her to one of them, wait until it dies, and then marry her to—*now* what?"

"My father said the marriage shouldn't happen. Hers and Ivar's. That it couldn't. That we should try and stop it."

"Your father said that to you? Then he does want you dead. *Listen.*" She lowered her voice and leaned closer. "Rory needs to be *queen,* Jaed. Which she won't be unless she marries your Prince. Her *second* husband can be a jumped-up Minister's son, sure. But not her first."

Jaed looked as if he might incandesce spontaneously. "He *encouraged* me to make sure Ivar didn't marry her."

"Your father did?"

Jaed's chin jerked up and down. The cords in his neck stood out like steel cables. "He said she was trying to use me. That she wanted me to rescue her from Ivar. He said—that the marriage shouldn't happen. That if it did, Rory was *his.* Ivar's." Color flared on his cheekbones, then drained. "And if she didn't, then . . . I could. You know."

"Marry her and live happily ever after, with your father ruling through the both of you."

Jaed looked at her miserably.

Thorsdottir weighed the merits of strangling him here and now, or letting Rory do it, and determined he might still serve a purpose. Besides, she was beginning to pity him. A child tried to trust its parents. It wasn't Jaed's fault his father loved power more than offspring.

"And how were you going to save Rory, then?"

"I had thought—maybe challenge Ivar. To a duel."

Thorsdottir stared at him.

He flushed. "Look. I know I'm not the best fighter, I know *you* can beat me, but Ivar can barely lace his own boots."

Thorsdottir found her voice again, and convinced it not to shout *you're an idiot*. Instead, she kept it low and reasonable. "A duel to what, the death?"

"First blood."

"And when the Prince used a proxy? Someone from security? Then what?"

Jaed blinked. "I—hadn't thought of that."

"That's because you're thinking royalty are normal people. They don't fight, unless it's each other. If you *hurt* Ivar, you'd be committing treason. Best case, prison for life. You actually kill him, you're dead. But if Ivar's proxy kills *you*, then Rory marries Ivar anyway, and he dies in a fortnight, and—"

"And then she marries Merrick. I *am* an idiot."

Jaed's expression was halfway between disgust and self-loathing. It did not look particularly comfortable from the outside. Thorsdottir imagined the inside felt much worse, but she had no leisure for kindness. Grytt was missing, and Rory in jeopardy, and both of those could be credited to Jaed's poor judgment and paternal misfortune. He had not quite betrayed Rory, but he had been fool enough to let himself be used. He had also been her best hope for help. In Thorsdottir's estimation, Jaed's usefulness would end the precise moment his father learned he'd assisted in the Vizier's escape, which had probably already happened.

She also knew that Rory did not measure people's worth by their usefulness to her. Whatever Jaed's errors—and there were several to which Rory would take offense—she would not leave him to his father's mercy.

"Let me help her." Jaed ground the words out. "Please."

Thorsdottir pinched the bridge of her nose. "I don't think Rory needs rescuing. I think *you* do."

As it happens, Thorsdottir turned out to be only half correct.

CHAPTER NINETEEN =====

On Eggs And Omelets

M odern science, as it is practiced today, consists of two primary branches. The first, designated strictly on the basis of alphabetical serendipity, is alchemy, and concerns itself with the study of the transmutation, manipulation, and understanding of substances. The second is arithmancy, and focuses on understanding and manipulating the mathematical principles which underlie, according to the famous treatise by de-Morales, "alle thinges grete and smalle in this Universe, fromme Aether to Man Hymeselff." The k'bal say, simply, that arithmancy is the language in which the song of the universe is sung. Even the mirri, who deny the science of arithmancy and instead refer to it as magic, say it is the breath of the universe, present in all things. (We exclude here the opinions of both vakari and alwar, whose discovery by the multiverse's human inhabitants is still some time in the future by this chronicle's timetable, and whose opinions do not fit as well with our metaphor here.) Arithmancy is, therefore (and despite its place in the alphabet), considered the first principle science, the one on which all others rest. The egg, if you will, that comes before the chicken.

Alchemists, naturally, object to that claim. Not to its objective truth, but to the prejudices and attitudes which accompany the title. Because of arithmancy's claim on first principles, alchemy is often seen as a lesser science, concerning itself with the mere physical manifestations of a more pure arithmantic truth. Some alchemists attempt to argue—the most eloquent of whom is M. Fantome—that it is the interaction with the physical, the intersection of matter and arithmancy, that is the most important course of study, since everyone, even arithmancers, must exist in their bodies (a fact which no arithmancer will dispute). Much energy, ink, and effort has been expended on this debate, from both sides, and to no real resolution; but the debate has produced an assumption, by the layperson, that alchemy and arithmancy do not overlap in practice. This is, of course, untrue.

The one fact on which both branches of science agree, however, is that the practical applications of arithmancy and alchemy do not play well together.

It was past midmorning and creeping up to early lunch when Rory finally declared breakfast finished, and herself and Zhang ready to meet with the Regent. The patisserie up-ring had proven to be out of the specific eclair she had wanted, which entailed a further search, culminating in the most populated café in the entertainment district, nearest the public voidport and, not coincidentally, a twenty-minute walk from the administrative offices.

The cumulative effect of the delay would, by Rory's calculation, be nearly sixty minutes, from her exit from her flat to her arrival in the Regent's office. Enough time, surely, for Thorsdottir to find Jaed, though Thorsdottir's escape and presumed rendezvous were not the sole reasons for Rory's delay.

She had a plan. One, she was sure, that Messer Rupert and

Grytt would have disapproved of; but they weren't here, and that left her fewer options.

Rory's academic interests lay predominantly with arithmancy, and Messer Rupert had encouraged this; but he had been too conscientious to neglect the other sciences. She had done her time with alchemy, both theoretical and applied (having argued, while pointing at a skinned knee, that a Princess needs some knowledge of first aid). But her most useful alchemical knowledge came from history, and the various uses to which compounds and elements had been put, particularly by arithmancers.

The Vizier had encouraged her scholarship. He had also cautioned her against practicing arithmancy while alchemically altered. He could not, therefore, be blamed if she did so anyway, using as historical precedent a catastrophic incident in which Hermet, Vizier of what had then been only the Kingdom of Thorne, had attempted to revolutionize void travel by circumventing the requirement to tesser-hex through a gate. He had attempted to do so using a particular pharmacological substance which purported to expand consciousness, and thus facilitate his ascent (or descent, depending how one views it) through the many layers of aether. No one had ever found his vessel, the station from which it had launched, or the moon around which the station had orbited; the planetary system itself, absent a gravitational feature, had never quite recovered, necessitating the exodus from—which was a finer way of saying abandonment of—the homeworld.

Rory had no intention of tesser-hexing anywhere. Nor did she have access to Hermet's alchemical resources. She had only what she had scrounged from the Vizier's personal medical supplies, and her academic alchemy, to approximate the effects she required. She only needed to be able to hold a defensive hex while carrying on a conversation. It was a small requirement, compared to a tesser-hex. Standard battle-hexwork. But as she was no battle-arithmancer, it would require all her wits, intellect, and concentration in equal measure, and she was short of all three. Messer Rupert had never imagined a scenario in which she would be without himself and Grytt, and thus feel compelled to rely on the weapons remaining to her, though he would have, Rory was certain, protested the word weapon as a synonym for arithmancy.

So, while sharing a table and a pair of eclairs with Zhang, Rory slipped a tiny capsule from her sleeve and swallowed it, along with a bite of eclair, taking care to do so while the Tadeshi security pretended not to watch her every move (and were not, in fact, watching at that moment). Rory was certain that if they *had* been watching, it would not have helped. The capsule was small, and her movements natural, and only Zhang noticed, and that was because Zhang was sitting across from her, back to the Tadeshi, stabbing unhappily at the eclair as if reducing it to crumbs and custard would approximate actually eating it. Zhang paused in her assault on the pastry when she spied the capsule. She was not Thorsdottir, who would have asked about and possibly objected to its presence. But she frowned as thunderously as her partner, and pressed her lips together in a white line that said *your Highness* more clearly than words.

Rory ignored both the Thorsdottir in her mind, and the Zhang across her table, and chased the pill with an unPrincesslike gulp of coffee, which had the additional effect of scalding her throat as it washed the capsule down.

"A stimulant," Rory murmured, "for mental clarity. Messer Rupert kept it," she added, a little defensively, when Zhang continued to stare. "It doesn't last long."

"Princess," said Zhang.

It wasn't quite a *your Highness*, but it wasn't a stirring endorsement, either. Rory took greater care with the second capsule, a precise ten minutes later, dropping it into the last forkful of eclair and conveying it to her mouth that way. Custard did not require much chewing, and the capsule slipped down easily. This time, Zhang pretended not to notice.

Then Rory finished her coffee, set her fork in the middle of her plate, and pushed the plate to the center of the table.

"Finished?" she asked.

Zhang put her own fork down with obvious relief. "Yes."

Rory nodded, then raised her hand and crooked her fingers at the Tadeshi. It was the sort of gesture reserved for social inferiors by people who forget that servants and waitstaff can, and do, spit in the soup. The three security, having no access to food or revenge, simply grimaced and stood and came over.

"We're ready," she said. "You may escort me to the Regent, now."

A precise twenty minutes later, Rory, Zhang, and the Regent's security arrived at the Regent's office. The doors opened as they approached, which could have been courtesy and was, more probably, an indicator of how very expected (and how very late) their arrival was.

Rory set her feet on a straight line toward the doorway, commended her forward progress to balance and momentum, and closed her eyes. The first of the capsules pulsed red across the back of her eyelids, in time with her somewhat accelerated heartbeat, which was itself an effect of both capsule and coffee. Her mind felt extraordinarily sharp. Clear. Unfogged by sleep or worry. Her pressing problems—Grytt, Ivar, the Regent—receded to the edges of her awareness. There, certainly, and no less dire; but absent the chest-tightening worry, and the knot in her belly, and the tendency of her breath to catch in a throat gone tight with panic. What remained: the problems themselves, laid out like equations, spiked with variables and constants, begging solution.

The Regent figured highest among those problems. The longest equation. The most variables. The one most in need of solving.

She had perhaps four steps to go, before the doors. Rory required three of them, and Zhang's hand on her elbow (for balance, when her left toe discovered an imperfection in the deckplate unaccounted for in her initial calculations), to shape a false aura for herself. It was an elementary arithmantic ruse, but a good one, though its effectiveness was dependent on the skill of its creator. Messer Rupert had seen to it that she was very skilled indeed, but against the level of defense she expected from the Regent, she would need to sustain the hex, and adjust it as necessary. Thus, the second capsule, which enabled her to tap a deeper level of the aether, and anchor her hex to that. She should, if she'd done it right—and the doubt, that gnawing uncertainty, was banished to the same place as the worry-knot—seem perfectly normal, perfectly unthreatening, to any local defenses in the Regent's office. A mantis-lion, fully camouflaged. The perfect leaf.

Rory found the Regent exactly as she'd hoped: visibly annoyed, his long fingers strangling each other, a tic beating in his jaw, his eyes glacially furious. A part of her noted the intensity of his displeasure, and the corresponding tension in Zhang. She would have been nervous herself, perhaps even unsettled, forty minutes ago. She would be again, in another forty, when the capsule wore off, so it was in her best interests to move, and speak, quickly.

Rory unfurled her haughtiest smile and struck first.

"Thank you for seeing me on such short notice, my lord Regent. You are most generous."

The Regent noted the difference in her, and disapproved of it:

that was clear enough from the shifts in his posture and the manner in which his gaze traveled over her face and figure.

"Princess. How very kind of you to come. I had hoped to see you earlier. Perhaps my men did not explain the urgency of my request."

where is your damned body-maid

Rory kept her smile firmly in place. "*Your* request? I'm sorry, Regent. I don't understand. I asked to see you."

His nostrils pinched, then flared. "Well.

the hell you did

You're here now. Please. Sit."

There was exactly one available chair in the room, not particularly well-padded or comfortable in appearance, turned precisely square and centered in front of the Regent's desk. The other chairs had been drawn back to the room's perimeter, making the office look a little bit like an interrogation chamber. The arrangement was intended to make Rory feel like a recalcitrant child or a frightened detainee. She considered, for an alchemically accelerated heartbeat, playing to the Regent's expectations; but that was not the kind of leaf she was, today.

"Thank you," she said, and took her time arranging herself in the chair. She dragged it a half meter back from the desk, and off-center, and tilted it forty-five degrees to the plane of the desk. She sat, and crossed her right knee over her left, and folded her hands neatly around it.

"My lord Regent, I came to ask you about Prince Ivar."

"Prince Ivar." The Regent, for one blank moment, stared at her. Then he recovered, clearing his throat and glancing at his turing. Looking for an aura report, Rory guessed. From his expression, she guessed her hex was working; or at least, the Regent did not blurt *liar* at her.

"Yes, my lord." Rory frowned. "I received a message from him. A very strange message."

The Regent sat up straight, as if someone had poked him unexpectedly with a pin. "You. Received a *message*."

"I did. Last night. Midway through third shift." Rory paused. Her heart kicked at the confines of her ribs and chest. She willed it to calm down, and took slow breaths to drive the point home. An unexpected side effect of the alchemical enhancements, perhaps, which would be tolerable so long as the capsules *worked*.

The Regent interpreted her momentary silence for hesitation. His lip curled. It was, Rory thought, supposed to be a reassuring smile. It failed rather spectacularly.

"Are you certain it was from Prince Ivar? I ask, Princess, because the Prince is currently on Beo—as you know—and his opportunities for communications with Urse are limited by his duties there. There is also the matter of the electromagnetic storms, which render ordinary messages quite impossible."

"I *am* aware." Rory permitted her own imposter smile to appear. It had teeth, and a half-life just long enough to ensure the Regent noticed it. "But that's the curious thing, my lord. The message did not originate on Beo. It came from *Urse*."

"That's simply not possible. I'm afraid someone must be playing a prank on you, Princess. May I, ah, inquire about the contents of the message?"

Rory shook her head, feigning embarrassment.

"You mean, was it a love letter? No, my lord. That's why I'm here. It was . . ." She winced, and not entirely for dramatic purposes. Her heartbeat had given up its kicking, and had begun galloping in earnest, leaving precious little space in her chest for her lungs. Her skull had evidently shrunk two sizes as well. "Disturbing. The letter *said* that he wished to dissolve our engagement.

That he was being forced into the marriage, and did not desire it, and wished my collusion in finding a solution to our, oh, how did he say it, *mutual problem.*"

The Regent shook his head. He offered a thin, tepid smile. "That does not sound like Prince Ivar. It's likely a prank, Princess. A poor joke."

damn you Jaed

The fairy gift had not caught Rory entirely off guard since her adolescence. She had almost forgotten the sensation, which had inspired many unfortunate incidents before she had learned to control her reaction. Even so, the sensation was so unexpected, here and now, that she was grateful for the sturdiness of the chair. She had expected the Regent to be unsettled, even alarmed by her mendacity. She had not expected him to believe in its feasibility, and she had not, would not ever, have predicted that he would blame Jaed so easily and automatically. It was as if he'd *expected* Jaed to send such a letter, which was absurd, unless—

Her brain pushed against the confines of her shrinking skull. She pressed her fingers hard into each other, grounding her focus in that discomfort, and stared at her bloodless fingertips.

"A prank played by whom, my lord? And for what purpose?"

The Regent heaved up a sigh that was entirely sincere in its exasperation. "A romantic fool,

Jaed

who, having seen the public spectacle you and my son have been making with each other, wishes to see it made real."

"But to work to dissolve our engagement would be *treason*, my lord."

"Indeed, your Highness. Highest treason."

Rory had rehearsed the expression of offended innocence a dozen times, and it still felt odd from the inside. "Jaed and I are not laboring under any illusions, my lord. I assure you. Our liaison is honorable."

"And yet, Princess, you
know very well
can see how the behavior might look to
my stupid son
individuals who are not aware of the intricacies of diplomacy."
The Regent tried on a smile two sizes too small. His teeth winked through the thin stretch of his lips like bone in deep cut. "I'm sorry you were disturbed, your Highness. If you could forward the message to me, I will have my security ascertain who sent it, and
might be too soon to arrest him
deal with him accordingly."

Rory nodded, and knowing she failed to conceal her distress, hoped the Regent misinterpreted its cause. She wanted to leave now, retreat to her apartment, and consider this new knowledge. She needed to see Jaed, and talk to him, and determine his culpability.

Then she recalled that any discussion of the Regent or Jaed would take place only among her, Zhang, and Thorsdottir, which reminded her what the true purpose of her visit was. Baiting the Regent had been the excuse, and it had yielded more information than she'd anticipated, but that couldn't distract her.

Rory remembered to breathe, and did so. Her skin felt hot. All of it, except the palms of her hands, which felt like half-melted ice. She turned the palms flat on her trousers and rubbed them surreptitiously.

"But that brings me to the second reason for my visit. I would like to see the Vizier. It has been several weeks, my lord. I have received no official advisement of his arrest, or his prosecution, *or* an order for deportation. So unless you are counting him a prisoner of war—which would be curious, since the Free Worlds and the Consortium are at peace, and my presence here is proof of that—I have a right to see him, my lord Regent. I am his sovereign representative."

"I'm afraid that's not possible."

he's missing

Well. That was interesting. Rory made her eyes wide as eggs. She suspected the expression fooled no one, exaggerated as it was; but the fog on the borders of her vision was drawing closer and more insistent, and she needed all the light she could get. "I must *insist*, my lord."

"I've explained my position. The man is suspected of crimes against the Free Worlds of Tadesh."

"You have, my lord. But now I've explained *my* position, so perhaps we can negotiate."

A smile flickered across Moss's lips like oil over water.

the hell

"I would be happy to

marry you off sooner than later

consider your request, Princess, except I fear there may be greater violations of treaty to consider."

"My lord?"

"Your body-maid. Grytt."

She let herself hesitate. Her false aura should, at this point, be turning an anemic shade of puce.

The Regent steepled his fingers and tapped them against his lips. It was a credible imitation of thoughtful consideration, laced with pity. "I feel I should remind you, Princess, that you are responsible for your staff. No, wait, let me finish. I *also* understand how one might be deceived by individuals in whom one places one's trust. There is a great difference between a failure in judgment—and the treason of a close associate—and a deliberate act of sabotage. Do you understand me?"

"Of course, my lord. Though I do not understand your implication."

"I don't believe that is true. Your loyalty to your people is commendable, but I must insist, for the security of Urse, on an honest answer to this question. Do you know where your body-maid is, at present?"

"No, my lord." Rory shifted in her chair, taking the position the Regent had first intended for her: hands white on the arms, knees together, exposed as both supplicant and accused. "She's been missing since last night. I fear something has happened."

The Regent spent a long, deliberate moment staring at his turing. The lines around his eyes deepened. Whatever he saw there, it did not please him.

"Something has," he said. "It pains me to be the one to tell you, Princess, but I believe your body-maid is part of a conspiracy to rekindle the war between our people."

"Impossible," said Rory, too loudly. She hoped she wasn't overdoing it. "There must be some mistake."

"No mistake. We have

nothing

extensive video records. Grytt attempted to

abscond with my prisoner

steal a shuttle during third shift. When confronted, she responded with violence. She

killed three of my men

did not survive."

Rory put both hands over her mouth. She hoped the portion of her face which remained visible approximated shock and horror sufficiently. She did not quite trust her lips, which were not sure if they should smile—Grytt had rescued Messer Rupert—or scowl—

why hadn't Grytt *told* her she was mounting a rescue?—or smirk—because the Regent had lost that battle entirely.

Then she remembered that he was lying to her and attempting to provoke a reaction, and that she needed to produce an appropriate response. She bit her disobedient lip, and made fists and pressed her knuckles against her cheeks.

"Are you telling me that Grytt is *dead*?"

"I

wish

am. You understand," the Regent added with poisonous gentleness, "why I am reluctant to return the Vizier to you, or to permit a conversation. I believe you are a victim, Princess, of terrible advisors. It is only fortunate that you don't know anything about their machinations, or suspicion would fall upon you. And that really would jeopardize

your usefulness to me

the treaty between the Free Worlds and the Consortium."

The fairy gift did not include audio accompaniment, but the flavor and tenor of its report suggested diabolical laughter.

Rory forgot, for a moment, just how awful she felt. She forgot she was sitting in a chair, unarmed, in front of a man who had murdered his King, his Queen, and very probably his Prince, and that any action she took against him would be both ineffective and counterproductive. She very nearly forgot to be a leaf.

"Princess?" The Regent leaned forward. His brow creased in a new pattern. "Are you all right? You're flushed."

Which was when she realized that the first of her alchemical advantages had expired, which meant the second would fail soon, too. Without her hex, her aura would be visible to him, and while reading an aura would not reveal the same level of detail as her fairy gift—she knew, having compared their effects with great rigor—it would reveal clues about her emotional state. She needed to terminate the interview, and quickly.

An ideal leaf would, at this point, burst into tears while protesting her innocence. Rory feared she would choke if she tried to speak. Instead she covered her face completely, and let her shoulders round. She sniffled loudly, amplified by her palms, and scrubbed her hands hard across her cheeks. And she was entirely surprised when she lifted her face out of her hands and found her palms smeared with blood.

Nosebleeds are a common side-effect of arithmancy taken too far. Messer Rupert had warned her of that, by example. Rory considered, for a horrified heartbeat, whether or not the Regent would know that, too, or whether she should attempt to conceal the seepage. Foolishness, she realized a moment later. The Regent could not help but notice. He would draw whatever conclusions he drew. At the moment, she had the element of surprise and a desire to end the interview. Time to end her leafiness, and become the mantis-lion—running away from a bird, rather than devouring a beetle, but still.

She shoved her chair back, tipping it in the process, and lurched to her feet, spilling a little of herself in the process.

"My lord," she said. "Please excuse me."

"Princess?" The Regent looked sincerely surprised. He began to reach for her, registered what was happening, and leaned back as far as his own chair would permit. His face drained of the very substance dripping onto his carpet.

"It's nothing," she said, sniffling past her fingers. "Station air is very dry. If you could direct me to a water closet, however—"

"Of course, yes, out there." He stabbed a finger at the doorway.

Zhang was already beside her, hand under Rory's elbow. *She* knew about Rory's breakfast supplements.

"Your Highness," she said, and took a bruising grip. She steered Rory out of the office and promptly turned toward the main foyer, exactly away from the water-closet.

Rory guessed their destination, and decided to give the order anyway.

"Thorne embassy," Rory whispered to Zhang. "Now."

"Yes." Zhang propelled her forward at a pace which suggested she expected pursuit.

So did Rory. She had startled the Regent, perhaps even frightened him, but he would recover. A man did not achieve his position otherwise. But she had learned that he did not adjust rapidly to surprises. He was a planner, a schemer, she'd known that; but he was not, as Grytt would have said, worth beans in the field.

That had to be useful. Somehow.

Rory let a breath go when they cleared the municipal complex's doors with only shocked stares from the security, though two of them reached for their comms. This was an advantage of the Regent's control; no one acted on his own initiative, and asking for orders took time.

The fifty meters across the plaza between the Tadeshi municipal complex and the Thorne embassy were the longest of Rory's life. She did not dare run. She walked briskly, pinching her nostrils together, thankful for the practical properties of her garments, into whose black fibers all manner of stains could be lost. She was less thankful for the stares and attention. *They probably think someone hit me,* she thought. And then: *Wait. That could be useful.*

Rory let her hand drop a little further. Made a point of looking around, making eye contact with as many faces as possible. There were usually media personnel loitering in the vicinity, waiting for a story. *Bleeding Thorne Princess Flees Tadeshi Municipal Offices* sounded promising.

The security at the Thorne Embassy were not the caliber of the royal guards, but they were Consortium military, and disinclined to let their Princess linger in apparent distress, whatever their orders to remain at their posts. A handful came out and met Rory and Zhang a little less than halfway across the plaza. They formed a breathing barrier around the Princess, though none quite dared Zhang's white-knuckled familiarity.

"Are you all right, Princess?" asked the duty sergeant.

"Yes, thank you," said Rory. "It's just a nosebleed. You know. Dry station air."

"Of course," said the sergeant. She looked dubious.

"No one struck her." Zhang's voice rivaled the deckplate for cool, hard, and flat. "But the Regent may pursue. Let's get the Princess inside."

They did, rapidly, sweeping Rory through the embassy doors past a growing throng of the curious.

"No one appears to be following," the sergeant said.

"No," said Rory. "And I don't think anyone will." Rory accepted a damp cloth from one of the secretaries and blotted her face carefully. "Thank you. The Regent believed me. He thinks I'm a victim. And he doesn't know that *we* know about, ah." Rory registered her audience, at that moment, and amended herself. "What we know about. It's all right. Return to your posts. I'll be in my office. Zhang?"

"Princess."

"You can let go, now."

"Yes, Princess."

"Have you gotten any messages from Thorsdottir?"

"No, Princess."

"All right. That's probably a good sign. Let her know to come here. We'll be waiting."

CHAPTER TWENTY ═══════

The Twelfth Gift

Since the invention of something to write with and something to write on, writers—and in this category, we include particularly historians, but also novelists, poets, and the odd journalist—have enumerated the qualities most admirable, and most reviled, in the human psyche. While there is some variance, there are some virtues which appear to transcend culture (and, in some cases, species).

Among these so-called universal virtues, courage may be the most popular, for the sheer volume of words spent defining, refining, and offering examples of it. The ancient homeworld sage Aristotle posited that true bravery requires a man to be aware of the consequences of his actions: to whit, he must face threat of pain and death, *knowing* those are possible outcomes, and proceed anyway. Courage is neither instinct nor honorable obligation. It is a deliberate choice. While the Kreshti poet-philosopher Kahandir was not the first to note the limitations of Aristotle's definition, she did, in her collection *On Ashes*, offer the most compelling argument that the form courage takes is a matter of circumstance, as much as of character: there are situations in which a woman simply *cannot* act, but instead must wait; and that waiting itself—patience—is itself a form of courage, as important as the moment when action becomes possible.

It is ironic, then, that courage is a virtue most associated with adventurers—knights, princes, kings—and very rarely with princesses and queens, who are expected to be patient, but never brave. It has been noted that none of the fairies gave Rory patience, with no attempt at explanation (fairies defying that by their very nature); but it is perhaps telling (of what, we remain uncertain) that the twelfth fairy's gift to the tiny princess was courage.

The Vizier's embassy office did not have a porthole. It had, in fact, very little decoration at all, except for the tastefully inoffensive artwork spaced at tastefully precise intervals to alleviate the otherwise distressingly blank bulkhead. With the exception of a small Kreshti fern (a sullen, disconsolate pea-green) on the desk, there were no personal items. An appallingly neat desk, with the turing at right angles to its access pad, and to the quantum-hex comm globe, and a bound copy of the treaty between the Consortium and the Free Worlds, with well-worn edges. Rory's own face hung on the wall, flanked by her mother and brother. The official portrait had been taken during her fifteenth year. She noted the remnants of baby fat on her cheeks, and touched the bones in her face. She didn't look like that now. A window—or a porthole—would have given her something else to look at. Even the ominous void, with the Brothers creeping past, towing their moons and flashing their poisonous atmospheres, would have been a comfort.

She checked the chronometer for the twentieth time (in the past thirty minutes), and heaved a sigh that sent the fern into yellow stripes and lavender polka dots.

Zhang eyed the fern, and her Princess, with equal alarm.

"Fine," said Rory. "Try Thorsdottir again."

Zhang nodded. She hesitated anyway, giving Rory a good looking over. Probably checking for nosebleeds, or other indications of brain hemorrhage or whatever it was Zhang imagined happened to foolish arithmancers.

Then she looked at her pocket comm. "Nothing yet, Princess. No response."

"Thank you." Rory stared at the fern. The edges of its bottom leaves turned bright yellow. As it happened, brain hemorrhage was a possible, even probable consequence of mixing alchemy and arithmancy, a little more than halfway up the scale of catastrophe. At the mild end, headaches. At the other, the explosive rupture of ophthalmic tissue.

Rory elected to keep that knowledge to herself.

Despair sloshed against the back of her throat. She had exhausted her options. She had no Vizier, no Grytt. She had avoided arrest and incarceration, for the moment, although the Regent could decide to take her into protective custody. She was a minor under Thorne law, and the *treaty* stated her marriage must wait until eighteen, but she guessed the Regent would lobby for an earlier date, in light of recent circumstances. Her mother would lodge a protest, but with Grytt's murder of Tadeshi personnel and the possibility of a renewed war, Rory did not expect Samur to intervene beyond a diplomatic protest.

At which point she would marry a clone, endure a short marriage, endure a longer period of official mourning and widowhood, and then, as soon as was decent, be compelled to marry again. The alliance between the Consortium and the Free Worlds required royal participation, not the stop-gap union of Regents and Regent-Consorts. But more vitally, the peace required heirs. Assuming Ivar did not succeed in siring any—and Rory supposed he would not, or could not; Moss would see to that—she would need to choose an acceptable husband and produce offspring.

How long she survived after that depended on what Moss knew, or suspected. Accidents happened, out here in the void.

Rory entertained briefly the fantasy that Ivar was fine, that he would break their engagement, that he would sign a peace treaty in perpetuity and require nothing more of her than a brief bi-yearly conversation. Then she dismissed that fantasy. *Happily ever after* was for children's stories. What her happily ever after would entail, she had not yet considered. She had a civil war in her possession, after all.

She had the documents proving the Regent's treason, if she could get anyone to believe them. She suspected those files would survive in the turing exactly ten seconds longer than the Regent's initial realization that she'd read them. She had separate copies, of course. She debated trying to send one set to her mother through the quantum-hex, and discarded the idea. Diplomatic communication was supposed to be secure, but no one believed that. And if she tried to hex it, then she would only be giving the Regent's arithmancer a puzzle to solve before he learned what she knew.

Rory wished Thorsdottir would check in. She was becoming increasingly concerned that something untoward had befallen her, and she was uncertain that her composure could withstand a second personal loss in as many days.

Then Zhang's pocket-comm chimed, and they both jumped. Zhang reached for it, while Rory made useless fists and failed at patience and the fern acquired periwinkle spots. It was not tradition for princesses to carry pocket-comms, for privacy and security and a host of reasons dreamt up before the existence of pocket-comms. Rory decided the tradition's days were numbered.

Zhang keyed in her pass-string and frowned at the tiny screen. "She's at the flat. She's sending Stary to get us."

"What? Why? Is she hurt? Is *Franko* hurt? Did she find Jaed?"

Zhang tapped obediently. The comm murmured and chirped to itself. Then it chimed again. "She's fine, Franko's fine, and she acquired the target. She says Franko's standing guard duty."

"On *guard* duty? Since when do we need a guard?"

Zhang sighed, faintly, and typed, and frowned more deeply. "She says . . . don't ask. She'll tell you when you arrive."

The fern turned bright scarlet. Rory held out her hand. "Give me that."

Zhang held out the comm as if it were a live, particularly unappealing insect. It chimed, just as Rory took it. A new message flashed up. Rory read it. Then she returned the comm to Zhang, who also read it.

They looked at each other for a long moment. The fern, unable to process the emotional morass, turned itself taupe and attempted to blend in with the desk. Rory picked it up.

"Right," said Rory. "We'll wait for Stary."

Thorsdottir, as it happened, did not much enjoy waiting, either. She enjoyed it even less when she anticipated the end would be less pleasant than the waiting itself. She did not require Zhang's confirmation to know that the Princess was angry. Rory liked *no* as much as any teenager, and she was unaccustomed to hearing it from Thorsdottir. It was a miracle, or a testament to the Vizier's tutelage, that she had agreed to wait for Stary.

Stary and Franko hadn't liked what Thorsdottir had said and done so far today, either, but their chain of command was clear enough in this instance.

"Hope you know what you're about," Stary had said. Franko had been less succinct and more profane in his response. But they hadn't argued. Truth was, neither of them wanted Thorsdottir's job.

Thorsdottir didn't want it, either. She wanted Grytt back, in the same fierce and futile way she'd wanted wings when she was four. She'd gotten a pony, instead: a beautiful, stubborn animal with a talent for self-destructive behavior and well-aimed kicks.

Things hadn't changed all that much.

Thorsdottir read Zhang's last message and flipped the pocket-comm off. She set it carefully on the desk, as if it were a grenade with a loose pin.

"The Princess is on her way," she said.

Jaed Moss looked at her from the very farthest corner of the divan as if he wanted to recede into the gap between the cushions, to take refuge among the loose coins and stray fountain pens.

"She's angry, isn't she?"

"Oh. Yes." Thorsdottir tried, and failed, to summon up any words of comfort. Instead, she heaved up a sigh, met Jaed's anxious gaze, and said, "Wait here. Don't touch anything. Don't even *move*. I'll meet her outside. Talk to her first."

"You mean, take the brunt of the yelling. I deserve that, not you."

"Yes, you do. Don't worry. She'll have enough for both of us." Thorsdottir tried to retrofit her grimace into a smile. "She probably *won't* yell. And she won't deny you asylum, either. But I suggest you use the time to consider exactly how you want to tell her everything. And you *do* have to tell her everything."

And so it was that the Princess of Thorne arrived at the tiny cul-de-sac of Thorne sovereign territory, gripping a small Kreshti fern (wan yellow) tightly in both hands. She was preceded by Stary, who was armed to the limit of treaty, and followed by Zhang, who had resigned herself to feeling underequipped for the day's shenanigans. Franko was, true to Thorsdottir's warning, standing guard just inside the corridor's threshold. He had a long-barreled 'slinger propped on his shoulder, and a helmet that made him look a little bit like a beetle. His uniform creases looked sharp as axe blades.

He saluted. "Princess."

Rory paused. Another day, she might have returned the salute and wrested a smile out of him. Now she glanced past him, further down the corridor, where Thorsdottir waited in front of the flat, unarmed and out of uniform. She recalled what Grytt had told her about the various personalities of their tiny garrison, and about pointing a weapon if you didn't mean to shoot it. Or in this case, two weapons. Franko on guard, armed like this, was no matter for levity.

"Any trouble?" she asked.

"No, Princess."

"Good." Because if there had been, there would be pieces of it spattered across the decking. She looked at Thorsdottir again. "Stary, stay with Franko. No one comes in without my order."

"Yes, Princess."

She continued the remaining seven paces, Zhang at her heels. The fern in her hands still throbbed scarlet.

Thorsdottir glanced at it, and at Zhang. "Princess."

"Our guest is an unwelcome complication."

"I'm sorry, Princess."

"No, you're not. *Why* is he here?"

"He told Grytt that the Vizier was being moved. He was *supposed* to tell you, to prompt some sort of reaction. Clearly he didn't. I thought—by now his father probably knows what happened, or what didn't happen, and so he's probably in trouble. So he asked for asylum."

The fern shivered. Orange lines crazed the red.

"He asked, or you prompted?"

"I suggested it. My judgment, Princess." Thorsdottir let that hang between them, for a beat. "I also told him he had to ask *you* before it's official. I also told him to tell you the truth."

"Which you're telling me now."

"Only the parts I know."

Rory closed her eyes and pinched the bridge of her nose. Her mouth worked around what was either a pair of angry badgers or the grandmother of all reprimands. Then she let go of her nose and her breath.

"Fill Thorsdottir in on the morning's events," she told Zhang. "I'll be inside with our guest. Give us at least ten minutes, and knock first."

Jaed stood up as she came inside. He had his back to the porthole. Cherno's dark hulk gnawed at one side of his silhouette. Reflected sunlight limned the other half of his hair silver. A shadow bisected his face, giving her one wide eye, the knife's edge of his nose, a downturned mouth, and concealing the other half.

Appropriate.

Rory set the fern down on the edge of the kitchen divider, and pushed it carefully away from the edge. Then she crossed the expanse of decking in three short strides, neatly angling past the desk. She stopped an uncomfortable less-than-armslength from Jaed.

"Rory," he said, and stopped. His hands hung at his sides, the tendons ridged over stiff fingers.

"You should have told me about the Vizier. Not Grytt. *Me.*"

"I was trying to protect you. I thought you'd do something—"

"Stupid? Rash? *Who* told you about Messer Rupert's transfer? Oh, don't bother sputtering at me. Your father did, I know that. You were supposed to tell me, and then betray me."

"Right. And I didn't."

"Which is why you're here and Thorsdottir's taken your side, instead of burying you in the arboretum under some unlucky shrub. You know how I found out what happened? I lied to your father this morning. I told him Ivar sent me a message, wanting to dissolve our engagement. I was *trying* to distract him with what I thought was something too preposterous to be true. Instead, he immediately suspected *you* of writing it. Why would he think that, Jaed? What have you two decided to do with me?"

Jaed took a cue from the fern, then, and turned two uncomplementary colors at once. "We didn't *decide* anything. I thought—he *said* he didn't want you and Ivar to marry."

"He said that so you'd do something stupid."

"Which, evidently, I am alleged to have done. Writing a letter to you, pretending to be Ivar, trying to break a political engagement? That's the stupidest thing *ever*."

"It's your father who thinks you're an idiot, not me."

"And what do you think I am?"

"Politically naive."

"Maybe. Yeah. Okay. But I didn't betray *you*. My father, yes. My—everything else. But not you." He gulped a mouthful of air. "I wanted to believe—it doesn't matter."

It did matter, very much. The fairy gift was quite adamant on that subject. Rory considered pushing the matter, then discarded the idea. Her head throbbed. She wished for a dark room, a cool cloth, and cup of green tea. Instead, she had Jaed Moss, a political crisis, and an hour before lunch. At this rate, they'd be at war by dinner.

"So," she said more gently, "your father thinks Grytt is alive. He thinks she escaped with Messer Rupert."

"Good—wait. He *told* you that?"

"No, he told me that she was dead. He was lying."

Jaed shook his head slightly. "How do you know? Were you running a hex on him?"

"No. I just do." She did not want to explain the fairies to Jaed. "He's not an arithmancer, your father. He's just got some good hexwork which, yes, I got around. Don't ask me—"

"How?" Jaed's expression made clear he would repeat that question until he acquired a satisfactory answer.

"By poisoning myself. Oh, *don't*. I'm fine."

Jaed looked as happy about that revelation as Zhang had witnessing it. And like Zhang, he did not comment, though it took visible effort. His jaw clenched around recriminations until Rory pitied his molars. "Oh, sit down. You're making my neck hurt."

Jaed did, somewhat warily. Rory maneuvered to the other side of the coffee table and perched on the back of Messer Rupert's favorite chair, feet dangling off the side. She propped her elbows on her knees and leaned forward, so that her eyes were level with Jaed's and her head felt less like it wanted to roll off her neck.

"I think your father wanted you to make an attempt on Ivar's life, either before the wedding, or after, when the clone dies. Jealous Jaed murders the Prince. Grief-stricken Regent forced to execute his own son. Which would leave Merrick for me."

"Thorsdottir said as much."

"Thorsdottir's said a lot today."

He winced. "So will you grant me asylum?"

"Yes. Provisionally. If we're lucky, your father won't know *where* you've gone for a while."

"And if he figures it out?"

"Stary and Franko can hold that corridor for a while."

"Rory."

"I'm not serious. Shut up and let me think." She cradled her forehead in her palms. Her brain banged on her skull like a prisoner on a locked door.

"You are *not* all right."

She heard him get up, a too-loud rasp of clothing on couch cushions. She sensed his hand hovering over her shoulder: an artifact of the alchemy, perhaps, that made him buzz like an exposed tesla coil. It was as if she could *hear* his aura, and feel it. Perhaps she was turning into a Kreshti fern.

His voice was blessedly quiet. "Can I get you something?"

The door chimed, just then, with a shriek like a thousand cats thrown simultaneously into a blender, or a single blast of the Lanscottar pipes.

"Get *that*," she said. "It's Thorsdottir and Zhang, anyway."

She listened to the boom of his footfalls, and the metallic howl of the door on its slide, and the rumble of a barbarian horde— three people, all speaking softly, a room away—preparing an invasion. Then another set of footsteps emerged, thumping across carpet and ringing off the deckplate underneath. Thorsdottir's boots appeared in the circle of Rory's vision. Thorsdottir's agitation buzzed across her skin like live wasps. She squatted down and peered up at Rory. Her eyes were fury and worry combined, and very, very blue.

"You need to go to bed, Princess," she said. "Now."

For once, Rory did not argue.

Rory woke to the smell of Thorsdottir's cooking, and a murmur of voices and the fuzzy chrysalis dark of her chamber, cut only by the patient glow of her turing. Someone had activated the opacity hex on the porthole. Rory banished it, and the stars faded into view. Cherno had retreated for the evening—it was evening, wasn't it? That smelled like garlic, not breakfast. Her head still felt scuffed on the inside, but her stomach had recovered sufficiently to demand something in it besides the memory of eclairs.

Rory sat up and discovered that although she did not recall undressing, she clearly had, or someone had done so for her. Likely the latter: the clothes she'd worn to see the Regent were absent entirely. There was a bulb of water on the bedside table, and a pair of pills of a more benign alchemy than her earlier ingestion. She took them both promptly, and swished the water around in her mouth before swallowing. She did not feel *quite* human yet, but her condition was improving.

She swung her feet off the bed, facing the porthole, and squinted at her reflection, which was little more than a translucent afterthought in the porthole's silicate alloy. A ghost, lost and—she leaned forward. A ghost whose braid was a mess. Rory grimaced and combed her hair out with her fingers. Her ghost self acquired a cloak of pure void in which the stars winked and glittered. A lovely image for some poet or artist. The ghost girl, hair made of stars.

Rory made a very unartistic face at her reflection, and reached for her robe. Then she remembered the political refugee in her living room and reconsidered. There was more modesty in the robe's concealing folds than there was in her tum'mo leggings and shift, and Jaed had seen her *that* way often enough; but there was an intimacy to the robe, too, reserved for the household, her sole garment which was not also a costume.

You are a Princess, said Messer Rupert, a hundred-hundred times in her memory, with all that implied. A constant performance of someone else's script. And on the other hand, there was Grytt, who—

Rory sighed. Grytt would not say anything, because Grytt usually didn't. But she also wouldn't stand in opposition to Messer Rupert. She never had. She'd just hand Rory a pair of trousers and a sweater and expect no argument, because to Grytt, Jaed had been, was, and would be forever the outsider, which was half a step from enemy.

Except he wasn't. He was maybe a fool, sometimes, politically naive. But he wasn't *bad*. She *liked* him, for some version of like. And he was the closest thing she had to an ally on Urse, not because of his personal qualities (or lack thereof) but because he and she had mutual interests. Outmaneuvering the Regent, mostly, and avoiding prison. Or marriage. The distinction was fuzzy.

So, at the moment, was the distinction between Princess and person, and she was tired of playing roles.

Rory shrugged the robe around her shoulders, taking extra care to wrap it close and belt it firmly. She left her hair loose, too, and her feet bare, and, having fortified herself with a breath and a hard stare at herself in the porthole, turned on her heel and marched into the corridor.

The garlic smell was much stronger out here. Rory waded through it, toward the murmur of voices, which, upon closer proximity, resolved into a conversation. The subject appeared to be a recounting of an event from Thorsdottir's youth, in which a basket of stolen eggs, brothers, and practical jokes figured prominently. Jaed was laughing and stirring a pot, while Thorsdottir wielded a substantial cleaver in pantomime, and Zhang smiled and arranged cutlery on the table.

At that moment, Rory missed Grytt and Messer Rupert with a ferocity that quite stole her breath. It should be curry in the pot, not stew. It should be Grytt muttering, and Messer Rupert fiddling with a turing, and herself wielding the spoon. Thorsdottir and Zhang would be across the corridor, and Jaed would be avoiding his father and brother elsewhere on Urse. But that normal was over. Gone. Even if Grytt and Messer Rupert had survived—and Rory chose to believe that they had—they could never return to it, even if the Regent turned into a ball of blue smoke and they were permitted back on Urse. Too much had happened. Thorsdottir and Zhang and Jaed.

And Rory could not regret it, not really, because in that normal, Messer Rupert and Grytt had intended she marry Ivar. Now Rory had different plans, new plans, and for the first time, an opportunity to act on them. She was no longer *their* Princess. She was becoming her own.

Though what those new and different plans were, well. She didn't know yet. She needed to think of them first.

Zhang noticed her, then. She absorbed Rory's informal attire, the loose hair, the bare feet, with a raised eyebrow. Then she offered one of her small, spare smiles.

"Princess," she said, exactly timed for one of the pauses in Thorsdottir's story.

"Princess," echoed Thorsdottir, looking up.

"Ah." Jaed also observed Rory's attire, and found something very interesting to examine in the depths of the stew pot.

"Sorry," said Thorsdottir. "We're almost ready."

"No, go on. Finish your story. Tell us how you outwitted Sven and got out of the loft *and* recovered the eggs."

Thorsdottir snorted. But she continued, narrating a successful scaling of the old barn wall with bare feet and hands ("Didn't you get splinters?" "Oh yes. Shed-loads.") and the rescue of the eggs *and* the subsequent descent and flight across the farm, with Sven in pursuit, the recounting of which lasted until the bowls were on the table. Rory was grateful for Thorsdottir's excellent sense of timing. She was spared any need to make conversation, or to respond to someone else's attempt. After a day in which she had been the center of everyone's attention, in a lifetime where that was often the case, Rory found anonymity at her own supper table to be a welcome thing. It left her time to think, and to see to the ingestion of her own supper for a few spoonfuls.

Knowing what the trap was, how it would close, was no help if she could not also see a way past it. The Regent had outmaneuvered everyone. There was no way to undo his maneuvering. She *could* endure, at least for a while, and hope an opportunity presented itself. Except *endure* meant marriage, first to a doomed clone, and then to Merrick. It was what a Queen would do. What her mother was doing.

Rory realized, with her spoon halfway to her mouth, that she did not *want* to endure marriage.

Nor, for that matter, did she wish to endure monarchy.

It was a startling realization.

What *good* was the thirteenth fairy's gift, if it showed her a truth she could not avoid?

Messer Rupert would have remarked on her silence by now, reminding her that stew is for eating, and eating is best accomplished by conveying the contents of the spoon into one's mouth, rather than reorganizing it in the bowl. Neither Thorsdottir nor Zhang did so. Nor were they likely to do, having no history of prompting princesses to eat. So it would fall to her to direct the conversation, and to jeopardize everyone's enjoyment of what really was an excellent stew. Messer Rupert would have found a graceful way to do so, an anecdote or an observation to segue naturally into the topic at hand.

Rory had exhausted her own supply of grace for the day, though hopefully not cleverness. Still, she thought she should save that for the actual plan, rather than spend it on pretty preamble.

"So," she said, and waited for three sets of eyes to find their way to her face. "I think some clone of Ivar is going to arrive on Urse very shortly, and my wedding will happen even more rapidly thereafter, and we need to see that it doesn't. The wedding, that is."

Jaed blinked. Thorsdottir and Zhang looked at each other. Then Zhang squared her shoulders.

"How?"

"I don't know yet. I was hoping you had some ideas."

Thorsdottir stirred her soup as if the answer floated somewhere among the potatoes. "If you don't marry Ivar—or some version of him—the treaty could fail."

"And if I do marry him, I'm a widow in two weeks and Merrick's wife in twelve months *and* the real Ivar dies, if he hasn't already. Look. If I thought marriage would save us from Moss, I'd do it. But I think *my* life won't last much longer than the arrival of my first heir. Then I'll have an accident, or I'll end up on Beo while a series of my clones legitimizes another round of Moss sovereignty."

"You could always challenge the Prince to a duel. That was my original plan."

Rory sat up a little straighter. "What?"

"It's an archaic law, I know. Barbaric. Bloodsport to settle an argument. Or in this case, an engagement." Jaed twisted his face into a self-deprecating grimace. "I thought it'd get you out of the marriage, but it's a stupid idea. Thorsdottir pointed out why it wouldn't work."

Rory rescued her spoon, pinching it between thumb and forefinger. She examined it as if there might be gems encrusted on the handle. There were not; but she was beginning to see something better than gems. She was beginning to see a move the Regent wouldn't be able to counter.

And so the littlest fairy's gift worked its magic, unnoticed and unacknowledged, as the most powerful magics so often do.

CHAPTER TWENTY-ONE

Contact With The Enemy

There is an old adage, among generals and schoolteachers, that no plan, however well-constructed, survives contact with the enemy. While this maxim can be seen as one part cynicism, two parts irony—since of course both battle and lesson plans *do* in fact survive engagements, and people either die or learn, accordingly—the proverb's underlying wisdom is sound. No plan, however thorough, can be guaranteed success. The enemy often will behave in a manner unanticipated, and random elements can skew the scenario. A wise general must, then, be flexible, able to adjust in the moment. They must, in other words, be ready to *react*.

It is an uncomfortable position.

A Regent, too, must possess some degree of flexibility and foresight, particularly if he wishes to wrangle a headstrong Princess into marriage before her majority as delineated by treaty. He must have reasons why the ceremony should be hurried, and responses to the inevitable objections, and responses to the next round of protests. But the Regent of the Free Worlds of Tadesh despised *reaction*. He preferred to act, and to keep his opponents reacting. In his mind, it was forever better to be on the attack than on the defense, and he had considerable pride in his strategic skills. He had, after all, engineered the death of two kings and one queen on his path to power, and removed his political enemies, *and* repurposed potentially benevolent research into what would, were it widely known, provoke outrage both within and without the Free Worlds. He considered himself a success, and predicted more of the same for his future.

He was not, therefore, pleased with two surprises in as many days. The loss of the Vizier was unexpected and inconvenient, and Grytt's participation in that loss was entirely unforeseen. On the one side, it removed two of Rory's most irritating allies from play. On the other, he did not control them and, in fact, had no idea where they'd gone. The missing shuttle had not turned up on Beo at its appointed hour. Nor had its wreckage been found in the system, despite extensive sweeps and searches. It appeared to have vanished utterly. The Regent did not require an advanced degree in astronomy to understand that the void was a big place, and the ways in which a small shuttle with two fragile biological entities could disappear were many, varied, and lethal; he had employed some of them to rid himself of the Queen, after all. So when his advisors assured him that the Vizier and the body-maid must be dead, he agreed. In private, he stared at system maps and brooded.

The second surprise—the stupidity of his younger son—offered both greater immediate vexation and a simpler path to resolution. He knew how to solve that difficulty: he would confine the boy to the Moss family apartments, until Rory's marriage, widowhood, and remarriage—in short, until the public forgot him—and then send him to some inhospitable, inconvenient corner of the Free Worlds—Lanscot, perhaps—with a political position just barely befitting his rank.

The problem was that he couldn't *find* Jaed.

The Regent was not the sort of man to focus on frustration. He dispatched a missive to his distant wife, informing her that circumstances required a more rapid union of their kingdoms than anticipated. His fool son, rumors, and so on. When Samur responded, insisting on a real-time quantum-hex conference, he acted the part of the embarrassed father (which required very little acting) and the diplomat concerned for maintaining the peace (which did). Samur, to her credit, requested a conference with her daughter, which the Regent could not find sufficient grounds to forbid. But since the only equipment for quantum-hex conferencing lived in the Tadeshi municipal complex, he was not concerned that mother and daughter might conspire to surprise him. The conversation would be monitored.

He dispatched a second shuttle to Beo, with orders to prepare his Highness for a wedding. And he sent a messenger to Rory, requesting her presence to discuss "matters of import to the Free Worlds and the Thorne Consortium." He included a specific date and time, allowing her three days for preparations, tantrums, or frantic (monitored) calls to Samur.

Then, with the important business in motion, the Regent turned his full attention to finding Jaed.

"He wants to tell me about the wedding." Rory grimaced. "I wonder how he managed to move it up a year. What if I refuse?"

"You can't." Jaed had not expected the twin knots in his stomach and his throat, upon hearing Rory pronounce the word *wedding.*

"I most certainly can. I can have feminine complaints. I can have a cold. I can have five days of indigestion."

"He'd send his alchemists and his chirurgeons to treat you

personally. Rory." Jaed leaned forward and fixed upon her a stare of such mingled earnestness and vexation that his face threatened to crack under the strain. "I've been living with my father my whole life. He doesn't make a move like this unless he knows he can win. You don't want this to come to a fight. Do you?"

"Of course not. And of course I'm not going to simply defy him." In truth, the last thing she wanted was the Regent or any of his personnel coming through her door to compel a conversation. Better to meet him on his territory.

"What concerns me more," she added, a little snappishly, "is that he's going to find *you*. He's running out of places to look. The rumor that you're here is all over the network."

"There's a rumor he's holding me under house-arrest, too. So much for rumors."

"Yes, but he knows that one's not true. The only reason I can think that he's not banging on the door already is that he doesn't believe we're that stupid."

"Or I'm just not that important. There won't be any scandal if I'm found here. It's not like the Free Worlds require virginity in a Princess."

Rory cast her eyes heavenward. "I'm not worried about my reputation. I'm worried what your father will do when he gets hold of you. Which he will, if you stay here."

"Do? Probably confine me to my room, under guard, and thus render true the tragedy of the star-crossed lovers, forced apart by cruel political circumstance. He won't *execute* me, Rory." Jaed sat up straight, of a sudden. "Wait. If I stay here—*if*? Where else would I go?"

Rory held up a finger, forestalling the next utterance. "I prom-ised you asylum, yes. I have very few options for enforcing that, except hiding you from your father, and we can't do that indefinitely. Even if the Regent won't storm our doors, he *will* be monitoring our household expenses. Our water consumption alone will alert him. Never mind the increase in groceries."

Jaed's face embarked on a journey from shocked betrayal, with brief layovers at hurt and resignation, before stopping at surprisingly thoughtful. "Okay. So you have an idea. Tell me."

"I do, and I will. But first, tell *me*, Jaed. What is the state of relations between Lanscot and the rest of the Free Worlds? Specifically the relationship with your father?"

Rory knew the answer already, of course. She had pored through the histories herself. She had read a half-dozen treaties late into third shift, sipping tepid coffee and acquiring a legendary backache. Lanscot had been an independent colony, later absorbed—badly and bloodily, through a war of occupation and two generations of civil resistance—into the Free Worlds, with the marriage of their Princess to the second son of the Tadeshi King.

It was not an unfamiliar story. The Lanscottar Princess had not fared well, accused of treason before her thirtieth birthday and executed, leaving behind heirs to be raised as Tadeshi. Since that time—some two hundred years, give or take—the Lanscottar had sulked and suffered at the margins of the Free Worlds, fiercely independent and, at the same time, marginalized as an archaic curiosity. They had produced, along with a surfeit of animal-derived textiles, the economist-philosopher deCharry, who had spent a full third of his life imprisoned for sedition, and whose treatise on the feudal roots of contemporary customs of employment and remuneration spawned no fewer than six reformation movements, two of which had succeeded. It was deCharry's fault, if one could use the label, that the Tadeshi King must share governance with a

Council of Ministers and that he was accountable to public constituents. It was that very system, in fact, that had enabled Vernor Moss to rise from relative obscurity to Regency in fewer years than deCharry's imprisonment.

Messer Rupert had always said that history offered the best prediction of future events. Rory interpreted the Lanscottar Princess's tale as both cautionary and, if she did not act, prophetic. She had no intention of toppling the Tadeshi monarchy, or of instigating another Lanscottar rebellion. She wanted only to ally herself with a people who took pride in their defiance, and use that pride to secure a safe place for Jaed.

She had a *plan*.

That very afternoon, at precisely fourteen-hundred, Ursan standard time, two Thorne guards were observed by the 'bots across the corridor from the Thorne compound exiting the premises. The 'bots dutifully recorded their images, which the bored junior arithmancer minding that particular feed then dutifully attempted to identify. There were only four guards, after all, and their faces were well known; but they had all taken to wearing full uniforms, lately, including the antiballistic visors, presumably so they could use their internal, crypto-hexed communications and thus thwart any monitoring by Ursan equipment.

The junior arithmancer knew very well that her superior could hex his way into Thorne HUDs, if he so desired. She also knew he had been given no such directive, because she had no feeds from the HUDs on her own console. Such information would have identified the guards instantly. Instead, she was compelled to guess, based on body-type. The woman of the pair was easy. Zhang was smaller than everyone else. The male, however, was more difficult to identify, Stary and Franko being almost of a size. The apprentice settled on Franko, finally, and made a note in her logs.

She followed the pair's progress through the 'bot-feeds. It was unexciting. They stopped at several grocery establishments, one cosmetics shop, and a patisserie before arriving at the door to the Lanscottar embassy. After a brief exchange at the door, they were admitted.

So engrossed was she in the progress of the Thorne guards that the apprentice failed to notice that the feed from the 'bot watching the Thorne compound flickered for a period of three seconds before it stabilized. She failed to notice that a man's black boot passed through the bottom edge of the screen and that three seconds later, that same boot reappeared in the same place and repeated the same trajectory, and repeated the process exactly every three seconds thereafter. It was exactly the sort of motion that a person in front of a bank of monitors all displaying various grainy moving images would not notice, unless she was particularly astute.

Astute individuals, however, are not assigned console-minding duties.

The not-particularly-astute junior arithmancer made another note in her logbook. The visit from the Consortium to the Lanscottar was somewhat unusual, but also not without precedent. At least one exchange of sweaters and brightly colored plants had already occurred, shortly after the formal presentation of the Princess to the Prince. That was a customary first move in further diplomatic relations. This visit was probably an invitation to some dreary social event or another. The junior arithmancer considered adding that to her logbook, then discarded the idea. Her supervisor did not approve of personal speculation.

At fifteen hundred twenty, the Lanscottar embassy doors

opened. At this point, the 'bot watching the doors suffered a malfunction. Its visual feed turned entirely pink, with pixelated infusions of lavender, orange, and yellow. The junior arithmancer followed procedure. First, she struck the console with the flat of her hand. Gently, once, and then harder. When the visuals failed to resolve, she turned that 'bot off, waited three seconds, and turned it on again.

The feed resolved. Five minutes later, the Thorne guards exited the structure, and proceeded by a more or less direct route home. This time the apprentice *did* observe a flicker in the Thorne 'bot's feed, but before she could follow procedure and hit the display, the image steadied. The Thorne guards had returned and, laden with their packages, re-entered the premises.

The black boot, and the three-second span of video in which it had been the sole actor, did not reappear, and was never noted in the logbook. The presence of the hex which had produced that repeating segment was also not recorded.

And so Jaed Moss passed into Lanscottar custody, and with him, copies of Prince Ivar's medical records. Rory had hesitated over sending the latter, before finally deciding that the only independent copies should not be kept in her residence. The records were her best evidence of the Regent's perfidy, but only if they remained hidden. The moment he knew she had them, he would move—against her, the Lanscottar, Ivar, the Thorne Consortium—to protect himself. Rory reckoned that he would destroy the physical evidence, fabricate other documents, arrange a catastrophic accident on Beo—in short, that he would do nearly anything to protect his power.

In that, she was correct.

Where she erred, however, was in her assessment of the Lanscottar, and particularly, Dame Maggie.

————

When the Tadeshi security arrived the following morning, encountered Franko standing sentry at the mouth of the narrow corridor, and demanded entrance, Rory thought at first that they had come about Jaed, and congratulated herself on having moved him the day before. Her demeanor, therefore, was calm, even a bit smug, when she went to meet them.

Her calm slipped a notch when she noted the formality of their uniforms, and the bulk of body armor beneath it. Either they were expecting a fight, or they wanted her to believe that they were. Franko had stationed himself exactly in the corridor's center, symbolically and suicidally, should it come to actual conflict. Rory gauged the tension levels on her side to be *high, with increased chance of violence*, and their side to be *oh yes, please start something*.

Decorum said keep walking and pretend to notice nothing. Prudence said dive back into the flat and bar the door. Rory compromised, stopping precisely where she was and pretending to adjust her sleeves, which, being attached to a Lanscottar sweater, required very little adjustment. It was an obvious stalling tactic. Rory just as obviously did not care.

"Thorsdottir?" she said. "Get Zhang."

"Yes," said Thorsdottir, and whipped around with equal parts precision and desperation and did not quite dive back into the apartment. Ten seconds later, she emerged with Zhang, at which point Rory appeared satisfied with the disposition of her sleeves. Together the three of them walked up the corridor.

She was considerably less sanguine when the leader—the same medium blond fellow from her last encounter—declared that she was, per section forty-two-dash-seven-dash-one of the Treaty between the Free Worlds and the Thorne Consortium, hereby remanded into custody of the Free Worlds of Tadesh, and that she must come with him for her own protection.

He was serious. His companions were serious. And heavily armed. Rory thought she could see a small hedge of similarly outfitted security waiting just beyond easy eyeshot of Franko's position.

Sweat prickled along her scalp, under her arms, across her palms.

"Do you have orders to take me into custody by force, sir?" she asked, while her heart made a credible attempt to crawl up her throat. It was one thing to know what the Regent was capable of doing (anything, really) and to prepare for such an eventuality. It was quite another to experience the effects firsthand.

Grytt had been right: she would be a fool not to fear Moss. Rory began to suspect she had been a fool, lately.

"I hope that will not be necessary," the medium blond security man said. That, too, was honest, and no comfort at all.

Be calm, she wished her heart. It retreated obediently, leaving her throat clear, and resumed pacing the confines of chest and lungs. She could not bluster her way through this situation, but she could perhaps paralyze with politeness.

The smile slipped into place, old armor, well-practiced. "Against what threat, exactly, am I being protected?"

"The Regent will explain. Please, Princess. If you could come with us."

The small hedge was moving, in Tadeshi threes, into more visible, and strategic, positions. Franko had noticed. Rory took note of the absolute rigidity of his spine, and the bleached knuckles gripping his 'slinger. She felt, rather than saw, Thorsdottir's gathering tension to her right. Behind her, Zhang was as still and silent as aetherless void, which meant Zhang was also upset, prepared to act, and waiting for a signal.

It was a moment in which wars could be (re)started. The Regent had to know that. He was perhaps trusting her to respond diplomatically. He was also perhaps hoping she did not; if she *did* resist, he would still take her into custody. She recalled the Vizier's arrest, and what Grytt had said about stray bolts. If she fought back now, she would lose, and she would truly be alone.

"Stand down," Rory said, and laid a hand on Franko's arm. To her distress, she did not have to feign the tremor in her hand. "I appreciate your concern for my safety, but I must ask, sir, what provisions have been made for my personnel?"

The medium blond's face relaxed a fraction. His smaller companion let go a visible breath. The largest continued to stare on a vector that suggested he and Thorsdottir were eyelocked and stalemated.

"Your body-maids are welcome, too, Princess. The remainder of your guards might prefer lodging in the embassy's guest quarters."

So. The Regent's men were here to search both apartments, under the thinnest of political shields, and to effectively take her prisoner. A spike of anger joined the prudent terror, hot and cold by turns.

"May I at least pack some belongings?"

"I have no orders to that effect."

There was a small crowd gathering now. Rory considered rushing among them, throwing herself at the certainty that the Regent's men would not engage in public violence, and at the hope that the crowd might help her. She reconsidered, when she got to asking herself what help, exactly, she expected. The Regent *would* gain access to her quarters, and he *would* take her into custody. A civilian gathering armed with nothing more dangerous than pastries and personal communication devices would hardly risk themselves for what was, in essence, their favorite celebrity of the moment. It was *her* job to entertain *them*, not theirs to defend her.

All right. Entertain, she would.

"I will be happy to accompany you," she said, a little louder than was strictly required by etiquette and proximity. "But I insist one of my body-maids be permitted to pack for me, and that the other accompany me to whatever custody the Regent has prepared. It is not at *all* proper to have strange men in my chambers, unobserved."

Her voice remained steady. Her hands shook, where they pressed against her thighs. She resisted, only just, gathering fistfuls of sweater. If they refused, there was nothing she could do.

"I." Medium Blond looked like he wished he had someone to consult. He scooped his gaze sideways, at Large Blond, who was still engaged with Thorsdottir. Then he dredged up an ill-fitting smile. "Of course, Princess."

"Thorsdottir," Rory said at once. "Please oversee the packing with Franko. Advise Stary to see to the rest of our equipment, and to instruct the embassy to prepare suitable quarters for himself and his partner. And Thorsdottir. I'll want my fern at once."

"Princess," said Thorsdottir. She peeled away in a smart slapping of boots, breaking her staredown with Large Blond with a nearly audible snap. Her long legs took her to the flat's entrance, and through it, before the Tadeshi could react.

Rory employed a method learned in youth, on Thorne, when Messer Rupert had taught her how to gauge a storm's distance. Count, he had said, the seconds between lightning and thunder. The shorter the count, the closer the storm.

One purple tree-rat. Two purple tree-rats. Three purple tree-rats.

That quantity of tree-rats, of whatever hue, would ensure Thorsdottir sufficient lead-time to get inside the flat and secure the most sensitive materials.

Medium Blond's expression said he was well aware of what Rory had done, and that he saw no particular harm in it, which meant that the Regent was not particularly worried. That was not surprising. His security would go over every centimeter of both apartments, and likely an arithmancer or two with them. The capabilities of the Princess of Thorne to conceal anything from him was, apparently, of no great concern at all.

That realization restored Rory's calm. The Regent was expecting her to behave exactly the way she *was* behaving, which meant she had been a very convincing leaf. And now he was about to bring the mantis-lion into his territory, which sounded much better in her head than its physical reality, because in truth, a mantis-lion is a small insect, vulnerable to large boots and casual swats unless it is very, very careful.

While she waited for Thorsdottir to emerge with the fern (and, presumably, a small bag of essentials, that a Princess would need until the balance of the baggage could be assembled, transported, spied upon, and delivered), Rory, conscious of her several audiences, clasped her hands together in front of her, and rolled her shoulders in, so that the Lanscottar sweater seemed even larger.

You see? said that posture. *I am no threat at all. Little me, drowning in all this wool.*

Then she raised her chin and stared with studied indifference past the security, allowing her gaze to wander across the crowd. A great deal of curiosity there. Some sympathy. And even—though she did not stare, lest she draw attention—some shaking heads and frowns.

Thorsdottir re-emerged at that moment. She handed the bag—

a military-issued duffel, rather more stuffed than a Princess's immediate needs might suggest—to Zhang, and glared so forcefully at Medium Blond that he snapped his lips closed on a comment. To Rory, she handed the fern, which promptly divided its efforts between vermillion and magenta.

"Thank you," said Rory. "Franko, help Thorsdottir pack my apartment, please. Go now."

She waited two purple tree-rats, then said, "May I have your word, sir, that my body-maid and guard will be permitted to pack my belongings without interference?"

Medium Blond looked as if a sudden crop of nettles had materialized in his small-clothes. He could not very well say, "No, Princess, our own personnel will sift through everything." He was no longer certain they *could*, without incurring a conflict that he was under strict orders to avoid. He settled instead on a, "Yes, Princess," that earned him a sharp side-eye from Large Blond beside him.

Rory recycled her most gracious smile. "Thank you." She readjusted her hands on the fern. "Then please, whenever you're ready."

Medium Blond gestured, and a second trio of security moved to the end of the corridor. This set was more olive in complexion, and both taller and broader. They formed a spearhead, dividing the crowd as neatly as a boat's prow slices through water. A third triad, medium brown of both skin and hair, fell in behind, effectively surrounding Rory and Zhang with a fence of black uniforms. Rory was uncertain if she should feel like a prisoner or a precious commodity, and decided that she was both.

The Regent certainly didn't mind parading his prize through the station. They took the main thoroughfares, drawing stares and crowds where they passed. Word of her coming spread ahead, so that by the time they reached the diplomatic plaza, a small audience was already waiting. The Thorne embassy staff had turned out, nearly en masse, in an ominous clump. Rory feared (and hoped) for a moment that they would stage a protest, shout and surge at the Tadeshi, but they did not. The embassy guards saluted. The civilian staff bowed, male and female alike.

Rory risked the ire of her escort and stopped to wave, to smile, to offer reassurance that she fervently hoped no one believed. Surely a message had been quantum-hexed to her mother by now. *Surely* that. Although, on reconsideration, Rory imagined the quantum communications might be suffering outages today, or intermittent service, or just simply fail to work in the Thorne Consortium's embassy. Samur had been silent on the matter of Messer Rupert's arrest, which Rory had taken as evidence she'd been arguing with the Regent behind the scenes—but what if she hadn't known at all?

"Please," she said, and thrust an arm between the two halves of her escort. She walked up to the Acting First Ambassador of Thorne, who bowed a little more deeply.

"Please welcome Stary and Franko, when they arrive," she said. "And please don't hesitate to assign them duties, as you see fit."

"Majesty," said the ambassador, which was not technically correct, as Rory was not yet Queen; but it was a declaration of loyalty, and unexpected, and Rory's eyes stung and threatened her composure. She blinked hard and rapidly, and retreated into her escort—which was, predictably, scowling at her, at her embassy, at the fern—vivid orange, now, with spatters of furious pink—and permitted them to take her the rest of the way to the municipal complex.

The sound of those doors, when they whisked shut behind her, was the loudest thing Rory had ever heard.

CHAPTER TWENTY-TWO

The Gilded Cage

I t is a common practice, among Kings, Regents, and other sovereign personages who make plans which involve nations, colonies, and large investments, to protect those plans by limiting the ways in which they interact with chance. While the methods vary according to historical period and monarch—as detailed by Ghota in her excellent *Maintaining Control: A Historical Survey of Two Kingdoms*—a universal source of chance, and thus disruption, comes from the people involved. Arithmantic predictions can offer probabilities of likely actions and reactions, and many a sovereign has relied on those with great success. But the more conservative sovereigns—dubbed alternately conscientious or tyrannical, depending on the historian—attempt to control the most disruptive elements through fear, coercion, or, perhaps simplest, incarceration.

Of course, there are laws, most of the time, which attempt to limit, or outright forbid, incarceration without crime. Thus, a sovereign who wishes to act conservatively and prevent his plans from ever coming into contact with the enemy must use diplomacy, and sometimes force, to relocate a problematic individual to a location in which her potential for damage is eliminated. Narrative tradition is full of dungeons and towers employed for this very purpose;

because while prisons and detention blocks are very well for ordinary citizens, they permit too much potential interaction with fellow prisoners, allowing for conspiracy, sympathy, or escape.

Thus, in keeping with tradition, both political and narrative, the Regent ensconced Rory in the least accessible location in the Tadeshi municipal complex. He could not put her in a dungeon for two reasons. Firstly, a dungeon is impractical on a void-station, not because of its cramped confines and windowless chambers—which are standard, and unremarkable because of that—but because the horror of a dungeon relies on its damp walls and vermin, and the Regent was short of both. Ordinarily he did not consider that much of a loss. Today, he mourned their absence, though not necessarily for Rory herself; he did not like the look of her body-maids, one for her Kreshti complexion, and the other for her size, and both together for the looks of sheer murder they cast about like most men cast shadows. He comforted himself with the knowledge that he *did* have free cells in the detention block, and while those cells lacked mold or rats, they were designed to render their occupants miserable. They remained an option, should the Princess require incentive for good behavior, though the Regent did not *expect* that she would. Rory had proven herself resourceful and clever, but still, at the end of it, too pragmatic to offer resistance for its own sake, particularly when the consequences would be borne by others.

The second reason for avoiding a dungeon—or a detention cell—as Rory's residence was this: prisoner-princesses do not fare well in dungeons, not because of any inherent incompatibility, but because, *politically*, a princess in a dungeon invariably wins the sympathies of the sovereign's own allies—children, cousins, siblings, and, most damning, the jailors themselves. The Regent was well aware of Rory's charm, and while he was himself immune, he did not suppose everyone in his employ would be.

The other traditional destination for prisoner-princesses is a tower, and while *tower* as a physical artifact was impossible, *tower* for all practical purposes was not. The municipal complex of the Free Worlds permeated several levels of Urse, sealed unto itself. The Regent selected for Rory a suite at the very top level, against the outer hull, with a single double-wide porthole overlooking the dock, through which Bielo made daily traverse. It was a lovely set of rooms, appointed with fixtures more in keeping with planet-side luxuries than traditional void-born pragmatism. The tesla fixtures hung in glittering confections of metal and silicate crystals from ceilings paneled in warm polycarbonate amalgams and grained to look like old timbers. The carpets spread across the deckplates were thick, and richly patterned, and priceless. There was even a cast-resin mantle, framing a 'caster facsimile of a fire, on which was moulded fantastic beasts that sneered and snarled at the room.

Rory sympathized.

There were also 'bots in twenty locations, both audio *and* optical, and a layer of high-quality hexes on the turing, 'casters, and 'bots. Rory ascertained that immediately, having taken one turn of the premises under Medium Blond's watchful eyes. She choked up a thank you, dismissed him, and resisted throwing what looked like a genuine antique candlestick at the door. Instead, she held it in her right fist like a club, and prowled her new prison's confines, marking the location of each 'bot. With the exception of the lavatory, each room was covered from multiple angles; the lavatory had only one 'bot, rather boldly mounted on the freestanding mirror in the corner, where it could not *quite* see the interior of the shower. The toilet cubicle had no 'bot at all, but Rory discovered a pressure plate under the ridiculously shaggy rug, which would report excessive occupancy by weight.

Rory stomped on it, pure pique, before returning to the main chamber. She looked at Zhang. She looked at the fern, which was trying to hide by turning itself ecru.

Zhang followed her gaze. The fern's barest edges flared crimson. Zhang's expression did not change. She looked at Rory, who had fixed her stare at the elaborate light fixture overhanging the even more elaborate table.

"Shall I help you unpack, Princess?" she said.

"Yes," Rory told the chandelier. "I'm sure Thorsdottir will be along soon."

Whether in response to Rory's exhortation, or by coincidence, Thorsdottir did indeed arrive shortly. She came with several bags draped over her person, with a half-dozen Tadeshi security in her wake, serving both as porters and as insurance of Thorsdottir's good behavior. None of them seemed happy, especially the Tadeshi in custody of Rory's harp case. He was red-faced and damp at the hairline and collar and looked as if he wished to deposit the instrument on the decking with all the ceremony one grants a sack of tubers.

Though Rory was predisposed to kindness, she was also only sixteen, verging on seventeen, frightened and angry, and unable to reach the source of her distress. The security were the only targets available.

"I'd like that over *here*," Rory called, from the far end of the room, and watched as the man wrestled the case—real harvested wood, not vat-grown, and almost as valuable as the instrument inside—across the carpets, which seemed to snag and grip the case with fibrous fingers. She directed the harp's disposition to the minutest detail, *this* angle, *that* angle, over by *this* chair, before dismissing him at the conclusion of his labor with an impatient hand gesture. He left, with the rest of his companions, even redder of face, his jaw ratcheted tight around anger.

Zhang watched, impassive. Thorsdottir frowned. While Thorsdottir, at least, would not have objected to violent expression of her own frustration, she also realized the futility of harassing people whose personal goodwill could be an asset later on, whatever their professional alignments.

"Your Highness," she said.

Rory held up a finger, just that: imperious gesture and warning together. She neither looked at Thorsdottir, nor spoke, and, after a heartbeat, returned her attention to the harp case, opening the brass latches, easing the instrument out of its prison, setting it beside the porthole.

Thorsdottir shook her head and retreated, dragging several bags with her. After a moment, Zhang followed.

The Princess remained, alone in the front room, drawing her fingers across the strings with apparent idleness. Then she pulled the chair to a more convenient distance, sat, and began tuning the harp with a savage expression at odds with the care and precision of her play.

And so Rory's imprisonment began.

The same narrative tradition that places imprisoned princesses in towers neglects the details of their confinement, as though the princess merely waits, patient, for her circumstances to change. Instead, the story refocuses on the adventures of the individuals who eventually arrive to liberate the princess from captivity. The reason for this neglect is easily explained: long literary descriptions of people doing nothing is boring for an audience. This explanation, however, rests on the assumption that the prisoner is actually doing nothing for the duration of her confinement—which is to say, physical actions may indeed be limited, but the actions of *mind* are not.

Rory did pass her first afternoon in captivity *doing* a great deal. She tuned her harp. She practiced tum'mo. She rearranged the contents of the wardrobe and the disposition of the furniture in the main room. And all the while, throughout each activity, she was thinking. Then she returned to her harp and began to play it, for a duration greater than any since leaving Thorne. Rory had an idea.

The Regent came to visit Rory that evening. He was not, as one might have expected, feeling particularly triumphant. He had summoned Rory to dine with him—phrased as a request, of course—and been rebuffed with an excuse of headache, so succinct that it bordered on impolite.

That might have amused him, on another day, as evidence of her pique. He did not believe any stories about headaches; the Princess was angry, and asserting her power the only way that she could. But he had failed to find Jaed in Rory's apartments, which left the Regent still unsure where his younger son—and the second most likely source of disruption to his plans—was. He was certain Rory had some information on the matter; he was equally certain she would not be forthcoming with it.

The Regent elected, therefore, to visit her himself, prior to the delivery of her evening meal, under the auspices of soliciting after her health. He was fully prepared for her ire, her demands, her tantrums—and once those were out of the way, he thought might manage to learn something. He did, although not the information he'd hoped to acquire.

Rory greeted his arrival with all the expression of the grotesques on the mantle, which is to say: stony, flat, and forbidding.

Nor did she rise to welcome him. She remained seated beside the porthole, her harp tilted back in the playing position. When the Regent came into the room, she pushed it upright with visible irritation.

"My lord Regent," she said. She did not invite him to sit.

He did so anyway, selecting the central cushion on the couch, which afforded him the clearest angle to see her face, past the harp's silhouette. He left his escort standing near the door, two black columns of uniform, armor, and weapons. He was mildly amused when the second of Rory's body-maids appeared from the rear of the suite, pretending to join the first in a game of chess near the porthole, in which, evidently, pieces never actually moved.

"I trust you find this suite acceptable," said the Regent, after a long moment in which he waited for Rory to adhere to protocol and make some polite inquiry about whether or not he'd like refreshment.

"Quite. Thank you."

"Good," said the Regent. "If there is any way in which I might make your stay here more comfortable, please do not hesitate to ask."

Rory's very dark eyes flickered, as if she were reading a HUD's optical display. The Regent cast his own surreptitious glance sideways, and encountered only the fern, which was clearly unwell, being a pale, venomous green.

"You could begin, my lord, by explaining why I'm here at all."

"I received intelligence that your life was in danger, Princess. An assassin. I thought you would be safer here."

Rory raised both brows. "I see."

She clearly did not believe him, and while he had not thought that she would, he'd expected a better show. The Regent found the dearth of emotional feedback disconcerting, accustomed as he was to seeing an aura report on a pop-up window on his turing. He resolved that next time, he would permit his arithmancer to accompany him, if only to gauge her emotional state more precisely than the obvious anger.

"An assassin," he added, more testily, "is a threat we must take seriously."

"Of course, my lord." Her lips flexed, visibly holding back whatever else it was she wanted to say. Her hands gripped the harp's curves so tightly they were bloodless.

The Regent waited. Silence was a powerful tool, he'd discovered, particularly against teenagers and amateur criminals. Wait long enough, and most subjects belonging to those categories would break.

Rory did, after a respectable minute or so, although *what* she said was not what he'd expected.

"We find the lack of a kitchen somewhat inconvenient," she said. "If I might, my lord, I request a portable refrigeration unit, a small cooking device, and a cabinet for storage."

He blinked. "We have an excellent kitchen in the complex, Princess."

"Then I will avail myself of its facilities."

The Regent imagined how his chef would respond to a princess banging about, disrupting his staff. Then he imagined the Princess with access to cutting implements and to everyone's food. "I am afraid that isn't possible. You will take your meals here, or in the formal dining room with me and Merrick."

The fern seemed to be dying as he watched. It bled through red, then drained white, even as the tips of its leaves turned a halogen green. Rory's face matched the fern for pallor.

"Then let me repeat my earlier request for portable kitchen materials."

"Princess, you will hardly be poisoned."

"Cooking relaxes me," she said. "And it provides structure for the day, which I believe I will find sorely lacking otherwise. Unless I will be permitted to leave these quarters at will? Perhaps resume my duties in the embassy?"

"Until we resolve the matter of the assassin, it would be best if you remained in our custody, Princess. But should you wish to travel *within* the municipal complex, simply request an escort from the security outside your door. There will *always* be two men there, Princess."

"I see. Thank you for explaining, my lord." She plucked a string on the harp, then pinched it into silence. "Was there something else you needed from me?"

The Regent marveled at the girl's audacity, to imply that she might dismiss *him*. His patience, already strained, creaked alarmingly.

"Where is my son, Princess?" he said sharply. "Where is Jaed?"

She bent her lips into the sort of smile that earns that classification only by shape. "Confined to his room, I'd imagine. Much like I am. Isn't he?"

She wasn't even trying to lie. He did not need an aura-reader to know that. She knew where Jaed was. She was *smug*. How she had contrived to conceal Jaed, the Regent did not know. The tip advising him of Jaed's residence with the Princess had been technically anonymous, originating from a public access terminal for which there was inadequate 'bot coverage, but the alchemists had found traces of his hair in the shower drain. The source had been correct. But Jaed had evidently vanished.

In another age, the Regent might have employed methods to

persuade the Princess to share her knowledge. It was times like these he was most ambivalent about the price of modern civility.

"I am afraid," he said slowly, "that my son is missing. Given the presence of an assassin, you understand my concern. Any information you could give me would be most welcome."

The Princess sat back and folded her hands in her lap. "Of course, my lord. Should any information find its way to me past the men at my door, I will advise you at once."

Another evident dismissal. This girl was truly remarkable. "While I am here, Princess," the Regent said, "let us discuss matters of great importance to Thorne and the Free Worlds."

Rory raised her brows. "More important than this threat to my royal person?"

The larger body-maid clamped her jaw so tightly the Regent thought she might crack a tooth. He sympathized.

"Sarcasm is an unattractive quality," he murmured, "and one unworthy of the future Queen of the Free Worlds of Tadesh. What would your mother say, your Highness?"

"Whatever best served the interests of Thorne. But it seems premature to discuss a royal wedding, if that is what you meant. My eighteenth birthday is a little more than a year in the future."

"The wedding will take place on Prince Ivar's eighteenth birthday, Princess, not yours, to coincide with his coronation. And before you protest: I have already discussed the matter with my ministers, and with the Regent-Consort of Thorne, who has undoubtedly discussed it with *her* council. We believe it in the best interests of our people if we amend the treaty to accommodate Tadeshi law. You *are* familiar with it?"

Rory did not look as shocked as the Regent had anticipated. In fact, she did not look shocked at all. "Perhaps my lord would supply me with the necessary books and documents, so that I may familiarize myself with the finer details. I have noted that the turings in this suite have a very limited access to the public networks."

The Regent chose to ignore that. "I will do so, Princess. Expect visits from the tailors, and reports from the Minister of Finance, detailing the preparations. You will be needed for consultation on some matters."

"*Thank* you, my lord." Rory bowed her head. "I will cooperate to the best of my limited capacity."

The Regent stared at the crown of her head, and the blue gleam of Bielo reflected in her black braid, and revised his opinion of Rory's resemblance to her mother. Physically, certainly; but where Samur was convincingly cooperative, Rory had clearly been permitted an excess of agency, the effects of which must be handled before her ascension to the throne.

"I am certain you will," said the Regent. "Good evening, Princess."

He took his leave under the distinct impression that, although he had come away best from the encounter—she would not have her improvised kitchen, nor freedom to leave her suite unescorted—he had not entirely triumphed.

Jaed Moss did not find his own confinement especially comfortable. Lanscot's compound was among the older and least well-maintained sections of the municipal wing (by design), and smelled pervasively of wet sheep. It was also filled with Lanscottar who were suspicious in general of all persons Tadeshi, and in particular of him. It might have been easier if all he had to deal with were scowling eyes peering out of tartan-wrapped faces, but inside the compound, the Lanscottar dispensed with their woolen wraps, dressing in perfectly reasonable, unremarkable tunics and trousers like anyone else. Jaed endured full-facial scowls, beetled brows, and the flat, uncompromising unsmiles of every person in the corridor as he was escorted to his new quarters by a pair of equally unsmiling security.

"You stay here," said the taller of the two.

"Dame Maggie'll call for you when you're wanted," said the shorter one. Her tone suggested Jaed might languish a very long time.

"Thanks," he said. "I mean it."

The smaller escort had already turned her back on him. The taller one's expression softened a jot. "You've got run of the place," she said. "If you want it. We've got a rec room, and a little gym. There's a terminal in there, has maps and mealtimes on it. You're not a prisoner."

It was a kind thing to say, if not entirely true. Jaed thanked her again, and resolved to be a model not-really-prisoner and stay in his quarters.

The following afternoon, the first reports of Rory's relocation to the Regent's compound surfaced on the station news reports. Jaed watched the footage of Rory, Thorsdottir, and Zhang marched through Urse surrounded by a hedge of his father's security, while the reporter alleged an assassination plot and extolled the cleverness of the Regent's security in having foiled it. The Princess, said the reporter, had requested relocation, and the Regent had extended his personal hospitality.

Jaed thought his father must be slipping, if he hadn't concocted an entire conspiracy already, complete with names, to blame for this alleged assassin. Assassination attempts played well on Urse since the death of King Sergei, but even so, a lack of specific details hurt credibility. Either his father didn't care, or—no. That must be it. His father didn't care. He didn't think the details would matter, because no one would question whatever tale he told.

It was all *very* vague. Jaed began to suspect his father had acted quickly, before he'd had a good story in place. But then the following day, the newsfeeds were quite overtaken by announcements of the upcoming nuptials, three months hence, between Princess Rory Thorne and Prince Ivar Valenko. No further mention was made of the assassination attempt. Clearly the Regent was counting on the excitement of a coronation and a wedding to keep the station entertained and distracted, though from what, Jaed had no idea.

That evening, seeking his own distraction, Jaed ventured exactly far enough from his quarters to request of the kitchen staff a bottle of Lanscottar single malt. The cook, a closet romantic and ardent follower of the Jaed and Rory romance, gave Jaed one of his better bottles along with his best sympathetic expression.

Jaed seemed to be feeling rather sorry for himself. While it is not a chronicler's task to guide a particular interpretation on the part of the audience, it may be appropriate here to advocate on Jaed's behalf. He regarded himself as essentially a prisoner—kind words aside—to a people to whom he was at best a political hazard, and for whom he might also be a hostage. He reckoned his worth to his father was purely political, and that Dame Maggie was politically ruthless enough to spend him if the situation required it. So if the reader finds themself impatient with Jaed's demeanor, well, perhaps they might dredge up some sympathy. This historian would not waste time reporting a man's self-pity unless it becomes something more interesting and germane to our chronicle.

The following morning, Jaed awoke with a headache and an epically foul taste in his mouth to the beeping of his terminal. He staggered, squint-eyed and graceless, across the room, intending to swat the machine to silence. Instead, his hand slipped and turned it on. It was then that Jaed realized the beeping was not an errant alarm, but rather an alert of a special broadcast. He noticed both the broadcast's origin—*not* Urse's news network, but rather the Outer Colony Independent Link—and the content in the same ragged, indrawn breath.

Lanscot Referendum Passed by Unanimous Vote

The name was misleading, as the report soon revealed. The referendum wasn't a political act local to Lanscot, but rather a collective proclamation, of which Lanscot was only the largest and primary signatory. There were at least a dozen others (truthfully, Jaed stopped reading after the first few), all colonies and stations on the fringes of Tadeshi influence, all victims of annexation. Only three of the signatories—the Kymric, Zhenovian, and Tzoumi, who also had violent, difficult histories of assimilation into the Free Worlds—even maintained a presence on Urse.

Jaed knew that the Ursan newsfeeds would be broadcasting their own version of the story, in which the Lanscot Referendum would be reduced in significance to merely a political gesture by ungrateful malcontents. And because he knew his father, Jaed suspected that the accelerated wedding, and perhaps even Rory's arrest (he, at least, would call it what it was), was a result of the referendum, which his father would've known about before any public broadcast got hold of it. Any non-local broadcasts were held at least one Ursan day before release on the station. Jaed reasoned Maggie must have dispensation to get hers so promptly.

Jaed wondered if Maggie had known when the Referendum was to be issued *before* Rory'd asked for his asylum with Lanscot. Or if Rory had known. Or if *everyone* in the multiverse figured things out before he did. And then, because he was not the same young man Rory had approached in a gym some months before, or even the same young man who'd gone a few rounds with Lanscottar single-malt the previous evening, he turned off the report, took a shower and two painkillers, and dressed. Then he accessed a map of the embassy on his terminal and figured out where Maggie's office was and, after a moment, decided against calling ahead to ask for a meeting.

Sometimes surprise is a strategy.

There weren't any guards outside of Maggie's office. There was only a lone secretary who got up and scuttled into a side passage, intent on some errand, either unaware of Jaed's approach or assuming he would wait in front of her desk until her return. He didn't. He went to Maggie's door and banged the flat of his palm on the metal. Then he looked up where there should be a camera over the door—there was—and stared at it.

From the corner of his eye, he saw the secretary coming back with a couple of what must be security at her heels. He had a moment's sick certainty that he'd been, what was it Rory called him? Right, *politically naive*, which was a nice way of saying stupid, and that he was either going to be dragged bodily back to his quarters or perhaps thrown out of the compound altogether.

Then the door to Dame Maggie's office whisked open.

"Well," she said, "Come in, then. I wondered when you'd show up."

Jaed wasn't sure what he expected to find in Maggie's office. Something . . . neater. His father's office was ordered. Spotless. Possessed of portholes. This office was none of those things. There were tablets and styluses piled haphazardly on one end of the desk, with a small Kreshti fern from Rory's previous visit perched on top. One of the massive woolen wraps was half-draped, half-fallen from a chair in the corner. A 2D 'cast of Lanscot hung on one bulkhead, the planet revolving on its axis, its constant cloud-layer splitting and sealing again over surprisingly bright slivers of ocean or glimpses of the habitable landmass, a collection of large islands in the cooler end of the northern hemisphere's temperate zone.

And, most fascinating, there was a quantum-hex globe perched on the edge of the desk.

Jaed sidled up to it. Every quantum communication device was linked to one or more others specifically and exclusively by a series of hexes that bored holes in the fabric of the void, and was of sufficiently advanced arithmancy that it might as well have been magic. Such globes were common enough in the municipal offices, but all of them were registered to Urse and monitored. This one was not one of *those* globes. It was smaller and a bit scuffed on the surface, as if it'd shoved in the bottom of someone's rucksack and smuggled onto the station (which it had).

Jaed jabbed his chin at it. "That's. Um."

Dame Maggie eyed him. "A quantum-hex communications globe."

"I was going to say against regulations, but I suppose that's the point. This one isn't standard Ursan issue. Just how many other globes does that link to, and where are they?"

Maggie leaned back in her chair and folded her arms. "You don't expect me to answer that, surely. What do you want, Jaed Moss?"

"My terminal woke me up this morning with an OCIL report about a referendum. They're saying it's a declaration of independence. Is that true?"

She raised an eyebrow. "What do you think?"

"I think you gave me asylum on Rory's asking, and you wouldn't have agreed if there wasn't something serious going on, something that is better served by my survival than my capture and execution as a spy or whatever charges my father came up with as an excuse. This referendum. I just don't get what help you think I'll be."

Maggie's expression softened. "Your father's a hard man. We

know that as well as anyone. You're here specifically because Rory Thorne asked a favor. That's all."

The Kreshti fern, visible in his periphery, turned profoundly green.

Jaed chewed over a retort that would have felt good to say and probably landed him back in his quarters, this time with a guard on the door. Then he dumped the wool wrap onto the floor, dragged the chair in front of Maggie's desk, and sat down. "I know Lanscot wants independence. But there's no way my father's going to give up a *planet*. You know that. The Free Worlds of Tadesh has a shortage of planets with actual biospheres, and the stations need the resources. Rory won't be able to get you your freedom. Even when she's Queen. No matter how big a favor you think she owes you for saving me."

"The Princess said you were sharper than you seemed. Oh, peace, lad." Maggie held up a hand. "It's not an insult. What were we supposed to think of you, being your father's son, trotting around in Merrick's shadow?" She plucked a data crystal from her terminal and laid it on the desk between them. "Have you read these files?"

"If those're Ivar's medical records, then no, I haven't read them, but I know what's in them."

"Treason, that's what." Maggie turned the crystal between her fingers. "It's the sort of thing that could start a revolution. A rebellion, among some of the outer colonies. It's the sort of thing that takes down dictators. It's the sort of thing we can use, if your father decides to fight back on the referendum."

"That's not why you gave me asylum. You didn't have those files yet when Rory asked. And it's not why you held the referendum, either, because something like that's been in planning for a long time."

"Right on both counts."

"Then why?" Jaed wanted to stare at his hands. Instead, he stared at Dame Maggie. "Do you intend to . . . what, trade me to my father? Use me as a hostage? Don't look at *me* that way, Dame Maggie. You're a politician. Though I think I should tell you, I'm not worth much to him these days."

Maggie smiled. She was a woman in shades of brown—medium skin, darker hair, lighter eyes—but her smile was wide, white, and startling. "Oh, I think that's not true. I've been watching you lately, carrying on with the Princess." She paused, in case Jaed wished to protest the term. When he said nothing, her smile tightened. "I thought maybe her request to give you shelter was a matter of sentiment. But then . . ." She leaned over and dragged the quantum-hex globe over a few centimeters, until it had edged into the expanse of desk between them. "Then I got a call from one of the other globes linked to this one. *That* globe's on a ship we have out there on the fringe of this system."

Jaed examined that knowledge with careful mental fingers. Urse's astronomical neighborhood was large, he knew that. Vast distances from the central star to the rocky, aetherless inner planets to Bielo and Cherno. The tesser-hex gate lay even further out, in the same plane and just past a belt of asteroids that must've been planets before some cosmic catastrophe. Galactic law and good sense said any ship through the gate announced itself, via automated transponder, so that local ships (and Urse) knew who was in the neighborhood. If the Lanscottar had a ship out there Urse didn't know about, that was—well. A lot closer to armed conflict than Jaed had supposed.

"Big ship?"

"Oh, no. Little. Surveillance skiff. They intercepted a Tadeshi shuttle running for the gate. It's a good thing that shuttle didn't get to the gate, mind you. You don't tesser-hex without a turing to do the math, even if you *are* an arithmancer." She waited while Jaed thought that through.

Jaed side-eyed the fern. It was smugly cerulean, with striations of violet. Not a hint of mendacious green.

"The Vizier." His heart stuttered hopefully on Rory's behalf. "And Grytt?"

The fern deepened its self-satisfied blue. "It's *her* recommendation I'm taking, telling you all this, and only because you came to me, first. To answer your initial question: the referendum was intended as a gesture. You're right: we were counting on Rory's influence once she ascended the throne. Now *this*"—she jabbed at the data crystal—"suggests she won't get the chance to help us. But this also means we have actual leverage."

"Maybe. But you only have until the wedding if you want to act on it. After that, my father will have the Consortium's warships to draw on."

"Technically, by treaty, he has them now."

"No. He doesn't. His marriage to the Regent-Consort is provisional. It's a treaty to stop the war, that's all. The full alliance doesn't happen until Rory marries Ivar. That's *why* she has to marry him."

Dame Maggie sat up straight. Her fern flickered through the spectrum of surprise. "How do you know that?"

"Rory told me." Rory had explained, at length and with detail, the conditions of her future marriage, during one of their many public strolls through Urse. Jaed could recall with perfect clarity the way her hand clenched around his arm, and that bright, false, furious smile she deployed like a weapon. The gossip forums were full of those photos, Rory looking happy and amused, when Jaed had known she was furious and frustrated and leaving marks on his skin through his sleeve. "I think we both know who's going to be running the Free Worlds after Ivar's coronation. That means we can't let it happen."

Maggie appeared to be considering what Jaed had said, which frankly surprised him a little. The next words out of her mouth surprised him even more.

"All right. What do you suggest?"

CHAPTER TWENTY-THREE

Life In The Tower

Arguably chief among a historian's tasks is the recording of information, which must be collected and presented in such a way as to appear objective (these events *happened*) while still affording a framing narrative (and here is *why* and *how* events happened as they did). As such, a successful history makes note of the moments and decisions which contribute to major events. When discussing the union of Rory Thorne and Ivar Valenko and its consequences, then, it is necessary to examine the effects of the Regent's so-called "tower treatment" of the Princess, which was designed to isolate her from external influences and events. In that, it was successful, to the letter of its intent.

Time, as has been noted, seems to pass at different rates for a subject, inversely proportional to how much the subject enjoys her current situation. There is a corollary, however, that there is never enough time for adequate preparation, no matter how bored, frustrated, or miserable one might be.

Rory, for her part, was not idle. She had three months and two days before Ivar's eighteenth birthday to thwart the Regent by saving Ivar and avoiding any plans to marry her to Merrick. But the mechanisms of how she might accomplish that goal were not immediately evident.

She needed more information. She also needed to appear very much the leaf, and not at all the mantis-lion. She reasoned that the Regent would expect her to follow the accepted stages of teenaged outrage. She had already attempted defiance. Now she would appeal to another authority.

She demanded to speak to her mother.

The Regent, with great magnanimity, promptly delivered a quantum-hex unit to Rory's prison-apartment, without any attempt to dissuade her or force her to come to a location of his choosing. That suggested two things: that he was confident he would hear whatever was said, and that whatever was said would have no effects on his plans.

Rory was certain the quantum-hex machine would have its own layers of spyware. Rory was also certain that her mother knew nothing of the Regent's plot against Ivar. She was less sure of her mother's complicity in the accelerated marriage arrangements. She wanted to believe that Samur did not approve of them, and that her acquiescence was an indicator of how little she could inspire the Consortium to intervene in Tadeshi affairs; but there remained the possibility, however slim, that Samur was genuinely in favor of the Regent's plan. She had, after all, arranged the marriage in the first place.

So it was that Rory found her heart beating too fast and her stomach tying itself into knots. While she waited for the hexes to make their connection, she straightened the already orderly arrangement of her desk. Tablet *here*, squared and exactly one centimeter from the terminal keypad there. After a moment's consideration, she set the Kreshti fern where it could be easily seen by the camera, and thus, by Samur.

She considered hexing her aura into good behavior; the fern was an unhealthy shade of chartreuse, with veins of cerise and tomato spidering along its leaves. She discarded that notion in the next moment. Her distress was expected; therefore, the Regent (or whomever he had reviewing the recording) should see exactly that distress.

The quantum-hex machine beeped. The viewing-globe, heretofore blank and black, acquired a small white dot at its center, which rapidly expanded into a profusion of bright light and blurriness that resolved, rather rapidly, into Samur's likeness.

The Regent-Consort of Thorne sat behind her own desk, arranged almost identically to Rory's, except for the prominent 2Ds of her children. Samur's fern was a larger specimen and it, too, bore an unhealthy pale green hue over large parts of its leaves. But its accents were deep orange-magenta, bordering on plum: distressed, but resolved, with none of her daughter's active anxiety.

Interesting, Rory noted; and chased that thought aside before her own fern's leaves could change color.

Mother and daughter regarded each other for a moment, silent, taking note of ferns and desks and faces. Then Samur brought out a smile of sufficient brightness and enthusiasm that someone might fail to notice that her fern remained determinedly puce.

"Rory! My darling. How are you?"

Rory could count on one finger the number of times she'd been called *darling*. She did not need the fairy gift to tell her Samur was unhappy, and that Rory figured close to the center of that unhappiness.

She plastered her own smile into place. "Mother! The Regent says I'm to marry Ivar on his eighteenth birthday, and that is in just three months!"

Samur's fern turned a little bit greener, like wheat newly

sprouted in spring. "Yes, dear. I thought you might be calling about that. The Regent

is up to something, smug bastard

and I discussed it. We thought it best to move up the nuptials, in light of the

Lanscottar referendum

rumors about your romantic inclinations. Something about his younger son?"

"Oh, that." Rory rolled her eyes, grateful for a chance at unfettered, unpolitical honesty, while her mind leapt toward the *Lanscottar referendum* and began making a list of questions she wanted to ask. "Jaed is my *friend*. I told the Regent as much."

"Nevertheless." Samur leaned onto her elbows, in a posture the Vizier would have recognized all too well. "Appearances matter, Rory, sometimes more than the truth."

Rory let her smile wilt a little bit. She need not pretend enthusiasm; everyone watching knew better. "So I've been told."

Samur's eyes narrowed. She studied her daughter's face, searching for signs of rebellion. "We have a treaty with the Free Worlds of Tadesh. You

don't have the luxury of friendship

will marry Ivar, and you will be Queen. That is necessary to keep the peace between our nations."

Rory's fern flashed bright as sunset. She choked out one of those small, self-deprecating laughs that people expect to hear but no one ever truly believes. "I suppose, then, that maintaining *appearances* is why the Regent has been so generous with our new quarters."

"New quarters?" Samur said it softly, as if repeating a new and strange word to be sure of its pronunciation.

Rory made herself look up just as slowly. "Oh yes. The Regent has found the most *astonishing* residence for us. It's actually *in* the municipal complex. I suppose that's more appropriate for a future Queen of Tadesh than our old apartments." Rory leaned sideways, allowing Samur to see past her shoulder. "And it's so much larger. Thorsdottir and Zhang can *each* have their own rooms now. No more need to share with Stary and Franko. They're being quartered in the embassy now."

The hardness of Samur's smile spread like frost across glass until it reached her eyes. "That is certainly generous of the Regent."

The fairy gift indicated otherwise, in syllables more profane that Samur was wont to utter.

Rory's relief translated into a flash of temporary violet along the edge of her fern's leaves. Her mother had not known about the move, then. Her pragmatic politics did not extend to her daughter's imprisonment, at least.

But to Rory's astonishment, Samur's fern did not turn a cold analytical blue. Instead, it turned decidedly pink, with tremulous strands of orange. "I'm surprised the Vizier

why hasn't he written?

has not kept me informed. He must be very busy."

Rory could not quite control her flinch, nor intercept the stricken look she cast at her mother's image. So her mother *didn't* know about Messer Rupert's arrest. That probably also meant she had no idea about what'd happened to Grytt, which made Rory suspect their escape had not gone well. (And indeed it had not; although the ill-luck in this case was a matter of convenience rather than survival, having to do with the vastness of the void and Grytt's claustrophobia, and the delay before the Lanscottar spy-skiff scooped them out of the dark.)

Rory rolled several lies around on her tongue, trying for the one least likely to flag the Regent as *seditious behavior.* Rory knew if she began shouting that the Vizier had been arrested, that he was missing, that he might've been involved in violence with Grytt, that the communications-globe unit would likely cease functioning.

Politics is about appearances; in that, it bears much in common with theatre arts.

Rory nailed a smile to her lips. Her fern, permitted the luxury of honesty, acquired a set of bitter black stripes, jagged and irregular. "He's been busy, lately." That sounded lame and unfinished. She could imagine the Regent leaning forward, finger hovering over the connection, ready to come crashing down. She groped for a plausible excuse and seized upon something Samur had (not) said. "He, ah, said it was something to do with the Lanscottar referendum."

Samur stared at Rory's fern. Her lips tightened, then drew together. Then the mask of Regent-Consort fell back into place, even as her fern melted into a browned butter color. "Then I'm certain he told you the same thing Regent Moss told me: it's

serious

nothing to worry about."

Rory was gratified to hear that Lanscot was distressing the Regent. She wondered if the timing had anything to do with Jaed's sudden arrival at the Lanscottar embassy, and if the Regent's plan for a fast marriage was indeed a response to Lanscot, or the other way around. Either way, it was interesting information, in the same way that curses were interesting, which is to say—beyond her ability to avert or affect.

Rory added it to the ever-expanding list. One's options for action, when one is locked up, are somewhat limited. Rory was beginning to suspect that royalty in general involved some sort of confinement. She allowed herself to imagine a future conversation, herself with *her* daughter, discussing an arranged marriage. Her stomach clenched around the remnants of breakfast.

Samur looked like she, too, was regretting her last meal. Yellow and green crazed along her fern's leaves, which had otherwise turned maroon. She sat back a little bit, as if trying for safer distance. The edges of her office bled in on the edges of the screen: the familiar paintings, the very edge of the window overlooking the koi pond, the watery winter cast to the light coming through the glass.

The familiar dimensions and colors conspired to make Rory's throat tighten until she was not at all sure about swallowing. She decided a leaf could knot her fingers together and stare at them, but that she could *not* bite her lip. "I'm not ready to marry yet, Mother. I thought I'd have more time."

Had Rory been watching her mother's fern at that moment, she would have seen helpless fury sheet crimson over the leaves, until the whole plant looked as if it might combust. Had she been looking at her mother, she would have seen that same crimson darken Samur's cheeks, tarnishing the warm bronze. But Rory was not looking at either mother or fern, and so heard only Samur's controlled, cool, "You have three months, Rory. You will have to be ready."

Truth, absolutely.

Here, the chronicler must interject a brief defense of Samur, against whom historians have already rendered a mostly unflattering judgement. The Regent-Consort was, above all, a woman of duty, dedicated to its fulfilment in the best manner possible, with little regard to personal happiness. Like all mothers, she wanted what was best for her daughter. But even though all her sacrifices, personal and political, had been made to ensure Rory's future, Samur had always intended Rory to fulfill her royal duty at the probable expense of personal happiness. In other words, Samur's notion of best was bound by the limits of what she believed was possible. Thus, if Samur has a fault for which history can condemn her, it is a lack of imagination.

Once the call had ended, Rory sat for several minutes, brow knotted, fists clenched. She lifted her face and stared at the elaborate light fixtures. There was almost certainly a colony of spybots up there. There were probably 'bots in every room, tucked in various nooks and crannies. This was not at all like the old apartments, which had masqueraded as Thorne sovereign territory. The Regent and his arithmancers could enter at any time, replace any 'bots she disabled. That was bad enough. But disabling the 'bots would also reveal her arithmancy to the Regent, and she could not afford to yield up that secret.

She could also not afford to be spied upon every moment of every day. There was always the lavatory, assuming some shred of propriety from Regent Moss; but even that sanctuary might be taken from her if she and Zhang and Thorsdottir began cramming in there together. There was always leaving notes under the soap-dish, but that wasn't practical for conversation, and certainly not for planning.

She needed to maintain both her leafhood and her privacy. As her gaze traveled around the living room, over the boxes and crates of recent relocation, she noted her harp in the corner. Knowing she was still being observed, she did not smile. She even got up from behind the desk and walked out of range of the fern, lest it give her away with its sudden profusion of pinks and purples and the deep, clear cobalt.

The Regent's men wasted little time in coming to reclaim the quantum-hex globe. Rory withdrew to her harp as they did so, and began plucking a scale. When those same men returned an hour later, bearing the promised full set of Tadeshi law books, both in priceless hardcopy and in more practical annotated editions for

Rory's tablet, she did not even look up, much less thank them. That was a pointed, unaccustomed rudeness, and while she regretted it on some level, she thought the Regent would attribute that rudeness to pique, and congratulate himself on impressing upon her how impotent she was to affect her environment.

Rory continued to contribute to that impression when, after the law books had been delivered, she dragged the harp into the center of the room, with her back pointedly to the porthole and baleful Bielo, and continued to play.

And so the Regent's spybots reported hours of footage of a girl bent over her harp, the law books apparently ignored. He supposed that, when confronted with the hedge of legal jargon, she had given up and found something more productive to do: hours a day with her back to baleful Bielo, tuning and playing her harp. The Regent had no ear for music, and no skill in that sphere, but he could appreciate the Princess's technical precision, and the harp's acoustic effects were pleasant enough. It was, at least, a more traditional pastime than her previous habits. It was *proper*, and far less worrisome than a Princess poring over law books would have been.

The Regent understood nothing of musical theory, nor of the overlap between arithmancy and music on at least a theoretical level. What is more fortunate for Rory is that his chief arithmancer also possessed little expertise in that area (and, as we have observed, possessed little inclination to admit any doubts or professional shortcomings to the Regent). The Princess's surveillance seemed uninterrupted (according to the personnel whose sole task it was to monitor the Princess's suite). The 'bots in her old apartments had ceased function almost at once, the fault for which the Regent assigned the Vizier; but he had harbored some suspicions about Rory's arithmantic capacities. But since the 'bots in this apartment continued to function, the Regent concluded that the Princess possessed insufficient arithmantic talent to pose any threat.

This conclusion, while grounded in logic, was also incorrect.

The harp could, and did, achieve a sympathetic resonance with the 'bots. Through the careful, constant, invariable application of sympathetic tones, Rory gradually—over the course of several days—hexed her way past the audio and video, convincing them to report a girl and her harp and not the other doings in the room. The hexes were not invisible, but they relied, like the mantis-lion, on camouflage. Rory worried that the Regent's arithmancer would discover them, but until he did, she had things to accomplish. One of those things *was* reading the law books. The other was not.

"I want to resume my martial training," Rory announced. She had been curled in the largest chair, a tome of Tadeshi law cradled in her lap. Her tablet bore evidence of detailed note-taking, accompanied by several marginal drawings, one of which appeared to be a diagram of the atrium. Now she sat up, set book and tablet aside, and bounced to her feet. "I think if we move that couch over *there*, and shift the table back to the wall—what?"

Thorsdottir and Zhang had already shared a look, and were now both watching Rory with a mix of dread and distress that Rory had come to associate with variations on the theme of *no, that won't work, and here's why*, often accompanied by a *Princess* or a *Highness* for emphasis.

Rory pinned her attention on Thorsdottir, expecting any verbalization would come from that quarter; so she was startled when it was Zhang who said, "We aren't entirely adverse to the idea."

Rory blinked. Even though the fairy gift was most clear on

Zhang's statement's veracity, Rory felt compelled to repeat: "You discussed this already? When?"

"We've been leaving notes in the lavatory," Zhang said. "Under the soapdish. We thought you might've noticed."

Rory opened her mouth and shut it again. She weighed the sting of betrayal—and it wasn't, really, she knew that—against her pride in the stealth of her guards. "I didn't. Well done."

Zhang bowed, very slightly, and nearly smiled. "Since Grytt's disappearance, we've been trying to figure out the best way to defend you. Grytt had the advantage of authority and experience. We don't."

Rory frowned. "You mean, I'd take her advice."

"No, I mean—" Zhang flung Thorsdottir a pleading look, clearly hoping for rescue.

Thorsdottir sighed. "That's partly it. But mostly it's that Grytt is just older. She's seen a lot more. What the Regent's done here is beyond our experience. We don't think he would have dared do this if Grytt were still here."

Rory cocked her head. She did not need the fairy gift to hear *we failed you* in Thorsdottir's speech. "Perhaps not. But it was Grytt's action that precipitated this confinement. Mine, too, granting Jaed asylum in the first place." A worm of worry curled in her belly. She had taken to eating one meal a day in the dining hall, and while her escorts kept her at a private table, she still overheard bits of conversation, particularly when she lingered over the dessert buffet. So far, she had heard nothing at all about Jaed. She took that as mostly good news—she imagined, not incorrectly, that the Regent would have come to gloat if he'd been recaptured—but she still worried. (And had she known the full extent of Jaed's activities, she would have worried even more.)

Thorsdottir, too, was worried about Jaed, though not because she felt responsible for him. The Ursan networks had finally offered commentary on the Lanscottar referendum: as Jaed had predicted, they were calling it an empty political gesture by a small, bitter collection of colonists, it was a threat without teeth, it was meant to distract the people of the Free Worlds from the triumph that was the approaching wedding and the realization of an alliance with the powerful Thorne Consortium. Thorsdottir, who had discussed the referendum with Zhang and with Rory, suspected the reality far more serious than the official, breezy dismissal, though what the referendum's signatories could actually do to realize their independence remained unclear. She also thought that handing Jaed Moss over to people who made a virtue of defying authority, particularly his father's, might have been like adding a cat to a bag of tree-rats. (And had *she* known the full extent of his activities, she would have felt the grim satisfaction of being right.)

But neither she nor Rory did know Jaed's disposition, and Thorsdottir was faced with a situation for which she felt unprepared: namely, a princess determined to pursue activities expressly forbidden by both Grytt and Messer Rupert. But unlike those two, Thorsdottir was unconvinced of her own correctness, and so she did what Grytt and the Vizier would not have done. She asked,

"Why do you want to learn?"

Rory had been preparing for a refusal and marshalling her arguments, so the honesty and simplicity of the query took her by surprise, particularly since she had not been planning to tell the actual, unvarnished truth behind her request. She settled for a half truth. "Because I don't like feeling helpless."

"No one does, Princess. But it's our job is to protect you. That's going to be a lot harder if you're charging head-first into a fight alongside us."

"What if I promise I won't do that? My word, Thorsdottir. Zhang, you too. My word I won't try to do your job for you. I'll only fight if it's my responsibility to do so."

Thorsdottir was inclined to agree; Rory was, in Thorsdottir's experience, honest. But Zhang had been present for the Alchemical Incident, and, while she did not doubt Rory's basic sincerity, also knew that the Princess had been raised by viziers and politicians and would, if she deemed it necessary, leave out important bits of information to engineer her own way in things.

So when Thorsdottir looked at Zhang for agreement, she was surprised at her partner's expression. "I think we need to know what you consider your responsibility," said Zhang. "We are *not* Grytt or Messer Rupert. We don't have their authority, and you don't have a habit of obeying us. We don't want that anyway." Zhang paused and licked her lip. "But we do need your honesty, Princess. You keep things to yourself, and then you act, and we are left to react. That's worked so far, but only because we've been lucky. So again, Princess: *why* do you want to learn, especially now?"

It was perhaps the longest speech Rory had ever heard from Zhang, and certainly the most impassioned. She also understood, without any benefit of fairy gifts, that she did not need to answer. She could command martial instruction, and Thorsdottir and Zhang would comply; she was their sovereign, after all. She had to trust her own judgment; but so did Thorsdottir and Zhang, because her decisions could get them hurt or arrested.

Or killed.

Rory looked down at her hands. There were callouses on her fingertips from playing the harp. She could make a curry with those hands, or hex a turing, or braid her hair. But it was the power she held that she felt most keenly, for the first time in her life. She imagined lives balanced on her palms. Whole worlds. All of the Free Worlds of Tadesh, as Ivar's Queen (and then Merrick's, if Moss's plan succeeded). Lanscot, with its referendums and rebellion, would rest in those hands. She would hold *lives*, too, more than just Thorsdottir's and Zhang's: citizens who had never met her, who knew her only as a name, would be affected by her decisions. It was *her* duty to carry that responsibility. Her mother and Messer Rupert had aimed her whole life to that end, shaping her in their hands, so that she might eventually hold power over others.

She wondered, for the first time, if everyone might not be better off if there were simply more hands sharing that kind of responsibility. Messer Rupert, she thought, would be horrified at the suggestion. She thought Dame Maggie of Lanscot might approve. But ultimately it did not matter what they thought, what anyone thought, because all those lives were currently in Regent Moss's flawlessly manicured, incapable-of-making-curry hands, and he was more interested in the power than the responsibility.

Rory flexed her fingers and spread them wide. Then she flipped them, palms down, and lowered them to her side. She cast her gaze at the law books. "I'll do better than tell you. I'll show you."

If the Tadeshi seamstress, who spent hours measuring the Princess's dimensions (and who was also Lanscottar on her mother's side), noted Rory's revolving collection of bruises—and it was unclear how she could not—she never commented; and as the Regent made no attempt to curtail the activities, Rory presumed she did not report on them, either.

Rory's conclusion, equally as logical as the Regent's suppositions about her activities, had one important difference: it was correct.

The Regent had larger, more pressing concerns. The station network, which had made Rory its darling for weeks, took note of Rory's change in residence, and the manner in which that change had occurred. The Regent assumed that, once the initial flurry was over, the public would find someone else to occupy their interests. But it seemed that the Princess's relocation catalyzed a new nest of conspiracy theories, in which the words *imprisonment* figured widely. More disturbingly, Urse security reported increasingly frequent minor acts of vandalism, particularly in the residential areas nearest the schools and the industrial zones, consisting of painted slogans on the bulkheads which said *Free Rory* and *Free Jaed* and *Free Rory and Jaed*; in the commercial districts, signs advertising the upcoming coronation and wedding were routinely defaced with doodled mustaches.

The Regent might have dismissed those as youthful romanticism. But other slogans bumped up on treason: *Down with the Regent* and *The UnFree Worlds of Tadesh* and *Support the Referendum*, and the associated defacing of *his* likenesses consisted of anatomical amendments more obscene than facial hair.

Coincident with the graffiti came a rash of 'bot failures, always in the vicinity of the vandalism, always at the times when the vandalism occurred, but not always *where*, so that a dozen 'bots would fail more or less at once, forcing the dispensation of repair and security teams, inevitably to a location in which no vandalism was taking place. There was clearly a rogue arithmancer on the station, or perhaps more than one, aiding the vandals.

That it never occurred to the Regent that Jaed might be that arithmancer, we can't hold against him.

His subsequent actions, however, we can.

Vernor Moss was unhappy. His chief arithmancer, Ashtet-Sun, did not require hexes to see that. The Regent of the Free Worlds of Tadesh was not sitting behind the gleaming expanse of his desk, but was in fact standing behind it, chair askew, arms folded. When Ashtet-Sun entered the office, the Regent jabbed out the hand nearest the desk, fingers spread.

"Do you see this?"

Ashtet-Sun side-eyed the desk. It was no longer orderly and gleaming, but rather smudged with fingerprints and piled haphazardly with tablets on which Ashtet-Sun could see varying reports from Maintenance, and at least one from Finance, and a small, disheveled stack from Security. "I do, sir."

"The curfew is not helping. You said it would help, and it's not."

Ashtet-Sun *had*, in fact, suggested that a curfew—specifically, a lockdown on second and third shifts which required everyone abroad in the corridors to carry identification and, if stopped, produce a verifiable reason for being out—would limit civilian traffic on Urse, which it had. He had *not* suggested that the Regent should institute random security checks of suspicious persons during all shifts, which was in fact the cause of that tottering stack of security reports. The curfew had made station citizenry wary of the security, which prompted them to behave more suspiciously as a result.

It did not seem wise to point that out, however, so Ashtet-Sun sifted through an array of responses. After he had discarded the ones Moss could interpret as excuses, he was left with another iteration of, "Sir," this time accompanied by a well-timed drop of his gaze to the deck.

Moss aimed his ire at the top of Ashtet-Sun's head. "The detention block is full. It is, in fact, overcrowded. I have Legal filing complaints about the treatment of suspects. I have just authorized *more* overtime for Judicial to process the cases, but I am being told that won't help. Do you know why, Ashtet-Sun?"

"Because there are so many hours in a day," said Ashtet-Sun. "Because the judges are overworked."

"Exactly so. If *only* there were a mechanism by which we could monitor activities in the corridors, instead of relying on the physical presence of security personnel. Oh! That's right. We have 'bots to conduct our surveillance! Only the 'bots do not seem to be working."

"Yes, sir."

"You assured me you would find out whoever had been hexing the network."

"Yes sir, I did."

Moss and Ashtet-Sun stared at each other for a long and uncomfortable moment. "And," Moss asked, in his most quiet and menacing voice, "have you?

Ashtet-Sun delayed his response long enough to muster enough saliva to oil his tongue. It would not do to rasp at the Regent. Or to mutter. "Not yet. But"—he hastened to add, as the temperature in the office dipped several degrees—"we have discovered how this vandal is doing their work. They have stolen a pass-string. Or perhaps several pass-strings, all of which have sufficient clearance to bypass the 'bots."

"So revoke the clearances for those strings."

"Well. I did that. But this vandal, whoever they are, has hexed the strings to recombine their clearances each time they are used, while at the same time convincing the turing that they are, in fact, legitimate. It's a quite clever bit of hexwork."

Moss's nostrils pinched around a hissed inhale. Ashtet-Sun

observed, from the corner of his eye, the slow crawl of red up Moss's normally masklike visage, culminating in a pair of asymmetrical blotches at the top of his cheekbones.

"I was under the impression that you were a paragon in your field, Ashtet-Sun, which I took to mean as both experienced and highly skilled and, one presumes, also intelligent, and you are being stymied by *clever.*"

Ashtet-Sun had no defense to offer. He had examined the personnel records of every arithmancer for every embassy and delegation, and found a great deal of competence, but no cleverness, and no exceptional skill or abilities. He would have laid blame for this vandalism on the Vizier (the hexes bore the delicate precision of Rupert's work), if he had not known for a fact that the Vizier was no longer on Urse.

(Ashtet-Sun would have derived some comfort from the knowledge that the vandal was actually two arithmancers, both receiving regular assistance from the Vizier over an illegal quantum-hex globe in the Lanscot compound. He would have been mortified to realize that the one of the vandals was Jaed Moss.)

And so, thinking it better to be thought a fool and remain silent, than to open his mouth and draw down the Regent's wrath, Ashtet-Sun said nothing.

The Regent, frustrated by that silence (and half-convinced Ashtet-Sun was a fool anyway, or at least less competent than the Regent had supposed), decided instead to declare martial law.

The decision prompted several diplomatic protests, including one from the Regent-Consort of Thorne, and the station chatrooms continued to speculate about Rory's well-being and Jaed Moss's whereabouts, but the station corridors grew quiet, and both graffiti and 'bot-hexing ceased. The Regent assumed the worst of the upheaval to be over.

He was wrong.

Activity on the turing network intensified, with conspiracy theories about Rory Thorne and Jaed Moss giving way to complaints about the unfairness of martial law and anecdotes about friends and family detained or harassed by overzealous, overworked, and overtired security.

At the same time, new conspiracy theories appeared concerning the Prince's health and whereabouts, in which the terms *cryostasis* and *illegal cloning* figured heavily (and were of course true, though no supporting documentation accompanied them).

And finally, there came a new crop of stories, this time about similar abuses of power taking place on Lanscot, Kymru, Zhenovia, and Tzoumish. Those stories were not true, but conceived of and composed by Maggie. However, they served to link the Regent's unpopularity and the despised wedding (which had become a symbol now of both monarchy and thwarting a beloved romance) with the referendum and the pursuit of freedom (of which Rory became a potent symbol). And while there is little doubt that the Regent's declaration of martial law provided the fertile ground for sedition, the rhetoric Maggie cultivated contributed greatly to the events that followed—which the more generous among historians call her plan, and which this chronicler calls a convergence of complementary events.

CHAPTER TWENTY-FOUR

In Which A Wedding Almost Happens

T hree months, two days, and seven hours after the Regent took custody of Rory Thorne, on the eighteenth birthday of Prince Ivar Valenko, a wedding, and then a corona-tion, were scheduled in the arboretum of Urse.

The events began at the rather arbitrary, unfriendly zero-eight-hundred of Urse's first shift, coronations being lengthy affairs in which many ceremonies and speeches take place, and weddings being only slightly less so, and the day itself being required to play host to both. The wedding was first on the schedule, so that the Prince and Princess could be crowned together, as required by the treaty.

The Regent was a patient man. He could endure years of wait-ing, of planning, and *had*, without betraying his intentions. But the proximity of his plans' culmination corroded his fortitude, leaving him snappish and fretful. Jaed's whereabouts remained a mystery, and there was substantial (though whispered, and then only in secure chatrooms) anticipation that he would disrupt the wedding and abscond with the Princess in a fantastic blaze of 'slinger fire and martial skill.

The Regent was not especially concerned with his second son's abilities to actually *prevent* the wedding. The bridegroom and future King was a greater worry: Prince Ivar appeared, to the untrained eye, to be recovering from a night of debauchery. Pale complexion, verging on grey, pink-rimmed eyes, tremors in his knees. It seemed more likely that Ivar would collapse than that Jaed would breach the layers of security surrounding Rory and somehow rescue her.

The Regent was, however, determined not to underestimate the Princess of Thorne, who, having exchanged her metaphorical prison for a carapace of velvet, beaded embroidery, and a headpiece superseded in its complexity only by the crown of braids upon which it sat, epitomized serenity. Her smile hung perfectly balanced, neither too wide nor too fixed. She balanced the weight of her finery without apparent effort, gliding the length of the arboretum with her bouquet clasped in front of her heart, dragging the small garrison of Tadeshi security in her wake like shadows. Her own body-maids, uniformed and (under protest) unarmed, walked at her sides. They, at least, looked grim and unhappy. The Regent found that more reassuring than Rory's performance.

She was too calm. The Regent didn't like it. The Regent's arithmancer Ashtet-Sun hovered at his shoulder, eyes soft-focused, watching the kaleidoscope of auras. He would alert the Regent if there was an emergency. He hadn't, so far.

Rory, for her part, timed her steps to the deliberate—some might say sluggish—pace of the wedding processional, and took advantage of the pace to familiarize herself with the current disposition of decorations and delegates along the aisle. The dangling tesla strands were back, but in greater numbers, resulting in a twinkling starlight effect of bright white and red, the Valenko colors, which washed a dim pink in the corners, spangling off the polished metal accents of the Tadeshi military standing honor guard at the perimeter. There were elaborate protocols in place concerning which group stood where, how many members a delegation might have, how close it might stand to the dais. The Lanscottar, predictably, had been relegated to the back. She deliberately did not look at them, as she passed. She didn't know what Maggie had done with Ivar's files, but Maggie's presence here suggested she'd done nothing, so far. She also didn't know where Jaed was, or in what condition, her only proof of his continued freedom being the Regent's grim silence on the subject.

The small brace of Consortium uniforms, among them Stary and Franko, clustered around the acting Consortium ambassador and her delegates. They were close to the dais, a position of honor, acting as the Regent-Consort's proxy. Samur's intended attendance had been prevented by an outbreak of mirri plague beetles on Thorne, which had caused a planet-wide quarantine. Rory mourned her mother's absence (and blamed the Regent for it), but even more, she wished for Messer Rupert and Grytt, even though they would have encouraged this marriage, even though they would have opposed, with their collective wisdom, Rory's own plans for the day.

A fairy's gift is not a miracle. It can shape a person, delineate trends and tendencies, prescribe a set of preferences. But it cannot make a person *be* a certain thing. It is a gift, not an imposition. As with any gift, it is subject to wear, to damage, to displeasing its recipient. It can be ignored and stuffed in the back of a metaphorical wardrobe.

In that moment, as she walked past a sea of eyes—some curious, some hostile, some glazed over and bored—Rory wavered. The thirteenth fairy's curse loomed large in her awareness. She *knew* that her future, the one to which wiser, more patient heads had counseled her, was only the beginning of a longer, more complicated political dance. The curse would allow her to see the steps. She might gain sufficient skill to outmaneuver the Regent. She might see the jaws of the trap closing and be unable to stop them. But at least she would *know* what was coming, and why.

The littlest fairy's gift was a lonelier prospect. Courage always is, because it takes us into the unknown.

At last, Rory achieved the far end of the arboretum, and climbed the small step up to the dais. The official wedding party waited: Ivar and two marines, Merrick, the Regent, and the Minister of the Interior, who was acting as officiant, the position of Lord Bishop having been dissolved in favor of popular atheism. Zhang took her place opposite a stern-faced, steel-haired Tadeshi marine. Thorsdottir's own opposite number was a slightly younger, taller version, whose eyes, the color of wet stone, bounced from Zhang to Thorsdottir with force enough to leave bruises before coming to rest on Rory with exactly the same hostility.

Rory let her smile drift away, having no audience left except those on the dais. She handed her bouquet to Thorsdottir and sank into a much-practiced curtsy, spreading her hands wide across the expanse of brocade and beads that glittered like fresh snow at twilight, the shadows fading grey and blue. She rose again, a beat later, and clasped her hands at her waist. Her knuckles made a brave attempt to out-white the dress, chasing all the blood out of skin pressed flat against bone.

"Princess," the Regent murmured. "You are radiant."

Rory ignored him. She leveled her gaze at Ivar, expecting him to continue his rapt examination of the top of his own boots. She was startled, therefore, to find him looking back at her.

The Prince cut a poor figure, stoop-shouldered and huddled into himself like a wet sparrow. His hair flopped across both eyes in a poor imitation of current fashion. He blinked through it, rapid fluttering of pinkish lids. It took *effort* to look this unappealing.

Rory suspected the Regent's hand in this, a cosmetic meddling to further skew public opinion. No one would mourn when their King died. Not really.

Prince Ivar knew it. Sweat glittered like beads at his hairline, collecting at the rim of the simple circlet around his temples. He looked like a man condemned, who, having exhausted all prayers, only hopes that his end comes swiftly.

Rory had learned to pity Ivar as an abstraction. At that moment, she pitied Ivar the man.

She offered him a small smile. "My lord Prince."

"Princess," he blurted. Then, "Rory." He thrust out his hand. His lips trembled, twitching toward what he evidently intended as a smile, but which looked more like impending tears.

Rory took Ivar's fingers, which latched onto hers with a papery determination. She squeezed, very gently. Then she turned her attention back to the Regent, setting her gentleness aside, and bared her teeth.

Ashtet-Sun frowned slightly. He swayed toward the Regent, then stopped himself just short of whispering.

The Minister of the Interior stepped forward. Round-faced and red-cheeked, she should have looked jovial, but her eyes sat in the folds of her cheeks like two chips of coal.

"My lord
idiot
Prince," she said. "My
Kreshti strumpet
lady Princess. It is with great joy that we join you today, in this
travesty
celebration of your marriage and the union of our nations."

Rory let her attention drift. The formula was traditional. The greeting, some small speech extolling her virtues, then Ivar's, then a meditation on the nature of marriage, usually the one by Herrick, and then the exchange.

"... and there is no greater gift than that peace," said the Minister. She paused, to allow the audience to understand that the dull bit of the ceremony was over.

"Prince Ivar," she said in stentorian tones. "Do you accept the responsibility for the Princess of Thorne's well-being, her happiness, and her comfort?"

"Yes," said Ivar faintly. His hand in Rory's shook like a palsied tree-rat.

"And Princess Rory," said the Minister, "do you accept the Prince Ivar as your sovereign, your guardian, provider for your happiness?"

Rory took a deep breath, and took hold of the littlest fairy's gift with both mental hands.

Ashtet-Sun stiffened, and snatched at the Regent's sleeve, but it was too late.

"No," said Rory. "I do not."

The arboretum got very, very quiet, so that everyone in it could hear her say:

"I challenge this man's ability to provide for my well-being, happiness, and comfort. I issue a challenge to Prince Ivar Valenko to prove his worthiness in unarmed combat, where the loser must yield or die. And," she added, after a moment, "I name no proxy. This is a *personal* challenge."

The Regent moved so rapidly that he created a small gust of displaced air, which ruffled the arithmancer's robes and Merrick's hair and startled his security into reaching for the weapons. He drew up a scant half pace from Rory and leaned down until their eyes were level.

"Absurd," he said, in a voice as quiet and controlled as his face was red. "You cannot."

"By the Laws of the Free Worlds of Tadesh," said Rory, "I *can*. I refer to heading three, in *On Succession*, subsection five: *The bride, or her guardians, may elect to challenge the sovereign's worthiness, and may name the terms of the contest.* And in that same section, paragraph seventeen: *If a challenge is issued, the right to a proxy may be waived.*"

She paused, while various Ministers consulted their tablets and the Regent turned an alarming shade of burgundy.

"She is correct," said the Minister of the Interior. She looked as if she'd discovered a live crab in her trousers.

Rory nodded. "Does the Prince accept my challenge?"

Prince Ivar squinted at her. He licked his lips. He looked at the Regent, and at the older marine, as though he expected someone to tell him what to say. The marine did not even blink. The Regent took a half step forward.

"He does *not*. I am the Regent, and—"

Ashtet-Sun laid a hand on the Regent's sleeve, and set his lips close to the Regent's ear. That ear, and the rest of the Regent's face, grew even redder. A vein throbbed across his forehead.

"Prince Ivar," said Rory. "I ask a second time."

The older marine laid a hand on the Prince's shoulder, whether for reassurance or to keep the Prince from bolting off the back of the dais, it was not evident.

Ivar looked past Rory at the wedding guests in the arboretum, and saw them perhaps for the very first time. He stood up a little straighter.

"Yes," he said. "I accept."

Rory twisted and leaned forward, rounding her shoulders so that the rigid bodice of the dress gapped away from her breasts. She reached down between them, while Merrick and both marines gawped and a murmur rose like a flash flood through the arboretum. She turned, holding a slim, unassuming blade in her fingers.

"Thorsdottir," said Rory.

"Princess." Thorsdottir took the slender blade, unsheathed it, and with two quick strokes undid months of careful stitching. She laid the bodice open along the lacing, front and back, and it sprang away from Rory's ribs like a manacle unlocked. The skirts, unsupported, succumbed to gravity and slid down off the Princess's hips.

Zhang scraped the fabric aside as the Princess stepped free of skirts and shoes at once. Beneath the gown, she wore a scanty second skin of tum'mo clothing, the sort a practitioner might wear in tropical climates during the heat of the day. The yellow-green legacy of her martial practice marked her shins, her thighs, her ribs. A fresher bruise, still purple, smeared her upper right arm.

The susurrus crested into an audible commentary, among which the words *indecent* and *lovely* and *holy shit* figured prominently from several points in the room.

Ivar pinked.

The Regent, by contrast, paled. "When," he said, "did you do that? *When?*"

"The harp," said Ashtet-Sun. His eyes were wide. "It's the *harp*. You've been hexing the 'bots."

Rory inclined her head. "I was surprised that you didn't notice."

The arithmancer shook his head. His mouth looked like a string with a knot in the middle. "Well done. Who taught you to do that? The Vizier?"

"No one," said Rory. "It was my idea."

Ivar had, with help from the steel-haired marine, managed to divest himself of his outer layers. He stood reduced to a silk shirt and trousers, and though his boots lent him several extra centimeters to Rory's bare feet, they gave him no greater illusion of martial competence.

"Clear the dais," snapped the Minister.

For the second time that morning, silence reigned in the arboretum. Personal communication units crept out of pockets and sleeves, nestled in palms, angled like solar panels toward Rory and Ivar. Everyone had meant to steal pictures of the event, private mementos of *I was there.* But no one had expected a battle instead of a wedding.

Rory, for her part, did not expect a battle even now. She stalked a slow semi-circle, flexing her toes against the brushed steel, acquainting her skin with the chill. Then she turned sharply toward Ivar, who simply stood where he'd been left, and came within arm's reach.

"As the challenged," she said, "you may strike first."

"Strike," he whispered, and looked at his fist as if he had never seen it before. Then he thrust it forward, the whole of his body weight behind it, in Rory's very general direction.

Rory noted that the Prince's eyes were squeezed shut, making it simple matter to fold sideways and let momentum carry him past. He pinwheeled for balance at the dais edge while his boot's very excellent heels gripped the metal and, in a stroke of luck, prevented him from spilling off. He flailed, and came around, and charged at her a second time.

This time Rory stepped to the outside of his punch, took his outstretched wrist, placed a hand against the back of his shoulder, and levered him to his knees. She leaned down, twisting the arm up behind him. A struggling opponent could dislocate his shoulder; Ivar, however, went limp as a tree-rat playing dead. He turned his head as far as the limits of shoulder and neck would permit.

The unfortunate hairstyle surrendered its fight against gravity and slid over his forehead, revealing round, unblinking, terrified eyes. His lips quivered, buckling as if under great weight, then steadied into something like resolution.

"Help me," he whispered. "Rory. I remember you. *Help me.*"

It seemed to Rory that void had replaced all the aether in her lungs.

The Prince was not lying. The gift said so. He *did* remember her. It *was* Ivar. The real Ivar. The boy who had been so afraid of koi. The man she was supposed to marry—here, on his knees, asking

begging

her to help him. She had prepared herself for a clone, whose life would be measured in weeks. She had not imagined—considered—that the Regent might supply the real Ivar. It occurred to Rory then that she might have been wrong, given the sliver of optimism in which a girl predisposed to kindness feels guilty because she's assumed that someone else is unkind, about the Regent's intentions. Perhaps he meant to let Ivar rule, which would mean leaving Ivar alive.

More likely he couldn't guarantee an heir in a clone's allotted lifespan, assuming they can reproduce at all, said Rory's cynical self, which sounded like Grytt. *And if you didn't know about the clones already, switching out a new husband every few weeks might clue you in.*

Rory sent her guilt packing. She leaned over Ivar, so that her lips came within a finger's width of his ear.

"Yield," she breathed, "and I will help you. I swear it, Ivar."

The Prince's lungs heaved, producing a sound very much like a sob. "I yield."

The Regent made a small, strangled noise. The older marine

closed his eyes. The younger marine grimaced. Somewhere behind Rory, Thorsdottir blew all her breath out slowly, like a leak through a cracked seal. The Minister of the Interior only watched, unblinking, doing a credible imitation of a woman turned to stone.

Rory let go of Ivar, rocked onto her heels, and straightened. Ivar remained on his hands and knees, looking at the floor as if he hoped it would open and swallow him.

"The challenge is decided," said the Minister. The words crept out from between her teeth and fled to the far edges of the arboretum, where the assembled dignitaries picked them up and repeated them. The Minister listened to the echoes for a moment, then sneered.

"What *now*, Princess?"

CHAPTER TWENTY-FIVE ═══

Happily Ever . . .

Rory had rehearsed this moment in her mind a hundred times. She would declare the marriage null and void, denounce the Regent's perfidy, expose the cloning facility on Beo. Then someone could retrieve Ivar, and restore the true Prince, and. . . . She hadn't gotten much farther than that, unwilling to imagine too thoroughly how the Ministers might respond, or the diplomats. Or security. She could feel them staring holes in the back of her head.

Rory had *not* imagined Ivar being *Ivar*, however. Isolated on Beo, perhaps in cryonic suspension, he had not had the benefit of a Messer Rupert, or a Grytt, or even a wretched Deme Isabelle. The Regent would, if his schemes were revealed, face arrest, trial, execution. But those things wouldn't help the Prince. Vernor Moss was an ambitious, amoral man, but he was hardly unique. True Prince or no, this Ivar, *her* Ivar, was no sovereign. The Free Worlds of Tadesh would be ruled by someone, in Ivar's name. That hadn't mattered six months ago, three months, three *minutes*. But it did, now.

The Regent, emboldened by her hesitation, peeled a smile and hissed, "Dissolve this marriage, Princess, and the peace dissolves with it. The treaty is very specific. There will be *war*."

Rory matched his tone. "You have no power to declare that,

Messer Moss. You are no longer the Regent. You have not been, since the Prince turned eighteen, and that was almost four hours ago." She turned to Ivar and reached out a hand. Ivar took it, warily, and let her pull him to his feet. His fingers clutched at hers, still cold, with a grip surprising for its force.

"You are the King, Majesty," she told him. "The coronation is a formality. Tadeshi law, Section One, subsection forty-three, paragraph two. Which means *you*"—and she rounded on the Regent—"have no power at all now, save what your sovereign grants you."

"The Pri—King has not relieved me." The Regent stared fire at Ivar. "*Majesty*. I am your humble servant—"

"That man is no king," said a voice from the rear of the arboretum. "The true Prince is dead. That man is a clone."

This time, the surprise lurched past murmur and straight into commotion, with voices—both human and otherwise—striving to shout the loudest.

"We have proof." The voice and its owner, the Lanscottar ambassador, just-call-me-Maggie, shook free of the crowd and stood alone and surprisingly tall in the middle of the empty path. "We have medical files on Prince Ivar, detailing the methods by which Regent Moss cloned his Highness in three separate attempts. The real Prince, *our* Prince, died on Beo, where he was prisoner."

"Nonsense," said the Regent. "*Lies*. Arrest her!"

Tadeshi security moved to do so, converging off the perimeter like ants toward spilled sugar. Their progress was hampered by the sudden surge of the crowd, who, having found themselves between security forces and their target, attempted to move out of the way by pushing at everyone around them and shouting a great deal. This, in turn, proved helpful to some individuals wearing the formal dress of Kymru, Zhenovia, and Tzoumish, several of whom had produced sticks of varying lengths, and who accreted into a barrier around Maggie, who ignored all of them.

"Truth!" she bellowed. "We have proof, which we have uploaded to the station's turing. We've also quantum-hexed it out to Lanscot, Kymru, Zhenovia, and Tzoumish. The word will spread."

The Regent whipped around, staring at Ashtet-Sun. "Is this true?"

The arithmancer produced a small, sleek pocket-terminal and poked at it. His eyes widened. "On all the major news channels," he said, in a grey voice. "And the social feeds. She's telling the truth, my lord."

The noise in the arboretum damped several notches, as people nearest the conversation retrieved their personal devices and began checking the newsfeeds, at which point their neighbors followed suit, and so on, until everyone, with the exception of the security forces and the ring around Maggie, was bathed in the glow of small handheld screens.

"Shut it down," said the Regent. "Now."

Ashtet-Sun grimaced. His fingers flickered across the touch-pad of his terminal. "I can't. They're *your* codes, my lord." He looked poison at Rory. "Your doing, too?"

"I stole the medical files," said Rory. "I can't claim credit for the codes."

"Those files are false," snapped the Regent. His expression hovered between scorn and righteous anger. "Clever fakes, but *false.* There is no proof."

The first Tadeshi security had reached the ring of Maggie's defenders, and hesitated. There were protocols about firing projectiles in public places that did not apply to swinging sticks, and as a result, the defenders held momentary advantage.

"We have proof," said Maggie. She looked over at the knot of

Lanscottar, wrapped in their wool. Her arm thrust out, imperious finger settling on a tall man, wrapped to obscurity in a violent plaid, wearing a ridiculously elaborate hat with a floppy brim and an excess of feathers.

For a moment, the arboretum held its collective breath. Hand-held devices turned toward the tall man and followed him like flat glowing eyes.

"The Regent's own son can testify!"

Jaed tugged the hat off. His hair, which had grown to brush his shoulders, crackled in the sudden absence of hat and stuck out at all angles. He was looking at Rory. She could see the blaze of his eyes, could feel them, all the way across the arboretum.

There came a tiny cheer behind the ornamental pears, which was picked up by other brave voices around the arboretum. Hand-helds winked and flashed, immortalizing the moment for later dispersal onto the networks.

"You," said the Regent. Then he shoved Merrick forward, so that he stumbled into the middle of the dais, and threw himself at the rear, the three blond security at his heels. At the same moment, the younger marine grabbed for his sidearm. Thorsdottir promptly tackled him and they went down in a heap, which had the effect of clearing the dais and its immediate perimeter of by-standers. Rory dragged Ivar aside, Zhang leapt at Merrick, and the Thorne delegation swarmed to surround their Princess.

The conflict did not last long enough to earn the term *battle*. Thorsdottir laid the young marine out with a decisive right cross to his jaw, and was back on her feet, exploring the blood on her lip with the tip of her tongue. Merrick offered no resistance (to Zhang's evident disappointment), and passed quietly from her hands to Franko's, while Stary took ungentle custody of the younger marine. The steel-haired marine lunged for the Regent, though too late; the Regent had already disappeared, presumably having escaped through the maintenance hatch hidden behind a small decorative hedge on the rear bulkhead. The old marine rounded on Ashtet-Sun instead, who promptly raised both hands, empty.

"I will testify for immunity," Ashtet-Sun said. "But I suggest you take control quickly."

"Ministers," Rory said sharply, and seven heads whipped toward her. "Which of you is in charge?"

"You're the one who knows the fine points of law," snapped the Minister of the Interior. "Maybe you can tell us." But she called out two of her colleagues, War and Energy, and the three of them put their heads together.

The Ministers of the Interior, War, and Energy, with sheer force of will and tremendous volume, imposed order in the arboretum. They were helped by the older marine, who loaned his bellowing to the Ministers' efforts and reminded the security forces, all of whom had been soldiers at some point, that an angry sergeant's order is more compelling than a politician's. Six of them set off in pursuit of the Regent, shouting into their handheld communication devices.

It may seem, to someone well versed in dramatic narratives, that Prince Ivar, at this point, would discover new depths to his person: step forward, find his voice, command the security to stand down. Instead, Ivar remained huddled at Rory's side, as she stood in the middle of the barely controlled chaos, and breathed. She was alone on the dais, except for Ivar, Thorsdottir, and Zhang. The Thorne embassy staff, including security, was imposing an ever-increasing ring of order on the area immediately around the dais. The armed delegates of Kymru had secured the arboretum's main set of doors. The Zhenovian and Tzoumish delegates were mingling with the crowd, offering reassurance and threats of violence, as was most appropriate.

Rory's knees sent a tentative plea to her brain, asking if they might not buckle and just *sit*, since everything would make more sense on the ground. Rory's brain denied their request. She'd caused all of this. The least she could do was watch its resolution. Besides, she could see more than a few handheld screens gleaming in her general direction. Whatever she did now would be on the Ursan network in five minutes, and from there it would travel to all the corners of the Free Worlds, and to the Consortium, and—

She was suddenly conscious of just how scant her clothing was, and how lurid her bruises, and she wondered what her mother would think.

"Princess? Here." Zhang did not wait for acknowledgement or permission. She draped Rory's cast-off wedding dress over her shoulders.

Rory clutched it with her free hand, Ivar still having possession of the other and showing no inclination to let go. Zhang tipped a meaningful look at the Prince, which Rory interpreted as an offer to pry him loose.

Rory shook her head. "It's fine."

She had more pressing concerns than possession of her fingers. She could see Jaed Moss wending his way across the arboretum, heading straight for the dais, moving with the brisk determination of someone who knows exactly where he wants to be and won't be stopped by anything like shouting ministers and nervous crowds. He was stopped briefly by a young man who wanted a 2D, which Jaed permitted and for which he even produced a smile, but after that single interruption, he did not break stride again until he reached the edge of the dais.

He exchanged a nod with Thorsdottir, an almost-smile with

Zhang. But his real smile, he saved for Rory, as he stepped up on the edge.

"Hey," he said, but what the fairy gift heard was *I love you.*

Rory hitched her dress-cloak over her shoulder more firmly, jammed a swath of skirt tight between her Ivar-side elbow and her ribs, and freed up an arm to throw around Jaed's neck. His arm snaked around her, helping to keep the dress-cloak in place. His heart and hers attempted to engage in an exchange of Morse code, each knocking against the respective ribcage.

"I'm glad you're okay," she told his shoulder. "I didn't know if you were."

"Likewise," he said. "I thought those bruises were my father's doing, at first."

"Thorsdottir's and Zhang's." Rory gave his neck another squeeze. "You hexed the turing with your father's codes. Well done."

Jaed shrugged. He was trying, and failing, to look nonchalant. "I had help from Messer Rupert. He and Grytt got picked up by a Lanscottar spy ship, and Dame Maggie's got an illegal quantum-hex globe, so we've been talking. Also, the Lanscottar arithmancer, Tess, is really first-rate."

Rory had been about to extricate herself from Jaed's arms. Now she was glad of their support. "Messer Rupert's *alive*?"

"And Grytt. They made it. Are you sure you're okay?"

"Yes," Rory said, and she meant it. "Now. Jaed. This *is* Ivar. The real Prince Ivar."

Jaed looked past her shoulder. His eyes darkened. "Your Majesty," he said, after a moment.

"Jaed," said Prince Ivar. He released Rory's fingers.

Jaed worked his mouth around what was either a small sack of stones or a difficult sentiment. Then he added, "I'm glad you're all right, Majesty. We thought—you know."

"Thank you," said Ivar, with a credible attempt at sovereign dignity.

"So," said Jaed. "Now what?"

They both looked at Rory.

She sighed. "Wait here."

Rory readjusted her dress, squared her shoulders, and marched toward the current seats of Free World government, which appeared to be a wrought iron bench, a small glass-topped table, and a conveniently low collection of garden statuary, on and around which the Ministers and several ambassadors, including Maggie of Lanscot, congregated. She arrived near the end of the Minister of War's update on the Regent's impending arrest, which was being hampered by the protests in the main corridors, as it seemed every malcontent had emptied into the station's thoroughfares and begun waving signs and chanting for Rory's freedom, the Regent's arrest, or the end to the monarchy. All three, in some cases.

The Ministers greeted that news with variations on the frown and the scowl. Several ambassadors, including Maggie of Lanscot, beamed. Then she noticed Rory and beamed wider.

"Princess!"

The Minister of Energy scowled. "Princess."

"Princess," said the Minister of the Interior. Her face was carefully neutral.

The Minister of War puffed his cheeks. "Princess," he said. "You've made a fine mess of our station."

"I'm sorry, my lord, but I'm not sure how this is *my* fault. Moss is *your* Regent." Rory smiled with only her lips. "Dame Maggie, a word?"

The Minister of War opened his mouth. The ambassador of Lanscot stepped on his foot, hard, and his teeth clicked together. "Of course, Princess," Maggie said. "Excuse me a moment, my lords."

She walked with Rory a few paces away, still beaming.

"Princess, is there something I can do for you?"

"Tell me you planned this. Riots? *Rebellion?*"

"Reform," Maggie said firmly, "begins at the popular level, when the people express their discontent with the corruption of the aristocracy."

yes

Rory nodded. A cold seed sprouted in her chest. "I see."

Maggie nodded, as if it were the most natural thing in the universe, that a princess should understand and approve of rebellion against the ruling class. "We owe you a great debt. People were incensed at your incarceration. No one wanted your wedding to happen. Everyone blamed the Regent, and we used that. And those files—they were all the proof we needed to give the referendum some teeth. Thank you. You've helped save the Free Worlds from tyranny."

The seed grew roots and spread. "You're getting rid of the monarchy. *That's* what you want. And I am intended to, what, return to the Thorne Consortium?"

Maggie's smile dimmed and hardened at the edges. "If you renounced your title, we could offer you asylum on Lanscot, but you would be only a citizen, same as the rest of us. But you can't stay here. No offense, Princess, but we're done with royalty. What the Thorne Consortium does is its business, of course, but the Free Worlds must be *truly* free."

Rory was conversant enough with history to know the answer to her next question already, but she asked it anyway. "So what happens to Ivar?"

Maggie's smile ossified. "Prince Ivar is dead, of course, on Beo. Killed by the Regent's treachery."

"No. *That's* Ivar. Over there. The fellow standing beside Jaed on the dais. That's the *real* Ivar."

Maggie abandoned her performance. Her face settled into the topography of a woman well acquainted with insomnia and hard choices.

"We know. That marine there, Ian Jones—he's a Mac'Hoi'y on his grandmother's side."

"A spy."

"A patriot. He didn't like what he saw, down in those labs. No more than *you* did, Princess, when you read those files. Ian couldn't get us proof, though, and you did—

"Then you know Ivar's a victim, not a criminal. Certainly not a *tyrant.*"

Maggie shrugged. "He was used, Princess. So were you. But true Prince or no, that man over there is not fit to rule. Everyone can see that. Leave him in place, and we'll have governance by Ministerial faction, and that only after a fight. Better that everyone believes him a clone, and the real Prince dead."

"Not better for Ivar. Let him go into exile. I'll take him with me."

"And have him act as a rallying point for royalists? That would be civil war. And if they won—then there would be a larger war with your people again. Do you want that?"

"Of course not. But you're saying he's a clone, and a clone dies in a few weeks," said Rory. "So officially, there won't *be* anyone to rally around. Right? There will just be some young man of unknown parentage puttering around on Lanscot."

Maggie considered. "I see your point, Princess. I'll have to think about it."

not worth the risk

"Thank you," said Rory.

She inclined her head, turned on her heel, and marched back to the dais. Security had removed Merrick and the arithmancer, leaving only Thorsdottir, Zhang, and Jaed in possession of the dais, with Ivar there only because he had nowhere else to go.

"The Regent's gotten away so far," said Rory. "And the station's rioting. Evidently I need to be freed, the Regent needs to be arrested, and the monarchy needs to yield to popular elections."

"Ah," said Thorsdottir. "That last one could be a problem."

"I know." Rory squinted across the arboretum. "The Ministers seem to be busy, at the moment. I don't want to interrupt them again. Thorsdottir. Zhang. Do you think it's safe to go back to our embassy?" She laid a dramatic hand on her forehead. "I'm very tired."

Thorsdottir snorted. "I'll get Stary and Franko. We'll make it safe."

"Good," said Rory. She turned to Ivar. "I promised I'd help you. That means you have to come with me now."

Ivar licked his lip. He had been so afraid of koi, of planets, of things unknown. Perhaps the cryonic suspension had been a kindness, a cold cocoon in which he was entirely safe. Rory had a moment's panic in which Ivar refused her, in which she would have to contrive to abscond with him, or resolve to leave him behind to his fate.

Then Ivar stood a little straighter. He would never achieve Jaed's square shoulders, never cut so impressive a silhouette; but in that moment, he became a giant.

"Let's go."

Jaed had been watching the exchange with increasing agitation. "Wait. You're leaving. You *can't* leave."

with him what about me

"You haven't asked me to stay," said Rory. "You've assumed that I will."

There were, in fact, a great many assumptions floating around.

Maggie's, that Rory would simply return to Thorne. Jaed's, that she *would* stay on Urse, and presumably attempt to take control of the Free Worlds in some sort of coup. She had defeated their Prince, after all. By their laws, she could assume—that word again!—the throne. All those Tadeshi lives would rest in her hands. So would the reform Maggie was so intent on enforcing, which Rory suspected would be neither simple nor peaceful to achieve, and perhaps even impossible, with a popular sitting monarch. And she *would* be popular. She needed only continue on her current path, the one for which she'd been raised, trained, and prepared since the fairies had come to her Naming. Eleven of them had bestowed gifts upon her intended to make her an adequate queen. The thirteenth fairy's gift would make her a *great* queen.

None of that would help Ivar, however. Only the twelfth fairy's gift could do that. And once she'd saved him, that gift would help her, too. Courage is the best companion when going into the unknown.

She looked at her hands. They were empty. She liked that. Then she looked at Jaed, and offered him one of them. "I've *been* a political symbol as a princess. I don't want to be one again. And that's all I'll be, if I stay here, whether or not I become a queen. That's all *you'll* be, too, if you stay." She took a deep breath. "There are Consortium warships on the border. All we have to do is get there. Come with us. Come with *me*."

A sensible man would, at that point, have hesitated, or argued, or offered a dozen good, solid reasons why *getting there* was not a trivial endeavor. Jaed did none of those things.

"How?" he asked.

"Zhang," said Rory. "I think it's time we stole a ship."

"Yes," said Zhang. "I think so, too."

. . . AFTER

I t is a historian's task to adhere as much as possible to material facts: when a woman is born, what she did and said of lasting import. Her deeds, her choices, act as rocks thrown into a pond, with the effects spreading like ripples; a historian might simply point to those metaphorical rocks: here is what happened, this event, then that one, and now the subject passes out of history.

And so:

Having escaped Urse in the stolen military transport, Rory, Thorsdottir, Zhang, Jaed, and Ivar were rescued by the same Lanscottar surveillance vessel which had been lurking on the edge of the system. Once on board, they were reunited with the Vizier and Grytt, at which point, they all returned to Consortium space, and from there went to Lanscot, Maggie having relented about extending asylum to Ivar.

It is *this* chronicler's opinion that such a mechanical approach renders the narrative unpalatable, like stale bread rubbed all over with dust. History rarely happens in neat order; events bump into each other, cross each other's paths, hiss and quarrel, and then flee in opposing directions.

Let us say instead that the choices that Princess made were less like ripples in a pond and more like the shockwaves of an explosion, where solid stone may be reduced to dust, and glass to shrapnel, and fragile bodies to wet pulp.

Is that unlovely? Well. So are wars, and Rory Thorne's decisions spawned several. The sound of an explosion alone does damage, so great and violent is its force. But the sound also travels well beyond the blast radius, heralding the destruction, announcing it, so that those far distant can be warned of its coming.

And so:

In the chaos that followed Rory's wedding—an ultimately failed pursuit of the Regent, which involved two days and through each level of Urse, several stolen weapons, one firefight, and a civilian casualty (an amateur journalist attempting to acquire exclusive footage)—it was noticed that a Tadeshi military shuttle was missing. It had been the Prince Ivar's vessel, scheduled to depart after the coronation, and so it was fueled and waiting, unattended, in a secure bay.

There should have been extra security assigned to it, but with the Regent and Merrick at large on the station, and the first disturbances of what would become a civil war, there *was* no extra security. The local station security forces had taken sides, and were either engaged in pursuit of the Regent, or conducting internal investigations to root out traitors. It would be poetic, perhaps, to say that no one at all noticed a small party of dockworkers (who of course were not dockworkers at all) moving cargo through the secure sections of the aetherport while the station ran to riot. It would also be untrue. People noticed, and made reports; Rory and Jaed were somewhat distinctive, even when wearing a dockworker's canvas coveralls, which are designed to make observers dismiss their wearers as *the help*. But there were simply not sufficient personnel available to investigate in a timely manner. When security finally arrived, the dockworkers had penetrated the military half of the aetherport using codes fabricated from at least three Ministers' pass-strings, and the shuttle had disappeared.

It was at that point that the Ministers realized that Rory Thorne was also missing (the Consortium embassy having filed no such report), as were her body-maids and Jaed Moss (whom the Lanscottar had also not reported as missing, having, as the saying goes on Lanscot, better sheep to steal). It was presumed that the Ivar clone had accompanied them.

Ivar's loss was a worry, but as everyone knew a clone's lifespan is measured in days, the urgency to recover him faded after the first month. Since, by all accounts, the monarch of the Free Worlds had died years ago on Beo, the recovery of a clone was not important except as evidence in the Regent's trial, and the files themselves were sufficiently damning.

Unfortunately, to hold a trial, one needs the accused, and although Merrick Moss was recaptured while trying to crawl into a maintenance shaft, Vernor Moss managed to escape. He resurfaced clutching a distant Valenko cousin some months later, exchanged the title of Regent for the neologistic Primarch, and promptly launched an attempt to weld the fractured Free Worlds of Tadesh back together. It was noted by people less immediately involved in the conflict that *primarch* seemed to be functionally equivalent to *monarch*, and that the distant Valenko cousin was at best a puppet, and at worst a fiction, and in either case, Vernor Moss had not altered his ambitions of sovereignty.

Unluckily for those ambitions, the unrest begun on Urse had spread during the intervening months throughout the Free Worlds. Local governments were finding themselves challenged, and in some of the more extreme cases their members were escorted out of aetherlocks without hardsuits. Dame Maggie of Lanscot, feeling (correctly) some responsibility for the violence, collected the secessionists into the Confederation of Liberated Worlds, aptly (and unimaginatively) named after all the colonies, stations, and planetoids who shared Lanscot's discontent and desired some measure of political freedom. Although they represented the majority of the former Free Worlds of Tadesh, they were not perhaps the wealthiest or best equipped of those worlds. The wealthiest saw nothing wrong with the monarchy, as they benefited most from it, and chose to remain with the loyalists.

Dame Maggie named Lanscot as the Confederation's capital and set about attempting to organize her far-flung constituents into some kind of functioning organization, a task akin to herding cats or trying to schedule an interdepartmental meeting of academics. Her eventual success was brought about in part because when Vernor Moss resurfaced at the head of the royalist faction, he did so with the majority of the Tadeshi navy intact. He proclaimed his intent to reunify the Free Worlds by firing on a Confederation station and seizing control, at which point the recalcitrant Confederation members set aside their differences and started cobbling together a navy of their own.

And so a very uncivil war began and, as such wars tend to do, soon spilled beyond its own borders. The remaining monarchies collapsed with varying degrees of alacrity and violence, including the Thorne Consortium, though the Regent-Consort's deft political maneuvers delayed that inevitability until Jacen's ascension. The independent pan-galactic corporations in the Merchants League, including Johnson-Thrymbe, survived the upheaval without significant bloodshed. The Tadeshi civil war inspired the creation of no fewer than seven separate, inter-company workers' unions; rather than disrupt their war-profiteering, the various CEOs and presidents together entered into negotiations with their workers, prompting the philosopher-economist Rand Pin-Ko to write his treatise on anarcho-syndicalists, war, and economic justice, which sparked a further series of wars (this time, thankfully within academia, and thus mostly bloodless) that would last almost a hundred years.

And then, as is well documented elsewhere, the League encountered both the alwar Harek Empire and the tenju merchant clans, raising the number of known xenos to four. Humanity had little time to marvel at how crowded the multiverse was, however. Shortly after meeting the Harek Empire and the tenju clans, the vakari Protectorate and their Expansion—a pretty way of saying a war that walked on the twin legs of conquest and religious fanaticism—reached human space.

Perhaps we can declare Rory Thorne's story *finished*: for having set off the chain of events which destroyed the multiverse, surely the Princess of Thorne has earned a bit of privacy. The official record aids us in this endeavor, for it shows that shortly after her departure from Urse, the Princess renounced her title. Thus we may say with honesty that Rory, Princess of Thorne, literally disappears from the records.

We might imagine that, having managed their escape, everyone settled on Kreshti, where Rory became a successful musician and tutor of arithmancy, while Ivar took up raising fancy koi. Perhaps Zhang became a bush pilot, Thorsdottir a local constable, and Jaed a horticulturalist, raising Kreshti ferns for export. Or perhaps everyone emigrated to Lanscot instead, having earned the regard of the Confederation (and the Consortium being somewhat uncomfortable for a former princess), and so lived their lives in happy obscurity.

But because we pursue accuracy here, rather than seeking comfort (we leave those sorts of accounts to popular entertainments that are *inspired by true events*), we must note that Rory, Jaed, Thorsdottir, and Zhang did *not* settle on either Kreshti or Lanscot, to which they were invited (nor, in fact, anywhere else). The four of them elected to remain in their stolen vessel, christened it *Vagabond*, and struck out for the unaffiliated human settlements on the edge of the k'bal Verge, where they turned to a life of salvaging, privateering, or piracy, depending on one's perspective. The Vizier, Grytt, and Ivar *did* settle on Lanscot, where they took up farming sheep and attempted to retire from public life.

They all failed.

But that is another story.